THE CONTROL

A Psychological Thriller

M.W. LAYNE

OTHER BOOKS BY M.W. LAYNE

Ashes Still Burn Urban Fantasy Series:

Ashburn (Book 1)
The Demon Slayer of Ashburn (Book 2)
The Blood of Ashburn (Book 3)

Horror/Thrillers:

The Gate
Running Club (A Short Dystopian Thriller)
Thirst (A Horror Short Story)

THE
CONTROL
A PSYCHOLOGICAL THRILLER

Published by Writer Layne, LLC

Cover Art and Design by M.W. Layne

ISBN: 979-8-8690-3788-6

"The course of true love never did run smooth."

William Shakespeare

"There is always some madness in love. But there is also always some reason in madness."

Friedrich Nietzsche

PRESENT DAY

Jim

CHAPTER ONE

WHEN I WAKE from my nightmare, I'm sitting in a dusty office. Across from me, on the other side of the desk, my psychology professor, Benjamin Mooken, is hunched over his laptop. At first, I wonder if he's taking a nap. But his caved-in skull and the dried blood on the back of his neck tell me otherwise.

"Professor?"

There is no response.

The black hands of the wall clock tell me it's three in the morning—the time when demons are supposed to roam the land of the living, according to old superstitions. But there are no evil spirits here. Only scattered piles of paper cluttering a large wooden desk, an open drawer with a notebook sticking out of it, and an empty cedar chest on the floor. Adding to the chaos around me, every wall is lined with floor-to-ceiling bookshelves stuffed tight with artifacts and tidbits from more countries than I'll ever visit in my lifetime.

"Professor Mooken?" I say, louder this time.

I stand up and reach toward him. My shaking hand is covered in itchy, dried blood.

"This isn't real," I assure the unmoving professor. "You're fine. All of this is…fine."

But Professor Mooken isn't fine.

Not at all.

I press on his shoulder, enough to wake him, but he still doesn't move.

My heart beats hard and erratic—a prisoner pounding inside my chest, desperate to escape his cage. While Mooken remains motionless—a cold stone statue only resembling a man.

Despite his stillness, the dead weight of his hand on the keyboard continues to cause the letter *m* to be typed over and over.

Because of this, the document on his screen is filled with that single letter from top to bottom.

mmmmmmmmmmmmmmmmm

A low hum floods my nervous system, and my body buzzes.

With two fingers, I lift Mooken's icy hand from the keyboard, treating it like a disgusting bug I have to touch. I've watched enough television shows and read enough mysteries to know better than to disturb a dead body. But I need the letters on his screen to stop.

They remind me too much of how Mooken used to make his awkward *hmmm* sounds in the middle of his lectures when pondering a point his students weren't getting.

Being this close to a dead person, my body revolts at the heavy cocktail of copper, feces, and urine in the room—a combination I've never encountered before.

Well, *once* before. But that was so long ago I sometimes wonder if it wasn't another one of my nightmares.

But my stomach tells me the scene in front of me is real. My guts convulse and threaten to spew everything from inside of me, and I swallow hard, choking back my sickness…barely.

I bury my nose in my sleeve, breathing through my mouth. Other than the shallow in-and-out of my air, the room is quiet.

Inside my head, however, things are very loud.

Along with the loud buzzing, my father is telling me to run.

Leave now and save yourself, boy. Before they blame you for all of this.

I ignore him and stare down at Mooken.

After five minutes, his screen starts to fade to black, but I move the mouse, and the screen returns to full brightness.

mmmmmmmmmmmmmmmmm

I lean over my professor's body like I'm showing a dead man something he might find interesting. I hold the mouse lightly in my hand and scroll up. There are so many pages of *mmmm*s that the document appears to stand still as I scroll. I climb through a hundred pages of that single, lonely letter before I make it to the substance of the file and slow down to skim its contents. I scan blocks of Mooken's text, reading snippets from the bottom up.

classic signs…
early schizophrenia…
chronic sleep deprivation…
acute depression…
disruptions in personal affairs…

My head throbs as I continue further up the document.

delusions…
romantic interest…
auditory and visual hallucinations…
sleep paralysis…
irrational anger and suspicion toward therapist…
potential for extreme violence…
formal evaluation recommended…

I speed to the very top of the document to see who Mooken was evaluating, and my stomach freezes when I read my name.

Jim Straub.

But this can't be. I didn't kill the professor. I know this for certain.

Professor Mooken was my teacher and trying to help me. That must be why I came here tonight—to get his help.

Not to kill him.

The *delete* key stares at me, cooing, tempting me to erase my name—to fix this.

But I can't do that—not yet, at least.

I disable Mooken's screen saver, stagger to the other side of his desk, and sink back into the leather chair.

When I check the clock on the wall, fifteen minutes have passed.

My phone vibrates in my pocket, and on reflex, I check it. As happens so often lately, it's a missed call from my father, who suffers from dementia and calls and texts daily.

I love and miss my dad, but I can't deal with him and his altered, severe personality right now.

My present situation is too dire, although there are still a few hours before other professors and students begin entering the building to start their days.

I squeeze my eyes shut to help me remember the events that led me here, but when I do, I hear my father giving me advice again, yelling at me, ordering me.

Leave.

"Not yet," I say through clenched teeth. "I need to remember what happened first."

My father quiets to a whisper in my head as I sift through everything I know.

First and foremost, although I'm not his murderer—*someone* killed Professor Mooken.

More significant than that, they ended his life and spared mine.

Images swim and swirl through my brain—ghosts of memories fighting to be seen.

I close my eyes tighter, forcing them to line up in an orderly queue. Some shove their way to the front, assuring me they're more important than the others, but I force each memory to show itself one at a time in the order it occurred.

Finally, the bedlam calms down, and memories begin to play against the back of my eyelids—a choppy movie hastily assembled in my head.

I settle deeper into Mooken's guest chair.

I watch, and I remember.

PART ONE

SIX WEEKS AGO

JIM

CHAPTER TWO

I AM HURRYING along the narrow path that runs along the side of the road, crunching gravel and dried leaves under my sneakers. I take this route to avoid passing through the central *Grounds*—the term students and faculty use here at the University of Virginia instead of *campus*, because, well, that's how Mr. Thomas Jefferson wanted it.

As I head to Gilmer Hall, the home of UVA's Psychology Department, Nirvana's *Smells Like Teen Spirit* plays in my head. It is the background track to my favorite recurring fantasy, where I'm walking to class, trying to keep a low profile so none of my fans notice who I am. In this fantasy of mine, a trio of female students see through my disguise and recognize me as a semi-famous grunge rocker who was out partying too much the night before.

But, like I said, this is only a fiction of mine—a happy delusion that helps me survive as an introvert in a social college town like Charlottesville.

In other cities, I'd be mistaken for a drifter—unshaven, with disheveled hair, mismatched clothes, and hiding behind cheap sunglasses that cover my bloodshot eyes. But my eyes aren't red because I was out drinking. They're puffy and veined because I don't get enough sleep, and when I do, it's plagued by nightmares.

Bad ones.

My phone vibrates, and I answer it to talk to my father. He lives in a facility specializing in his type of dementia, and, as usual, he calls whenever his addled mind remembers he has a son.

"Why aren't you here with me?" he says, and I take a deep breath before responding.

"I'm on my way to class at UVA, remember?"

Silence on the other end.

The black bird perched atop the yield sign on the opposite side of the road shakes his head, scoffing at me.

Coming at me from the opposite direction, a female student passes under the same yellow sign, and I recognize the curve of her nose and her chapped, pouty lips.

I've never met her before, but I've seen her often on my way to class. I'm not a giant of a man, but I'm wide-shouldered and tall enough that I'm sensitive about making women I don't know feel nervous or threatened. So, like usual, I aim my gaze at the ground, and we pass each other without a word.

"How are you, Dad?" I ask.

"How do you expect me to be?" he says. "Are you being careful like I told you? Keep your head on your studies, and watch out for women. They only want one thing."

This is something my father tells me a lot, but when I've asked him what that one thing is, he answers differently each time.

Your money.

Your freedom.

Your life.

I've learned not to ask anymore.

When I look up from my phone, an older student with an unkempt beard turns the corner up ahead and walks straight toward me. His black lab is on a leash, trotting by his side, wagging its tail.

The guy smiles at me, and his dog opens its mouth, flopping its tongue around in a friendly greeting. I get that a lot from animals. They usually love me, even when their humans don't.

Out of caution, I cross to the other side of the road and give the guy a wide berth. Instead of being appreciative, he glances at me as if to say, *what the hell is wrong with you*?

I focus on my phone call again.

"Are you eating your food and doing what the doctors tell you?" I say as I step onto the flyway that stretches over the highway.

"Doctors aren't any good," he says. "You're better off listening to yourself. And me."

I cross University Avenue and soon stand in front of the red-bricked Gilmer Hall.

"I hear you, Dad," I say. "But I have to go now. I'll talk to you soon, okay? Love you."

My father grunts, then ends the call without saying goodbye—his usual way of finishing our conversations.

I slip my phone into my jeans pocket and merge with the crowd of students and backpacks funneling through Gilmer's heavy double doors. Once inside, I run-walk down a musty hallway lined with corkboards and displays, late, as usual, for my Intro to Experimental Psych Lab.

When I reach the room Eugene, Amber, and I are using to conduct our experiment, I catch my breath before I open the door and enter with as little noise as possible.

Even though I know what to expect, the scene is surreal to me every time. Eugene hunches over a compact control panel, his back to me, as he peers through a wall of one-way glass. He's observing a young man and woman in an adjacent room sitting on opposite sides of a thick wooden table, studying a pile of oddly cut, geometric wooden shapes.

Without acknowledging my entrance, Eugene switches on a digital recorder and speaks into a microphone, bringing the antiquated PA system to life.

"Again, thank you both for coming today. I have your filled-out questionnaires and your signed NDAs, but for the record, please state your first and last names, age, whether you are a student, and, if so, your major. Lastly, please confirm which of your hands is dominant. Amber, you may go first."

"My name is Amber," the attractive, mocha-skinned brunette says into the air, appearing to be uncertain whether she is doing this correctly. "I'm nineteen and an English major with a psych minor…probably. I'm not sure yet. Also, I'm left-handed."

"Are you here to take part in this experiment of your own free will? And are you being compensated with an hour of required lab work for the semester?"

"Yes."

"Great. Go ahead, Anthony. Your turn."

The man sitting across from Amber is older than her. His face is as dry as old leather—a result of spending too much time outside without sun protection. His hair is dark brown and parted on one side, and he is bone skinny like he doesn't eat enough.

"I'm Anthony," he says. "Tony's fine. I'm not a student. I'm just here for the Amazon gift cards. I'm twenty-five years old. Right-handed. And, yeah, I'm here of my own free will. You don't have to ask."

"That's great," Eugene says.

His intonation is flat and betrays none of the impatience he must be experiencing as he continues reading from the printed page in front of him—the same introductory script we've both used dozens of times over the past few weeks.

"The object of this experiment is to test whether left-handed or right-handed people are better at motor function skills that require coordinated analytical thinking and problem-solving. If you would please look at the wall opposite the observation mirror, behind which I am sitting, you will see a photograph of a wooden cube constructed of irregularly shaped blocks similar to the ones on the table in front of you."

Both Amber and Tony glance from the table to the wall and back again before nodding.

"When I tell you to start, each of you will begin constructing your version of the cube shown in the photo to the best of your ability. Please note there is only one solution to this puzzle. But there are enough of the correct pieces for each of you to build your own cube. The first to do so will receive double the advertised credit for this experiment or double the number of gift cards if you are not a student. If neither of you completes your cube, the one closest to being done will win. You may examine the photograph, but all puzzle pieces must remain on the table while you do so, and you may not remove the photograph from the wall. Also, you may not speak to one another or to me once the test has begun. If you do, *neither* of you will receive any compensation for your participation here today. Is that clear?"

They nod.

"You have ten minutes. Good luck to you both. You may begin."

Eugene mutes his mic and turns to me.

"What the hell is wrong with you?" he says before turning back to observe Amber and Tony fumbling with their puzzle pieces.

"Sorry I'm late," I say.

But this is not what Eugene is talking about.

"Leaving a woman as gorgeous and as horny as Amber was a real loser move," he says. "Good luck finding someone better than her. Seriously, I can't believe you two ever dated in the first place."

Eugene isn't lying about Amber's beauty. She moves with a curvy athleticism, has sensuous lips, and smells of honey. He's also not wrong about her appetite for sex, even though I've never shared that with him. Eugene is my lab partner, but he's not a friend, and I would never tell him intimate details like that.

"Why'd you do it?" he says, laughing as my cheeks redden. "Was she too crazy in bed? Did she scare you?"

Don't listen to that idiot, my father says in my head. *That woman was dangerous. You did the right thing breaking it off with her.*

My father's said that about every female I've ever been interested in. They've always been too *something* for me.

Still, he's right about me making the right choice, although dating Amber had its bright sides. For instance, sex with her was exciting, although it often turned too dark for my liking. But her over-amped libido wasn't what ended things between us. I broke up with her when I found out she'd been fucking her *other* boyfriend all those weekends she was supposedly out of town, visiting family in Jersey.

A mutual friend ratted her out one day at lunch. Said she couldn't stand by while Amber cheated on me. I stopped eating my sandwich mid-bite. My body trembled, and my heart ached at Amber's betrayal. But more than anything, I was embarrassed because there I was, learning the same lessons I've learned over and over again—that I have zero ability to tell when someone close to me is lying and that people can't be trusted.

When I ended things with Amber the next day, she listened to what I had to say, accepted the situation with a nod, and let me walk away without a word. I had tears in my eyes, but she was as cold and unknowable as anyone I'd ever encountered.

Her ability to detach herself made her a shitty girlfriend, but it's also why she's so good at being the control subject in our little experiment.

Eugene and I take our turns being the control to ensure there's no inherent bias toward Amber. But she's a natural in the role—I think because she enjoys the deception—or maybe because she doesn't care.

"I predict Tony *almost* loses his shit the first time Amber cheats," Eugene says. "But at the last second, he contains his temper and makes goo-goo eyes at her instead. He rated her a nine out of ten on his questionnaire."

I shrug, but I'm not surprised.

Yes, rating the attractiveness of experimental subjects is not normal. But it's critical for testing our *real* hypothesis—that a person's anger and aggression threshold increases if they find their perpetrator attractive.

I think of it like we're trying to prove the existence of a Halo Effect for good-looking people when it comes to anger and aggressive behavior.

And, since Professor Mooken insists all subjects fill out a questionnaire to help collect statistics about the type of person who volunteers for these experiments, we sweetened his questionnaire with a few additions of our own.

How good are you at puzzles?

How much do you trust the person sitting across from you?

And, of course, *How attractive do you find the other subject in today's experiment?*

You might think that last question would give away our secret to participants. I mean, why would we care if one subject thinks the other one is hot or not? But no one has ever complained or asked about it.

In fact, Tony looks perfectly happy to be stuck in a small room with Amber as they study the photograph of the completed puzzle from their chairs. But soon, with the promise of all online gift cards driving him forward, he's on his feet, analyzing the photo close-up, trying to identify which pieces go where.

Amber stands up, too, and pretends to do the same, but unlike Tony, she isn't trying to build a cube at all. She's only there to cause trouble. And, unlike Tony, she knows there is no actual way to construct the cube that's shown in the photograph from the pieces we've given them.

Unburdened by this knowledge, Tony sits down, takes two pieces from the center pile, and fits them together.

Amber simply smiles, looks at Tony, and giggles.

It's a classic Amber move and highly effective.

Tony looks up at her, frantic, as she picks through the pile, calm and certain. She places two pieces together in front of her and nods with satisfaction. Then she selects another piece and flashes Tony a grin of certain victory that causes him to twitch.

He jumps up from his chair to study the photo again, stressed now that he thinks he's losing the chance to double his gift cards. While he's distracted, Amber removes one of his pieces and places it back into the pile.

Tony scrunches his eyebrows when he returns to his seat.

He stares in disbelief at his defiled construct, then he glares at Amber, who keeps a straight face as she continues to build her own cube. Tony is desperate and angry as he studies the *No Talking* sign tacked to the wall. Then he turns to the one-way mirror. He remains silent, barely, but it's clear he's appalled at Eugene for not stopping the experiment to chastise Amber.

But that will never happen. It's not part of our script, but Tony doesn't know this.

Instead, Eugene and I study Tony and take notes on everything he does.

How long before his face turns red?

Does he try to communicate with Amber non-verbally? If so, how?

Does he confront her with words, even though it would mean both of them losing credit for their participation?

And ultimately, *Was Tony more, equally, or less likely to exhibit aggression and rage toward Amber than our other subjects?*

According to our hypothesis, Tony will be less likely to get angry at Amber because he's attracted to her. This made sense to us when the three of us came up with it at the start of the semester. Attractiveness bias is real, after all. Good-looking people are treated differently all the time and in many ways.

But even though we haven't analyzed our results, the *only* conclusion I can draw so far is that subjects never get mad or turn hostile when I'm the control, regardless of whether they find me attractive.

I don't know why this is.

Eugene thinks it's because of my round face and lopsided smile. He thinks people simply don't find me threatening.

Maybe he's right.

Maybe if I were in Amber's place, Tony wouldn't be nearly as upset as he is right now.

He stops glaring at the one-way mirror, checks the clock on the wall, forces himself to chill, and gets to work on his cube again.

A minute later, Amber walks over to the photograph and pretends to study it.

When she does this, Tony stretches across the table and wrecks her cube.

Brilliant.

I love when subjects fight back.

He thinks he's getting even with her—dealing out his own form of karmic justice—but all I see is a Rhesus monkey throwing feces at an infuriating stranger.

Amber returns to her seat, ignores what Tony's just done, and begins building her cube from scratch, as cool and calm as ever.

Furious, Tony rises from his chair and returns to the photo again, desperate, searching the image for some clue to a solution that doesn't exist.

He looks back and checks on Amber, watching her for any more misbehavior.

And Amber is more than happy to oblige.

She locks eyes with Tony as she knocks down his blocks while simultaneously showing him the slightest glimpse of cleavage. She doesn't even attempt to hide her actions this time, and she displays no emotion as she follows our script.

Like I said, she's the perfect control subject.

Tony's eyebrows shoot up, and his eyes widen, his sense of right and wrong demolished. When he returns to his chair, he's breathing hard, struggling to control his shaking hands as they fumble with the mess of wooden blocks in front of him.

He slams two pieces together and then another and another, each time glaring at Amber, waiting for her to cause more trouble…which she soon does.

While he tries to shove a complex polyhedron into a square hole, Amber reaches across the table and slaps his horribly assembled pieces, toppling them.

This is her most blatant sabotage yet, and Tony has taken all he can bear.

"What the hell is your problem?" he shouts at Amber, then turns to the observation mirror. "Hey, over there. She's cheating! This is bullshit."

On our side of the glass, Eugene clicks the stopwatch app on his phone. He shakes his head in disbelief, disappointed.

"Four minutes and twenty-three seconds. He didn't even come close to lasting the full ten minutes. So much for our fucking hypothesis."

"Maybe Tony doesn't really think Amber's a nine," I say. "Or he could be gay."

On the other side of the glass, Tony is out of his seat, waving his hands in the air, flapping his lips as he berates the stoic Amber.

I get out of my chair, ready to defuse the situation, as I think about how quickly humans abandon civility, given the right situations and circumstances.

With a sigh, Eugene unmutes the mic as I step into the testing room.

"Please have a seat," Eugene says, using his deepest, most authoritative tone. "The experiment is now concluded. You will both receive double credit and/or payment for your participation today."

When I close the door behind me, Tony sits down and clears his throat as Amber observes him like he's an insect pinned to a board. Her face remains flat and gives nothing away. She is as cool as someone who knows the entire story and doesn't have to guess what's coming next.

Before Tony can open his mouth to complain again, I begin the official spiel and explain that we are, in fact, *not* testing for problem-solving acuity.

"Thank you for your patience," I say. "We conducted this experiment to measure your responses to those who break the rules and cheat. We are sorry to have misled you, but it is essential subjects do not realize the true nature of the experiment in order to obtain objective results. If this has caused you any distress, once again, we apologize. That being said, please remember the NDA you signed, in which you agreed not to disclose the details of this experiment or its true purpose to anyone for at least one month from today."

Tony nods slowly, still angry but breathing easier, accepting his situation. His silence won't last a full month, but that's okay because we only have two more experiments before we're done gathering our data. After that, we'll compile and analyze our findings and begin writing our lab report—the final group project for our Intro to Experimental Psych class.

When Tony leaves with his Amazon gift cards in hand, Amber closes the door, then sidles up close to me. The heady sweetness of honey engulfs me.

"How'd I do?" she asks.

"Perfect, as always," Eugene says. "I don't know how you stay so calm during these things. We never do as well when we're in the chair."

I can't disagree with him on that count because Amber is a pro at not showing her emotions. For all I know, she doesn't have any.

CHAPTER THREE

PROFESSOR MOOKEN IS speaking in front of a packed lecture hall. Next to him sits a wire-frame cage on a wobbly table, and inside that cage, two rats pace back and forth, separated by an opaque, removable wall.

They know something is up.

As I stare at the trapped rodents, I remember the time my uncle asked me what kind of job I expected to land with a degree in psychology.

"It's better than majoring in English," he said. "But not by much. Why can't you be an engineer?"

This is a valid question, but I don't *want* to be an engineer. Then again, I also don't *want* to become a clinical psychologist or to practice as a therapist one day. I have the rest of my life to make money and earn a living, but for my four years of college, I want to learn as much as possible about everything I *won't* get paid to do in my adult life.

When it comes down to it, I'm taking as many psych classes as I can to understand how the human brain works, hopefully, so I can figure out what's wrong with mine. To find some clue as to why I'm plagued by nightmares, sometimes hear voices from people who aren't there, and see shadows that aren't real.

I clear the memory of my uncle from my head and focus on Mooken's Teaching Assistant, Beverly McDane. Even though I love learning about psychology, Beverly is my TA and the real reason I *never* skip this class.

She's intelligent and well-spoken—supposedly getting master's degrees in psychology and Russian studies at the same time. Add to that a smile I can only dream of being on the receiving end of, and Beverly is the definition of stunning. I don't actually know her very well yet, but I'm certain the two of us would connect deeply and really get along if we ever had the chance. And after my relationship with Amber, that's what I'm looking for—an emotional connection with someone. A person with whom I can fall in love.

"Let's talk about love, shall we?" Mooken says as if reading my thoughts.

The rest of the class erupts in laughter, but I lean forward and pay closer attention.

Professor Mooken is friendly, and I can tell he enjoys teaching. He especially loves experimental psychology, so much so that he is the author of our textbook.

"We all know how mysterious love can be," he says, continuing his lecture.

Then he lifts his chin and hums while he thinks.

Hmmmm.

"But how many of you are aware that love is nothing more than a conditioned response?"

I almost jump in my chair, startled by the loud moans and laughter erupting around me.

"This doesn't mean love is any less valid, true, or magical," he says. "However, in certain circumstances, and at some level, the emotion of love can be controlled and even predicted. To demonstrate this, let us look to our favorite human experimental analog, the beloved laboratory rat."

Every student turns as one, watching the nervous rats scuttling about in their enclosure.

"Do rats fall in love?" Mooken says. "I don't know. I've asked, and they won't tell. However, let us recall Maller's experiment, where he applied a mild electroshock to rats that induced them to feed. As it turns out, when a female rat is nearby, that same electroshock will also prompt a poor little male rat to do something much different from eating.

"You may have noticed my two assistants today, Micky and Minnie. They have the—some would say—enviable job of copulating whenever allowed. And please, the vegans and animal rights activists in the audience need not worry. Neither of these fine specimens will be harmed today. Quite the opposite.

"We have conditioned Micky on the left to associate a mild electric shock with sexual release whenever he has access to his girlfriend. And now, even the slightest tingle of electricity puts him *in the mood.* Observe as I administer a mere .6 milliamps of current for a split second to the floor on his side of the cage."

Mooken turns a knob on the box wired to the cage, and the hum of electricity pierces the quiet classroom for an instant.

As promised, Mickey doesn't writhe in pain. But, unable to see Minnie yet because of the cage partition, he speeds up his pacing, suddenly frantic and unsure of what to do with himself. He is all revved up with nowhere to go.

"The stimulus has been delivered, and Micky knows very well what to expect next. But when he does not immediately get what he seeks, notice how his ardor turns to anxiety and nervousness—similar to an addict being denied a dose of their preferred drug. Hold on, Mickey. Your shock shall not have been in vain."

With a well-placed smile aimed at his students, Professor Mooken lifts the cage partition, and Mickey dashes toward his girlfriend. The two start going at it, and all is well…in Mickey and Minnie's world, at least.

Half of the students groan or laugh uncomfortably while applause breaks out here and there throughout the auditorium.

"Don't think less of Mickey for being a cad and wanting Minnie only for sex. He is merely a product of his own chemistry and how it responds to the stimulus of the shock combined with the presence of a familiar female.

"*Great*, you say. But they're only rats. Well, we don't shock humans—not anymore, at least—but we are not much different from our rodent friends. For instance, it has been shown in controlled experiments that both men and women become more aroused when watching an erotic film *if*, before the movie, they are exposed to a vivid and gory depiction of a car wreck. They don't find automobile accidents sexy, and neither would any of us. But watching a horrific event increases their levels of adrenaline, cortisol, and other internally produced drugs, priming their bodies and making them more susceptible to erotic movies.

"Trust me. No matter how much of a prude or an old-fashioned gal or guy you might consider yourself, the same would happen to you, given those circumstances."

One of the students who always sits in the second row, a young woman with shoulder-length blonde hair, raises her hand. Mooken nods at her, then peers into her eyes over the top rim of his thick spectacles, waiting.

"You're saying love is nothing more than heightened arousal and conditioned sex?"

Mooken's eyebrows raise, eliciting patches of laughter.

"I am *not* saying anything of the sort. But those two things are certainly a good start. Freud believed *all* behavior was triggered by biological energy—and that we spend our lives trying to reduce the tension inside ourselves as it relentlessly builds. It turns out that one of the best ways to do this is to have sex. And we allow ourselves to think this is okay by believing in the human myth called *love.* And make no mistake about it, class—romantic love only exists because we believe in it. On its own, love is not real."

Mooken waits for his assertions to sink in before continuing.

"Love is the result of repeated stimulus-response interactions. One person meets another, and perhaps they have sexual intercourse. Afterward, their internal stressors and tensions are diminished…for a while. The next time they have sex, the same thing happens, and soon, both of them associate their repeated reductions in stress with…"

"The big O!" someone shouts from the middle of the lecture hall.

"Yes, that is correct. The big O. Nirvana. Shangri-La. La Petit Mort, as the French would say. But whatever you call it, every time two people experience that intense, shared sensation, they reinforce their concept of romantic love."

With all this talk about love and sex, I glance at the back of Bev's head, wondering if I can make her sense my gaze by concentrating hard enough. The notion is ridiculous, but the romantic part of me wants to believe she'll be able to feel my intentions from across the room.

I snap back to reality as the class fills with laughter again in response to another one of Mooken's jokes—one I totally missed.

"A few things before I release you into the wild," he says. "You should have gathered most, if not all, of the data for your final lab reports by now. Remember, your final report is due at the end of the semester."

On cue, Amber, Eugene, and I look at each other, stressed because we still have more people to test and because our stupid hypothesis isn't being borne out by our results.

"Last but not least," Mooken continues. "Every Wednesday during October, your beloved Psychology Department will be hosting the Classics in Psychological Thrillers film series, led and organized by our very own Ms. Beverly McDane. Everyone, please give her a hand."

Bev turns part-way in her chair, giving us a token gesture, raising her hand but barely waving. It's clear to me she's not too excited about hosting the movie series.

Regardless, she stands up and faces the class.

"We have some great films for you this month," she says. "Tomorrow we start with *A Clockwork Orange*—a tender romance about a gang of hoodlums who roam the English countryside in search of…love."

I haven't seen this movie yet, but judging from the trickles of laughter in the classroom, *A Clockwork Orange* is *not* a love story at all.

"And, although there is no requirement to do so, anyone who would like to volunteer to help with the show tomorrow night would be greatly appreciated. Unfortunately, you will not be compensated in any way, but please come see me after class if you're interested. Thank you."

As far as I'm concerned, the movie could be about a cartoon mouse. All I hear is an opportunity to interact with Beverly outside of class, and I practically sit on my hands to keep them from shooting into the air to volunteer my services.

When Beverly sits down, and Mooken dismisses the class, sixty students stand as one, eager to move on to wherever they're going next. But I'm one of the lucky ones with no more classes on Tuesdays, which means I'm *not* in a hurry. With my most disarming face locked and loaded, I start making my way to the front of the class, where Bev is gathering her books.

But Eugene grabs me by the shoulder before I make it two steps.

"Dude, what are you doing? We need to talk about our report."

"Email me what I need to do," I say. "I'll get right on it."

The unhappy Eugene grunts as I walk away, but I don't care about him. A few seconds later, I'm standing in front of Bev, hovering above her, inhaling her almond scent.

She looks up, half-covered by my shadow that's blocking the stark fluorescent ceiling lights hitting her from above.

"I can help tomorrow night," I say.

"That's great," she says, looking up at me. "Meet me in the basement auditorium at six-thirty. I need someone to sit at the laptop in case something goes wrong with the movie file. Does that sound okay?"

I stammer through my next words, bolstered by the belief that my face will make Bev trust me and not feel threatened.

My face is my superpower, I repeat in my head. *My face is my secret weapon.*

"I was wondering if you also maybe have a minute to talk," I say. "On your way out now. It's semi-private."

Her eyebrows arch. Maybe intrigued. Maybe frightened. But after pondering my offer, she glances at Mooken and finishes gathering her books.

We leave the lecture hall together and walk down the hall. And even though we don't talk, this is already one of my favorite college moments. I awkwardly throw my hand above her head and push the building's heavy exit doors open, letting her leave first.

Outside, we stand on the brick-paved walkway, soaking in the cool autumn afternoon. When she looks up at me, I'm barely ready for the sparkle of her hazel eyes.

She really is beautiful, but after a second or two of staring, I catch myself and realize she's waiting for me to say something.

"I have nightmares," I say, spitting out my words. "Well, not all of my bad dreams are really nightmares, but they're all pretty intense and stressful. I was thinking I should see someone, but I don't know where to start. I was wondering if you had any time to talk, maybe I could get your opinion. You know, buy you a meal in exchange for pointing me at some books that might help? I know it's a lot to ask, but anything I can do to repay you, just name it. What do you say?"

She examines me, trying to decide whether this is my feeble attempt at asking her out or if I'm a sincere, stupid underclassman in need of actual help.

Now it's my turn to stand and wait for her to say something as a group of students splits long enough to maneuver around us.

As they do, I imagine I can hear their thoughts.

Look at that fool trying to make something happen with the TA.

That is so sad.

"I can't give you free therapy if that's what you're asking," Beverly finally says. "Actually, I couldn't give you any kind of therapy, even if you paid me. I don't have my degree yet, and I'm far from being licensed to practice. Plus, you're one of my *students*."

Her formal tone sucker punches me, and I'm too stunned to do what I should, which is turn and run. But thankfully, her next sentence is kinder, more hopeful, and helpful.

"I *am* interested in the study of dreams, though," she says.

Her mind spins, putting together pieces to a puzzle I can't see, and I wonder if she's considering my offer or thinking about something totally different.

"You remember what Freud said about dreams, right?" she says. "He believed they were unconscious activities that provide direct insight into the workings of our unconscious minds."

"So these terrible dreams probably reflect how I unconsciously feel in my waking life?"

She shrugs, nods, and turns to walk away, but she motions with her head for me to follow her.

And I do—an apostle intent on his master's teachings.

"That could be the case," she says. "But like I said, I won't and *can't* give you any kind of therapy or even hazard a guess about any underlying mental health issues you might have."

I don't know how to, or even if I'm supposed to, respond to this.

"What was your name again?" she says. "I'm sorry. We have a lot of students in this class."

"It's James, but I prefer Jim. And for sure not Jimmy, please."

She emits an authentic laugh, and my shoulders relax. Even as untouchable as Beverly is, she still reacts to humorous banter.

"I have a meeting with Professor Mooken in a few," she says. "But *maybe* we can go to lunch sometime if you want to talk more about what the literature says about dreams. But if you think you need a therapist, I suggest trying Student Health. They offer free counseling to students."

She stops walking, looks away briefly, and squints before turning to me.

"You know, you *could* ask Professor Mooken for help. He's not practicing, but he's licensed in Virginia. Depending on how generous he's feeling, he might meet with you a few times. Off-the-record, of course. Maybe he could assess you enough to recommend a therapist who specializes in your issues."

"Thanks for the advice," I say, and I mean it.

Her upper lip twitches almost imperceptibly, and she squints harder, even though the sun has moved behind a bank of clouds. There's an edge to her in this moment I haven't seen before, and as I study her face, I'm certain she has plenty of secret layers most people will never see. She's a complex person, and I'm intrigued by what's going on below her surface.

While I stand there, stunned that Beverly McDane has agreed to have lunch with me, she gives me a tight smile and signals it's time for her to go.

"Thanks again, Beverly," I say. "See you tomorrow night at the movie."

"Right. Wonderful," she says. "And please, call me Bev."

I wave goodbye as she leaves, heading back to Gilmer Hall to meet with Professor Mooken.

When I turn on my heels, ready to return to Lambeth, a gray-green lizard the size of a ballpoint pen pokes its head out from a nearby bush. It flashes its tongue almost too quickly for me to see, then fixes me with its cold eyes.

As I stand, transfixed by the reptile's alien expression, my dad's voice fills my head.

You're not fooling anyone, boy.

CHAPTER FOUR

I LOVE GOING to the movies. But watching a film in the basement auditorium of the Psych Department is a different experience than I'm used to.

No popcorn.

No previews of upcoming blockbusters.

No drinks, other than hidden flasks of vodka and the occasional beer bottle rolling beneath the rows of fold-up auditorium seats.

At some level, we're here to enjoy a movie, but we're also here to study it. To learn from it. After all, we are attending an institution of higher learning. And tonight's show promises a lot to analyze, both for film students and for psych majors. I haven't seen *A Clockwork Orange* yet. But after an online search, it's clear that the packed audience of students and faculty is buzzing because of the movie's controversial reputation.

Those who haven't seen the film, like me, wonder if the hype is warranted.

Those who have seen it are busy watching the rest of us. For them, we're the main attraction tonight, not the movie.

But I'm only here for one reason—Bev. And that is why I almost turn and leave when a round-bodied young man named Carl greets me and says he's running the show tonight instead of her.

"Where's Bev?" I ask, but Carl's face scrunches up as if he's not allowed to share such sensitive information with me.

Before I can flee, he walks me up a short set of stairs in the back of the auditorium to a cramped control booth, fully equipped with a digital projector and a wide observation window, from which I can look down upon the audience as they continue to pour in.

"When I give you the signal from the stage," Carl says, "turn on the projector and hit the play button on the movie file. That's all you have to do. And don't worry. I've already deactivated the screen saver."

"I think I can handle it," I say, but Carl looks doubtful as he hurries away, leaving me with his open laptop.

Seconds later, I see him through the wide window as he greets Professor Mooken in the front row. Carl nods his head repeatedly as Mooken pelts him with questions I can't hear.

As the place fills up with people, my phone vibrates. It's Dad again, texting me.

I hope you're studying.

In class right now, I text back. *Can't talk.*

My heart aches when I blow him off like this, but I can't be there to talk with him every time he wants. Life doesn't work that way, and communicating with him is always a one-way street.

He never speaks with me, only *at* me.

With fifteen minutes before show time, I scan the crowd for Bev, but she's still not here. I do, however, recognize a few familiar faces from class.

There's the blonde who always sits in the second row.

There's the jock who does his best to stay awake during Mooken's lectures. He's sitting among a row of attractive sorority girls down below. They hurriedly type on their phones, texting each other, even though they're only mere feet away. And as usual, the jock yawns while all of this goes on around him.

I have nothing in common with these people, but here we all are. Tonight we are all sitting together—subjects in the same big experiment.

Ten minutes to go, and my thoughts land on Bev again.

Has she been in an accident?

Is she sick?

Or is she on a date with another man?

Out of all my imagined stories, the worst is that she's stayed home because she doesn't want to see *me*.

No, that can't be it, I think.

You're right, my father says in my head. *She doesn't care enough about you to miss her movie tonight.*

"Leave me alone," I say, as I stare straight ahead, concentrating on Carl, waiting for my cue.

Soon, the lights dim. Carl steps on the stage in front of the screen and holds up his hand—the universal sign for everyone to shut the hell up and pay attention.

As I said, this is a movie, but it's also an educational event.

"Welcome to the first feature in our Classics in Psychological Thrillers film series," Carl says into a hand-held mic. "Tonight's film is the infamous *A Clockwork Orange*, written by Anthony Burgess and adapted for film and directed by Stanley Kubrick. The movie stars Malcolm McDowell, known for his controversial roles, such as playing the Roman Emperor in the semi-mainstream, erotic movie, *Caligula*."

The crowd collectively squirms in its seats, a giant worm feeling the first drop of water as it falls from the sky. We all know about the Roman Emperor Caligula and his orgies. But the mention of an X-rated movie stirs up the men in the audience as if the mere allusion to sex will increase their chances of getting laid tonight. Meanwhile, most of the women glance from side-to-side, more acutely aware than usual of the cavemen surrounding them.

Carl runs through a few more announcements about events the Student Union is hosting.

A comedian will perform at the amphitheater this weekend.

A local band is playing at the Pavilion.

There will be a pickup game of disc rugby at Lambeth Field on Sunday.

And finally, Carl looks up at me and points.

"Enjoy the show," he says.

I turn on the projector, start the movie file, and settle in to watch the show like everyone else.

After the first fifteen minutes, the film has already lived up to its reputation. Handfuls of students leave the auditorium in silent but clear protest after an explicit rape scene.

The young protagonist, if that's what the main character, Alex, can be called, is vicious, with no conscience, and mentally unstable.

But somehow, he's also likable and oddly innocent. I would never want to meet him in real life, but watching his exploits projected in front of me is mesmerizing.

With a considerably less crowded audience, the movie continues to unfold, one violent scene after another. To me, it's both provocative and disturbing, but the film also centers around experimental psychology, which explains why it was chosen.

Why *Bev* chose it.

After Alex is apprehended by the authorities and imprisoned, he volunteers for a new type of state-issued rehabilitative program in return for a shortened prison term. The scientists, who don't look at all like Professor Mooken, Eugene, Amber, or me, strap Alex to a chair in the front row of a movie theater.

They force his eyes to stay open and barrage him with filmed violence and porn.

Alex can't avoid what he's watching, and neither can we. There's nowhere for any of us to hide.

The difference between him and me is that I am disturbed by the violence on screen, whereas Alex enjoys it and wants more. It's not until the doctors inject him with nausea-inducing medicine that he begins to wretch and recoil as the images flash past him.

Adding to the horror and serving as a dark contrast to the events in this scene, Beethoven's beautiful Ninth Symphony—Alex's favorite piece—plays in the background while he's being reconditioned.

After his treatment is complete, Alex is released back into society—a cured man. He is no longer physically capable of committing crimes. But he also can't get angry enough to stick up for himself without getting sick, nor can he listen to Beethoven's Ninth. Soon, pathetic and defenseless, he becomes the victim of the people he's terrorized in the past.

I imagine most audience members are happy when Alex finally receives a dose of his own medicine. But I see him as a sad character—a young man no one understands or cares about.

He needs help, but all the doctors do is strip him of his humanity.

In the end, the state reverses Alex's conditioning. Once again he is able to enjoy his favorite classical composer while simultaneously dreaming of violence.

And that's the end of the show.

After the credits roll, I close the movie file and turn off the projector, dutifully concluding my role in tonight's event.

When the lights come up, the audience is buzzing. Discussions pop up everywhere about this visceral story. Nothing about the movie was settling or pleasant, but it was compelling, and no one can dispute that.

A quick look reveals that Bev still isn't here, and when Carl starts the questions and answers, I'm completely uninterested.

If I only knew where Bev was, I could check on her, but I know nothing about her personal life.

And then I realize I'm sitting alone with Carl's laptop. I remain still and listen for footsteps, but once I'm confident I'm alone, I open his list of contacts.

A few seconds later, I find Bev's information—her cell phone and address. I only feel a little guilty when I snap a quick photo of her file because my intentions are pure—and I only want to make sure she's okay.

After I close her file, I stand up and leave quietly with Beethoven's Ninth Symphony booming in my head.

The evening is chilly, and I should go home, but it's Wednesday, I'm in college, and the night has not yet started.

I leave Gilmer Hall and cut across the Grounds until I'm walking along the lightly populated, paved paths that skirt the hospital at the edge of the university's property. Soon, I end up at the strip of restaurants, bars, and shops known as the *Corner.*

I'm tempted to hit Shenanigans, where I've hung out plenty of times before. But I've never seen Bev there, so I head to the St. Maarten Cafe instead, where an older crowd parties.

As I make my way to the bar proper, I'm surprised Amber and Eugene are talking in the middle of a group of older guys. Amber is the only female, and that's the way she likes it. She's the center of all attention, even in this crowded bar.

They're not the only ones I recognize.

My poetry teacher is here. He is a pale, gaunt man who speaks with precision and perfect pauses, every line pouring from his mouth as a perfectly metered stanza.

My English Lit TA is here, too. He's a pure introvert unless he's drunk, like now. Tonight, he commands a small audience of students and peers. He is a Shakespearean character come to life.

Before I can catch the bartender's attention and order a drink, a switch turns off inside me. My stomach sours, and I lose my appetite for alcohol and people. I am only focused on one person tonight, and *she* is not here.

Before Amber and Eugene spot me, I reverse course and exit the way I entered, nodding at the bouncer and humming Beethoven's music as I step onto the sidewalk.

People pass me—walking right through me. I am a phantom to them, and I'm fine with this.

I stay still and think for a moment. I could continue looking for Bev out here in the wild, but she's probably at home sick. Why else would she not have attended her own movie presentation?

I start walking again, leaving behind the commotion of the Corner.

Fifteen minutes later, I am standing on a buckling and cracked sidewalk, staring at the old house where Bev lives. Judging from the number of cars parked in the driveway and the size of the home, she lives here with several housemates.

I can't determine anything about how Bev is doing from so far away. But I did the right thing in coming here.

How else am I supposed to watch over and protect her?

CHAPTER FIVE

THE NEXT MORNING, I shower, shave, and pick out one of my nicest, buttoned, long-sleeve shirts—one made of soft black cotton. I take a different route to my psych class than usual, heading down Emmet Street, then winding my way to Gilmer Hall, where a black-tailed squirrel clutches to the side of a tree, looking down on me as I enter the building and make my way to the lecture hall.

For once, I am early for Mooken's class.

I station myself where Amber, Eugene, and I usually sit and keep an eye out for Bev. I don't want her to think I'm a stalker, so I search only with my eyes and remain motionless.

Amber pops in five minutes later, and Eugene enters from the other side door shortly after. With only a minute before class is supposed to start, we three are together, exchanging quick greetings and opening our textbooks and laptops.

Professor Mooken enters at the stroke of the hour and walks up to the podium alone. My breath leaves me when he welcomes the class because Bev is still nowhere to be seen.

I barely listen to his discussion about classical conditioning that day. And I don't snap out of my daze until the end of his lecture, while he's thanking everyone who showed up to see *A Clockwork Orange* the night before.

He summarizes the questions and answers but doesn't mention Bev being absent.

I study his face and decide he knows something about her the rest of us don't.

Of course, he does. He's her professor.

Mooken dismisses the class, and the usual mad rush ensues. But I take my time, ignoring Eugene and Amber, who want to talk about how to start compiling our notes and writing the actual *damn* report.

"Only two more to go," Eugene says. "Try not to be late to them, Jim."

Amber doesn't say a word, but I can feel her judging me as I make my way down the center aisle to where Mooken is packing up to leave.

"Professor Mooken?" I say, unsure of how to start the conversation I really want to have.

I *want* to ask him about Bev. But before I do something stupid and demand he tell me what's happened to her, I remember Bev's suggestion about discussing my *issues* with Mooken.

"Yes, young man?" Mooken says, waiting for me to proceed.

His voice is deep, almost comically so, as if he were auditioning for the role of a wise father in a play.

"I was hoping I could stop by your office sometime and…maybe talk?"

Mooken flashes me a flat smile and returns to stuffing notes into his well-worn leather briefcase.

"Not about class," I say. "Which I'm really enjoying…But, your TA, Bev. She thought you might be able to help me with something."

Mooken's face dims, and his eyes sparkle at the same time. Both are involuntary reactions to the mention of Bev's name. He glares at me, but at least he's paying attention.

"About what did my illustrious teaching assistant suggest you speak to me?"

I glance at my feet, deciding between telling him the truth or making something up. I haven't shared details of my dreams with anyone before—not since I was a kid, at least. And even though Mooken is a professional psychiatrist and counselor, being honest about the horrible things I see and do when I sleep won't be easy.

"She said you're licensed to practice in Virginia," I say.

He gives me a half-nod, urging me to continue—to speed up whatever I'm so painfully trying to say. When I remain silent, he sighs.

"Am I licensed? Yes," he says. "Practicing? No. Practicing on students? *Definitely* not."

"Bev thought you could help me find the right person to talk to, though. Maybe you could do an initial assessment or something and suggest a specialist who could help me."

He stares at me—through me—like he's already assessed everything about me and knows exactly what's wrong with me but doesn't want to say. After exhaling loudly, he speaks, and now his voice is calm, metered, and without judgment.

"Next Tuesday," he says. "My office, at three-thirty. Does that work for you?"

I don't even review my schedule in my head because my answer is *yes*, even if I have something else already planned at that time.

"Yes, sir," I say. "And thank you very much."

He nods and turns to ignore me again. I want to leave, but I need to ask about Bev directly, even at the risk of annoying him more than I already have.

"I wanted to thank Bev for her advice," I say. "But I didn't see her today. Or last night at the movie."

Trying to outwit a psychologist is a foolish endeavor. The man in front of me has seen and heard it all. And he knows I'm fishing for information about his TA.

I wait for him to tell me that Bev is none of my business, but instead, he looks up and studies my face—my unthreatening, perfectly harmless face—and his scowl softens.

"Ms. McDane is out on a personal matter. But when I see her, I will let her know you and I spoke. And that you expressed your gratitude and concern. You are…Mr. Straub. Isn't that correct?"

Now, it's my turn to scowl. How does he know my name? Yes, I'm his student, but I'm only one of many, and it's not like I've been participating in class.

He sees the confusion on my face.

"One of your laboratory partners," he says. "A Ms. Louder stopped by my office to discuss the use of tables in your lab report.

She said you and another young man were in a group together. She *also* mentioned that the three of you have not yet finished gathering your data."

I try to smile, but even on the best of days, it comes across as fake.

"We only have two more experiments to run," I say. "We'll finish on time."

Mooken gives me a flat grin devoid of any emotion other than maybe a trace of pity.

"Perhaps you might aim a little higher than simply meeting the deadline," he says. "I will see you in my office next week. Now, if you'll excuse me, I must be going. Have an enjoyable remainder of your day, Mr. Straub."

I mumble something that sounds like *you, too*, as I step back and let him leave.

I remain standing at the front of the class, fantasizing that I'm the teacher providing insight and knowledge to my students. But the truth is, I have nothing to impart to anyone and nothing worth passing on.

By the time my daydream dissolves, the lecture hall is empty. Even Amber and Eugene are gone, and for a moment, I wonder why Amber didn't tell me about her visit with the professor.

I shrug. Maybe she mentioned it to Eugene.

I don't care either way.

Since Bev didn't show up for class, I'm now hungry, dressed nicer than usual, and without plans for lunch. I decide to treat myself to a meal at one of the restaurants on the Corner—perhaps a Nukem' sandwich from *The Corner Deli*.

I begin my cross-campus trip, but with each step, something feels *off* and gnaws at me.

A trio of sorority girls walks toward me. Their hands flail and flutter, conducting their loud, shrill conversation. I don't have enough time to cross the street and get out of their way, so I turn sideways to let them pass. They separate just enough to walk around me, and soon, all that is left of them are lingering particles of perfume and body oil.

Coconut butter, I think, as I continue on my way.

A minute later, the birds and insects around me all go silent.

It's a subtle warning others may miss, but I'm always listening. I pay attention to my surroundings and what the world has to tell me.

The creatures have done their job warning me. Now it's up to me to discover the threat.

Before I consciously process the slapping of feet behind me, my nape hairs stand on end. I don't have to turn around to know that someone is approaching more quickly than normal. I speed up and take a sharp turn at the next street. And as soon as I'm around the corner, I walk faster, almost running. When I turn down the next street, I look back and finally glimpse my pursuer.

I recognize Tony—the local from our experiment—and his wiry frame immediately.

Despite the distance I've put between us, the snarl that distorts his weathered face is enough to tell me he is not here on pleasant business.

Maybe he resents being duped in our laboratory drama. Perhaps he thought he was making headway with Amber, and he's angry that she was part of the act. Whatever his reason, I increase my pace, walking as fast as possible without running. When I do, the cadence of his feet hitting the asphalt behind me speeds up as well.

I'm not a runner. I never have been.

But as my adrenal glands flood my bloodstream with a huge batch of epinephrine, I break into a full sprint. When I look back, Tony's in full pursuit. But luckily, he's not in that great of shape, despite being rail-thin. His heavy breathing is louder than the sound of my pounding heart.

Even so, the next time I check behind me, his form is bigger as he continues to gain.

I turn another corner and move onto the sidewalk that runs

along Rugby Road. The Greek-inspired fraternity and sorority houses blur by on my right as I jump onto the shoulder to avoid the crowd of students as I approach Beta Bridge.

As my heart slams inside my chest, my surroundings snap into clear focus.

The graffiti on Beta Bridge is newly painted in spring motifs of flowers and Easter eggs.

A female student steps on an earthworm without realizing it, smearing its body on the concrete as she crosses the bridge.

I inhale the sour odor of wet mud from Mad Bowl—the field on my right where popular guys, muddy and drunk, play rugby in the wet grass.

My brain processes all of these things in a single instant. And I silently thank evolution for the chemicals in my bloodstream allowing me to maintain this pace for much longer than usual.

But I don't kid myself. My body is only responding this well to being chased because Tony is the dog and I'm the rabbit running for my life.

When I glance behind me, Tony has taken to the street, running against traffic, and has halved the distance between us. I should stop and let him say what he wants to me—allow him to vent his anger in front of all these student witnesses.

Being in public should keep me safe from any serious harm. Besides, even though he's angry, he's not a psychopath—not if Mooken's questionnaire is as good as he claims at screening out psychopaths, sociopaths, and people with other serious mental issues.

While thinking about all of this, I spend a second too long looking over my shoulder and almost wipe out when I run into someone.

The person grabs me by my shoulders and spins me around, and I struggle to move past him. I'm an unwilling partner in this dark dance with him, and the sounds of bassoons and kettle drums from Beethoven's Ninth flood my head as I ball my right hand into a fist, ready to fight if he won't let me go.

But before I can throw a punch, Eugene speaks.

"Calm the fuck down, man. What is going on with you?"

I can't construct a complete sentence. Not yet. But even though Eugene is not my favorite person, his face is more welcomed than Tony's.

I leave my hand clenched in a fist, then turn around, ready to face my pursuer head-on. But he's not there anymore.

"It was that guy," I say to Eugene between staggered breaths. "Tony. The townie from our experiment."

"Slow down," Eugene says, jutting his square jaw forward. "What are you talking about? I don't see anyone. And who the hell did you say Tony was?"

I wave my hand at him to stop talking. He helps me step up onto the sidewalk, and we walk over to a patch of grass away from the flow of students.

I bend forward and brace my hands on my knees, trying to return my breathing to some level of normal.

Eugene starts to talk, but I hold up a hand and shake my head, silencing him again.

Ten seconds later, I am together enough to try to explain.

"The local guy, Tony, from our experiment last week," I say as slowly as possible. "He chased me from the Corner all the way here."

Eugene furrows his brow.

How can he not remember Tony?

But his face shows no signs of recollection.

Despite this, Eugene scans the street with me, but Tony is gone. The coward probably dove into the crowd and hid when he saw I was no longer alone.

Even though I feel fine after a few minutes, Eugene walks with me back to Lambeth, pretending to be a good guy. But I figure he must want something from me.

"Amber and I were a little worried about you, man," he finally says. "You looked kind of out of it when we left Mooken's class. You didn't even answer us when we were talking to you. You just stood there with your mouth hanging open."

"I was thinking about something," I say. "Sorry about that."

"We saw you talking with the professor. Did you ask him about our lab report?"

I squint, trying to process Eugene's question.

"I was talking to him about something else," I say. "And checking to see how Bev was doing."

"Bev? You mean Beverly McDane, our TA? Tell me you're not really going after her, please. I mean, holy shit, man. She's a grad student, and gorgeous, and smart. No offense, but she is *way* out of your league."

"You think everyone is out of my league," I say.

"That's not true. You went out with Amber," he says.

I don't want to tell him anything else, but I can't resist putting him in his place.

"She said *yes* to lunch."

"Who?"

"Bev."

"You are shitting me," he says. "You asked out the TA. And she said *yes*? In what reality does that happen?"

"Must be my personality," I say. "Or my non-threatening face."

I wait for Eugene to respond to me. But he's tuned out, staring through the columns of the Colonnades at a game of disc golf in the field below, oblivious to me.

I think of my father, and even though he isn't here, I've listened to him all my life and can predict with one hundred percent accuracy what he would say to me in this situation.

Nothing good is gonna come of this. That woman is trouble.

CHAPTER SIX

BY THE TIME I step inside my apartment that night, I'm exhausted.

I make a quick stop in my bedroom, but when I return to the living room, a nude woman is waiting for me, sitting on an antique wooden chair. Her hands are wedged between her spread legs, steepled together to form the silhouette of a heart.

My own heart speeds up at the sight of her round, natural breasts. But her face frightens me. Or, rather, it is the lack of her face that is terrifying. Her head is covered by a burlap sack with black buttons sewn into it for eyes and heavy stitching that forms a lopsided smile across its rough material.

As I stare into the dull plastic of her button eyes, I am no longer sexually excited.

I am only afraid.

From the side of the woman's neck, a shining prehensile tail curls outward, an octopus's tentacle without suckers. I stand frozen in front of her, terrified and wondering why she is in my apartment.

She remains still and quiet, waiting.

I want to get away, but as soon as I think that, I realize I'm standing only inches away from her.

She opens her legs farther and tilts her head, proposing a silent question.

I could easily reach out and touch her, which is what she wants me to do. But becoming one with her would have nothing to do with love. Despite this, the animal inside me overrides my terror, demanding that I lean closer.

Close enough that the burlap scratches my cheek.

Something here reminds me of Bev, although I thank God this isn't her.

My blood rushes and recedes so powerfully inside me that I can measure my pulse without touching my skin.

I extend my fingers, and when the woman's warmth wraps around them, my breath catches in my throat, and I can't breathe.

When I sit up in bed, it is early in the morning and hours before dawn.

I am alone.

My heart is tap-dancing in my chest, and beads of sweat dot my forehead.

My body is still alert but also terrified as I breathe deeply, relieved the horrible apparition of the woman was only in my dream.

As the last strand of sleep dissolves around me, a strange guilt tugs at my gut—a gnawing sickness because it feels like I've cheated on Bev, even though that is ridiculous.

First, we aren't dating and hardly know each other yet. Secondly, the woman with the bag over her head was a figment of my dream, and I can't be blamed for the dark things I do while I'm asleep.

Can I?

I didn't ask to be visited by a nightmare succubus tonight.

Yet, here I am, electrified as if the entire encounter had been real.

My body doesn't care about my complicated thoughts and justifications. All it knows is what it *wants* and what it *needs*.

And it needs release.

I close my eyes, and the woman is there again, sitting on the hard wooden chair. But this time, she's not wearing a sack, and nothing is growing from her neck. She has Bev's face, which alone is enough for me to surrender to her. My breath grows more harried with each passing second, and it's not long before a flood of endorphins overwhelms me, and I am wracked with pleasure.

Afterward, I keep my eyes closed and drift back to sleep.

CHAPTER SEVEN

WHEN I DRAG myself out of bed, it's almost noon, and I'm thankful for the leftover lo mein in the fridge. It's a greasy brunch, but it satisfies me.

Today is Saturday, and my day is free. As a luxury, after eating, I linger in the shower for half an hour and scrub the darkness from my skin until my flesh is pink.

When I finally step outside, it's late in the afternoon. As I walk through the common area, surrounded on either side by three-story apartment buildings, I imagine I'm in a prison yard with my fellow inmates. The truth is, the students buzzing around me are my people, and I'm one of their Resident Advisors—an RA entrusted by the university to take care of them.

Unlike my colleagues, however, I do not thrive on interaction with tons of people on a daily basis. And I certainly wasn't chosen for this role because of my outgoing and shiny personality. But, as we're discovering in our psych experiment, I have other strengths, such as people feeling comfortable opening up to me. One of those people is Bob, who sits at the bottom of the metal staircase outside his first-floor apartment. He's holding his head, and his flesh is pale green, making him look close to death.

"Hi, Bob," I say, approaching him like it's any other, regular day and not one where he has the pallor of the undead.

"Hey, Jim," he says, barely glancing up at me. "Sorry I look like such shit right now. I gave up cigarettes yesterday, and I'm having a rough time kicking the habit."

I'm no doctor, but Bob's shaking hands tell me he's withdrawing from something far more sinister than nicotine.

Part of my job as an RA is to support students like him whenever possible. But invading his privacy isn't an option. I stand there for a few seconds, giving him the opportunity to elaborate, to reach out to me for assistance. But he only groans. He doesn't want to tell me anything further, and he's not hurting anyone. So I make a mental note to check up on him later.

"Let me know if there is anything I can help with, okay?" I say.

He nods, and his face softens—relieved I'm about to leave him to his suffering.

I continue past him and walk until I reach Lambeth Field, a crumbling, open-air amphitheater crowned by two rows of parallel columns known as the Colonnades. I climb the steps that lead up to the columns and walk between them, heading for the Corner, where I can get a proper meal.

I don't make it half-way through the columns before something snaps in the woods off to my left.

My senses sharpen, and I scan the trees for whoever or whatever made the noise. A pit in my stomach hardens, and I worry it could be Tony again, hiding, waiting to attack me. Even though I don't see him or anyone else, I catalog every fallen stick and pointed rock within arm's reach that I could use as a weapon if I had to.

The relaxation from the slow start to my day has vanished, and I am once again a lone traveler threading my way through a hostile land.

When I make it to the street, I remember St. Maarten's from earlier in the week and decide it's the perfect destination for me right now. It's dark enough inside, even while the sun is out, and I'll be able to sit alone while pretending to be a participating member of humanity.

Fifteen minutes later, I step onto the sidewalk that runs along the Corner, passing the ATM, Mincer's souvenir shop, and Bobo Bagels, before turning down Fourteenth Street to St. Maarten's. The place is as dark as I was hoping it would be as I sidle up to the bar, order a beer, and pretend to enjoy the sports game everyone is watching on the television.

I've never understood how people can become so involved in the physical accomplishments of others. But I know that applauding when the local team scores is essential to blending in, and so, when everyone else makes noise, I join in with them to complete my disguise of normalcy.

The bartender passes me a beer without asking to see my ID. Something about drinking during the day validates it as legitimate adult behavior and less like an underage kid trying to get drunk.

That first beer is ice cold and goes down smoothly. When I look up, my reflection stares back at me, unflinching, in the bar's mirror. I shift my head, hiding from myself behind a row of bottles. But when I sit up straight again, my face is still there, unmoving.

No matter how much I twist and turn, I'm the one person I can never escape.

I sigh and order another beer.

The grad student working the bar slides me another Yuengling and glances past me. I stiffen, ready for anything, but then I recognize Amber's scent of honey and the flash of her dark brown hair as she sits down next to me.

"Hey," we both say, overlapping one another.

"Nice shirt," she says. "Waiting for someone?"

I sneer and take a long swig from the beer the bartender places in front of me.

Amber is in jeans and a form-fitting, buttoned blouse that shows the top lace of her maroon bra and enough of her breasts that I'm forced to remember the last time we had sex.

For a moment, the same dread from my recent nightmare starts to mount inside me. Except this time, the darkness of the woman next to me is no mystery. I am well familiar with it.

She wants to talk, and I will be polite, but I can already hear my father warning me.

Don't be stupid, he says in my thoughts. *Don't get mixed up with her again.*

I know he's right. But I'm drinking. I'm lonely. I have no idea if Bev will or won't work out. And Amber is here right now—a lioness sizing up her prey.

Surprisingly, it isn't the promise of potential sex that softens my mood toward her or the third beer I order and subsequently chug. It's the fact that I rarely had any bad dreams when the two of us were dating.

With that much sex, I was worn out most of the time and slept soundly at night.

And God knows I could use a good night's sleep right now.

"I thought I might find you here," she says, nodding at the bartender to bring her a beer. "Eugene told me a local guy from one of our experiments chased you yesterday. Are you okay?"

She punctuates her words with a quick rub of my thigh—her fingers like syringes dumping opium into my nervous system.

Not succumbing to her is going to be difficult. Maybe impossible.

But I can do this because I want more than just intense sex.

I want to connect with someone.

I want to be more than the *other guy*.

So I change the discussion to focus on her.

"Since you walked in here," I say, "almost every man and a few women have been staring at you. You could have any one of them if you wanted. Tell me, Amber, how does that feel?"

"Meh," she says. "It's okay."

We both laugh, mainly because her answer surprises me and because she's being totally candid.

She's dealt with attention like this all her life. Unlike me. I'm more of a niche, acquired taste. But for some reason, even though Amber knows it's over between us, she peers right into my eyes and grins as she sips her beer.

God help me.

She rubs my lower back delicately while we talk about little things. The weather. Homework. She even asks about my dad as her fingernails gently scrape across the back of my shirt and send chills up and down my spinal cord.

I close my eyes—an involuntary reflex.

"I know you don't want to be in a relationship with me," she says. "I get that. But the sex *was* pretty good, wasn't it? I mean, it was really good. Don't you want more of that? Don't you want more of…this?"

Fuck, fuck. I will not survive this.

My eyes roll into the back of my skull, and my veins fill with a potent mix of internally created drugs so strong that my body shivers, unsure of what to do with itself.

Amber sees this happening and knows she has me in her snare.

"Still dating your boyfriend in Jersey?" I say, hoping for some part of our conversation to remind me how much I want nothing to do with her.

With most women, a comment about the guy she was cheating with would cause a visible impact, but not with Amber. She doesn't even flinch before she answers.

"I still see him when I'm in New Jersey," she says. "But that's not where I am right now. And, Jim, it's been a while since I've been to Jersey, if you know what I mean."

"Why me?" I say, turning to her, asking her the one question I've always wanted to ask. "Just about every guy I know would kill to get into bed with you."

She smiles—a chess player who's realized she has checkmate in two moves.

"Who said anything about a bed?"

Her comment hits me directly below the belt.

"Finish your drink," she says, then slides her beer over to me. "And mine. I want to show you a shortcut I discovered out back."

Both of our beers are down my throat, and the glasses are empty in less than a minute.

I've given up, and we both know it. And to be honest, I've surrendered to worse things in my life.

Amber throws a twenty on the bar, takes my hand, and walks me out. I know I'm stepping down a dark path—one my body will love but which will leave my soul empty.

As she leads me outside, the other patrons stare and judge.

What does that guy have?

He must be rich.

Must have a big dick.

If only they knew none of those things apply to me.

I walk in silence—marching to my moral execution, even as my body is geared up and excited. It's been a month since I've indulged in flesh, and as unfulfilling as this encounter will be, it can't be worse than waking up from another nightmare and masturbating about a demonic woman wearing a bag over her head.

Once outside, Amber pulls me over to a strip of trees at the back of the tiny parking lot.

This used to be one of our favorite things to do as a couple.

After we find a tree wide enough to shield us from other people as they enter and leave the bar, she leans in and kisses me deeply. Her taste is familiar and dismantles any defenses I have left.

She looks me in the eye and doesn't say a word.

I know the game.

I know her kink.

My old reflex returns, and I spin her around, pressing her hard into the tree's rough bark. She wraps her arms around the tree as far as they will go. If this had happened back when we were dating, I'd have been prepared and would have already tied her wrists together with whatever I could find. As it is, I unfasten her jeans and pull them down so they're bunched above her knees, preventing her from spreading her legs. Her panties would typically be the next to go, except she isn't wearing any.

In the parking lot next to us, a group of students walks past, entering the St. Maarten Cafe.

A stray cat runs across the alley, its tail high in the air as it hunts for its next meal.

A worker from the bar empties the trash.

And Amber and I start to fuck.

How romantic.

But that's part of what turns her on—the lack of tenderness and emotion. That, plus the possibility of getting caught, fills the air with electricity. To ensure she doesn't scream—which she's done plenty in the past—and because she likes it, I move my hand to her face and cover her mouth.

I never did anything like this before I met Amber, but she likes to pretend she's being held and taken against her will. And even though that's not my *thing*, my inner caveman reacts, and soon I'm breathing hard and fully engaged.

I release my hand enough so she can breathe, but not so much that it ruins her fantasy. When she moans and pushes back against me, I force my brain to imagine I'm in a calm meadow so the experience won't end too soon.

As we push against the tree, again and again, her pleasure mounts. She goes up on her toes, and her legs shake.

Within seconds, she convulses and emits a guttural moan that is only partly human.

But she's not done yet.

She pushes against me even harder, not giving me a chance to stop, even if I could.

Then she takes my hand from her mouth and moves it to her neck. I know the next step she wants me to take. Her first wave of pleasure was only the warm-up for her full orgasm that has yet to come. And we both know what she needs to achieve her final goal.

I push up and under her chin, cutting off some of her circulation.

This is the part I both hate and love.

I *wish* the mock violence didn't turn me on. But I'm wired the way I am, and Amber knows this.

I tighten my grip, only enough to make her light-headed, while I do my best to remain standing. I hold both of us perfectly still, frozen in time, like I'm trying to prevent a scorpion from injecting its poison.

"Don't stop," she whispers.

I listen. I obey.

After I begin moving again, we make it less than a minute before she trembles as if possessed by an ancient Voodoo spirit, and I lose myself in our pleasure.

Afterward, she goes limp, and I hold her up, supporting her body, pinning her against the tree, but gently this time.

She's a rag doll in my arms, not unconscious, but somewhere in-between worlds.

Few could resist Amber's raw, unfettered lust, but even though my body is satisfied, my mind and soul are *not.* Call me old fashioned, but I'd like to have sex with a woman without having to almost kill her to have an orgasm.

Despite this, I'm grateful for how light and devoid of darkness I am as we separate our sweat-slick bodies.

I smile because, even though I will be alone in my bed tonight, I know I will sleep soundly.

With the formality of two colleagues ending a meeting, we straighten up and pull our clothes back on. She spins around lazily with her back against the tree and kisses me.

I kiss her back.

It's not as if we don't like each other, but I know what Amber's kiss means. It's her way of saying *thank you*—nothing more.

A few minutes later, we're walking back to the Corner, moving in slow motion, looking at those around us as if we've recently awoken from heavy sedation. With a simple hug, we go our separate ways. There's no emotion in our embrace. Just a slight grin on her face as she waves, turns, and leaves.

I take a deep breath and walk in the opposite direction.

When I look up, Tony is a block away, glaring at me—a shark studying its food. While I stand still, waiting for him to approach, my sex-drained mind struggles to shift into high-alert mode.

But to my surprise, Tony doesn't come any closer.

On a different day, I would confront him and demand he tell me what the hell he's doing. But right now, I don't even think about it. Instead, I continue on my way and stagger back to my apartment.

I still check a handful of times to make sure Tony isn't following me, but he is nowhere to be seen.

CHAPTER EIGHT

I SLEEP SO well that I don't wake up Sunday until noon. I stay home all day, watching TV and thinking about being with Amber the day before. Since I've already committed the sin, there's no harm in savoring the memory. And I do. A few times.

By the time I go to bed Sunday night, I'm dehydrated and tired, but only one bad dream plagues me while I sleep. An anxiety dream about being late to class. When my alarm wakes me, I'm rested, but I'm heavier than the day before, weighted down by the darkness building inside me again.

Monday passes by smoothly, filled with my non-psychology classes. We discuss José Saramago in Modern European Literature, and I listen patiently to my biology professor lecture about patterns of organization in living organisms.

And not surprisingly, on Monday night, my nightmares return.

I dream of attacking a stranger as we pass on the sidewalk. I beat him close to death, and before I can make it home, the police catch and arrest me. I am quickly sentenced to prison, and my life is effectively over.

I wake up drenched on Tuesday morning, with barely enough time to shower, eat, and get to lab.

Because I run to class, I end up being five minutes early for our psych experiment, which is unusual for me. I pause in the hall as I remember that Eugene is the control subject today. This means Amber and I will be in the observation chamber.

Together. Alone.

I wouldn't put it past her to mute the mic, lock the doors, and jump on top of me right there. And I wouldn't put it past me to surrender completely to her sensual assault, despite my lingering hope of having lunch with Bev after class today.

On my way to our lab, I pass a flat-screen monitor displaying photos of the Psychology Department staff. Mooken's face is near the top, although there are several other professors higher up in the hierarchy. In a smaller photo, below and to Mooken's left, Bev smiles, warming all who pass by.

When I make it to the room we are using for our experiment, Amber is there, grinning at me as I enter.

"Hiya, stud," she says with a lopsided smile that makes her look hungry.

She runs a fingernail down the side of her throat, pretending it's by accident. But she knows exactly what she's doing.

"Are Eugene and the subject almost ready to go?" I say, ignoring her flirtations.

She looks at her phone, then back at me.

"You know, I've been thinking about something," she says without answering my question. "You asked me why I don't go for other men. Why I want you. And trust me, I've wondered that same thing myself. But I think I know. I mean, you're not the best-looking guy out there. No offense."

She's not lying, but I don't appreciate her bluntness.

"It's because you don't have any limits when it comes to trying new things. At least none I've found yet, and that's saying something. And you're a nice guy, which I like. But you *also* have a little demon inside you. And all that makes you *not boring*, at least not in bed."

I know I shouldn't get into this again with her, but before I can still my tongue, the words fly from my mouth.

"Then why all the lies? Why did you need a second boyfriend if I was so much damn fun? Was he the side dish, or was that me?"

She shrugs like my questions aren't even registering with her.

"What about Eugene?" I say. "I'm sure he'd be up for anything and everything you tell him to do."

Amber scowls.

"That's exactly what I don't want," she says. "I don't want to have to *tell* someone to do stuff to me. I want someone who just *does* it. Someone who's a natural at getting me off the way you are.

Besides, Eugene's all right to hang out with…but only *outside* the bedroom."

She peers through the one-way glass at Eugene, who is sitting with a young, blonde woman, waiting for the experiment to start.

"I don't know. Maybe if I got desperate," she says. "Speaking of which, I broke up with Mr. Jersey. He and I are no more. He was too…clingy."

"You mean, you're actually single for real?" I say with a snort. "No boyfriend hidden away somewhere else, like Idaho? No fuck buddy in one of your classes?"

She fails to suppress a devilish grin.

"I said I'm single, Jim. Not dead."

I close my eyes and chide myself for indulging her in this conversation. Of course, she's having sex with someone, somewhere, even if he's not an official boyfriend. That's what Amber does, and it seems I will never learn that about her.

Eugene coughs in the other room, and Amber and I turn to look.

It's his way of reminding us that it's time to start the experiment.

I take a deep breath and sit in front of the mic while Amber enters the testing chamber and retrieves the filled-in questionnaires.

Amber returns and sits behind me, close enough so the scent of honey from her hair fills my head as I unmute the mic.

"Good morning, April and Eugene," I begin.

Then I pick up the script and read my lines while glancing at the only question I care about on April's questionnaire.

She's rated Eugene as an eight out of ten. Not bad. They have a calm, reserved energy between them that escalates when Eugene gives her the eye, pretending to be more interested in her than the puzzle.

It's his version of flirting, although in this case, it's hard to tell if it's working.

A minute and a half into the experiment, Eugene knocks down April's blocks for the first time—right on schedule. April doesn't witness it directly, but she's not happy when she sees the mess Eugene's made of her work, and she does little to hide her displeasure. Without talking, she communicates clearly to Eugene with her eyes that he'd better leave her shit alone, *or else.*

Amber observes what's going on over my shoulder, studying our subjects through the one-way glass but I get the sense she's not interested in the experiment as much as she is in Eugene. Maybe it's because we were just talking about him, but in the back of my mind, I wonder if she's thinking about screwing Eugene to get back at me, to make me jealous.

There's a reason the line about hell having no fury like a woman scorned has survived this long.

Because it's true.

But why do I care?

Let them both fuck each other until the end of time. It won't be real. It won't be love. It won't be what I'm interested in finding with someone like Bev.

As Eugene goes for his second knockdown of April's cube, I root for her to reach over and slap him. Her doing that would further destroy our hypothesis even more than it already is, but at this point, I don't care.

April doesn't last as long as Tony did before she loses her mind, throws Eugene's blocks to the floor, and starts yelling.

Amber goes in and breaks things up while I utter soothing words through the mic, informing April the experiment is over and they'll both be receiving full credit for their participation.

After April leaves, only slightly red in the face, it's the three of us again, sitting, not talking—stuck in our messed-up little love triangle.

Eugene wanting Amber.

Amber wanting me.

And me wanting Bev.

CHAPTER NINE

IT'S POSSIBLE PROFESSOR Mooken presents firm evidence to our class that aliens are real. But I could neither confirm nor deny this.

Because Bev is here today, sitting in the front row, and she has my full attention.

An hour later, when Mooken dismisses us, I stand up and am surprised by how hard my heart is slamming inside my chest.

But before I can do or say anything, Bev smiles at me and waves.

My legs walk me down the aisle to where she waits, and I smile—a simpleton presenting myself to his dream girl.

"I missed you last week," I say.

"I was under the weather," she says, with a short laugh and a smile. "I didn't want to give whatever I had to anyone. So I stayed home, drank magnolia bark tea, and ate rice for three days."

My body grows weightless, and I try to suppress a grin. I shouldn't be happy Bev was sick, but the truth is, I'm ecstatic she was actually ill and not simply avoiding me.

"Do you have time for lunch today?" she says. "To talk about your dreams, I mean."

I check my watch, not because I need to, but because it's a habit.

"I have a meeting with Professor Mooken later this afternoon," I say. "But I'm free now if you're hungry."

Her eyebrows shoot up—an involuntary reflex to my mention of Mooken's name, but she tamps down her surprise and tilts her head, questioning.

"You told me to ask him, remember? To see if he would talk to me. Maybe give me a consult."

Bev still seems stunned, processing something in her head.

"I was surprised he agreed," I say. "I…sort of mentioned your name. I hope that was all right."

Bev considers my question before answering. But at last, she smiles and gathers her things.

"No, that *is* great," she says. "He's very good, but I'm a little surprised he agreed to talk with you. He must like you a lot, or he's intrigued by whatever you told him."

We leave the lecture hall together, our arms bumping once or twice as we walk along. It feels…nice to be this close to her.

It feels safe.

We settle on having lunch in a secluded but popular nook called the *Cavern*. Built into the inner structure of Cabel Hall, it stands like an ancient castle's stone turret. Anyone can eat there, and the food's decent, but almost no first-year students know it exists or how to even get there, so it's rarely crowded.

We each order a sandwich and bottled water, then settle in at a table near one of the aging windows that overlooks a secluded inner courtyard.

"So, what did you and Mooken talk about?" she says. "If you don't mind me asking?"

"I told him I was having bad dreams and not getting any decent sleep. That I was thinking about seeing someone but wanted to go to the right person. He said he'd help me figure out who to see. He was super nice, actually."

Bev laughs and snorts, which makes her even more beautiful than she already is.

"He knows his stuff," she says, with a lopsided grin, as she bites into her turkey and cheese. "But he can be a bit…quirky."

"Isn't that a requirement for someone who teaches psychology?"

She laughs again warmly.

"Now that you have the boss to talk to, I guess you don't need me," she says, lowering her head and looking up at me as she sips her bottled water.

"Maybe," I say. "But Mooken's not nearly as attractive as you are."

There.

It's out.

I've said it, and there's no way to take it back.

I stop breathing and wait for her reaction. Thankfully, she blushes and smiles.

"Where do you live?" she says. "Off grounds somewhere? I assume you're a second- or third-year student, right?"

I grimace.

"Second. I'm an RA at Lambeth."

She nods while chewing more of her sandwich. If I'm lucky, she's impressed I'm responsible enough to be a Resident Assistant for upper-class dorms.

"I remember living on Grounds," she says. "Those were the days."

She sighs and tilts her head to one side.

"You know, you can tell me about your dreams if you want."

"I thought you weren't allowed to give me therapy."

She closes her eyes and chuckles.

"I'm making conversation. You don't have to share any details. Just…are they frightening? Are they…erotic?"

It's my turn to laugh, and I almost choke on my sandwich.

I shrug.

"Sort of both," I say. "Which is one of the things that disturbs me the most. I dream about doing a lot of dark things I'd never want to do in real life."

"That was vague but enticing," she says, almost spitting water out of her mouth.

"What about you," I say. "What's it like being a TA for the guy who literally wrote the book on experimental psychology?"

Her face goes dark, and this is the first time she doesn't laugh. She's not offended, but she crinkles her perfect nose like she smells something rotten.

"At first, working with Mooken was an honor," she says. "He's very selective about choosing his TAs, and there's a lot of competition for the positions. I had him for a couple of classes as an undergrad, and we got along well enough. I was a good student, and he could tell I was really interested in experimental psych—not just trying to get a grade and a diploma."

"Do you want to do research one day or actually practice?"

She cocks her head again, which is becoming one of my favorite things she does.

"Maybe industrial or organizational psych. I'd rather be a social worker, I think. But I'd starve on a social worker's salary. What about you? Are you majoring in psych?"

I nod before I speak, making sure she knows I'm listening and paying attention, interested in everything she's saying.

"Currently majoring in psych and minoring in English, my mother tongue," I say.

She's back to laughing again, and we settle into finishing our food. When I check my phone, an hour has passed like it was barely a minute.

This is a good sign.

While we continue to chat, the guy at the table across from us glances up at Bev and stares at her for a little too long. I'm not happy about him scoping her out, but I understand. Bev is gorgeous, and it would be impossible for others not to notice. This is something I will have to get used to if we are ever to be together.

After a pause in our conversation, Bev and I look into each other's eyes and say nothing.

Usually, maintaining eye contact with a woman is next to impossible for me. Not this close-up, for sure. But with Bev, we are two magnets pulling, tugging at each other. And I could stare into her eyes forever.

"What time are you meeting with Mooken?" she says, breaking our gaze and looking down at the table.

I check my phone again. I have only half an hour to get back to Gilmer Hall for my meeting. To be honest, a part of me doesn't want to go anymore. Even though this is only the start of Bev and me—the start of *us*—I am already lighter inside, and therapy is far from what I want to do.

"I should be going," I say, letting my obvious disappointment color my words.

I wish I could stay with her longer, and I don't *want* to leave.

She nods like she understands, and we get up, throw away our trash, and leave the Cavern together.

As we walk down the hallway, the sides of our bodies touch in silence, but the lack of words between us remains comfortable instead of awkward.

Just outside the building, we turn to face each other. I don't know about her, but my heart is racing like I've just finished an all-out sprint.

"I share a house a few roads down from Rugby Road with four of my girlfriends," she says. "You'll have to come over sometime. We throw a party every once in a while, and I'll make sure to invite you. Or you could stop by if you're in the area. If you want to say *Hi,* I mean."

I mumble something I hope sounds like "sure," or "that would be cool," or some other clumsy phrase meant to disguise my excitement.

This is not the behavior of a TA simply trying to help one of her students. These are the acts of a woman who is interested in me as a man.

My assumption is confirmed when she asks her next question.

"Tell me about that girl in class you sit with. Amber. Are you two an item?"

I'm surprised she's observed this much about me, and for a split second, I panic, wondering if there's some way she could know I had sex with Amber last weekend.

But that would be ridiculous.

"No, that's all over," I say. "We broke up a couple of months ago."

"She's very pretty."

I nod and stand there, transfixed, as she taps my phone with hers and airdrops her address and cell number.

It is only through a supreme act of will that I don't allow my face to betray the fact that I already have her contact information in my phone.

I start to thank her, but she shuts me up by leaning in, standing on her toes, and kissing me.

On the lips.

She steps back and looks at me, pleased—admiring the piece of art she's created on my face. And I have no problem at all being her painting.

"Give me a call if the dreams get too bad," she says. "If you want to talk."

I am stunned and not sure what I end up saying next. But whatever it is, she smiles and bites her bottom lip, then turns and leaves, while I remain paralyzed, blocking the entrance to Cabel Hall.

I am not equipped to deal with such an onslaught of positive emotions today, and I close my eyes as they flood my soul. When I open them again, a couple is standing inside the building glaring at me, for what reason I don't understand.

A crowd of students makes its way to the entrance, then stops to stare at me. Their faces show no emotion, but I'm obviously in their way.

A centipede scrambles out from under a bush and undulates across the sidewalk. Before it hides under the next bush, it turns back, judging me with cold insect eyes.

I scan the immobile group of students and the other people mulling around the parking lot, worried suddenly that Tony might be near, about to leap out at me.

Thinking of him reminds me of our experiment, which reminds me of Mooken and the fact that I now only have fifteen minutes to make it across the Grounds to his office.

To the sarcastic cheers of the students trying to enter and leave the building, I move away from the door and break into a full run, brushing past an older man browsing on his phone in the parking lot.

My feet and heart are light, and soon, I am flying down the sidewalk on my way to meet Professor Mooken.

CHAPTER TEN

I BURST THROUGH the doors of Gilmer Hall with three minutes to spare. I race through the hallway, barely dodging a student staring at his phone, not looking where he's walking.

Outside Mooken's office, I try to regain control of my breathing and to store what just happened with Bev somewhere separately in my mind, so I can make it through my meeting.

After my heart rate settles to a reasonable pace, I gently knock on his door.

Mooken calls for me to enter, and when I step inside, he's sitting behind a large wooden desk surrounded by a dense clutter of books, papers, and other strange objects that fill the floor-to-ceiling shelves lining his walls.

I can only assume all these things are from his travels—figurines and religious totems carved of wood and black onyx from ancient lands that now serve as makeshift bookends and paperweights. An old military officer's helmet perches next to a black velvet Stetson. A Japanese katana sword lies horizontally on one of the higher shelves next to a jade statuette of the Buddha. And an old wooden chest sits on the floor, looking like it belongs in the dark hold of a pirate's ship more than in a psych professor's office.

Everything is covered in a layer of gray dust except for Mooken, his laptop, and a giant computer screen connected to it.

Behind him, four diplomas hang on the wall, each mounted behind glass and framed. These comprise the official proof that this man knows more than any of his students—way more than me.

"Please, close the door and have a seat," he says, motioning with his hand.

Despite the fact I'm meeting in a closed room with an authority figure, I don't feel threatened here. Maybe this is because I've watched and listened to Mooken lecture all year about experimental psychology and the motivation of action. I feel like I know him better than I really do.

"How is Beverly?" he says. "I saw the two of you leaving together after class, presumably for lunch."

It's an odd question to begin our discussions about my dreams, but he's the king here and probably trying to make me feel at ease and to get me talking.

"She's well," I say. "We ate lunch, and I told her I had an appointment with you. She seemed…surprised that you agreed to talk to me, but she also said you were a brilliant psychiatrist."

Mooken laughs in a pleasant enough manner, and my shoulders loosen a little more.

"Young man, flattery will get you *everywhere* with me! But seriously, I am happy to hear she is over her sickness from last week. Good TAs are hard to come by, and she is one of the best, you know. But let us talk about you. Why do you think you need to see a counselor? And remember that even though I am *not* your therapist, I am still bound by my oaths here when we talk—as a board-certified psychiatrist and as your teacher. You may speak openly with me, and I will not judge you."

I inhale deeply as I switch mental gears from Bev-induced euphoria to the topic of my disturbed sleep.

"I have bad dreams," I say. "Dark nightmares, where I do awful things to people. Or sometimes they do awful things to me. And *sometimes*, the dreams are just plain awful all on their own."

Mooken tilts his head, prompting me for details. So I tell him about the button-eyed, bag-head lady and wait for his shock.

Instead, he only nods.

This is not the weirdest thing he's ever heard. Strangely enough, the lack of impact my nightmare makes on him relaxes me even more. There is power and comfort in being heard and accepted and not feeling like you're the only person in the world suffering from your problems.

"The thing is," I continue, "the only times I sleep well and get a decent night's rest is when I do… certain things while I'm awake."

His right eyebrow arches up.

"What kinds of things?"

"Nothing illegal. No drugs or anything. More like having…intense, sometimes dark sex."

I'm uncomfortable saying these words out loud, but he can't help me if I don't explain my problems to him.

"Do you have a lot of this *dark sex*?"

"Not at the moment," I say. "I did with my ex, though."

"And how long ago was that?"

"We met in your class, actually, and dated all last semester, then broke up a couple months ago. We got together last weekend, but that was a one-time thing and a mistake."

"And yet, you slept well that night?" he says, suddenly serious.

I nod. Blood rushes to my cheeks, and I regret telling Mooken about sex with Amber. But at least I didn't mention her name. I think I believe him when he says he'll keep my secrets, but what if he tells Bev I'm still sleeping with my last girlfriend?

"Go on," he says. "Tell me what you mean by *dark sex*."

"Sometimes, it can get sort of violent. Pretend violent, I mean. No one got hurt, but my ex liked to fantasize she was being…you know…taken…and choked and other stuff. That turned her on, and I'm scared because it turned me on, too, and…well, this is really embarrassing to mention. But whenever I had sex with her, it was like…a release valve."

"That is a normal byproduct of satisfying sex," he says.

"I understand feeling relaxed after sex," I say. "But this was more than that. It was like all these dark feelings in my head spilled out of me and drained away. The crazy sex doesn't bother me as much as the fact that there's always this darkness inside me. It feels heavy and gross, and it's always there, always growing. What kind of specialist do I need to see for that kind of thing? Is this even something you've heard of?"

"The DSM defines a little over two hundred mental diagnoses, and the ICD from the World Health Organization lists another fifty or so. And mental illness—not that I'm saying you are mentally ill, because that is not my place to determine—but mental illness often manifests with multiple diagnoses. That is, your issues could simply be a mix of generalized anxiety, sexual guilt, and insecurity—something all humans your age experience in abundance. If I were you, I would begin your quest for a better night's sleep by seeing a behavioral or psychoanalytical psychologist. We have several fine ones on staff at Student Health."

"You're saying all this could be because I feel guilty about having dirty sex? I don't get that. After I have that kind of sex, I *don't* have bad dreams. Not the other way around. And what about all my dark feelings."

Mooken pauses and nods slowly, like he's really heard me, instead of dismissing my idea out of hand.

He taps his middle finger on his desk and lets out a low-pitched *hmmm*.

"Imagine the following hypothetical model, if you will. For whatever reason, let us say you enjoy *fantasizing* and thinking about intense, rough, almost violent sex. You feel guilty about liking such *dark* intercourse, and your guilt results in anxiety-fueled dreams. Now, let us suppose you actually *have* this type of sexual activity for real. I assume that when you do, you…reach *nirvana*, correct?"

I nod and resist telling him that dark sex makes my pleasure more intense.

"Your sexual indulgences, however dark," he says, "are rewarded by the positive response of orgasm. Your orgasm, in turn, is paired with the physical release of your biological swimmers and plenty of endorphins and oxytocin—a veritable cocktail of pleasure. All of this lets you relax while also smoothing over your guilt.

"After a couple of days, the calming effects from the sex wear off. However, because your fantasies persist, your guilt returns. When that happens, your bad dreams also resume. This is not unusual. People often feel intense guilt over what brings them the most pleasure, especially in this country. As for the darkness you are so worried about, it is *possible* that it is a symptom and not the cause of your problems."

"So the darkness I feel is just me feeling guilty about liking that kind of sex?"

He shakes his head and chuckles.

"That is one possibility. I could be right, or there might be a completely different explanation for your dreams. There's a spectrum of possibilities that could explain your symptoms. Until you work with someone to unravel whatever is going on inside of you, you won't know for certain. How long have you been dealing with these issues?"

"The dreams have been there on and off since I was a kid, but they were never as bad as when I started college and started having sex. I've only had two real girlfriends, and the nightmares have gotten worse with each one."

"I see," is all Mooken says before glancing up at the stark black hands of the clock on his wall. "Let me mull this over and come up with a few names of local counselors I think would be best for you to speak with. Come back next week, same time, and I will see if I can arrange an intro for you with someone. In the meantime, I'm giving you homework.

"Write your nightmares down in a sleep journal this week. Nothing extravagant, but it might help me determine how to best direct you to the help you need. You also may want to try over-the-counter sleep aids to give yourself some short-term relief, although, to be clear, this is not medical advice—it's only something to consider."

"I understand, professor. And I really appreciate it. Thank you."

"One more thing," he says. "You might also try confronting

whatever is happening in your nightmares. Become aware they are only dreams. Some call this lucid dreaming. I'm not sure I agree with all the new-age thinking associated with *that*, but you *can* stand up for yourself in your dreams, the same as you can in your waking life. It might help."

I nod, ready to leave, and Mooken checks the wall clock again.

"Go on, now," he says. "I'm certain you have plenty to do on your lab report. I'm looking forward to reading about your experiment and your conclusions."

Right. The lab report. Once again, I've forgotten all about that.

A wave of stress tightens my shoulders as I think about all the work we haven't yet done on our report. And now, after Mooken has been so helpful, I have an increased desire to turn in the best product I can.

On my way out the door, I stop at his coat closet, turn around, and ask him one final question.

"Professor. About the lab reports. How much will it hurt if our original hypothesis isn't supported by our findings?"

He tilts his head before he answers, the same way Bev did at lunch.

"If every experiment resulted simply in a validation of one's original hypothesis, there would be no need for experimentation at all. We often learn the most from unearthing why our initial assumptions are wrong. Now, *shoo.* I have another appointment in a few minutes, for which I must prepare."

I smile and am strangely at ease—more than I thought I'd be. Something about Professor Mooken makes me feel safe like I'm a normal college student who worries too much about problems that may pass on their own.

I nod and leave his office, closing the door behind me. Between talking about my problems with Mooken and the kiss from Bev, my day is going much better than I ever expected.

I start down the hallway, but when I turn into the main corridor, I almost collide with Amber.

"What are you doing here?" I say.

She stops and places her open hand on my chest, rubbing me like I am one of her favorite pets.

"I have a meeting with Professor Mooken," she says. "I want to talk to him about my major. See you around, okay?"

"Sure," I say, as she walks past me with a final wave before continuing to Mooken's office. With no hesitation, she opens the door to his office without knocking and eases it shut behind her.

A second later, his office door lock clicks into place.

CHAPTER ELEVEN

THE EXCITEMENT FROM Bev's kiss has faded only slightly, as I sit alone in my bed, staring at the traces of light from the living room seeping under my door.

A faint scent of patchouli floats past me, reminding me of Rashmuni, my first college girlfriend.

She was fun, even though she liked the taste of my blood too much.

My lips throb as I remember her teeth raking across them until I bled. Maybe she was secretly a vampire, or maybe just really bad at kissing.

For a moment, I imagine Rash is outside, waiting. I don't know how she would have gotten into my apartment, but she's resourceful. She's also only five feet tall and not a cruel person. But scorned is as scorned does, and crazy is crazy. Plus, Rash was always as unpredictable as a wild animal, so I don't rule out the possibility she might really be out there.

My heart speeds up as I imagine the ways she could exact revenge on me for leaving her as she was becoming emotionally committed to our relationship.

She might use a gun, a baseball bat, or even a crossbow. I wouldn't put anything past her.

As I'm thinking about Rash, a shadow appears under my door, blocking the light. *Someone* is standing there, even if it isn't Rash.

My phone rings, and I jump.

With his usual uncanny timing, it's my father calling.

"What?" I whisper into my phone. "It's very late, Dad. Is everything okay?"

"Who's there?" he says, yelling so loudly I almost drop my phone.

I think about reminding him how he was the one who called me, but this would be pointless. His brain isn't working right, and he can't help that.

"Dad, it's me."

"I know that," he says, annoyed. "But who's at your door?"

It takes me a moment to register my father's words.

I almost ask him how he knows someone is here, but I want to know the same thing. I curl up tighter in my bed, and to my right, a shadow forms into a gnarled version of me and peels itself away from my bedroom wall.

I sit in silence, a human bat scanning the room with my sonar, but I detect nothing.

"Don't let her in, boy."

I shake my head, willing my dad to be quiet, but I have no power over him, other than to hang up and hope he doesn't call back.

"I have to go," I say and end the call.

Suddenly, a high-pitched gurgle erupts next to me—laughter from an inhuman, primeval creature.

The air in my room turns damp and musty, and moonlight breaks through a crack in my blinds, illuminating a puddle of black liquid spilling across my floor. The liquid is already inches deep, and it continues to spread and deepen.

Normally, one would call the RA in this situation, but I *am* the RA, and I don't know what to do.

As a reflex, I pick up my smartphone, but the screen remains dark no matter how hard I shake it and push the button to wake it up.

I get up and stand on my bed as the black liquid rises, getting nearer and nearer to the level of my mattress until it finally spills across my sheets.

Death's cold grip tightens around my heart.

I could break the window and try to escape, but before I can move, something under the black liquid explodes upward, grabs my ankles, and pulls me down into its depths.

Once I'm under, my world is as dark as ink, and someone's bare skin is rubbing against my leg. A woman climbs up my chest and places her lips against mine.

Is she here to save or kill me?

I pray she will fill my lungs with life-giving air, but instead, she pushes her tongue into my mouth and kisses me, ignoring the fact we are drowning.

Her front teeth drag across my tongue and bite down on my lips, and my eyes open wide. I am struggling, frantic, because I would know those teeth anywhere.

It *is* Rashmuni.

Her limbs, fingers, and toes tangle in mine, constricting my movement. She is *not* going to save me. She is giving me a final kiss before death.

I struggle for purchase—anything to which I can cling that will help me break free. But her grip is iron, and I cannot move.

Drained of strength and energy, I stop struggling, and I float, waiting for death's embrace, even as a speck of logic buoys to the surface of my suffocating brain.

This can't be happening.

I've been submerged without air, held down by Rash for several minutes now, but I'm still alive. I can't hold my breath this long in real life. Not even close.

Therefore, this cannot be real.

She cannot be real.

I open my mouth to scream at Rash—to tell her I've discovered her for what she is, but when I do, she forces her tongue in deeper and drags her fingernails down my chest, tearing strips of flesh from my torso.

I try again to reason my way out of my dream. This is a nightmare, and Professor Mooken told me I can control my dreams.

But nothing works.

My lungs struggle to expand, but nothing can get past Rash's tongue and her air-tight lock on my mouth. Whether a dream or not, I am *not* going to survive this. After all, people die in their sleep. Not all the time, but it *does* happen.

I prepare myself to make peace with a God in whom I don't even believe. But right before my last moment of life, I wake up, tangled in my bedding, kicking.

The floor is dry, but my sheets and pillows are soaked. My temples throb with pain, and I am trembling. My phone, which is working once again, tells me it's only a little after midnight.

For a college town and its students, this isn't late at all.

I'm exhausted and wired, but the last thing I want to do is fall asleep again and give Rash a chance to finish her dark work.

I don't think I could survive her twice in the same night.

I close my eyes and take three deep breaths before I pick up the small notebook on my nightstand and jot down as much of my dream as I can remember, as Professor Mooken directed.

When I'm done, I thumb through the contacts on my phone and bring up Bev's entry.

Before I can stop myself from doing something this stupid, I click her number, and it begins to ring.

CHAPTER TWELVE

"WHO IS THIS?" Bev asks.

Her voice is low, and her speech is a little slurred. I have woken her.

"It's Jim," I say. "From psych class? We had lunch today."

Silence on the other end of the phone.

"Hi, Jim."

"I'm sorry for calling this late. I…I had a really bad dream, and I don't want to fall asleep again. If this is a bad time…"

She is silent again, but not for very long.

"It's okay," she says. "I wasn't having any luck sleeping, anyway. If you need help staying awake, we can talk some."

She pauses.

"Or you could come over. I'm not far from Lambeth."

I nod, like she can see me through the phone.

"I could be there in half an hour, if you're sure," I say, as my heart rate soars and my mouth goes dry.

"I'll see you soon. Come to the back door and knock."

After we end the call, I move as quickly as I can. A five-minute shower. Clean clothes. A light jacket.

For a moment, I contemplate driving, but parking is horrible at UVA, and the night air will feel good. Soon I'm out the door, walking with purpose and certainty, because I've been to Bev's home before and know exactly where I'm going. As I hurry along, I can hear my father chiding me, but I ignore him and make it to Bev's place a little after one in the morning.

My footsteps crunch through the gravel of her driveway as I circle behind her house. It's surrounded by trees that have spread their branches over the roof, protecting the people who live inside.

I follow Bev's instructions and quietly rap on the screened-in back door.

Seconds later, she appears, and I am stunned.

She's in sweatpants and a T-shirt and is the most beautiful woman I've ever seen.

I manage a pathetic "Hello," which she silences with a kiss before taking my hand and pulling me inside.

We pass through the kitchen and go straight to her bedroom on the first floor. It smells of herbs.

"I made tea for us," she says and hands me a cup before sitting on the edge of her bed.

I take the hot mug in my hands and inhale. Light citrus notes and deep plums fill my head as I look around for somewhere to sit.

But there is nowhere other than her bed.

I ease onto her mattress, facing her, and sip the tea. It's hot—almost too hot—but the flavor is comforting. As it enters my throat and my stomach, my body wakes up even more than it already is.

I laugh, giddy and nervous because…well, I'm on a bed with Bev.

The Bev.

"Do you want to tell me about your nightmare?" she asks.

I do.

I want to tell her everything. There is nothing I *don't* want to tell this woman, but when I recall my dream with Rash, nausea rises in my throat, and I shake.

Bev sighs and inches closer. Whatever words I'm about to utter stick in my throat and never make it out of me.

I move closer to her, and we kiss again, trying not to spill the scalding liquid in our mugs.

"Finish your tea," she says, backing away. "I'm not going anywhere."

My heart softens when she says that. My shoulders relax, and I sip the tea as quickly as I can, waiting for it to cool off enough for me to chug it.

"We shouldn't be doing this," she says, nodding toward me. "Mixing with students on a romantic level is frowned upon ethically. It's part of the honor code."

"Oh yeah. The honor code," I say. "I'm not such a huge fan of that anymore."

She laughs and smiles into her mug.

"If we do whatever this is going to be," she says, "we have to keep it quiet, especially near Gilmer Hall and with the other students in the class. And definitely around Mooken. Especially him. I can't lose my position as a TA."

She makes sense, and I don't want to cause trouble in her life.

"If this is risky for you, then why am I here?" I ask. "Won't your housemates find out about…this, about us, or do we need to be careful around here, too?"

She inhales so close to me that she steals the air I am about to breathe.

"This house is sacred ground," she says. "What goes on behind these walls stays here. Also, none of my housemates are psych students. But to answer your question, you're here because I like you. And also because my last boyfriend was shitty and hurt me pretty bad, to be honest. *And* in fair disclosure, his name was Jim, too. Just so you know."

I nod and shrug. I don't care what her last boyfriend's name was.

She shrugs, too, and we drink more of our tea.

"I have an idea," I say and raise my hand.

She pulls away, flinching—a reflex beyond her control—as her breath catches in her throat.

"I'm sorry," I say. "I only wanted to do this."

I extend my pinky finger in the air slowly, and her body relaxes. The fear leaves her eyes.

"I have some trust issues from past relationships," I say. "And I understand why we need to keep this to ourselves for now. So I'll make a deal with you. We can lie to anyone we have to in order to keep us a secret, but we can't lie to each other. Ever. Do you pinky swear?"

She smiles, and her eyes mist up as she raises her hand and wraps her pinky around mine.

"I swear," she says in a quiet voice.

The die is cast. The promise is made. Whatever this is, it's going to be interesting and something I've never experienced before.

Hopefully, it will end up as love.

As if reading my mind, she releases my hand and leans in, locking me in a gentle, passionate kiss that sends my stomach fluttering.

But then her body turns rigid. Something is wrong. She pulls away and looks deeply into my eyes.

"I know you told me already," she says. "But you and that girl, Amber. You're not seeing each other anymore, right?"

"I promise," I say.

This must be the right thing to say, or at least not the wrong thing, because she leans in and kisses me again.

It doesn't take long before our hands stray into unexplored territory. Her fingers slip under my shirt and rub my chest, and all my neurons explode. I am as hot as the desert while also chilled to my bones.

We lie together in her bed, undressing one another. Each piece of clothing that lands on the floor is another piece of our puzzle. Soon, we make a clumsy move to slide under her covers, which results in both of us laughing.

Being bare and vulnerable with this woman feels right to me, and laughter has never felt so good. Because there is nothing dark or evil here. Just pure, wonderful energy bouncing back and forth between us, stronger than anything I ever felt with Amber or anyone else before.

I smile as we begin to make love.

The pleasure is overwhelming. But the real show is in her eyes, which let me see directly into her heart.

Less than an inch away from her, I hold her gaze, showing her my full self. This is amazing and terrifying, because there's nowhere to hide, but also because I don't *want* to hide.

I catch my breath and try shaking some sense into my head.

This is only our first time.

Her last boyfriend was horrible, and I'm nothing more than a rebound.

She probably doesn't even want a relationship right now.

These and more negative thoughts crowd my mind, and she senses the change in me.

"Where did you go?" she says. "Come back to me."

"I'm sorry," I say. "I was only thinking…"

"Don't do that," she says, and we begin to move again as one, linked in all ways physically and emotionally. We twist and writhe, climbing a ladder of pleasure together, rising above the invisible, dark fears of our pasts.

Soon, sweetness gives way to passion, and the chemical reactions exploding inside us urge us onward. Our breathing synchronizes until hers becomes panicked—short bursts of air as her eyes open wide—a mix of fear and sensuality.

And then, together, we explode in pleasure, and I smother her cries with my mouth.

When we finish, our hearts are slamming into one another through the walls of our chests.

Unlike how it was with Amber, we don't separate, and she doesn't leave.

This is the way I've always imagined it should be.

This is what I've been looking for.

We are so relaxed that we jump, startled when someone knocks loudly on her bedroom door.

"Beverly?" a woman's voice says. "Are you okay in there? Open up, or I'm coming in. Three. Two."

Bev groans.

"Hold on," she says loudly enough for whoever is at the door to hear.

She eases out of bed and slips into her robe.

"I'm sorry about this," she says before gliding to the door and opening it.

Two women stand there, one with a black mag flashlight in her hand and the other holding a bottle of pinot noir like a club.

The women register me as they look over Bev's shoulder.

"We heard you screaming. Jesus Christ, we didn't know you had someone here with you. When did *he* get here? No offense…"

I shrug and am thankful for the low lighting, so they can't see how embarrassed I am.

"Trisha and Sally, this is…Jim."

"You're kidding me…" Sally says before glancing at me and stopping in mid-sentence.

"It's okay. He knows about my ex," Bev says to the women as she turns to me with a hand on her hip. "But we do need to nip this in the bud right now. From now on, when we talk about my ex, he'll be known as *Evil Jim.* And when we talk about this Jim…"

She peers into my eyes and smiles.

"When we talk about you, we'll call you *Good Jim.*"

After they leave, Bev and I turn out the lights, entwine again, and fall asleep.

It is no surprise to me that I sleep like a child in his mother's womb that night.

No bad dreams. No drowning. No violence.

I am drowsy when I wake but also at peace—for a few seconds at least—before I start to second-guess my happiness again.

Maybe last night was a fluke.

There is no way she is really this into me.

Half an hour later, Bev wakes, turns to me, and smiles. When she does, my doubts flutter away.

After a slow choreography of kissing and hugging, we amble into the kitchen, and she cooks eggs for us, as her housemates gradually file into the small area. There are four in total, along with one boyfriend who stands relaxed, accustomed to being in a kitchen filled with attractive grad students in revealing nightwear.

"Hi there, Good Jim," Trisha says with a smile as she pads past me to the fridge.

"Good morning," I say, acutely aware I am the stranger here and also the youngest, visiting a foreign world not meant for underclassmen to see, much less partake of.

Seeing my nervousness, Bev takes my hand and introduces me to the members of her group I haven't yet met.

"This is Cynthia and her boyfriend, Dan," Bev says, nodding toward a tanned Asian woman with long black hair and slender limbs.

Dan, her boyfriend with shoulder-length, curly hair, reaches out to shake my hand—a typical but friendly bro greeting. He doesn't offer any information about himself, and I don't ask. But I know I have at least one ally in the house—if for no other reason than because he's the only other male.

"And this is Kathy," Bev says, as she points to a short, round woman with a scrunched-up face that looks permanent—like she spends too much time worrying about things.

"Hello, Good Jim," she says as she monitors a bagel in the toaster. "Make yourself at home, but please understand we label our food, and partaking of something that is not yours is grounds for eviction or continued harassment until you replace the items you've eaten."

Kathy ends her warning with a smile as the toaster dings and her bagel pops up, brown and warm.

As the discussion turns to the weekend, I half-listen to their plans to go to the Foxfield horse races, an event I know about but have never attended. While they negotiate who's riding with whom, I inspect a spot on the far wall. I do not belong in this conversation.

But then Dan grabs my shoulder.

"Are you coming?" he asks.

I prepare my excuse for not attending, but before I can say anything, Bev places her hand lightly on my chest.

"What do you say? Do you wanna get drunk around a lot of old people wearing hats and pretending to watch horses?"

My weekend is usually filled with homework, Netflix, and horrible dreams. So it doesn't take much to agree to join Bev and her friends.

"If you're sure," I say. "I don't want to intrude or anything."

They all laugh, and Bev rubs my shoulder.

"See?" she says. "He really is Good Jim, just like I told you."

CHAPTER THIRTEEN

THE FOXFIELD RACES are a huge tradition at the University of Virginia. I know this because, during my first year at school here, most of my dorm went, while I stayed home and read Mary Shelley's *Frankenstein*.

Again.

But now I'm going, and my date is the most wonderful woman I've ever met.

I volunteer to be the driver, to help Bev out, but also to ingratiate myself with the group. Bev sits up front with me, while Trisha, Sally, Cynthia, and Dan cram into the backseat of my Ford Mustang.

I obey every traffic rule to the letter because being stopped by a cop would not be good. Everyone in the car, other than me, is packing at least one flask of alcohol—vodka, gin, or tequila, to be specific.

"Are you sure Kathy didn't want to come?" I say to Bev quietly enough so only she can hear me. "I feel like I'm taking her spot."

"She hates these kinds of things, and she's working on a paper. It's really sweet that you offered to drive, you know. Thank you, Jim."

She punctuates her gratitude with a kiss on my cheek as the traffic slows about a mile outside the race venue. Soon, we're sitting still in a traffic jam filled with students who've *been* drinking, *are* drinking, and *plan on* drinking some more. It only takes five minutes of idling before a student five cars up from us gets out of her car, crosses the road, and runs across the grass to use the bathroom in the trees.

It's such a good idea, a mini exodus begins up and down the line of stopped cars. Young men and women drunkenly stumble through the dewy grass and disappear into the darkness of the forest to do their business.

I count the students as they step past the tree line.

Six go in, and six come out, then another three run into the cover of the dark, swaying trees.

Two of those return quickly, running and whooping back to their cars.

But the third student does not.

Maybe he has more business to perform in the forest than the others. Or perhaps he's passed out on the cold, wet moss, buried among the veins of forest floor ivy.

But also, maybe something else has happened to him.

I hear my father's voice in my head, what he would say if he were here.

That forest ain't right, son.

I reach out and squeeze Bev's hand, and the echoes of my father fade away.

I inhale deeply, but when Dan says he has to *go*, my heart tightens.

"I'll be right back," he says. "It's not like you guys are moving any time soon."

I start to tell him not to leave, to warn him, but he is fast and out the door before I can gather my words.

He speeds across the grass, drunk, but also a natural athlete. He makes the other bathroom goers look as if they're stumbling forward in slow motion.

Within seconds, he's past the tree line and disappears from sight.

I begin counting. Waiting for him.

One thousand one.

One thousand two.

I make it to ten before Dan's head pops out of the forest, and he scans the line of cars until he spots us. Cynthia waves her hand out of our car's open window, and in under a minute, he's back in the car, sliding underneath his girlfriend, who showers him with kisses.

I want to ask him about his experience in the woods. Whether he saw anyone lying on the ground in there. But this kind of questioning will only disturb him and my other passengers, and it might make Bev question my sanity, which is something I do not want to do.

For an entire hour, we inch along the final mile into the Foxfield parking area, stopping and starting over and over until we are finally directed to our own little plot of grass where we park.

Still in the car, Bev looks around, craning her neck, before she reaches into her dress pocket and removes a small white pill.

Everyone in the car does the same, and I realize I've been left out of whatever's going on.

"Oh my god," Bev says. "I'm so sorry. It's just *X*, but I forgot to ask if you wanted one. It's okay. I don't have to take it."

I've been around plenty of drugs in my life, although all of them have been prescribed for me. I've never done any illicit drugs, though. Not because I have a problem with them, in theory, but because I'm afraid they'll mess with my personality and alter who I am.

And I have enough problems without introducing psychedelics into the mix.

"You go ahead," I say. "I'm driving, anyway."

Dan grabs my shoulder and squeezes.

"Dude, you're a standup guy. If you ever want anything, let me know. Hard stuff. Soft stuff. Even weird stuff. I'm your man."

"Shut up, Dan," Cynthia says, pulling him back to her.

After everyone takes their pill, we get out, stretch, and instantly we're absorbed in a wave of students. Most of the males are dressed in chinos, shirts, and ties—the same as me. The women wear floral summer dresses and large, decorative hats. In our group, only Sally and Trisha have brought hats with them, and as soon as they put them on, it's difficult to distinguish them from anyone else.

We allow ourselves to be swept along by the flow of people making their way onto the outfield of the track. An announcer's voice echoes above us, announcing the next race. But I'll have to take his word for the fact that there are horse races going on nearby because all I see are drunk people.

As we move along, I take Bev's hand, and she gets on her tiptoes and gives me a kiss.

"Are you doing okay?" she asks. "I'm really glad you decided to come. I hope you're having a good time."

I nod and speak into her ear, giddy from the smell of her almond body oil.

"I'm fine," I say. "Anywhere with you is great. I hope that's all right to say."

She looks up at me and smiles before stopping and kissing me deeply. I don't know if the drugs are making her less worried about showing affection in public or if she knows Mooken hates horse races and won't be here. But either way, she doesn't seem to care about letting everyone know we're together.

And I am totally okay with this.

Her kiss places my crowd anxiety at bay, and we follow her housemates through the masses until we find Dan's fraternity, where we are welcomed with cheers and beers. Even I, the lowly underclassman, feel like I am a part of their organism. This surprises me, since I have never even considered joining a fraternity.

I have to admit that being a part of a group is nice, though. I can see the appeal it holds for normal people. And for once, it feels good to fit in.

I enjoy this euphoria until the first police officer walks past, staring me down behind his sunglass-shielded eyes. He wears a black baseball hat and tactical pants and carries a walkie-talkie. Clearly, he is not searching for people who are drunk in public, because, if he were, the local jail would be overflowing already. He passes by, then breaks into a run to join with two of his brethren who are forcibly escorting a sloppy woman with white powder covering her face.

I watch over the next few hours as more of these black-clad police officers weave through the attendees, searching for those who are too wild or too high, even for Foxfield. Every one of them casts a disapproving, dark eye at me when they pass, but none engage with me.

I tell myself they're not looking for me *or* at me, because I haven't done anything wrong. Because I am innocent.

Meanwhile, I spend my time watching the fraternity brothers and their guests drink, sing, hug, fall in the mud, and get back up.

Unlike them, I am a good Boy Scout, pacing myself and barely consuming a single drink every hour. This is not difficult for me, since I am the sober driver, and I will not do anything to risk Bev's well-being.

She and her friends will arrive safely back home.

Half-way through the event, with the sun baking everyone and adding to the general state of dehydration, the vomiting begins.

Men, women, tall people, short people—one by one, each gets sick. They run somewhere not nearly far enough away and expel the offending poisons from their stomachs. But most of the students here are professional drinkers, even this early in their lives, and it only takes half an hour on average for them to be back in line for their next drink.

Bev imbibes enough to be drunk as well, but she remains in control of herself, for which I am thankful. She sidles up to one and then another fraternity brother, chatting with those she knows. Each tries to win her over, usually with a bad pickup line or a story, but she always leaves them and returns to me.

I am her homing beacon of safety.

Brad is one of the brothers trying to impress her. He is handsome with a square jaw and wide shoulders—a friend of Dan's—and he is interested in Bev to the exclusion of the other women encircling him.

"You'll never believe what happened on the way here," he says to Bev, his eyes wide and his arms outstretched.

Bev takes his bait and crosses her arms over her chest, laughing. Even I am interested in hearing what lie Brad is about to deliver to impress Bev.

"I swear to God," he says. "We were stuck in traffic with everyone else, and this pledge, Dillan, says he has to go to the bathroom *really* bad."

Everyone listening to him grimaces. No one wants to hear a bathroom joke right now.

"He gets out of the car and runs into the woods along with a couple of our other pledges."

I focus on his every word now, because I know how his story will end.

"But he never comes back," he says.

No one laughs, especially not me.

"You left him?" I say.

Brad furrows his brow, pissed that I've interrupted his story. But I maintain eye contact with him, anyway, waiting for a response.

He shakes his head, ignores me, and continues.

"We got out and looked, but we couldn't find him. Not at first."

The crowd goes quiet.

"Turns out the asshole was asleep on some branches, passed out like the dumb shit he is."

"What did you do?" Bev asks.

Brad isn't offended by *her* question, though. He only smirks.

"I wrote a note on his arm saying we'd pick him up on our way home."

"That wasn't very nice," another woman says. "Something could happen to him."

Brad laughs and points to one of the entrance gates twenty feet away. A bewildered young man with leaves and pine needles in his hair and clothes stumbles through the crowd.

I don't ask, but I assume his name is Dillan.

Bev also laughs when the groggy pledge enters the circle and Brad hands him a beer. But after that, she turns away and starts to mingle with a group of women.

Not happy being ignored, Brad grabs the back of Bev's arm.

"No need to be so sensitive," he says.

Before Bev can turn around, I pull Brad's hand away from Bev and position myself between them.

I stop short of doing anything else for the time being, but my brain lights up with images of what I *will* do to Brad if he pushes matters further. I imagine slamming him to the ground and stomping on his face until his skull cracks. I fantasize about forcing his fingers into positions they were not meant to go, so he will never be able to grab Bev again.

In reality, I know I may not have the ability to make these scenarios come true, but I will try until I can no longer stand. Three of Brad's fraternity bros move in to help him, but I am not afraid, and I step closer to him, an inch from his face.

I am willing to do whatever it takes to protect Bev, even if it means getting pounded into the ground by a group of ill-mannered, drunk assholes. If I bleed, I will wear my wounds proudly, but I will ensure nothing bad happens to Bev.

Not while I am still breathing.

"Take it easy, guys," Bev says, stepping around me and facing Brad. "We're supposed to be having a good time here. No need to get so excited."

"Your little guard dog started it," Brad says, but Bev knows the truth and continues to stare him down.

Everyone goes silent, waiting to see what happens next. But luckily, Dan steps in, a bridge of peace between Brad, his brothers, Bev, and me.

"Everything's cool," Dan says. "My man, Jim, here is a little protective, but wouldn't you be if Bev was your girlfriend?"

There is no arguing with this logic, and Brad doesn't even try.

"Come on, before the cops get involved," Dan says.

At the mention of the police, Brad turns away and grabs another drink. Dan has diffused the situation and checks to make sure we're both okay.

Once he's satisfied that harmony is restored, he wanders off, and Bev places her hand on my chest and smiles.

"Thanks," she whispers, and slowly, my heart rate starts to slow, returning to normal.

Hours later, with no further incident, Bev finally says it's time to go. I am stone sober and more than ready to leave.

I help her gather our carload of passengers, and after the six of us trek through the muddy parking area and file into my car, I ferry us away, past the dark woods, back to the university proper.

It's well after dark when we pull into Bev's driveway, and I laugh silently at the fact that throughout the entire day, I never saw a horse or a single race.

Once inside, with the effects of the X long vanished, everyone is tired, and we all go straight to our bedrooms to crash. Once Bev and I are in her room, weariness comes on strong, and she only wants to have some tea and then sleep.

This is fine with me, and after our nightly ritual, we cradle each other in her bed. Soon, we are both out cold.

When I wake up early the next morning, I am refreshed and happy until I hear Bev crying next to me.

"What's wrong?" I ask, turning her gently by her shoulders and looking into her eyes. "Tell me."

I'm worried something has happened to her, but inside, I am horrified, wondering if I've done something to upset her.

Such are the insecurities of a new relationship.

"I'm so sorry," she says between sobs. "But there's something I have to tell you. And I'll understand if it's too much for you and you want to leave."

I pull her close and close my eyes, wishing I could soak up her pain and make it my own.

When she is able to speak without bringing on another fit of sobbing, we lie on our sides, facing each other.

"Please, tell me what's going on," I say. "You know I would never leave you, no matter what you tell me."

Her eyes are blood-red and puffy, but they are still the most beautiful hazel I've ever seen.

"There's no other way to say this, Jim," she says. "But…I need you to know I almost killed myself a couple of weeks ago."

I understand what she's just told me, but I'm also in shock and unsure of what to do or say. Although I have no personal experience with attempted suicide, I've thought about it—fantasized about leaving this world—and I know she's revealing something she's told few others, if anyone at all.

I remain silent and let her finish.

"I shouldn't have done the X yesterday. I think it jarred something loose in me. I had the worst dreams last night, reliving how the whole thing went down. And I…I had to tell you. Because I'm not as perfect as you think I am, you know? I have problems, and not too long ago, things got too overwhelming, and I couldn't take it anymore."

I do not want to say the wrong thing to her, because suicide is a serious matter best handled by professionals. But I also can't let her confession hang between us without letting her know how much I care for her.

"I'm glad you didn't kill yourself" I say as softly as possible. "And that you're still here with me. If anything, I feel even closer to you. I'm not going anywhere."

She wipes a tear from her cheek and nods.

I have so many questions to ask, but she doesn't offer any details, and I don't want to force her into talking about this anymore.

All I can do is hold her.

If we had been together as a couple longer, I'd tell her the one thing that is reverberating through my mind and my heart.

But it's too soon for that.

Instead, I hold her gaze and *think* the words I want to share with her.

I love you. I love you. I love you.

She looks deeply into my eyes and clings to me. And in that moment, I convince myself she can read my deepest and truest thoughts and knows exactly how I feel about her.

CHAPTER FOURTEEN

BY THIS POINT, my apartment is nothing more than a closet to me. I return every other day to pick up a few sets of new clothes, take care of bills, and perform the bare minimum of my duties as an RA.

"You need to empty your trash," I say to the suite of guys with disgusting hygiene.

"Pick up your beer bottles," I tell the apartment of young women who will not look so cute in a few years if they continue to drink this much every day.

"Stop pretending sweet-n-low is cocaine," I tell the lonely guy who is desperate for attention any way he can get it.

As far as busting up parties that get too out of hand, which happens often, I leave that to my colleagues, most of whom actively live in their apartments.

When I walk through the Lambeth courtyard, ready to head back to Bev's house again, my head RA, Barry, runs up to me.

"Haven't seen you around here much lately, Jim. Anything going on I need to know about?"

I shrug and try not to smile like the love-struck sap I've become.

"Not a problem in the world," I say. "Pretty busy, though. I just started this new relationship, and on top of that, my psych lab's been killing me."

He nods sagely—a mature father figure amongst children.

"I get that. I do," he says. "But your residents need to know you're here for them, especially in the off hours and at night. This time of year, when exams are getting closer, they're a lot more stressed than they let on. You know that."

I sigh because Barry is right.

A few of my tenants have serious issues, most of which I'm not qualified to handle. Even so, I'm supposed to be the fire detector at the ground level, the canary in the coal mine. If I can't solve something or help someone with a problem, I'm supposed to alert Barry, who can bring in the real professionals. And, to be fair, it's pretty difficult for me to do that if I'm not around much.

"I'll do better," I say. "I'll spend a few more nights here each week. I promise."

"Invite your new girlfriend over," he says, trying to be helpful. "Your place is as good as hers, right?"

I tell Barry I have to go, then head toward the Colonnades.

There's no way Bev will spend time here on a regular basis amongst all these underclassmen. And her friends won't visit and hang out like we're all part of one big sitcom.

Yes, I'll attempt to persuade her to stay at my place once, to show Barry I'm trying. But if she agrees, she'll treat the entire event as a camping trip instead of hanging out with her *boyfriend* at his apartment. Sleeping here will *not* become a habit, for sure. And I don't want it to be. Staying with Bev at her house, with her friends, is a glimpse of life after college.

And I like it.

I take the back way into the Grounds, and when I arrive at Gilmer Hall, I'm early for our lab because it's my turn to be in the hot seat with our subject today.

When I enter the room, Amber and Eugene greet me. She'll host our final experiment, and Eugene will take notes and observe.

"Good morning," I say, but Amber shoots me a tight-lipped smile and points to the *No Talking* sign on the wall. Through the open door that leads to the experiment room, I see a blonde woman with perfect, pale skin waiting. She is early, and that means our act has already begun.

I enter the testing room and take a seat across from the woman. She looks up and smiles at me as I pretend to study the questionnaire.

"Good morning, Lisa and Jim," Amber says over the speakers in the room. "Since everyone's early today, we'll go ahead and get started."

Eugene closes the door, and Amber goes into her spiel.

At Amber's direction, Lisa and I fill out our questionnaires. I'm truthful about all my responses, even though it doesn't matter what I mark down, and I rate Lisa as an eight. Eugene steps in to retrieve our questionnaires, then closes the door again, and finally, it's time to get down to business.

Amber reads the same script we've used in every single one of our experiments. It is all I can do not to mouth her words silently as she recites each line on cue. However, when she gets to the part about the rules, she goes off script.

"As you can see, the sign on the wall says no talking," she says. "If either of you speaks to the other during the experiment, neither of you will receive credit for participating today. That being said, there are no rules about interacting in other ways with each other."

Those last words are not part of our standard language.

"If you both finish early, you may choose to spend the remaining time however you want, other than talking. This may include any kind of physical contact you wish to make with each other. Making out and even foreplay is acceptable, but we ask for you to wait until after the experiment is over before engaging in full-out sexual relations."

I look at Lisa, who remains emotionless as if she hasn't heard a thing Amber's said. My face turns red. I am angry and don't understand why Amber would say such things. Not only could they invalidate the experiment, but we could get in serious trouble for talking to one of our subjects this way.

There is only one explanation I can figure.

Amber must be acting out, trying to get back at me for being with Bev.

But what does she hope to achieve? To embarrass me? Or is she only trying to be mean? The latter is more her style. Or maybe she hopes I fall for Lisa and screw things up with Bev, so she'll have an opportunity to wedge her way into my life again.

I ignore Amber and smile at Lisa, who grins as the experiment begins.

As per our script, I knock down Lisa's cube once, then twice, each time more aggressively and openly. Lisa doesn't lose her temper, but she pouts—hurt as if I've violated a sacred, unspoken trust between the two of us.

I wonder if she rated me as being attractive or trustworthy on her questionnaire. Or maybe both. I want to know, not because I'm interested in her, but because I'm genuinely curious.

The lab session doesn't come to an end quickly enough for me. Lisa maintains her composure the entire time, and both of us work on our cubes until Amber calls time and assures us that we'll be receiving full credit for the experiment.

Still fuming over Amber's transgression, I glare at her as I follow Lisa out of the room.

Instead of returning to reconnoiter with her and Eugene, I head directly to class, ready and in need of seeing Bev's beautiful face again to calm me down.

I am one of the first students to enter the lecture hall, and I settle into an aisle seat ten rows from the front of the class—a different location from where Amber, Eugene, and I usually sit.

When Bev walks in with the other TAs and glances at me, I turn away. Not because I don't want her to look but because I'm trying to honor our agreement about keeping things quiet around the other students in class.

But when I raise my eyes, she's still looking at me, her head slightly tilted to one side as if weighing a decision.

She sits down, but seconds later, she pivots in her seat and smiles at me again, and I wonder what's going on I don't know about.

When Mooken steps into the room with two minutes left before starting time, I settle in, ready for the day's lecture.

But before Mooken begins, Bev stands up and ascends the stairs to where I'm sitting.

"Hey there," she says, grabbing my hand.

She leans in and whispers in my ear.

"I can't wait to see you tonight. You're still coming over, right?"

Plenty of students, as well as Professor Mooken, are watching as Bev chats with me.

Maybe she's turned some unknown corner in our relationship. I don't know what has caused this change in her discretion, but since she lingers at my seat, I take the opportunity to push my luck.

"I would love that," I say, "But I think I need to stay at my place tonight. The Head RA chewed me out today and wants to see me around Lambeth more often. But tomorrow night, I'll be over after the movie, for sure. And, Bev, maybe we can sleep at my place sometime? Not tonight, but some other night if you're up for it. Just once to show Barry I'm taking him seriously."

A shadow from a student walking past us sweeps across Bev's face, but she smiles and looks at me with eyes filled with emotion.

"Sure, baby," she says. "I understand. Whatever will help you out. I'll miss you tonight, though."

I half expect her to kiss me, but she stops short of doing so, which is probably for the best. I'm just happy everyone can tell there's something between us now, and I can relax a little. Being someone's secret is exciting and fun at first, but soon, all you end up doing is living their lie.

And that sucks.

Bev squeezes my hand and returns to the front of the class, where she takes her seat. Professor Mooken watches her, then looks at me, his face impassive and dark.

After three long seconds, he turns his back to the class and begins his lecture by writing on the chalkboard.

Love=Addiction.

CHAPTER FIFTEEN

AFTER CLASS, I wait for Bev outside, pondering Mooken's bizarre lecture.

The professor is smart, but he is the most jaded person I've ever known when it comes to love. I understand the points he made about the similarities between being in love and being addicted to drugs. I mean, the chemicals our bodies produce when we're in love are potent, to be sure.

But if Mooken was trying to make a point or to warn me about falling in love with Bev, I am unfazed by his pessimism.

Five minutes later, when Bev emerges from Gilmer Hall, she hurries over to me with the level of excitement all people wish they could instill in their partners.

"Hey, you. I thought I scared you, and you ran away."

"I'm braver than that," I say, resisting my urge to kiss her in public.

She squints.

"Up for lunch?" she says.

I nod and smile because when I'm near her, I just can't help it.

The sharp fall air blows across our faces as we meander up the sidewalk with our backpacks slung over our shoulders.

Students study us as we pass. This is something I'll have to get used to.

They can't understand how such a woman has chosen to be with an average guy like me.

But hey, looks aren't everything. Isn't that what people say?

It's what's inside that counts, and I have plenty going on inside me. More than I know, sometimes.

Before we've gone far, Eugene intercepts us from behind and greets Bev with the largest, fakest smile I've ever seen.

"You must be Beverly," he says. "I'm one of your students, too. Eugene."

I mumble a quick introduction and calculate the quickest way to force Eugene to leave. Above all else, I will not allow him to eat lunch with us, even if I have to be rude to drive him away.

Before I can arrive at a plan, Eugene squints and points to the steady flow of students traveling up and down McCormick Road, one of the main streets that leads into the University's Central Grounds.

"Is that the guy from our experiment you were talking about?" he says. "The one you said was stalking you?"

I track to where Eugene is pointing and swallow hard.

Twenty feet away from us, a familiar, skinny figure stands, outfitted in jeans and a ripped gray T-shirt.

He glares at me, then looks directly at Bev, drooling as he studies her.

"It is Tony," I whisper.

While keeping him in my sight, I place my other arm through the strap of my backpack and secure it.

Tony understands my movement for what it is. He knows what's coming next.

"I have to skip lunch," I say to Bev. "I'm so sorry."

"Jim, what are you doing?"

"I have to take care of something. I'll call you later. I promise."

Bev scans the students while Eugene moves closer to her.

As soon as I take a step toward Tony, he turns and runs, and I accelerate to a full-out sprint, almost knocking over a pair of young women taking selfies.

Tony is fueled by adrenaline and fear, but I'm stoked by anger. Even so, the scene that unfolds is not like in the movies. I don't yell at him to stop. I don't shout his name to let him know I've discovered him. And there's no thrilling soundtrack playing in the background to pull the audience into the chase with us.

Instead, I am silent, focused on breathing and where my feet are falling, trying to make sure I don't trip or twist my ankle. I expend no non-essential effort other than to pull the straps on my backpack tighter as I jump off the sidewalk and follow Tony, who is pumping his skinny arms, running up the middle of the street.

The shape of him fleeing, along with everything else around me, is tinted red as I sprint after him.

To our right, the stream of students continues on, heading to and returning from class, with only a few kids looking up from their phones long enough to wonder what the hell is going on.

I'm not in good enough physical shape to catch Tony as quickly as I want, but he has to stop somewhere, sometime, and I have enough rage powering my legs to follow him until he drops.

And when he does, I'll find out what he's up to and put a stop to it.

My sneakers slap hard against the pavement as I hurdle a speed bump and slip when I land, almost wiping out. When I recover, I'm forty feet behind Tony and running as fast as possible up the steep road.

Each beat of my heart hurts as it slams into my chest. I ignore it and try to breathe deeply as I run. My backpack is slowing me down and hurting my back and shoulders, but in the middle of a school day, there's nowhere safe to ditch my books and my laptop. So I tamp down the pain and press on.

Up ahead, Tony throws a quick glance over his shoulder and curses out loud when he sees I'm still there. He takes a sharp left and crosses the street, narrowly avoiding the rear bumper of a Honda Civic. I do the same, sticking with him as he leaps onto a sidewalk that leads away from the road and runs between a set of underclassman dorms.

I am familiar with this path.

It's a shortcut to the Castle—one of my favorite places for burgers.

And sure enough, seconds later, he exits the dorm area, and I follow, passing through the Castle's comforting cloud of fried food scents. To our left, students hop around and run on salmon-colored basketball courts, joyful and free of stress.

Tony and I are on level ground, and I force myself to close the gap between us, pumping my body as hard as it will stand.

Within seconds, he's at the walking bridge that passes over Emmet Street—the main road that leads back to Lambeth.

Tony stops at the entrance to the walking bridge and pivots to the left, descending a set of cement stairs that switch back and forth and lead to the street below. I've been up and down these steps hundreds of times and am familiar with every crack and piece of loose concrete—something I'm betting Tony isn't, since he's not a student here.

With only one flight of steps to go, Tony trips on a piece of loose metal flashing, ironically meant to keep the stairs safer. He descends the rest of the way in a single, airborne dive that ends with him plowing into the concrete landing at the base of the stairs.

He struggles to his feet faster than I expect him to, especially since he's bleeding from his elbows and must be hurting pretty badly.

Instead of continuing down the sidewalk that runs along Emmet, he makes a U-turn and moves our chase off-road, onto the grass and gravel underneath the overpass.

I don't know why he thinks this is a good idea.

It's not.

We're now hidden from the students marching on the road above us, and before he's half-way under the concrete overpass, I catch him.

I swing my backpack from my shoulders and toss it into his legs, and the results are marvelous. His feet get caught up in my backpack straps, and he face-plants into the gravel, throwing up a cloud of dust and rock.

I follow him to the ground, and when I turn him over and straddle his bony chest, he looks relieved not to be running anymore, the same as me.

His eyes bulge as he tries to capture his breath, but my weight on top of him prevents him from doing that. I press my knee harder into his chest and take a few seconds to inhale enough air so I'm able to speak.

"What…the fuck…are you doing, Tony?" I say to him, growling my words and lowering my snarling face so it's only inches from his.

His wide-stretched eyes betray his terror when he speaks.

"My…my name is Andrew," he says, as if his words will make me leave him alone. "I don't even know you, man."

I shake my head. He's lying. I know who he is.

"I don't care what name you're calling yourself today, asshole," I say. "Why are you following me? If it's because of the experiment, you need to get over it."

"What experiment?"

"Stop bullshitting me, man."

"I don't know anything about any *experiment*," he says, almost crying.

"No more lies," I say. "Listen to me closely. If I see you following me or even looking at Bev again, you will regret it.

"Beverly?" he asks, pleading, as a glint of recognition sparks in his eyes.

"Tell me you understand what I just said."

He closes his eyes, still trying to breathe. He's not having a good afternoon, and I don't care.

"Do you understand?" I yell.

He nods, shaking, finally surrendering to the fact that there is only one answer I will accept.

I lift myself partway off of his chest, allowing his lungs to expand, and all is silent, other than his labored breathing.

Shit, son, my dad says in my head. *You'll be lucky if they don't arrest you for this.*

I close my eyes.

"Shut up," I shout.

When I open my eyes again, there's still a guy under me, but something is different. And very wrong.

I've never seen the man with shocking red hair who is bleeding and moaning beneath me. For a second, I think this must be another terrible nightmare. But when the man turns his head and spits his blood onto the dusty white gravel, I know this is real.

I chased the right person. I'm certain of that.

But this man is not Tony. Not even his hair color is correct.

Even though I'm not an overly religious person, I close my eyes again and pray this is only a dream.

I don't want to go to jail, and I don't want to hurt anyone.

But when I open my eyes, I'm staring at the same stranger. He is afraid, but so am I, and I have to force myself to stay where I am and not run away.

I lean closer to him and snarl.

"I have a deal for you. Forget my face, and I'll forget yours. I'll pretend this never happened."

My words are meant to sound tough, but they don't. I recognize the timbre of fear, even when it's coming from me.

I'm appalled that I've terrorized a complete stranger for no reason, but a part of me relaxes. I don't know who this guy is, but he doesn't know who I am, either.

And I plan on keeping it that way.

"Do we have a deal?" I say again, my voice still trembling.

He nods, but his eyes are drained of fear now and slowly filling with hate.

I stand up, grab my backpack, step away from him, and run.

Home is a straight shot down Emmet Street, but I still have my Tuesday appointment with Mooken. Plus, I don't want *Andrew* to have any clue as to where I live. So I head back up the stairs as fast as I can. When I make it to the top, I'm out of breath again as I merge into a group of students and lose myself.

When I arrive at the outdoor amphitheater—a semi-circle of tiered stone steps where students lounge and bask in the sun—I take a seat by myself, as far away from the others as possible.

Once I'm alone in the crowd, I place my head between my knees to hide my face, and I cry because of what I did and because of what I *almost did* to an innocent man.

CHAPTER SIXTEEN

THE UNIVERSITY OF Virginia is large, but not too large. It's one of the reasons I chose it.

The student body is big enough to lose yourself in but small enough that you don't feel like a number. Add to that the fact that the school is nestled within the mountain town of Charlottesville, Virginia, with all its non-college-related businesses and the locals who live here year-round, and the chance of me running into Andrew again is remote.

Then again, it's a year and a half before I graduate, and that's a long time to avoid someone.

So I take the back way to Gilmer Hall when I leave the amphitheater, keeping my head down and my eyes riveted to the path in front of me—being as low-key as possible.

Twenty minutes later, when I enter Gilmer Hall, I'm horrified and hopeful about my meeting with Professor Mooken.

Horrified, because what I did to that guy isn't normal, and I haven't processed it yet. And because, although I could use some sane advice from a professional, I'm not willing to take the chance Mooken would be required by UVA's code of conduct to report my assault to the authorities.

But I'm also hopeful because *maybe* Mooken can help me with my nightmares, which I think are connected somehow to what just happened.

I stand outside Mooken's door, staring at his name etched on the glass.

Benjamin Mooken, Professor of Psychology.

When my phone vibrates, it's my father calling again.

I let it go to voicemail, then gently knock on Mooken's door, remembering how Amber walked into his office unannounced. Maybe after seeing him a few more times, I'll feel that casual around him, but I doubt it.

"Enter," he says, and I step inside his cluttered, dusty office.

He motions for me to sit down across the desk from him, and I do. But instead of greeting me or asking me a question, he props his chin up with one hand and glares at me.

What have I done to anger him?

This is not the kind of session I need right now. I still don't have my shit together, nor am I feeling very patient.

After a minute of watching him watch me, I can't take it anymore.

"Is this one of those things where you stare at me until I say something?" I say. "If so, congrats. It worked."

Mooken chuckles, straightens himself in his chair, and clears his throat.

"Silence is one of the most effective interrogation techniques there is," he says. "Most humans in our society are quite uncomfortable with it and feel an unconscious need to fill in the gaps of a conversation."

It's my turn to stare at him now. His little factoid is interesting, but I don't care. I'm not impressed.

"You could have reacted in any number of ways to me sitting here like a bump on a log," he continues. "Some students politely wait, although there are fewer and fewer of those each year. Others—the majority—sit still for a few minutes before meekly asking if I want them to say something. Sometimes they'll ask if now is still a good time for our meeting. Only a *very* small percentage—actually, whatever percentage of my students you represent—have answered with sarcasm and a direct challenge."

"I wasn't trying to be rude."

He nods, unconcerned by what I did or didn't intend.

"I take no offense," he says. "Your reaction is simply a piece of data for me. But what it means…now *that* is the interesting part. Tell me, did you bring your dream journal?"

Shit.

As soon as he says it, I realize I've screwed up.

"I left it back at my apartment."

I close my eyes and inhale.

"But I remember exactly what I wrote about—the one bad dream I had."

"You recorded only one nightmare?"

I shrug.

"It's been…a good week."

"I see. Did you have any additional encounters with your ex-girlfriend?"

I shake my head.

"Did you try any over-the-counter sleep medication?"

"Nothing," I say. "I just…I slept better. Maybe because we're talking about things in here…"

He studies me, not buying my lame suggestion that he is somehow responsible for my improved sleep quality. He knows I'm holding something back, and my throat goes dry when I remember he saw Bev and me in his classroom earlier. He must have noticed the way she touched me—how I smiled back at her like a buffoon.

He *has to* know about the two of us.

In an attempt to avoid bringing up Bev, I tell him about my nightmare.

I explain how I was talking to my father on the phone when a shadow started moving on its own. I tell him about the dark waters of *blood* and the demon named Rashmuni I used to date.

I remember reading how most patients don't share the full truth with their therapists, which, in the end, only hampers their progress.

I'm still not a fan of doctors, but Mooken is more than that. He's also my teacher, and I need to learn to trust him.

Mooken listens as I finish the details of my dream. When I'm done, he shrugs and nods. My weird life isn't that strange to him or original. He's heard it all before from other students and patients.

A sense of normalcy settles over me, putting me at ease.

"I am curious," he says, rubbing his stubbly chin. "How did you feel when you woke up from your nightmare, and…what was the first thing you did afterward?"

I stop myself from blurting out what really happened—how I called Bev and went over to her place to spend the night with her for the first time.

So much for telling my psychologist everything…

"I was relieved," I say. "Like I could breathe again. I browsed a few social media sites and went back to sleep. Eventually."

He shrugs, although, once again, I'm not convinced he believes me.

"Has anything in your waking life ever elicited the same or similar emotional reactions? This sense of extreme relief?"

I squint and try to determine how much of the truth to tell him.

Before I can say anything, he continues.

"The woman in your dream was another ex-girlfriend, correct? After you awoke, you say you felt *relieved* and could breathe again. Was that how you felt, perhaps when you and this woman broke up?"

My mouth opens slightly. I'm not sure where he came up with that, but his insight is dead-on.

"Sort of," I say. "When things ended with Rashmuni, it felt like a burden had been removed for sure."

"I see," Mooken says. "And the rest of last week was without incident? May I assume you are still single? Or are you getting a little nookie somewhere?"

I'm not sure what *nookie* means exactly, but from the context, I'm pretty sure he's asking if I'm getting laid.

"No nookie for me," I say. "Not since a couple of weekends ago with my ex-girlfriend, like I told you last time."

Mooken pauses for longer than is comfortable before sighing.

"I feel as though I've let you down," he says. "It seems neither of us is prepared for today's meeting as well as we should be. As you have forgotten your dream journal, I have also not had the time or the opportunity to find the name of a therapist to recommend to you. And because of my lack of follow-through, I offer, in return, a possible interpretation of your nightmares. I must state, however, once again, I am not your therapist. I am simply proposing a potential explanation based on what the literature and data say."

I nod and lean forward.

I expect the professor to tell me how my dreams are subconscious attempts at dealing with my past relationship problems, but instead, he brings up something unexpected.

"But first, I want to dig deeper into the blood," he says.

I force myself not to look down at my clothing and am suddenly terrified that Andrew's bloodstains might be all over me.

"How would you describe the sex life with your ex-girlfriend—this Rashmuni from your dream?"

I'm relieved he's only talking about my nightmare, but now I have to explain my sometimes complicated relationship with Rash.

"We had fun together," I say. "Hanging out, going for drinks, and listening to live music. And the sex was good. Other than kissing her—which was painful."

"Why was that?"

"She liked to bite. And usually kissing involved blood—mostly mine. The taste of it was always there when we were having sex, too. But…eventually it became exciting…arousing, if I'm being honest."

Mooken nods again, and I hope I've said something sensible.

"I would be surprised if it hadn't," he says. "Paired conditioning is a well-established fact. And when you were dating her, you had fewer nightmares, correct?"

I nod.

"And the same with your most recent girlfriend, as well. You had fewer of your dark dreams, yes?"

"For the most part. I figure it was because I was less stressed from having regular sex, right?"

"Was there any blood or pain involved with your most recent ex?"

I shake my head.

"No blood, for sure. And the pain…well, maybe a little, but nothing dangerous."

He clears his throat.

"I apologize if I'm being too personal, but did sex with your most recent partner ever border on violence? Even if it was only acted-out or *pretend* violence?"

When he mentions violent sex, I wonder if Amber is also seeing the professor as a surrogate therapist the way I am. Knowing Amber, if she *is*, she's freely divulged every minute detail of our sex life and used my real name without giving it a second thought.

I look down at Mooken's desk and close my eyes.

There's no sense in lying to him about this. And besides, I want to understand what this has to do with my nightmares.

"Sometimes it became a little…intense and dark, yes," I say. "And violent, but only in a fantasy sort of way."

"I wouldn't dare offer a diagnosis based on such little information," he says. "However, consider the possibility that when you are having intense or violent sex on a regular basis, your pent-up aggressions—your demons, if you will—are given a release valve and allowed to dissipate into the real world. But when you cannot act out your darker inclinations in your waking life, perhaps your dreams step up to the plate, as nightmares, to offer you a means of release."

"But not *all* of my nightmares are about sex," I say.

"I wouldn't expect them to be," Mooken says. "Like with most people, your true issues are deeper than sex. Perhaps you experienced a traumatic incident or encountered some other stimulus at the root of your real problems. And, Jim, let me be clear about this—I believe you would benefit from seeing a dedicated therapist to help you figure out the true source of your issues.

"In the meantime, I suggest you avoid stress during your waking hours as much as possible. Try to exercise more. Put yourself on a regular sleep cycle, getting up and going to bed at the same time every night. And maybe it's not such a bad idea for you to become sexually active again as well. Even additional encounters with your ex-girlfriend wouldn't be such a bad thing. She may not be perfect for you, but she is someone with whom you can find the kind of sex you desire in a consensual manner. And it may help you sleep better.

"Well, we broke up, though," I say. "I want something deeper."

"I understand, and you deserve something more substantial. But nothing is forever, and for now, don't let the fact you two are no longer together stand in your way. I say you should go for it. Have fun. Relax a little. And remember, love and pleasure don't care a single lick about your self-contrived boundaries. Your first priority should be to stop whatever is inside you from building and exerting pressure on your psyche."

I hear what the professor is saying. But his theory about my nightmares getting better if I start having fucked-up sex with Amber again doesn't make sense to me. Because I know something he doesn't.

Even if Mooken suspects that Bev and I are dating, he can't know that, after making love to her, I sleep like a baby.

If anything, Professor Mooken, the expert in human psychology, unknowingly has confirmed what I already know in my heart—that Bev is the only answer to my problems.

CHAPTER SEVENTEEN

I LIE IN my bed that evening, my head propped up with two pillows. On the video call, Bev is in her bed wearing sweatpants and a white camisole.

"I wish you were here," she says, her voice soft.

"Me too. But I'll be over tomorrow."

She smiles, but her mouth stays shut because she's thinking about something else.

"What was that all about with the guy earlier today, Jim?"

My face reddens. I need to explain to her what happened. At least most of it. That's what people do who are in love. They keep no secrets from each other, because love is total acceptance.

So why am I nervous about disclosing to Bev that I chased down and pummeled a total stranger?

"He was one of the subjects in our experiment," I say. "A local guy who's been following me, and I had to find out why. I'm sorry I messed up lunch."

"Did you catch him?"

"Eventually," I say. "I think we were both glad the chase was over by that point."

"Did you find out what was going on?"

"I…don't understand how, but after I caught him…he wasn't the right guy anymore. He was someone else."

"You chased the wrong person?"

I shake my head.

"It *was* him. But when I caught up to him, it *wasn't* him anymore. I don't understand what happened or how it happened, but I could have really hurt that guy."

"Is there a chance the person you started chasing got away from you at some point, and you continued following a different guy?"

Bev's potential explanation offers a chance for me to redeem my sanity, but the scenario she suggests isn't likely, and I can't let this go.

"I had him in my sights the whole time," I say. "He didn't lose me."

"It's Occam's Razor," she says with a sympathetic smile. "The simplest of all competing theories is likely the truth. What's more likely? You mistook the guy's identity from the start? Or you chased the right guy, but he magically transformed into someone else at the last second? Or is it most likely that Tony lost you during the chase, and you accidentally started following someone else?

She wants me to see the potential for reason in my insanity, but none of her options are likely.

"What does Occam say about someone who's not right in the head?" I say. "I mean, even Mooken thinks I should see a therapist. What if I almost beat up this guy because my mind isn't working right?"

Her face darkens again, but not because I'm discussing whether I'm mentally ill. Instead, she sours when I mention Mooken's name.

"You saw the professor again?" she says.

I nod.

"He was supposed to give me the name of a therapist I could contact, but he didn't have time to find one, and I forgot the dream journal he told me to keep, so we…talked."

"About what? You didn't say anything to him about us, did you?"

I take a heavy breath and exhale.

"I didn't mention your name at all. All I did was tell him about my dream last week, the night I called you and went over to your place the first time."

"You told him you came over here? Jim…"

"Of course not. I *only* told him about my dream. But from there, we ended up discussing other things."

She leans forward, waiting for me to explain, while I squirm in my bed, uncomfortable. I hesitate before I respond. There's nothing I won't tell Bev, but I need to ease my way into disclosing the whole truth.

"Mooken asked about my past sex life," I say. "He thinks my nightmares might be tied to whether or not I'm sexually active. And don't worry. I told him I wasn't having sex with anyone right now."

Her shoulders relax as she thinks about what I've said.

"With past girlfriends, sometimes things got…you know, a little dark with roleplaying and some…pretend violence," I say. "I always felt weird and guilty doing anything like that, and it upset me that those things could turn me on. But I also slept really well on those nights and never had any nightmares."

"And the professor thinks having this type of sex serves as a pressure release valve for whatever's driving your inner anxieties?"

I nod, impressed, but not surprised. After all, she is Mooken's TA.

Bev glances down, and in the light of her phone, her face is suddenly fragile porcelain—able to be shattered by a single harsh word.

"Do you have nightmares when we're together?" she asks quietly.

"None at all," I say. "I sleep great when I'm with you. Which is why I don't think vigorous and dark sex is the only thing that helps with my nightmares. It's also feeling happy and less stressed, which is how I've been since I met you, Bev. It's one reason I already care so much for you, even though all this is so new between us."

"I feel the same way," she says, her eyes sparkling with the beginning of happy tears filling her eyes. "Do you…do you want to try something…dirtier in bed next time? Would that help you more with your bad dreams?"

Her words are shots of adrenaline through my system. My body wants me to say *yes*, but Bev is more than my lover. She is also my sanity, and I don't ever want to associate her with darkness. Despite the temptation of my old passions, I like making love to her more than I want to fuck her.

"I don't need anything dirty with you," I say. "Our sex is perfect the way it is. If *you* like it, I mean."

She nods, and my heart soars, making the previous jolts of adrenaline pinpricks by comparison.

I have to force myself not to tell her I love her right then and there. I can't change my feelings, but I don't want to ruin this by rushing her. So I remain silent.

"It's getting kind of late," I eventually say. "We should get some sleep."

"I guess so," she says. "But I still wish you were here."

"Me too," I say as we wave at each other, and my phone goes black.

I lie back in my bed, turn out the lights, and think about Bev as the blackness of sleep overtakes me.

When I wake up, I have no sense that time has passed, but the sun is shining through my bedroom curtains, bathing me in its warmth. I am well rested, and I had no nightmares. None I can remember, at least. My body feels good and strong, and my brain is healthy and light.

And I'm not surprised.

I had no sexual release last night, but I experienced something much more potent—my conversation with Bev and all the positive emotions it evoked.

At first, I smile because this proves I don't need a sexually deviant outlet for my darkness to help me sleep better at night.

All I need is love.

But when I close my eyes, my brain fills with memories of chasing Tony through the Grounds and tackling him in the gravel. But it also fills with images of Andrew's bloody face and bright red hair. And as I lie there, still confused about what really happened, I am also no longer confident my love for Bev is what allowed me to sleep so soundly the night before.

What if, instead, my nightmares were held at bay because I almost beat an innocent man to a pulp while I was awake?

CHAPTER EIGHTEEN

TONIGHT'S MOVIE IS *Primal Fear*, and Gilmer Hall is filled with students and faculty. It's another film I've never seen before, but I'm familiar with both its stars—Richard Gere and Edward Norton.

The place is packed, and I have to take whatever seat I can find, which puts me near the rear of the auditorium. I can see the screen with no problem, but Bev is much harder to watch.

Amber and Eugene, whom I've almost forgotten about, are there, too. But they're both up front, closer to Professor Mooken, Bev, and the other TAs.

I am isolated and left out of their group as the lights fade.

The movie is an old one and begins with opening credits. Before they can finish, the film jumps and loses a second of time. I guess Bev wasn't able to fix all the problems with the file, and I hope she isn't too stressed out about it.

The story is about a cocky defense attorney, played by Gere, and an altar boy, played by a young Edward Norton, who is accused of murdering the Archbishop. Gere takes him on as a client and starts to believe that when things get too rough for the innocent Norton, he transforms into another personality—a dark, brutal version of himself—one that has no qualms about hurting people. Or about killing the Archbishop.

During the film's last scene, after getting Norton's character a verdict of mentally incompetent to stand trial, Gere's character, along with everyone in the audience, discovers that the innocent altar boy persona is all an act.

Norton's dark side is the *real* Norton, and simpleton Norton is a well-played, elaborate lie he's successfully sold for the entire movie.

We are collectively duped, and we love it.

We are also strangely pleased that evil Norton will get away with killing the Archbishop because it turns out the Archbishop sexually abused Norton's character.

The ending is so good the crowd applauds, and the post-film discussion is robust and energetic.

Bev glances at me a few times between calling on students, and even though the Q&A is interesting, all I can think about is being with her again.

It takes a full hour before everyone clears from the auditorium, and I wait outside for Bev like before. This time, however, Professor Mooken, Bev, and the rest of the TAs leave together.

I'm not sure what to do—or what Bev wants me to do. In my mind, she made it clear to Mooken in class yesterday that the two of us have a personal relationship. And he knows we eat lunch together. But I don't want to take any chances of ruining things for her.

So I walk farther away from the group and wait for her in a night shadow made by an overhanging tree.

Bev and the others stand outside the building, talking. She looks around, wondering where I am. I consider sending her a text, but instead, I stand still and observe.

Carl is there, as is the other TA—a woman whose name, I think, is Maggie. Carl stands close to Bev. Mooken, on the other hand, stands across from Bev, gesturing with his hands, telling one of his stories, no doubt.

At the climax of his tale, all the TAs laugh, and even Bev flashes a smile I have foolishly assumed was reserved only for me. There is chemistry and comfort between the four of them, something to be expected from colleagues who work closely together, but even so, once again, I am isolated and left out.

After ten long minutes, the group disbands, giving hugs all around. But when Mooken goes to hug Bev, she stiffens as he wraps an arm around her shoulders.

It's normal for Mooken to be attracted to Bev on some level, no matter how upstanding a professor he might be. I can understand that. She is, after all, intelligent, beautiful, and witty. I would be surprised if he didn't have some special place for her in his most closely held fantasies. But I'm relieved when she doesn't reciprocate his embrace. Whether that's because she knows I'm watching or not, I'm not sure.

Nor do I care.

As the members of the group part ways, Bev approaches the path where I am hidden. She knows I'm somewhere but can't see me in the dark, and she walks tentatively, with fear. The unknown always frightens us, even when we think we know what's next.

"I'm here," I whisper.

I make my greeting as non-threatening as possible so as not to startle her. But she jumps anyway before she registers it's me and smiles.

She steps into the shadow with me, and we embrace. It's only been a day since we've held each other, but the electricity is stronger than ever between us.

She leans in and whispers into my ear.

"I remember what you said last night, Jim. But I was thinking…what if I want a little dirt with my sex sometimes? Would that be okay?"

My head swims, and I'm incapacitated, unable to process logic or reason, as she moves her hand down my body.

In response, I do the same, and soon she's leaning against me, her legs weak, her breath ragged. After only a few minutes, she clutches my shoulders and tries not to collapse to the ground.

I hold her up—a limp doll in my arms.

"Now, it's your turn," she says after she catches her breath and looks around to ensure we're still alone.

No one is near us, and the tree's shadow provides ample protection, but this reminds me too much of the last time I was with Amber.

I shake my head, trying to exorcise Amber's image from my brain. Thinking of her while I'm with Bev pollutes something holy and sacred in me. To help with this, I open my eyes and take in the reality of Bev in front of me.

She kisses my stomach, and I do that which is most difficult for me.

I relax and enjoy the moment.

Losing myself in a rush of pleasure and love doesn't take long.

As I pull her up to me, I don't care about my nightmares, the darkness inside me, or anything else.

All that matters is Bev, and nothing can change that.

Ever.

CHAPTER NINETEEN

NORMALLY, I DON'T get excited about Saturdays, but today is my twenty-first birthday, which means I can legally drink without fear of being caught using a fake ID. It also means I can more easily join Bev and her friends when they go out drinking, usually at some bar on the Corner.

We start the evening at *Shenanigans Pub*, where I meet up with Bev, Cynthia, and Dan and proudly order my first legal beer. Even though I'm the youngest in our group, Cynthia and Dan are both welcoming, and Dan is as friendly and as dude-like as ever.

"Congrats," he says as we hold up our beers and toast. "To you and Bev. Such a great couple."

I look over to Bev. She makes goo-goo eyes at me and smiles. Life is good.

While waiting for our next round of drinks, Dan raps a knuckle on the table and leans in, whispering.

"Hey, you two. I have a couple of extra pills if you want to party tonight. I'll sell them to you for half-price as a birthday present."

Bev squeezes my hand underneath the table. My reasons for not wanting his drugs are the same as they were the previous weekend. But Dan is being jovial and inclusive, and I can't get mad at him for that.

"You can have one if you want," I say to Bev, who laughs and flares her nostrils.

"We're heading to Chris Greene Lake after this," she says. "For some quality alone time. That's going to be our party tonight."

Cynthia rolls her eyes and laughs.

"Your room isn't enough privacy for you two sex addicts? You're the only one of us living on the first floor, for God's sake."

"Shut up, fucker," Bev says with a laugh.

Her insult is a term of endearment, and this is how Cynthia takes it.

"The lake is one of Jim's favorite places," Bev says. "And I thought it would be a nice way to end the evening."

I smile and sip what's left of my first beer, nursing it since I will be driving later. It's only a half-hour ride, but still…I will not endanger Bev.

We continue talking, and the other three drink heavily as it grows dark outside. Soon, the guitarist on the small, makeshift stage in the front of the dining area tunes his guitar and tests his mic.

"I wish I could play guitar," Bev says.

"I can teach you, if you want," I say, and she pretends to glare at me.

"You never told me you play. I call bullshit on you."

I laugh.

The truth is, I've messed around with guitars since I was a kid, but I've never gotten much beyond playing chords, strumming, and basic fingerpicking.

"Dude, play us something," Dan says. "Ask that guy if you can borrow his guitar before he starts his set. He's pretty cool. I bet he'll let you."

I shake my head. This does not sound like a good idea. But Bev squeezes my hand and urges me to try.

"I'd love to hear you play," she says.

And suddenly, performing a song in front of a growing crowd of inebriated students is a wonderful idea.

I get up, kiss Bev, and step over to the musician, who's set his guitar on its stand.

"That's a nice instrument," I say. "Gibson."

He nods and gestures to the red cherry sunburst Les Paul—his treasure.

"See that woman over there?" I say, pointing at Bev, who blushes. "She really wants to hear me play her a song. Any chance I can try a verse before you go on?"

The man scowls, then looks past me at Bev.

"You expect me to hand over my very expensive guitar to a total stranger? I don't even know if you can play."

"No, I get it," I say, disappointed. "But I had to ask. Thanks anyway, man."

He laughs, hands me his guitar, and walks away, headed for the bathroom.

"Have fun," he hollers over his shoulder.

Everyone at our table loses their collective shit, hooping, hollering, and clapping. The scene turns surreal as I register that I am now holding a live, amped-up guitar in the middle of Shenanigans.

I nestle my shoulder into the leather strap and step up to the mic. I haven't played in years, but my muscle memory is strong, and my fingers remember what they're supposed to do. Besides, it's a simple song I want to sing for Bev—an old one by Dire Straits.

I pick out the arpeggio that begins a story about two famous lovers named Romeo and Juliet.

The chords sound right, and the strings are bright, but the words that come out of my mouth are mostly wrong and slightly slurred from the beer. Nevertheless, I manage my way through the first verse, and as I'm beginning to feel more confident, the musician starts making his way back to the stage, ready to commence with the evening's real entertainment.

I skip to the part of the song I want to tell Bev the most through its lyrics.

I sing to her, explaining that I can't talk the way people do on the television and confessing that I can't sing love songs the way they *should* be sung. I assure her through the lyrics that I would do *anything* for her and that I can't help but be in love with her.

When I stop, I fantasize I've made a poignant, romantic gesture worthy of a scene in a movie. But in reality and from the way the audience reacts, I'm certain I came across as what I am—a love-sick, slightly buzzed amateur.

Even so, after handing the guitar back to the guy, thanking him more than is needed, and rejoining my table, Bev grabs my face and kisses me for a long time.

Her mouth sobers and intoxicates me. And after we kiss, I decide to stop drinking alcohol for the rest of the evening.

An hour later, after we finish our cheese sticks and Dan polishes off another half-pitcher of beer by himself, it's finally time for the next phase of my birthday celebration—the part I've been looking forward to the most.

All four of us walk back to the house, but when Cynthia and Dan head up to her room, I hop into my car and wait while Bev runs in to use the bathroom.

She joins me five minutes later and smiles, ready for the second half of our special night.

"I know you've been to the lake before," I say. "But I can't wait to show you my favorite place up there. Daytime's the best, but I go there at night a lot, too. You'll see."

Bev responds by rubbing my arm and resting her head on my shoulder.

We both wear goofy grins, and my body floods with potent, self-made chemicals and hormones that set my nervous system buzzing.

Professor Mooken would be amused.

We make good time, and soon, I slow the car as we near the park that surrounds the lake. It closed at nine, but I know how to deal with this.

I park my car under some trees on the side of the road, and we walk the remaining quarter mile to the lake. When we ease through the closed gate, moonlight illuminates the empty picnic tables and the unmoving kid's playground equipment.

"It's a little creepy out here," Bev says, gripping my arm.

I've never noticed that before, but I can see her point. I certainly wouldn't want to run into a stranger out here at night.

Walking along the dirt trail that leads to the water, we are engulfed by darkness, accosted by moon shadows, and refreshed by the crisp, cool air. Bev is safe with me, but I can imagine she must be acutely aware of how alone we are in this remote location.

If I were a murdering psychopath, this would be the perfect place to bring my victims.

Luckily for both of us, I am not.

After a short walk around the perimeter of the lake, we step onto a large, flat rock in a secluded part of the park that overlooks the unmoving water. Opposite from where we stand is the beach most students visit when the sun is out.

We sit on my special rock and hold each other.

"This is where you come?" she says.

"Yes. To think," I say. "It gets me away from classes and everything else. I enjoy looking at the water when it's still—the way it is now. It…calms me."

Bev nods but says nothing.

And soon, we kiss.

We've done this often by this point, but there's something different about tonight—something more natural about the act as we sit beside the lake. I inhale fragrant leaves and the sweetness of sap. And it is so quiet that all I can hear are crickets, nightbirds, and our labored breathing.

She moans, and I want to make love to her more than anything else, but I didn't bring her to the lake for that.

I brought her here to tell her something.

I slow down and gently pull away a few inches, smiling at her.

"What's wrong?" she says, confused.

"Nothing is the matter," I say. "Everything is right, at least, it is when I'm with you. I know I can't rely on you to solve my problems, and I don't want to pressure you, Bev, but…"

"It's all right," she says. "I'm not feeling pressured. Say what you want to say. Tell me what you need to tell me, Jim."

Her words encourage me, and I blurt out what I've been holding inside and forcing myself *not* to utter since our first lunch together.

"I can't help it," I say. "I know it's too soon for this, but I need to tell you that I love you, Bev."

Her eyes sparkle, and the corners of her mouth draw upward. She moves closer, holds my face, and kisses me deeply.

After a minute, she rests her lips on my ear.

"I want to teach you something," she whispers.

I nod and stare into her eyes.

"Ya vas lyublyu," she says.

"What does that mean?"

"It's Russian for *I love you.*"

The tightness in my chest releases now that I know she feels the same way about me. And in that moment, in all ways, I am free.

We make out more, and my insides fill with emotion more powerful than I've ever experienced. I'm filled with reciprocated love—that elusive state I've been searching for all my life.

We explore each other until midnight arrives and then decide to leave—to return to the comfort of her bedroom. A light breeze from the lake washes over us as we walk hand-in-hand back to my car.

Silence has never felt so sweet as we drive to her house for the night. I can't wait to be in bed with her.

After I park behind her house, we get out and walk across the gravel, our feet crunching the rough rocks with each step.

When we reach her back door, a dozen wildflowers greet us—a mix of yellows, violets, and reds wrapped in green tissue paper and propped against the door frame.

A small, white envelope juts out from the colorful arrangement.

"What is *that*?" she says.

I hand her the flowers and the envelope. I want to rip open the note to see who's left flowers on the doorstep of the woman I love, but it's not my place to do that. Besides, there could be a reasonable explanation.

Maybe the flowers are for one of her housemates.

Bev's eyes freeze as she opens the tiny envelope, and her hands shake as she reads the message.

"You didn't leave these for me, did you, Jim?" she asks.

I shake my head. It's a strange question since I am standing here with her, but when she hands me the note, I understand why she's asked it.

There, in the middle of the card, three words stare up at me, written in black ink—words I did not write.

With love for you always, Jim.

CHAPTER TWENTY

THE FLOWERS AND the note go straight into the trash, where Bev assures me they belong. I believe her, but my loving thoughts are now overshadowed by concern and fear.

After she locks the door to the house, we go to her bedroom. While I sit on her bed, fully clothed, she locks her bedroom door and checks it twice before joining me.

"Can we get ready for bed first and then talk?" she says.

I nod, and we go about our established routine, wordless.

I head to the bathroom to brush my teeth with the toothbrush she bought for me while she boils water in her hot pot. Before I met Bev, tea was never my go-to drink after a stressful event, but I am now a true convert. Whether it's the magnolia bark tea itself or the ritual of drinking it with her doesn't matter to me.

It is enough that it has become one of our most sacred rituals.

After I'm cleaned and in my boxers, she hands me my mug of tea and takes hers with her into the bathroom. I sit cross-legged on her bed and sip the aromatic, hot brew. My shoulders unknot, but my mind won't stop thinking about the flowers.

I have, on purpose, not asked about her ex-boyfriend, Evil Jim, because talking about him upsets her. But after the flowers tonight, I need to understand better what happened between the two of them.

I stack two pillows behind me, recline against the wall, and take another sip of tea while I wait for her.

When Bev returns from the bathroom, her posture is more relaxed but still more rigid than usual. If we hadn't just proclaimed our love for each other at the lake, I'd swear she was about to break up with me.

I shake my head to clear the soot of negativity from my brain as she joins me on her side of the bed. We sit there, each looking straight ahead instead of face-to-face the way we usually do.

Avoiding each other this way creates an imaginary buffer between us, which I hope will make it easier for us to start talking.

But she remains silent.

Eventually, my lips move, and I am about to ask her directly about the other Jim, but thankfully, she speaks.

"I met him a few years ago," she says. "When I was an underclassman. He was older than me, more mature than the other guys I knew, and smart. And I like smart men."

I nod and can only hope she means that as a compliment to me as well as a statement about her ex.

"He was a graduate student," she says. "A TA in my Russian class. I don't think you want to hear all the details of how it started, right?"

She is correct, and I nod my head. I do *not* want to hear about her falling in love with someone other than me, but I need to know more about this man trying to wedge his way back into her life.

"Things were good for a while between us. I don't think they were ever *really* good, though. Mainly because I didn't understand who or what he was back then. He never beat me or abused me physically—well, hardly ever. But he was a manipulator, and after our first year together, he started…he made me do things I didn't want to do. It gave him a sense of power over me. And I think that got him off."

"Sexual things?" I ask with a lump in my dry throat that clicks when I swallow.

It is her turn to nod and give a tight-lipped, half-smile.

"But not always," she says. "The manipulation is what he enjoyed and needed. It was never about the actual sex. I don't think. I'm sorry if sharing this with you is too weird."

I shake my head and straighten my spine.

This is a part of loving someone, I tell myself. One must love the good, the bad, and the wounds of the other person.

"Tell me, if it will help," I say.

"Sometimes, he would make me have sex in places we might

get caught. In his office. Or out in public. Sometimes he'd tie me up and…take me, pretending we were strangers. A few times, he hit me. Not enough to hurt me, but I could see how much it got him off, and I worried one day he'd take things further. Thankfully, he never did, but our relationship slowly turned into being *only* about him controlling me. One day, he made me take something from *The Corner Bookstore.* Nothing major. A stupid souvenir—one of those little statues of Jefferson—but I would've gotten in big trouble if I'd been caught. That was when I realized he wanted to prove he could control me."

"Is that when you broke it off?" I ask.

Bev is quiet.

"Yes," she eventually says. "Not right away, but I told him I didn't want to see him anymore. To be honest, it wasn't as easy as it should have been. I know this hurts to hear, but I used to be in love with him. I thought he was everything I ever wanted and needed...at first."

Bev reaches out for my hand.

"I wanted to leave him for a while, but I couldn't take the steps to escape. Then one day, I discovered he was cheating on his wife with another woman besides me—maybe more than one, but there was only one I knew about."

I can't imagine a man wanting to be with anyone rather than Bev, but the story of one person cheating on another is as old as time. After all, it happened to me with Amber, and I don't doubt what Bev is telling me for even a moment.

"When I found out…it was rough," she says. "Have you ever wanted to break up with someone, but then they end up doing it to you first? And when they do, it hurts more than you thought it would?"

I nod, even though I was the one who broke up with Rash and with Amber.

"I'm sorry he cheated on you," I say. "I know how much that hurts."

Bev squeezes my hand hard and chokes out her next words.

"Even though it pushed me to get out of our relationship, when I found out about the other woman, it shattered my heart so much I thought I was going to die. And it broke my mind, too. It damaged everything about me. I had no more purpose on this planet. No more reason to be alive. Do you know what I mean?"

I nod again as I dare to guess where her story is going and how it will end. But it's not my place to get ahead of her, so I wait for her to get it all out at her own speed.

"You remember when I told you I tried to take my life? I didn't tell you the details before, but I think I need to now. I want to."

Tears fill my eyes at the mere thought of Bev being dead and not in this world with me. The pain she must have endured that lead her to attempt suicide must have been beyond imagining.

"I used pills," she says. "I think I was too afraid to physically hurt myself, so I tried to make everything go away as gently and as quickly as I could. So I took Xanax. Lots of it."

I don't know much about the drug other than it's strong, highly effective for anxiety, and very addictive.

"Where did you get it?" I ask, even though I know her answer.

"I used to take Xanax…at the direction of a doctor," she says. "But since I stopped going to him, I still take it at the same dosage as before."

"From Dan?" I ask.

"When I need it," she says. "But *please* don't tell him I told you. Promise me. I would have gotten the pills from someone else—and maybe from someone I couldn't trust."

I hear what she's saying, and a piece of me understands her logic. And, yes, I'll honor her request not to say anything to Dan. But I don't like him very much anymore.

When I turn to her and wrap her in my arms, she starts to cry, and I do too. And even though flowers from Evil Jim was a shitty thing to come home to, Bev and I are closer now because of it.

I understand more about the situation with her ex, but we still haven't talked about the present he left tonight and what to do about it.

"And the flowers?" I say when we release each other. "Do you want *me* to talk to him about that?"

My heart offers this service to her, even though I'd rather not confront him if I don't need to. But if it will make things better for Bev—better for us—I will do so easily.

For her, I will do anything.

When she replies, she shakes her head.

"He can be unpredictable," she says. "Sometimes dangerous. This is him trying to fuck with me—to control me like he used to, even though he knows the two of us are over and that I'd never go back with him."

"I won't do anything, if that's what you want. But you're not going to contact him either, are you?"

"No way," she says.

"That's good," I say and give her another hug.

While we embrace, my mind races through everything I've learned this evening, and a single remaining question pops up, begging to be asked.

"How long ago did you two break things off?" I ask.

Bev grows quiet and takes a deep breath before releasing me from our embrace.

"About two and a half weeks ago," she says.

Her answer disturbs me, even though it shouldn't, because everything in life is about timing, and timing is never optimal. But until now, I didn't understand that her breakup with the previous Jim was so fresh—so raw. And this realization leaves me raw and uncertain about us.

Is she still in love with the other Jim? Am I a rebound guy only here to help her get over him?

While I try coming to terms with how recently her last relationship ended, I study her troubled face, and as I do, another question assembles in my head—part of my process for piecing everything together.

"Is that why you weren't at *A Clockwork Orange* or in class that Thursday?" I ask. "Because of the breakup?"

She casts her eyes down and studies her duvet before she answers.

"Yes and no," she says. "I wasn't at the movie because the night before is when I took all the Xanax."

I pull her close to me again and try to reach out to her with my heart. I love her no matter what. But as we hug, I can't help but stitch together her timeline in my head and realize what she's *really* just told me.

Not only did Bev try to end her life by overdosing, she did it on Tuesday night—only a handful of hours after I asked her to lunch for the first time.

CHAPTER TWENTY-ONE

"LET'S TALK ABOUT evil," Professor Mooken says to the classroom full of students huddled behind their laptops. "For now, ignore the end of the scale where someone such as Adolf Hitler sits. Instead, let's talk about Mother Teresa. Surely, no one considers her to be evil. Correct? But what if you were a local religious leader in a village where she converted your followers to Christianity? If you were a shaman or some other holy leader, you wouldn't think too kindly of our revered nun and her actions.

"Therefore, I posit that evil is a myth, a fiction, to which most of us subscribe. At the very least, evil is *subjective.* It has to be because nature knows nothing of it. And why do we care? Hmmm? Because our experiments can reveal a lot about the darker side of human nature."

Professor Mooken walks through the well-known prisoner experiment conducted at Stanford, the Third Wave experiment, and the Milgram experiment, where students operated a device they believed was delivering lethal electric shocks to the control subject.

As I listen to the incredulous results from these over-the-top experiments, I don't feel nearly as bad about deceiving our test subjects, watching them struggle to assemble our little puzzle. We hide the truth from them to ensure honest results, but what Milgram did was cruel, distressing, and mentally damaging to everyone involved.

I tell myself I would never do such things. I am my own person. I would have disobeyed Milgram's cruel orders to deliver deadly doses of electricity to a stranger.

But even as I think this, I know I'm lying.

What if Bev told me to deliver a lethal shock to someone right now? To her ex-boyfriend, for example. Would I do that?

I think I might.

That is the stark realization humming in my brain when Mooken finally dismisses the class.

Bev turns around and waves at me from the front of the auditorium as the students and the other TAs clear out.

I wave back, smiling.

"Hey, we gotta talk about our lab report," Eugene says, as he ambles over to me. "And I mean now. I'm getting really stressed about this."

Amber is close behind Eugene, but she stares past me, watching Bev as she makes her way up the steps.

Bev greets me with a hug and a quick kiss on the lips. Even though the professor is gone, this is still out-in-the-open affection, and plenty of students notice. Her touch excites me, but it also makes my hands shake because we are now exposed for all to see.

There is no hiding *us* anymore.

I try to figure out what has brought about this change in Bev. Maybe this is simply her way of sending a message to Amber—and establishing her claim on me.

"I have to skip lunch," she says as she releases me. "The TAs have to meet with Mooken right now. I'm sorry, babe."

I understand. The professor is her boss, and he has a lot of control over her graduate studies and her life right now. Missing the meeting with him is not an option for her.

"Will I see you tonight?" I ask.

She smiles and nods—an excited schoolgirl.

After she gives Eugene and Amber a quaint grin, she leaves us, and Amber bores into me with her glare.

"Is that why you haven't done anything for our lab report?" she says.

I shrug and pretend not to know what she's talking about, but her accusation isn't wrong.

Eugene snickers then leans in and whispers.

"How in the hell is this happening?"

He turns to Amber, who stands with her arms crossed in front of her chest, her lips pursed.

"Please tell me what this guy has that I don't," he says.

It is rare for someone to speak their mind so honestly, and when they do, it can be jarring. But Eugene has said precisely what I'm sure he's been thinking since he first learned about Amber and me.

Amber leans in close, and even though my heart belongs to Bev, Amber's honey-scented body oil and lotion make me sweat and turn my cheeks pink—a Pavlovian reaction I can't control.

"Because *Jim* is up for anything," she says. "Especially in bed. And he never says *no*. Unless that's part of the game."

I try not to smirk because, unless Eugene's become a talented actor overnight, he and Amber haven't had sex, or if they have, it wasn't very good.

Eugene's mouth opens, and his lips twitch as he processes what Amber has just said. I study his face, and instead of an asshole, I see a real person—one who is vulnerable and lonely. I'm sure he's dealing with Amber's implied insult. And that can't be easy. But mostly, he reminds me of a kid who's uncomfortable and horrified after learning more than he wanted about his parents' sex life.

In fact, his blank expression reminds me of how I must have looked the first day Mom complained to me about how *awful* Dad was in bed after one of their big fights.

Her tearful disclosure, combined with my personal knowledge of my father's temper, planted a dark, violent vision of their sex life—something my ten-year-old mind couldn't process—an image I have not been able to erase, even to this day.

When I was a child, every time the lock on my parents' bedroom door clicked into place in the small apartment where we lived, I fell into a mixed state of dread, sadness, and excitement. And for a long time, I accepted that whatever darkness they had together was the norm between a man and a woman. This is why, I think, sex with Amber felt so…comfortable and familiar.

At least, at first.

My lungs are heavy from these unwanted memories crowding my psyche, and I have to force myself to snap out of it by standing up abruptly. Even working with Eugene is preferable to remembering my early childhood.

"Come on," I say. "Let's go figure this lab report shit out right now."

A minute later, the three of us leave the lecture hall together in search of somewhere to talk.

We walk up McCormick Road, where only a week ago I was running, dodging cars, and chasing someone who was or wasn't Tony because I thought he was spying on me.

What a difference seven days can make.

Soon, the three of us arrive at the Lawn—that most sacred strip of UVA grass and a part of Jefferson's original historic university. It is a perfectly kept plot of land lined with ancient chambers where only the students of the highest distinction and achievement are allowed to live. The accommodations are primitive by current standards, but oh, the *prestige* these rooms convey is epic.

I am not, nor will I ever be, one of those students.

Instead, like the thousands of other undergraduates at UVA, I come to the Lawn mostly to play Frisbee, sit on blankets, and bask in the elite students' sun.

Eugene, Amber, and I plop down on this holy grass and form a small, closed circle.

"We are so far behind," Amber says. "We need a plan. And we need one now."

"Because not all of us have a special relationship with the TA and the professor," Eugene adds.

I scowl at Eugene because leveraging my relationship with Bev has never even occurred to me. And as far as the professor goes…I laugh at the thought of him giving me any kind of special treatment.

I don't think he even likes me.

Instead of disagreeing with Eugene, though, I press onward.

"How about each of us gets his or her notes ready by this weekend?" I say. "I'll take a shot at drafting our observations and conclusions, which I think I have a pretty good idea about. Amber, you write up our summary and assumptions. And Eugene, you draft the references and endnotes."

They both nod, even though Eugene isn't happy with his role. His assignment involves the least amount of writing, but it's also the shittiest and most tedious task we have to accomplish.

"I'm okay with all of that," Amber says. "But can we talk through our conclusions first? I mean, what did we even learn from this stupid experiment?"

She delivers her last line at me directly because I was the one who convinced her to work on this with me in the first place.

"Our hypothesis sucked," Eugene says, and Amber nods.

I channel Professor Mooken when I respond.

"If every hypothesis were correct, there'd be no need for the scientific method. I'm sorry we were so off-target. But what I *did* observe was that our subjects had milder reactions to me than to either of you two. And the only difference between us is that I'm pretty sure I consistently rated higher on the trustworthy scale. So let's go where the data leads us."

"And ditch attractiveness bias completely?" Eugene says, throwing up his hands.

"Yes. We keep the part about people modifying their anger and aggressiveness thresholds. But we say it was for a different reason than we initially thought."

"What do we conclude, then?" Amber says. "People like Jim too much to get angry, even when he acts like a dick?"

Ouch.

"How about we conclude that trustworthiness, rather than attractiveness, is a greater predictor of how likely test subjects are to become angry and aggressive when someone sabotages their attempts to solve an unsolvable puzzle?"

"Well," Eugene says. "That doesn't sound too bad when you

say it like that."

With the matter closed, Amber and Eugene stand up and brush grass from their jeans.

"Are you coming?" she says.

I shake my head and look up at her through squinted eyes.

"I have an appointment with Mooken soon," I say. "I'm going to hang around here until then."

"Whatever," Eugene says, now convinced I have a special in with the professor *and* his TA.

As the two of them walk away, Amber draws lustful stares from a group of male Lawn residents while they toss a neon disc back and forth.

I close my eyes and face the sun, soaking in its heat, wondering what I will say to Professor Mooken when I see him.

Life is going great, and I have nothing to complain about, professor.

Or maybe…

I have not chased or almost killed a single person since the last time I saw you. I think I'm fine now.

After more pondering, I realize I don't need to justify anything to him. After all, as he continually reminds me, he's not my therapist.

CHAPTER TWENTY-TWO

I STAND OUTSIDE Mooken's office, my fist hovering in front of his door, ready to knock. But when it's time for our appointment, I simply walk in, the same way Amber did.

Mooken looks up, irritated by my intrusion. But I'm on time, he's expecting me, and, after all, this is our last session. Even if he doesn't know this yet.

Bev's molecules linger in the air and seep into my brain as I sit in front of Mooken's large wooden desk. She's been here recently and probably sat in the same chair where I now slump, trying to appear more casual and relaxed than I am.

Bev told me the TAs had to meet with Mooken after class, so that explains her scent, but there's not enough room in here for all of them to fit—not comfortably, at least.

Maybe Mooken makes them stand when they meet in his office. I wouldn't put that past him.

As I wait to get started, an image of Bev forcing a handful of pills into her mouth attacks my brain, and I flinch.

"Is something wrong?" Mooken asks.

I shake my head, blinking, trying to recover my composure from the horrific image of Bev.

"My mind went somewhere for a second," I say. "It wasn't anything important."

"Do you want to tell me about it?"

I chuckle when he says that, since I'm here to inform him I no longer want to tell him anything at all anymore.

"You've been very nice to me," I say. "But I feel like I've been taking advantage of your generosity. I was hoping today I could get the name of that therapist from you, and then I'll get out of your hair. I know you're a busy person."

Mooken steeples his hands in front of his chin and raises an eyebrow.

"Jim, are you breaking up with me?" he says, with a dark laugh, amused by his own wit.

"It's not you," I say. "It's me."

"Well played," he says. "And yes, I have that name for you right here."

He picks up a business card from his desk and hands it to me.

Thomas Greelis, MD, PhD, LPC.

"Tom is a fine practitioner and psychiatrist—one of the few around here who provides top-notch psychotherapy *and* the right meds for what ails his patients. I'd bet at least one of my diplomas that he'll be able to help you get a better night's sleep."

My laugh this time is genuine, and my shoulders relax.

"Like I said last time, I'm sleeping pretty well lately."

"Ah, yes. The illusion of love has taken hold of you. I can see it in your tired but joyful eyes. I'm happy you are still under its blissful protection."

"So far," I say. "But I promise to make an appointment with Doctor Greelis if things get dark again. I really appreciate the referral."

"You are most welcome," Mooken says. "But I would consider seeing Tom sooner rather than later. You don't feel as if you need help at the moment, and that is wonderful. But it's always better to get ahead of a potential mental health issue than to play catch-up once your psyche is under assault."

I nod because he has a point—one I'll think about later.

But not now.

I place my hands on my thighs, ready to stand. As far as I'm concerned, there's no need to fill the entire hour. But Mooken wants to talk.

"How are things going with Beverly?" he says with a tilt of his head and a lopsided grin.

I freeze half-way out of my seat, then sit back down, ready for whatever's coming next.

"Oh, it's okay," he says, suddenly paternal. "Beverly explained the entire situation to me, and quite frankly, I think the two of you make a good couple. Although, as she and I discussed, any class-related issues or questions you have should be directed to one of the other TAs from now on, either Judy or Carl. They are both very knowledgeable and good with students. That is a reasonable request from me, don't you agree?"

I exhale, relieved but also horrified he knows about Bev and me.

At least he's not angry. Strangely enough, he almost seems pleased.

"That's very reasonable," I say.

He nods and smiles.

"Everything going well back home?" he says.

It's a strange question since we've never spoken about my family before, but I shrug and answer him.

"It's fine," I say. "Dealing with my dad is tough sometimes."

"I can only imagine," he says. "His loss must be very difficult for you, even now."

I don't remember telling Mooken about my father's dementia, but he's not wrong. Communicating, trying to relate to him while he's in this state, is like I've already lost him—or who he used to be, at least.

"I'm sure he would have been proud of you," Mooken says.

"I think he knows. Somewhere in his mind, he knows."

Mooken's eyes soften, and he nods.

And that's it.

I half-expect him to pull a Columbo and ask me a piercing question as I stand up and walk to the door. But he remains silent as I move past his open coat closet and leave.

I quietly close his office door behind me and float down the hall, wallowing in the fact that, for once, everything in my life is perfect.

There are still several hours before dinner with Bev, and with no more classes, I head back to my apartment.

I'm so at peace with the world, I don't even check for Tony as I walk through the Grounds.

Half an hour later, I am sitting on my scratchy, school-issued couch with the blinds open and the windows cracked, letting the residents and Barry know I'm here and available.

Over the next three hours, I watch four episodes of the latest crime documentary on Netflix, and during that time, only one student stops in. All he wants to know is how to obtain a parking pass for his parents. I direct him to the appropriate website, close my blinds, and go back to watching television.

After a shower, I change into fresh jeans and a clean shirt and text Bev to let her know I'll be leaving soon.

On the way over, I stop by the Corner and pick up a new tin of magnolia bark tea from the convenience store. It's the brand Bev loves—*Puka Organic Sleepy Time*—an essential part of our nightly ritual.

She hasn't asked me to do this, but love is not about waiting to be asked. It's about anticipating the other's needs and being thoughtful. Also, given the amount of tea we drink, I figure she must be low on her supply.

When I arrive at her house, I circle around to the back entrance like usual, and I'm relieved there are no surprise gifts from Evil Jim waiting on her doorstep.

I give a tentative knock on the door, then turn the doorknob and step in, since, by now, I'm a regular, expected guest.

The kitchen smells of takeout Chinese food—flat noodles and chicken—and my stomach clenches and growls. Bev steps out of her bedroom, greets me in the kitchen with a tight hug, and clings to me.

"I broke up with Mooken today," I say into her hair. "I know how stressful it's been for you having me talk with him, and besides, since I met you, I…"

Tears flood my eyes as I try to figure out how to explain to this woman that she's the one who's cured me of my darkness and eliminated the need for me to talk with the professor.

She releases me from her embrace and smiles, pleased with my news.

"I don't have anything to talk to him about anymore," I say. "No dark dreams. No depression or anxiety. I think I was missing a piece of me, and…"

Instead of waiting for me to finish, she hugs me again, this time even tighter. She buries her face in my neck and leaves my skin wet with her tears.

When she releases me, I wipe my face, and she wipes hers. Whatever words I should say to her elude me. Instead, I hold up the tin of tea I've brought for her and smile.

She reaches over to the counter and holds up a plastic bag filled with an aromatic dinner.

"Thank you so much, baby," I say.

"Thank *you*, babe, for the tea," she says. "You're absolutely the best. I love it. And you."

We have taken to saying the *L* word to each other, but usually only when making love. Hearing her express her feelings in the stark light of the kitchen is extra special to me—yet another milestone in our relationship.

Without another word, we move to her bedroom, and soon, we are eating Chinese food in her bed.

After dinner, we lose our clothes and get under the sheets. We know what each other's body wants by now and how to give pleasure as quickly or as slowly as needed. This evening, our tempo is slow and luxurious, and we revel in each other until we both finish, breathing heavily, pressed tightly against one another.

Her lips graze mine, but then she pulls away and curses.

For an instant, I think I've done something wrong, but I can tell she's preoccupied with something unknown to me.

"I'm sorry," she says. "I totally forgot. The movie file for tomorrow is giving me problems again. I want to lie here and fall asleep with you, but I have to fix this really quick. It should only take a few minutes."

She sits up in bed, naked and glistening, as she grabs her laptop from the end table, sets it on her legs, and signs in. She's still groggy and flushed from pleasure, and she types her password slower than usual.

I don't want to watch. I don't want to spy on her or invade her privacy, but I cannot help but see the letters she types in as her fingers depress the keys, one by one.

Jim102938.

At first, I'm flattered, but then my heart goes dark.

That's the other Jim, I realize. She hasn't changed her password yet.

Bev glances over at me, and I shift my eyes away from her as her laptop screen lights up.

"With today's tech, there's gotta be a better way," she says.

She laughs, and I try to match her mirth as she opens a file, and the title, *Memento*, flashes on the screen before freezing, refusing to play any further.

She closes, then re-opens the file in a video editing program and saves it in a different format. The file is large and takes several minutes to process, but when it's done, she double-clicks the new icon, and up pops the opening credits.

I lean in and kiss her on her cheek.

"Well done," I say. "Now close that thing, and let's get some sleep."

She sighs.

"I need some tea first. To unwind."

"How about another orgasm?"

"You have such a one-track mind," she says with a smile as she gets up, still naked, and starts to boil the water.

Ten minutes later, we are sitting in bed, cross-legged, with our backs against the wall, sipping from our extra-large mugs.

Blow, sip.

Blow, sip.

Mmmm.

A wave of calmness seeps into me, and we chat about a fight she heard Cynthia and Dan having and about what she wants for dinner tomorrow. By the time we finish our tea, my eyes are drooping, almost shut.

When we finally turn off the lights, I reach over and set my hand on her naked hip.

Despite wanting to pass out, I force myself to think through something that's started to bug me. Bev's ex. Evil Jim. He isn't finished with her. I can feel it. And, from what she tells me, he doesn't give up easily.

Even though she won't divulge any details about her ex-lover, I need to protect her from him because, after all, that's what you do for those you love.

As I drift off to sleep, I visualize confronting Evil Jim and setting him straight.

In some of my imagined scenarios, I calmly convince him to stop bothering us, and he turns away, leaving Bev alone forever. In others, he's stubborn and an asshole, and I beat him until he agrees to never contact Bev again.

The second scenario leaves me with a grin on my face as I surrender to blackness.

I sleep straight through until the morning—no nightmares, worries, or concerns.

And when I wake, I hope with all my heart this peace inside me will last.

CHAPTER TWENTY-THREE

DAN IS PLAYING Frisbee on the Lawn with another student—one of his fraternity brothers, I presume.

He tosses the disc—a plastic bullet that slices through the air and smacks when his friend catches it. When his friend returns the throw, Dan spots me, catches the disc without looking, and walks over.

Dan waves at his friend, who waves back, turns around, and leaves.

Maybe he thinks Dan is about to sell me drugs.

Maybe that's what Dan thinks, too.

But I'm interested in speaking with him for a completely different reason.

"What's going on, my man?" he says, clasping my shoulder with his meaty hand.

"I was hoping I could talk to you, if you have a few minutes."

He shrugs and checks over his shoulder—an instinct honed from selling illegal substances to students in the open.

We stroll up the Lawn together, staring at our feet as we go.

"What can I help you with?" he says. "Looking for something in particular?"

"Only a little information."

"Shoot," he says.

"What can you tell me about Bev's ex, the other Jim?"

He laughs and shakes his head.

"Dude, if Bev wants you to know about him, she'll tell you. I don't want to get in the middle of that. And I don't want to be on Bev's bad side, that's for sure. She's tiny, but she can be furious when she's in a mood."

"I've never even seen her get pissed off before," I say. "Guess I'm lucky."

He shakes his head and whistles.

"The guy she dated before Evil Jim? He was a *real* jerk. One time, she caught him texting a girl from class. I guess it was about homework, but they were also flirting. Bev saw the texts, and it was over that night. I was in the house when it all went down, and I never heard someone explode like that before. Cynthia forced me to go down to Bev's room to make sure she was okay."

"Did he hurt her?" I ask.

"Shit, man. I knocked on her door hard—gave it a police knock, you know? The arguing and yelling stopped, and Bev opened the door. Her face was red. All teary-eyed. But she wasn't hurt. The dude, on the other hand, was *not* in good shape. Had a gash over his eye and blood on his face. He was bigger than her, but she must have scared him something fierce. Because when he saw his opening, he shoved past me and left without a word. I think he was happy to escape."

This does not sound like the Bev I know and love *at all*. But everyone acts differently with different people and in different situations. I mean, I treat Bev a lot nicer than I ever treated Amber. And, I wonder how Bev would react if Amber told her stories about me from *her* point of view.

"Thanks for the warning," I say, but this is *not* what I need to know from Dan. "Back to the other Jim, though—you met him, right?"

I put it out there, letting Dan dwell on my question until he starts to talk.

"Look," he reluctantly says when we reach the steps of the Rotunda. "While those two were going out, they were at his place all the time. I only ran into the other Jim once. He came to the back door to pick up Bev one night, when I was taking out the trash. He seemed like an okay guy. Intense. Smart. Older. We barely talked. That's all I can tell you. Like I said, I don't want to get in the middle of this."

I nod and ponder the stairs at my feet. He still wants to tell me more about the other Jim, so I remain silent, waiting for something to come out of his mouth, the same way Mooken would.

"I can tell you one more thing about him," he finally says. "According to Cynthia, he was a total control freak, and he used to order her around a lot, you know? He was one of *those* guys."

"Interesting," I say and wait for more, but Dan starts tapping his foot and looks out across the Lawn.

He is done sharing with me.

"I appreciate the info," I say. "And I totally understand you don't want to get involved. But to let you know, there's no problem between me and Bev. We're doing great. But…"

Now it is my time to share with Dan, and he senses it.

"What?" he says.

"Did Cynthia tell you what the other Jim's been doing?"

"That asshole's been bugging her again?"

"This is just between us," I say. "But he left her flowers on the back steps with a note saying he was still in love with her. She won't give me any details about him, which is why I was wondering what kind of guy he is. In case I run into him and need to…have a talk with him."

"Oh, dude, I get that," Dan says, nodding vigorously. "If Cynthia's ex started messing with her, I'd be all over him. Look, I don't even know the guy's last name. He was always just *Jim*."

I nod, satisfied that Dan is tapped out for information, but then he looks up at me, his eyes wide open.

"There was this one time when he had to go out of town, and we were all sitting around getting smashed. I remember Bev mentioned he was a TA in her Russian class when they first met. Seriously, that's all I know. And don't even tell Bev I told you that much. Cool?"

"Completely cool," I say.

"Anything else?" he says. "Not that I don't like hanging out with you. We need to do it more often, brother. But, right now, I have business to conduct."

I laugh, but inside I am glaring at him because he is the one who gave Bev the pills she used to almost kill herself. And he is *not* without blame.

"Speaking of your business," I say. "I know it's none of *my* business, but do me a favor. I won't tell Bev you told me about her ex, but I'd appreciate it if you don't sell her so many pills next time, you know?"

His face sobers. He may be making extra cash to help pay for grad school, but he's not a bad guy at his core, and he seems worried.

"Why? Did something happen?"

At this point, I should shut my mouth. I don't want to betray Bev's trust. And even though their household is full of tight friends, either Bev hasn't told Cynthia about her attempted suicide, or if she has, Cynthia hasn't told Dan.

"Nothing yet," I say, lying. "But…I worry about her. This shit with the other Jim is really stressing her out, and I'd hate for her to try something…you know, stupid one day."

He exhales, and we start walking back down the Lawn.

"Thank God, man. You scared me for a second. I mean, the truth is, I don't know what people do with the stuff I sell them. I don't ask. But I'm glad to hear there's nothing wrong with Bev. She's like a little sister to me, and…well, to be honest, I sold her a fresh bottle earlier today."

My nostrils flare before I can control my facial expression.

"A bottle of what?" I say.

Dan leans in and whispers.

"Calm down, my man. It wasn't anything hard. Just some Xannies. Shit gets stressful around here with finals coming up and everything, right? And, look. No offense, but maybe you should ask her for one of them for yourself. To take the edge off. You seem a little tense, bro."

He has no idea about my edges or how tense I am. I laugh as I draw him closer to me, so only he can hear. But inside, I am fuming.

"Just remember," I say. "If something happens to her, I know where she gets her shit."

Dan pulls back, reevaluating me, then nods. My message has been received.

Only seconds after he walks away, he's already mixing it up with a pair of students, probably more of his customers. I turn and start making my way to Gilmer Hall. Even though I was thinking about skipping the movie this evening, I've decided I need to go. My lab report can wait.

I don't make it more than a hundred yards before Amber texts me.

Im bored. Hang out 2nite and wk on lab report?

I know Amber, and she is not texting me so we can work on our assignment. Some plans of hers must have fallen through, and she's throwing a Hail Mary pass my way, hoping I'll pick up the ball and run with it.

I text her back as I dodge an oncoming group of students.

On my way 2 a movie. Sry. Maybe try Eugene?

I watch my phone as three little dots shimmer, then disappear over and over again.

After a full minute of that, her response pops up, and I begin making my way down McCormick Road.

He can't help with what I need lol but thx.

I laugh when I read her text. One good thing about Amber is that she's straightforward about what she wants and needs. I respect that. And as I suspected, she isn't looking for someone to help her write the summary for our experiment.

She's in search of something a little more extracurricular.

I reply to her with a laughing emoji and drop the phone in my back pocket.

A few seconds later, it vibrates again.

What movie?

I debate about whether to tell her the truth. The last thing I want or need is for her to show up and sit next to me tonight.

Knowing her, she'll start groping me in the dark, trying to cause a problem between Bev and me. Not that it would really matter, because there's no comparison between the two. Even so, Bev might not appreciate it.

To avoid the situation entirely, I take a page from Amber's playbook and bend the truth to my benefit. Although I'm not actually going to the show with Bev, it's close enough to the truth that my conscience is clear as I type my reply.

Seeing Memento w Bev. Sry.

Knowing Amber, she might show up anyway. But as I wait for her reply, it never comes.

CHAPTER TWENTY-FOUR

MEMENTO IS INTERESTING, and I'm sure it was an innovative film when it was released.

The part I like the best is something Bev didn't even mention to me. The main character's chiseled body is covered in tattoos he uses as notes to himself since he has short-term memory loss. Each morning, he forgets everything from the day before, so when he wakes up, he reads the clues tattooed on his body to figure out what's going on in his life.

The guy could have used Post-it notes instead, but the tats are a nice dramatic touch.

When the lights come up, I catch a familiar flash of brown hair on the other side of the room. Amber showed up, after all. But to her credit, she didn't sit with me, or she couldn't find me. Either way, as long as she stays over there, everything will be fine.

Although half of the audience gets up and leaves, I hang around for the discussion afterward to support Bev.

"Did he kill his wife or not?" someone shouts.

The whole place breaks into laughter, because it's not a bad question.

The problem is, as with many film noir pieces, the narrator is *unreliable*.

"In some ways, we'll never know," Bev responds from the stage. "If the main character doesn't know the difference between reality and the fiction his mind has created, then how can the viewer? It's simple. The viewer can't."

Not only is Bev beautiful, but her mind is sharp, and I can't decide at that moment what I love about her the most.

A half hour of questions and answers ensues. One student complains about the segments of the film that were shot in black and white because they looked *too old* for her taste. Another student raises his hand, and when Bev calls on him, he speaks in a shaky, nervous voice.

"If he can't remember anything, can we blame him for the people he kills since he was being manipulated by the cop?"

Bev starts to answer, but Professor Mooken stands up in the front row, and she hands him the microphone.

"That is an excellent question. How many of you feel he is without blame, even for the accidental killing of his wife? Raise your hands."

More than half of the audience raises their hands, and Amber is one of them.

"And the opposite," he says. "Who believes the main character is a killer who is to blame for the deaths he caused?"

Less than half of the hands go up, including mine, which evokes a deep chuckle from Mooken.

"Remember this. Questions of morality never have a single answer or only one truth. They are ultimately decided at the individual level. And they always reflect how and from where each of us views the world."

The audience collectively stares at Mooken—some captivated, others confused—but no one says a thing. Amber leans forward in her chair, and for a second, I think she's going to make a comment. But she sits there, transfixed by Mooken like the rest of us.

At last, Mooken laughs and breaks the silence.

"Enough lecturing from me," he says. "I can take a hint!"

"Thank you, everyone, for coming tonight," Bev says after grabbing the mic back from Mooken.

While the auditorium clears, I wait for Bev at the end of my row as she packs up her stuff and chats with Mooken and the other TAs. I know all of them, but I'd be intruding in their special, closed world if I joined them. So I stay where I am, play a game of Word Masters on my phone, and wait.

When I look up, Mooken and Bev are alone, speaking to each other, gesturing excitedly with their hands. I bury my face in my phone again, but part-way through the word puzzle, Bev steps up and greets me.

"Hey there," she says, her voice markedly flat. "I have to go up to the projection booth and get my laptop before we go."

I follow her out of the auditorium and up the stairway that leads to the small, enclosed room where the projector sits.

The surrounding tension is thick as she closes the movie file, logs off, and slips her laptop into her bag.

"Something wrong?" I ask, using a soft voice so she knows I'm trying not to bug her.

"Mooken told me he reassigned you to Carl for your TA."

My extremities go cold.

When I told her about breaking up with Mooken yesterday, I forgot to mention being reassigned to another TA. It was a simple misstep, but Bev is not happy.

"Mooken said you told him about us," I say. "And he said you already knew about me being reassigned to Carl."

She stands straight and gets in my face, for once, not in a loving way. She flares her nostrils and purses her lips.

"Well, I *didn't* tell him about us, and I *didn't* know about Carl. Mooken's a smart man, Jim. He's a psych professor, for God's sake. That makes him not the easiest person to keep secrets from, you know. It sucks, but he lied to you."

"Are you in trouble? Am I in trouble?" I say, even though I'm having a difficult time understanding why Professor Mooken would lie to me.

"Why would *you* be in trouble?" Bev says.

She zips up her bag with a dramatic pull.

"You're the student. I'm the TA."

She takes a deep breath and releases it.

"Look, I'm sorry," she says, calmer now. "I don't think I'm in any serious trouble. But it doesn't reflect well on me, either. Mooken asked me why I hadn't told him about you and me, which was pretty awkward. But worse things have happened in UVA's Psych Department, I assure you."

I wait for her to share more—to let me in on a scandal—but

she doesn't.

"I wasn't trying to hide anything from you," I say. "I was so happy about not having to see Mooken anymore, it slipped my mind. That's all. Are you and I okay?"

She looks deeply into my eyes and tries to smile, but it comes out crooked and contrived.

"You really are *Good Jim*, aren't you?" she says, with a slow shake of her head. "There's nothing for you to be sorry about. But…well, maybe don't talk to Mooken anymore, even in class. He can be…eccentric like this at times, and it's best not to give his brain any more fuel than it already has."

She forces a laugh, and so do I, before we leave the projection room together, head downstairs, and step outside into the cool evening.

We've just survived our first quarrel, and as we walk back to her house, we hold hands without talking.

When we approach her back door, a package wrapped in brown paper is waiting for us, sitting on the top step, and we both stiffen.

She stoops to pick it up and opens it carefully, treating it like a bomb she doesn't want to trigger accidentally. In the dim light of the porch bulb, she unwraps the paper to reveal three blackened, iron nails melded together in the shape of a crude cross.

When she looks up from it, her eyes are wet, and I'm certain it's a gift from her ex.

Maybe Bev would have rebounded from her earlier blow-up with Professor Mooken and from our subsequent argument. But now that she's received another gift from Evil Jim, her mood will not be salvageable tonight.

"It's from him," I say.

She nods.

"It's a religious artifact from Russia. Made by Orthodox monks under the rule of Czar Ivan the Terrible in 1550."

Mostly what I hear is that the cross is from Russia—a fact I wouldn't have paid much attention to if Dan hadn't told me about

Bev's ex being a Russian TA. I listen to her next words carefully and study them, hoping for any information that will reveal more about Evil Jim's identity.

"I mentioned one time how much I liked this piece," she says. "He picked it up on one of his trips overseas. Bought it in St. Petersburg. Shit. I'm so sorry, but this really is a lot for one night. For me and for you too, I'm sure."

I nod because she's right. It is a lot.

She re-wraps the cross, and we enter the house. I make sure to close and lock the door behind us in case Evil Jim's still around or plans on returning during the night.

When we step into her bedroom, Bev is a hollow shell, holding the wrapped black cross in her open palms. And I am her nervous sentry, trying to protect her but not knowing how I will do this or from where the danger might come.

When she sits on her bed, I do the only thing that will make things a little better. I start to boil the water for tea.

She opens her mouth, about to stop me, but in the end, she smiles with tight lips and lets me cater to her for once. Some of her old tea is left, but I snap open the new tin I bought and load up the tea ball with fresh leaves. Soon, the water is bubbling, and the room smells of fresh flowers.

I fix a cup for each of us, and we sit in silence, sipping our hot beverages together, trying to force normalcy into our evening. The tea tries its hardest to drape a sense of calm over me, but I do not fully relax the way I usually do, because I'm too worried about Bev.

After our nightly ritual, we prepare for sleep. When I turn out the light, we're both in bed, naked as usual, but on this night, only my fingers lightly touch her back.

I do not try to make love to her. It's not the right time and not what either of us needs right now.

"Tell me who your ex is," I say as softly as I can.

For a minute, all I hear is her steady breathing. All I see is the rise and fall of her shoulders.

"Maybe I can talk to him and make him understand that he has to stop," I say, pressing the matter. "Each time he does this without any repercussions, he's going to feel like he can do it again or maybe do even more."

I seethe as I wait for her response. I am not afraid of Evil Jim. Our love is my armor, and I would leave our bed right now and drag her ex out of his home and teach him a lesson if I knew where to find him.

She doesn't turn over to face me, but when she speaks at last, her voice is weak and fragile.

"Please promise me you won't try to figure out who he is or find him," she says. "I don't want you to get hurt, Jim. He…isn't right. If you spoke to him, he'd seem like a reasonable person, but the whole time, he'd be deceiving you, waiting for a chance to hurt you. I know him. If I don't respond, he'll get bored eventually and move on and find another girlfriend. God, I hope so. That would solve everyone's problems."

"Is he dangerous?"

Her eyes go distant, and she swallows hard before answering.

"One time, I was on my way to meet him when a stranger on the sidewalk stopped me and asked me out. Just like that. Out of nowhere. Jim saw him talking to me, and I could tell he was mad. Next thing I learned was that Jim had found out where the guy lived somehow and beat him up pretty badly. And I can't have that happen to you. I can't. Promise me you won't go looking for him."

"I promise," I say into her back as I trace a line down her spine with my forefinger.

I'm sad tonight because of everything that has happened and because Bev is so stressed and upset.

But mostly, I'm sad because this is the first time I've ever lied to her.

CHAPTER TWENTY-FIVE

WHEN I WAKE, I am still imagining what I would do to the other Jim if I could find him. Even though I have no clear memory of my dreams, they must have been taxing because I'm exhausted when I roll over to see that Bev is no longer there.

Water runs in the background, and I assume she's in the bathroom getting ready for class.

But there was no good morning kiss from her.

No hello.

She went straight into preparing for her day. My stomach turns to ice because it knows something is wrong.

While I'm still under the covers, she steps out of the bathroom and smiles, although she hesitates.

"Hey there," she says. "I have to get to class early and didn't want to wake you. Sorry again about last night. I know it sucks. Did you sleep okay?"

I smile back, and even though my heart is with her, my smile is not as genuine as it usually is, and I'm sure she can tell.

"I'm okay," I say. "Don't worry about last night. I'm sure everything will work out fine, right?"

"Sure," she says. "And listen. Stay here as long as you want right now. But I really have to go, okay?"

I nod and close my eyes because this is bad timing for what I need to tell her next.

"I think I need to work on my lab report tonight," I say. "I promised Amber and Eugene I'd have my notes and our conclusions drafted by the end of the week, and I'm pretty far behind on it. I can talk about this kind of thing with you since you're not my TA anymore, right?"

My attempt at levity falls flat, and Bev does not laugh.

"This is better anyway," she says after calculating something in her head. "I could use the time to catch up on things. Especially my Russian studies, which I've been sort of ignoring."

"I have a great idea, though," I say, trying to salvage our morning. "Saturday night. Let's stay at my place. We'll get away from the house and the gifts from your ex, and I'll get extra points from Barry for being available like a responsible RA. Dinner on me first. I'll even pick up some tea so we can have some at my apartment. Sound good?"

Her eyes focus on me, darkening, but she nods and smiles. After all, she promised earlier that we'd spend the night at my place at some point, and I really do think getting away from her house for a night would be good for her.

"That is perfect," she says as she opens her door. "I'll see you in class soon."

She stops before leaving and blows me a kiss.

The fact the kiss is not a real one is not lost on me.

After she leaves, I lie there, still and solemn. I hadn't planned on this, but as I scan her room, I wonder if there are any clues here about Evil Jim.

I wait ten minutes to make sure Bev is gone.

While I wait, I decide on the first place I will search. Her bookshelves are stacked cinderblocks and wood planks—four tiers of paperbacks, textbooks, and paper. Her dresser full of clothes sits against the far wall, and her closet door is ajar.

Her living area is clean, for the most part, but plenty of her things are covered in a thin film of dust I don't want to touch, lest I leave traces of having searched her room.

First, I approach her bookshelf.

It holds a few thick tomes on psychology, abnormal psych, and experimental psych, of course. And last year's copy of the DSM—the complete therapist's guide that holds all the possible mental illnesses a patient might have. If it isn't in there, it's not a valid mental illness, although I've always thought that was a short-sighted view of the human mind.

I examine the top shelf books and don't see any papers inserted anywhere. On the next shelf, however, a book on the Russian language with a deep purple cover intrigues me. It isn't dusty, so I pull it out with my fingertips and gently page through it.

Her name is written on the inside in lovely, clear print.

Beverly McDane.

Inside, a printed copy of a syllabus raises my hopes, but when I check, there is no mention of a TA and no one named *Jim*. But the name of the class and the professor's name are both there.

Advanced Russian Grammar. Professor Sulke.

I take a quick shot of the information with my phone and replace the book. The other books on that shelf deal with Russian history and culture, but they hold no additional clues I can find.

On the bottom shelf sits her personal collection of books.

Zen and the Art of Motorcycle Maintenance, *One*, and *Das Energi.*

These are new-age novels I've heard of but have never read.

I open *Das Energi* and let the hard-back book open where it wants—the place Bev has turned to the most.

It's a poem, sort of, and it tells the reader that if they're in a pit with no way out, they should stop waiting for someone to rescue them. Instead, the author advises the reader to make their own rope, tie it to a stone, throw it out of their prison, and use the rope to climb out of their hole.

Great advice, except what the hell are you supposed to make a rope from when you're stuck at the bottom of a pit?

I shrug, replace the book, and move to her dresser.

I feel like a pervert as I open her top drawer and stare at a sea of underwear. Beneath a bunch of tangled thongs, a small vibrator sits, waiting, and I wonder if she will ever bring this into our love life.

I sift through silk and lace but find nothing more of interest. No cards from Jim. No notes from Jim. No old photos of Jim.

Although, I guess I wouldn't find any physical photographs because we live in the modern age where everything is stored in the cloud. When I think of this, it reminds me of her laptop and that I know her password.

But when I turn to check, her computer is not there and almost certainly with her.

My idea to search her room is proving fruitless, but I am not yet finished.

I step into her closet as far as I'm able, which is only a few feet.

Clothes hang everywhere, only some of which I've seen her wear. This is how they look when they're off duty—versions of her skin airing out while not in use.

Bev is short and wouldn't be able to reach the top shelf without assistance of some kind, and from where I stand, the boxes stored up top don't look like they've been touched in a while.

Except for a single black shoebox placed lower than the rest and crisscrossed with fresh finger trails made in the dust.

I grab it, confident that with so many marks, she won't notice any of mine added to the mix.

Inside, the black cross made of iron nails sits next to a small wooden box. Inside the box, I find another artifact—one I've never seen before. A shiny bracelet of silver charms—small animal shapes hammered from metal. I look closer and can make out faint images of Cyrillic letters that make me think the charms may have started life as Russian coins. Maybe the cross and the bracelet are unrelated. But because of their Russian connection, I figure either Evil Jim has left more presents for Bev than she's told me about, or he gave her the bracelet when they were dating.

Both possibilities concern me.

I check the box for other hints about her ex's identity but find nothing.

I photograph the bracelet and the cross, then hide the photos on my phone, just in case, along with the image of her Russian class information. I hate keeping secrets from her, but I'm doing this for her own good—for *our* own good—and I have to be careful.

When I replace the box on the top shelf, I check the time and see I have only twenty minutes before class starts.

I quickly use the restroom, and on a whim, I check the medicine cabinet behind the mirror. On the middle shelf, behind her birth control pills, sits an orange plastic bottle filled with salmon-colored, oval-shaped pills. There are no pharmacy markings on the bottle, only a white label with the number *90* and the letter *X* written on it.

Ninety pills of Alprazolam, known commercially as Xanax.

I don't have time to count the pills, but at a glance, I can tell there are a lot fewer than ninety.

"Fuck you, Dan," I say in a whisper.

I am out of Bev's room two minutes later, sprinting across the Grounds, on my way to Mooken's Thursday lecture.

When I arrive, I'm breathing heavily and open the door precisely one minute *after* Mooken has begun to speak.

He doesn't miss a beat, but he glances at me and shakes his head when he sees I'm late.

I take a seat at the rear of the auditorium, getting my breathing under control, and I try to catch up to where the rest of the class already is.

"Open your books to chapter fourteen," Mooken says in a booming voice. "Today, we are discussing biological motives for sex."

Excellent, I think. *Just what I want to hear about.*

"Let's start by talking about the male stickleback fish," Mooken says with a beaming smile. "This species has been studied more than humans, and its mating behaviors have taught us plenty about our motivation for sex."

I try to pay attention as Mooken explains how the male stickleback will attack any other male that comes near his nest while at the same time courting any female who wanders past.

Mooken launches into every little detail about how these fish have sex without actually touching each other. But all I can think about is Evil Jim, and how he is coming far too close to the nest

I'm building with Bev. If I see his bright red underbelly anywhere near us, I will attack him, the same as my stickleback brothers would.

I stare at the back of Bev's head and fantasize about new ways to hurt her ex while I struggle to take notes about motivational chains in fish. My obsession with Bev isn't the only thing that keeps me from focusing, though. Something else is buzzing in my head—a discordant, white noise between my ears that is getting louder.

I watch Bev for most of the class, but she never turns around to see if I'm there or to acknowledge my presence in any way. In all fairness, she doesn't look up from her laptop at all, not even to watch the professor.

When class is over, as much as I want to talk with her, I don't wait for her.

Instead, I duck out the door and head to Cabel Hall, although I'm not sure what, if anything I hope to find by scoping out the home of UVA's Russian and Slavic Studies Department.

CHAPTER TWENTY-SIX

LIKE ALL THE older buildings at the university, the exteriors take you back to the time of the country's founding fathers. It's not hard to imagine Thomas Jefferson himself walking through Cabel Hall as I enter and slowly proceed up the open set of stairs. My English classes are on the second floor, but the Russian courses are held two floors up, on the fourth floor.

When I step into the upstairs corridor, handwritten signs are plastered across a large corkboard that hangs on the wall. It's filled with social announcements and offers to tutor. All of this is also online, but some segments of the student body like keeping old traditions alive and unchanged.

To my right, a glass cabinet is filled with award plaques and photographs. Farther down the hall, black-and-white photos of the Russian studies faculty dot the wall. Most of the teachers are old white men, with only a few females and minorities represented. There are photos here and there of young people, and one of them looks familiar, although I can't place where I know him from. At the top of the display, I find a photo of Professor Sulke sporting long white hair and bushy sideburns.

At the end of the corridor, a man's voice echoes from behind a set of double doors that are slightly ajar. I approach and listen through the crack to a small class that's in session before quietly pushing the doors inward and easing my way inside.

The room is large—the size of Mooken's psychology lecture hall—but it's occupied by only a dozen students, all sitting at the front of the class, surrounding their professor.

Russian and Slavic studies must not be as popular as psychology.

I debate for a moment before I take a seat at the back of the auditorium. The instant I do, all heads turn my way.

I clear my throat, raise my hand part-way, and nod, hoping they will think I'm auditing the class.

I recognize Professor Sulke from his photo, and I raise an eyebrow without meaning to when we lock eyes across the room.

I resign myself to sitting and waiting as he continues his lecture. All of it is delivered in Russian, as are the questions from the students, so I don't understand a single thing being said. But I nod at what seems to be the appropriate times, and I laugh when the others chuckle.

When the class is over, the students stand and file out slowly, most of them continuing to chat with each other in Russian.

Two older students linger at the front of the classroom, speaking with Professor Sulke.

The professor nods to the students, then turns to look at me again.

Is he angry I've audited his class? Does he want me to leave so he can have a private conversation with his TAs?

But as the other two turn to face me, my heart stops beating, and it's a full count of three before it starts up again.

One of the TAs has a shock of red hair and is pointing right at me. My eyes widen when I realize it's Andrew, the man I almost beat up under the overpass.

He's as surprised to see me as I am to see him, but I don't wait around to find out what he is telling his colleagues.

I leave the room, run down the hall, and practically fly down the stairs. Finally, I slam through the heavy double doors and burst into the sunlight.

I don't stop running or look back until I've turned at least three corners, and when I do, no one is following me.

My heart is a hammer slamming into my chest, and I am fearful something inside me is about to break. But even as I press my back against the brick wall of a building, trying to recover, I have enough sense to note the time of day the Russian class has ended for future reference.

It's possible that running into Andrew in two completely

different settings is a coincidence, but it isn't probable. But what is likely is that his name isn't really Andrew. I mean, why would he tell me his real name?

My mind races through every possible explanation I can muster, but only one feels true.

The man with red hair was there when I was chasing Tony because he was stalking Bev or maybe because he wanted to find out more about me—her new boyfriend. I'm not sure. But combine that with the fact that he also happens to be a TA in the Russian and Slavic Studies Department, and I can arrive at only one conclusion.

Andrew is not Andrew.

Somehow, he is Evil Jim.

CHAPTER TWENTY-SEVEN

I TRY TO spend Thursday night as planned, reviewing and cleaning up my notes and drafting a conclusion for our lab report. My grade in Mooken's class depends on it. But I'm stressed and tense, and parts of my body randomly twitch, making it difficult to concentrate.

Also, I don't give a shit about this stupid lab.

It's my life that concerns me right now.

Without Bev, I'm lonely and spend much of the evening biting my fingernails, fantasizing about what I want to do to Evil Jim. Even though it was my idea to sleep here tonight and work on my lab report, between the way Bev walked out of her room this morning and the fact that she didn't even look at me during class, I can feel her pulling away from me—from *us.*

And the thought of that is killing me.

I tap the keyboard on my laptop and try to concentrate on the results of our experiment. But instead, my brain replays two imagined scenarios over and over again in my head.

In the first, Bev is laughing and having a good time, out with her girlfriends tonight and being hit on by every man in the bar.

The second scenario is worse.

In it, Bev is home, locked in her bedroom, alone, depressed, clutching a handful of pills. What hurts the most is that I can't tell if she's upset about our relationship going south or if she's secretly still mourning the ending of her relationship with the other Jim.

I hold off as long as I can, trying to work like this, but after half an hour, I surrender and send her a text.

Thinking bout u. Making progress over here. Everything ok?

It is fifteen long minutes before she replies.

Hi Jim. Doing fine. Hope you finish your work and get some sleep. Still want me to come over Saturday night?

I respond, maybe too quickly.

Yes.

Ok cool. See you on Saturday then, cause I have some stuff to do tomorrow night. Sry.

A single night without Bev was going to be bad enough, and now I have to spend two nights away from her. I want to ask her *why* and to understand what's going on with her. But if she has something important to do, I also don't want to get in her way.

I respond to her text with a thumbs up and a heart emoji. And that's it.

She *likes* my text, and then there are no more communications from her for the rest of the night.

I spend the evening stewing over her sparse responses.

And that she only *liked* my text instead of *hearting* it.

And that she used my first name instead of calling me by one of our pet names.

My mind reels at all these signs, and by the time I am ready for bed, my stomach is in knots, and I want to throw up.

Anyone who claims there is no direct connection between the mind and the body has never been in love.

After another hour and several abandoned texts to Bev, I give up. With tomorrow evening now free, I will finish the draft of our lab conclusions then.

I contemplate staying up all night because I fear my nightmares, but eventually, my eyelids grow too heavy, and I fall asleep.

I dream of being chased by a monster with hands made of knitting needles and not being able to run. I dream of walking into Mooken's class and not having my lab report done on time. And, of course, I dream of finding and chasing Evil Jim. When I catch up to him, no matter how much he claims to be Andrew, I am not fooled. I let him beg for his life before ripping him to pieces, literally.

When I wake up Friday morning, my heart is beating rapidly and is emptier than it's been in a long time.

After skipping breakfast, I force myself to get on with my day and walk through it as an automaton without purpose. I go through the motions of showing up to my literature class, eating some of what I order for lunch, and checking my phone for a message from Bev every five minutes. By the time I return to my apartment at the end of the day and crash on my couch, I am a man without his soul.

As night falls, Bev still doesn't reach out, and I force myself to complete a half-assed draft of our lab conclusions. Without reviewing it, I send it, along with my notes, to Eugene and Amber.

Almost immediately, my phone vibrates, and for a second, I think it is a note from Bev. But it's a text from Amber, along with a photo.

It's a shot of her at the Corner with Eugene mugging in the background like the smug dickhead he is. Her smile is wide, and even though the pic is blurred, she's sexy enough that it could serve as the centerpiece in a fashion ad.

A part of me misses being with her and having a physical relationship without the complications that come with emotions. Even though my shallow connection with Amber couldn't fulfill me in the long-term, at least it never hurt very much.

Still, when I think about Bev again, my strength returns enough to resist Amber's charm. I send back a laughing emoji before I get up and start boiling water for tea—my lame attempt at invoking Bev's spirit.

But Amber is not ignored so easily and responds with her blunt questions.

U with the TA again tonight? How's that going?

Hanging out solo, I reply. Being a good RA.

Come out and join us, spoil sport. I miss you!

I send back a hug emoji, mute all notifications on my phone, and set it face-down on the coffee table.

Solemn and quiet, I pour my tea and wait for it to cool before taking my first sip.

The brew tastes mostly the same as what I've become used to, but its calming effects are not nearly as strong as when I'm with Bev.

So I sip and think.

Sip and think.

What can I do to fix whatever is breaking down between Bev and me? I can think of nothing that will alter my fate. And certainly, here, alone on a Friday night, there is nothing I can do.

I slouch on my sofa, click on the TV, and scan the channels until I happen upon an old *Ren and Stimpy* rerun.

At first, the over-the-top but silly cartoon violence makes me laugh, but my mirth turns to stone when a shadow flickers off to my left.

When I turn my head to look, a dark shape the size of a cat retreats—a scared animal of night tucking itself into the dark corner of the kitchen. It breathes loudly, its black lungs rattling as it watches me.

Five minutes later, the shape eases out from its corner—an oil slick come to life—oozing across the carpeted floor, climbing my leg, my torso, and covering my entire face.

I want to scream, to demand what it wants from me, but my mouth won't work. I'm mute, frozen, and helpless. But the shadow is not.

Idiot, it says, using my father's voice. *Why the hell would someone like her want someone like you? She's been using you, boy. She's still in love with him. Not you. You were just a port in her storm.*

I try again to shout, to tell the shadow of my dad to *fuck off* and to leave me alone, but no sound escapes my mouth.

I struggle harder to regain control of any part of my body, but I am paralyzed. I strain so much that I worry my guts will pop out. But at last, finally, my leg tingles, even though it still won't move.

In my mind, I slam my shoulder into an unseen wall of darkness repeatedly.

This is not real, I say. *This is a dream. Nothing is holding me here.*

Pound.

Pound.

Pound.

The thuds in my head echo.

I order my lungs to expand, to breathe, to permit air to enter, but they don't. At last, as I'm about to die, I sit up on the couch, wet with sweat, and take a shuttering breath.

When I look to the kitchen, the shadow is gone, returned to its corner.

I am left not understanding if the shadow was my father haunting my dreams or something darker cloaking itself in his voice, but whatever it was, it injected cold fear and doubt about Bev and me into my soul.

Worse than anything is that, as I sit on the couch, shaking, I am beginning to fear the worst—that the shadow could be right.

CHAPTER TWENTY-EIGHT

IT'S EARLY SATURDAY afternoon, and unlike my residents who are engaged in properly fun college pursuits, I'm on my laptop digging for anything I can find about a Russian TA with red hair named Jim.

He's not listed on the Russia and Slavic Studies home page. But eventually I come across a single photo of him, caught in mid-discussion, speaking with Professor Sulke.

I save it to my desktop, but the photo is not captioned, and I glean no details from it.

Social media yields better results.

A Reddit thread about Russian as a second language seems the kind of place a Russian TA might hang out online. And indeed, one of the admins regulating a debate about whether Russian is more difficult to learn than English has a profile photo that looks a lot like Evil Jim.

After an hour poking around archived threads, I find his name on the site.

Andrew Wilson.

Not *Jim* or *James* or anything even close.

Just *Andrew*—the same name he gave me under the overpass.

I pound my fist into the sofa cushion, but I follow through and search for Andrew in the student directory.

With his first and last name, I find him quickly, and when I look into his eyes, I'm still certain that, somehow, he is Bev's ex. But even so, *Jim* is not a nickname for *Andrew*, no matter how I look at it.

I curse and curse until a student photo next to Andrew's offers a possible explanation. Jerold Lynn Smith has listed his middle name, and Andrew hasn't.

After a quick scan of the page, I see that plenty of students didn't include their middle names when they signed up for the student directory. I know I didn't.

Maybe Bev's ex is Andrew *James* Wilson. After all, going by *Jim* would be better than being known as *Andrew* or *Drew*.

This is all conjecture, but it's all I have.

I do another quick search to confirm the class where I ran into Evil Jim meets twice a week, on Tuesdays and Thursdays. I don't want to miss another lunch with Bev next week, but I have to learn more about Evil Jim before I lose my mind.

When I close my laptop, done being a private eye for the day, Bev texts me, telling me what time she wants to come over and asking for my address.

I respond, but she doesn't continue the conversation.

After rubbing my eyes harder than I should, I scan my living room. It's claustrophobic in here and dusty, like the apartment where my parents and I lived until I was ten—and like Mooken's office—although not nearly as cluttered as either.

I have none of Mom's collectible figurines or her crocheted blankets. And none of Dad's books or his music CDs. My college apartment is filled with *my* things and contains nothing that would evoke unwanted memories of home. It's comfortable and familiar here, and I like it as it is. But I also want to make a good impression for Bev, and there's a lot to clean before she comes over this evening.

I put on a pot of coffee and start wiping off months of dust from everything I can reach. The living room is presentable within the hour, but my room and the bathroom need help.

Hours later, I am sweaty and tired, but my place is neater and cleaner than the day I moved in.

I only have one last thing to do before she shows up. I run to the shower and start my pre-date ritual of cleaning and shaving.

It's not long before I'm back on the couch, finishing the last of the cold coffee in my mug, waiting for Bev to text me.

Ten minutes later, she sends a message.

B there soon, is all it says.

Another half hour passes before she glides past my window, and I spring to my feet, meeting her at the door.

She gives me a tight hug, but even though her closeness comforts me, something is missing.

"Is everything okay?" I ask.

She shrugs, and her eyes dampen.

"Jim—the other Jim—left me another present today, and the whole thing is really stressing me out. I'm sorry. I was hoping that coming over here would give me a night off from all of this, but…"

Hearing about Evil Jim's gift is a kick in the stomach. He's struck again, and inside, I am a starving dog straining at my chain, ready to attack the man ruining my relationship.

Bev sees how dark I've suddenly turned and touches my shoulder.

"I almost didn't tell you, but you have the right to know," she says.

I shake my head, tears of anger filling my eyes, unable to figure out the right thing to say to her. Thankfully, she speaks first.

"I'm hungry," she says. "And you promised me dinner. Let's go eat."

Once we are on the shaded trail that cuts through the woods behind my apartment, I start to calm down. The fresh scent of pine has cleared my head by the time we arrive at Asia Delight, the Chinese restaurant on Emmet Street. The food is good, and since it mainly offers takeout, seating is always available.

"I think this is our first dinner out," I say as we settle into a booth.

"It smells good in here," she replies.

Our discussion continues and is pleasant enough, but she's stalling—delaying whatever she wants to say to me. Before I can ask her directly, she reaches out and takes my hands in hers.

Her mouth opens, but as she starts to talk, the server interrupts, and we order dinner.

"What were you going to say?" I ask after the server leaves.

She sips her water and frowns.

"Can we talk about that when we get back to your place?" she asks.

"Sure," I say. "Do you want to tell me about the gift?"

"Actually, not right now, if that's okay. How's your lab report going?"

I shrug and explain my initial conclusions and my interpretation of our data.

She laughs, and it's the first genuine thing to come out of her all evening.

"That's interesting," she says. "You do have a nice face, you know. It was one of the things that first attracted me to you. You look like someone who can be trusted."

"Not like Evil Jim," I say.

She pauses before answering.

"Not like him at all."

The food arrives and saves us from more awkward exchanges. Bev pretends to marvel at how well I use chopsticks, and we fall into a comfortable chat, this time about Professor Mooken.

"Tell me more about him," I say.

Her eyes go dark, and her upper lip curls in a half-smile.

"He's a smart man," she says. "I mean, none of the professors around here are stupid, but Mooken stands out, even among them. I was lucky to get my position with him."

"I don't know anything about him," I say. "Does he have any kids? Married?"

"He...doesn't talk much about his personal life."

"Did he used to practice around here?"

Her eyes darken again, but at least she laughs this time.

"That's how I met him," she says.

"You were his patient?"

"I was so worried and stressed all the time when I was an undergrad," she says. "He treated me for some low-level anxiety issues and helped me get better. And he also got me past some of my…bigger issues. And one day, out of the blue, he suggested I apply for one of his TA positions. So I did. And I got it. I had to start therapy with a new psychiatrist, of course, but that was no big deal. For me, it was like having two doctors at my disposal."

"It's none of my business," I say, "but if you ever want to talk about anything with me, I'm here for you, too."

She squeezes my hand, and, for a moment, we connect like usual.

"You're so sweet," she says. "But I'm fine now."

"Are you still seeing your new therapist?"

She shakes her head and shifts in her seat.

"I stopped going a couple of weeks ago, actually. Sorry I didn't tell you. But like you were saying, I don't think I need to see anyone anymore—not on a regular basis, at least."

I lower my gaze.

Her admission explains why she's self-medicating with the Xanax from Dan since she's no longer seeing someone who can prescribe it for her legally.

"Tell me more about Amber," she says, eager to change the topic.

I'm not sure why she wants to know more about Amber, but I tell her about when we dated and how we never formed an emotional connection. I omit the details of our sex life, and I'm surprised when she asks about our physical relationship.

"I hope the sex was good, at least," she says.

I shrug and am careful with how I proceed.

"If I ever told her something was off limits or that I was unsure about trying something, that made her want to do it even more. If you called it *sex*, she wanted to try it. That can be fun for a while, but what I have with you is so much more than anything I ever had with her. You know how much I mean that, don't you, Bev?"

Bev glances down and grins.

"Of course I do," she says. "But I *do* like our sex life. Don't you? I mean the physical part of it, along with the emotions."

"Just thinking about you turns me on," I say, and at that moment, my body hardens and responds to the memory of the last time she and I were together in bed.

When we finish our food, I pay the bill, and for a moment, I think the night has turned itself around. But Bev doesn't wait long before she takes a deep breath and sighs.

"Come on," she says. "Let's go back to your place and talk."

CHAPTER TWENTY-NINE

AFTER A SILENT walk back to my apartment, we settle into my couch. I wait a few minutes for Bev to say something before I turn on a shitty true crime show so it's not so deathly quiet.

The opening scene is a reenactment of a man calling 911 after finding his wife dead at the bottom of the stairs in their home.

I shake my head.

"It's the husband," I say. "It's always the husband."

Bev nods but continues to stare forward. She pretends to be interested in the show but is clearly disconnected from me.

Soon, I can't take it anymore.

"What did you want to talk about, Bev?"

Before she can answer, my phone vibrates. I don't pick it up, but at the corner of my vision, a notification banner flashes—another text from Amber.

Bev sees it, too.

"More work on the lab report?"

"Doubtful," I say. "She's probably out with Eugene and wants me to hang with them."

"Why don't you?"

"I want to be here with you," I say. "You know that."

"I do, but...I've been thinking lately, and I'm wondering if both of us jumped into this too quickly. I love what we have, and I *adore* you, but with my ex leaving me gifts and your ex still texting you this late on a Saturday night...well, don't you think maybe both of us have unfinished business?"

I don't reply.

"Do you understand what I'm saying?" she asks.

My heart skips a beat, and I am left confused, panicked, and shallow of breath.

"I don't have any unfinished business with Amber," I say. "Are you breaking up with me?"

"I don't *want* to," she says. "But I need to deal with this Jim thing first. And I'm not sure how to even do that. But I…I can't have you waiting around for me when all of *me* isn't even here. It's not fair to either of us."

I inhale and exhale slowly, but no air enters my lungs, and I am about to pass out.

I want to argue with her, to convince her she's wrong. But I don't want to turn our love into a tangled court case of loopholes and plea bargains that I desperately hope she will consider. I ache in my bones, but even through my pain, I understand that emotions cannot be reasoned with.

Instead, I embrace her, and she returns my hug. Our bodies press together as they have done so many times now, and our reflexes take over. Her breathing becomes labored, and the scent of her almond body oil fills me. Soon, we are kissing, urgent and desperate, because we both understand this may be our last time together.

I unsnap her jeans, she tugs at mine, and we become lost in our safe, lust-filled world. I want to take her to my bedroom, but when I try to stand, she pulls me back down to her, insisting we do whatever we're going to do right here on the couch.

One minute later, we are both naked, and I hold on as she writhes and spasms.

She grabs my head with both hands and almost crushes my skull as she shakes, moans, and curses before her body releases. My fire still burns hot, but I'm not important right now. Only her pleasure matters. I start to touch her again, but the moment has passed, and she sits up straight and uncomfortable on the couch.

Without looking at me, she gets dressed, and I do the same, easing myself next to her, wanting to talk more, hoping she will not leave.

A tear rolls down her cheek. The pleasure we just shared is not nearly enough to sway her from her decision.

She is resolute, and I am crushed.

After she retrieves her bag and gives me a final hug at the door, she steps outside and is gone.

I am left alone in my clean living room, silent and in shock.

You're better off without her, my father says.

But he is wrong.

I ignore anything else he tries to tell me and let my sadness wash over me. I cry until my tears are stifled by a sudden clarity of thought and a singularity of purpose.

I can't blame Bev for this. She is simply trying to survive what life is throwing at her.

She is not the problem that has broken us apart.

The other Jim—Evil Jim—*he* is the problem.

He's the one who has to stop.

He's the one who must be held accountable.

And it is now clear to me that I must stop fantasizing about what I *want* to do to him and instead take care of him for real.

CHAPTER THIRTY

I AM LOST, thirsty, and hungry, walking through a maze of walls that are alive, built from human bodies stacked one on top of another that writhe and reach out to me with wanting hands. The only hope I have of escaping this place is to tear through its walls and make my own path. I hold my breath and dig into the interlocked human bodies until I squeeze through and force my way into the next passageway. I do the same thing again. And again. But I underestimate the size of the maze, and every time I burrow through one barrier, pulling at skeletal limbs and ripping putrid skin, I end up staring at yet another wall and another set of terrified, open mouths screaming at me, begging for mercy.

When I wake with a start, it's three in the morning.

I check my phone for a text from Bev but find none. I don't want to return to my land of nightmares, so I play a word-matching game, then look for notifications on my social media apps five times—doing anything I can think of to stay awake. But eventually, my body surrenders, and my head nods.

I avoid falling asleep at the last possible second and get up to make tea. This reminds me of Bev, and by four in the morning, I'm sitting in bed, alone, sipping the calming dark liquid.

But it's still not the same without her.

At last, when the sun threatens to rise, I slide into a restless early morning slumber where I dream of shadows that suffocate me and legs that won't run.

By the time I am awake again, it's mid-morning. My head throbs, my hands shake, and my top lip is twitching.

No part of me is working correctly.

All of this is because Evil Jim has forced Bev to push me out of her life.

I check my phone again for a message from her, but still, there's nothing.

I make coffee and open the Internet in search of more information about *Andrew Wilson, Andrew James Wilson, or Jim Wilson.* One site promises to give me Andrew J. Wilson's address and phone number if I sign up for their service. But when I do, the page downloads a virus before I can stop it. My desktop begins flashing ads for Viagra and Cialis and is soon useless. In disgust, I shut down my laptop and toss it to the floor.

I give in to the fact that I have no sure way of finding Andrew or Jim until Tuesday, when I know where he'll be attending class. But the thought of having to live two full days without confronting him makes me itch, and soon I am rubbing and scratching my arms, leaving behind dark red marks across my skin.

I have to do something, or I will go crazy, so I dress without showering and step into the outside world. I have no plan, but my agenda is clear.

Find Evil Jim.

Because Sundays are prime drinking days at UVA, I hope to find Evil Jim somewhere on the Corner, and I start at the St. Maarten Cafe. It's crowded because of the game, but it's not long before I confirm that Jim isn't there. I want to move along, but my stomach growls and aches, so I order two beers and a plate of cheap, deep-fried bar food.

I eat and drink faster than I should, and by the time I get up to leave for the next bar, my head is buzzing.

I stumble to the far end of the Corner and work my way back. At each bar, I step inside, order a drink, study the room, look for my nemesis, and leave once I'm certain he's not there.

Soon, with a gallon of alcohol floating inside me, I convince myself that the coward is hiding from me intentionally. Adding to that, my brain comes up with the dark idea that he could be with Bev right now at her place.

I imagine the two of them arguing in her room, which reminds me of my parents and makes me smile and want to weep.

But my fantasy quickly morphs into imagined footage of them

having wild, passionate sex as they release their frustrations and decide to give things one more try.

This makes me wretch, but I shake my head furiously and return to my mission. I have yet to check all the local bars, so I move on to Shenanigans and stay there longer than I should. Not because I think I'll find the other Jim there, but because I'm thirsty again and want to lose myself even more than I already am. After I order my third drink in half an hour, the bartender refuses to serve me further.

This is not a problem.

UVA has plenty of places to drink, and I pay my bill and move on to the next establishment.

By dinner time, I have canvased all the bars and restaurants at the Corner and have seen no sign of Andrew *Evil Jim* Wilson.

As I shuffle along the sidewalk, students stare at me and sneer, laughing at what they think is going on inside me. Lucky for them, no one touches me because I'd love an excuse to attack and release some of the darkness building inside me with each step.

When night finally falls, I don't have much more left in me, even though I want to stay out and catch the other Jim and his little Russian friends as they party without a care in the world.

I make a final stop at the *White Spot*—the university's famous greasy spoon—and order a Gus Burger. The cheeseburger with its oily fried egg on top is a life-giving elixir, and by the time I've consumed it, I'm re-energized and ready to try another bar.

But there are no more bars here. I have been to them all.

So I start over. When I turn down an alley and take a shortcut to St. Maarten's, I recognize the back of a familiar figure standing in the parking lot.

I stop walking and blink until I can see clearly enough to recognize that it's only Eugene.

I sneak up behind him without a sound. I fantasize that I am his shadow, and I whisper his name once I am close enough to touch him.

He turns around, startled, then laughs, but his laughter dies when he sees how drunk I am under the pale light of the streetlamps.

"Dude, what is going on with you?" he says. "You look like shit, man."

I try to say *thank you*, but my words come out slurred and fuzzy.

"I think you need to go home, buddy."

"Where's Amber?" I say coherently enough that he understands me.

He shrugs.

"How should I know? Out with the new guy she's been seeing, I think. That train has left the station for you, my man. And you only have yourself to blame."

"Fine," I say as I stumble past him and enter the bar.

I hold myself together long enough to sit, order a beer, and pull out my smartphone.

The day has gone on for too long, and my brief burst of energy from the burger is gone, drained by my encounter with Eugene. At this point, I hope I *don't* run into Evil Jim because my motor functions are not working properly, and I would have no hope of punishing him appropriately.

While swaying on my bar stool, I manage to send a text—not to Bev, because that would be unwise in my current state—but to Amber instead.

What u doing? I text.

Half a beer later, the three dots on the phone start dancing, and she texts me back.

Hey there. Busy right now. You ok?

Yes, I bet she is busy. Everyone's busy tonight except me. And maybe Eugene.

I laugh darkly and imagine Amber riding her new boyfriend and pausing in her gyrations to respond to my text. Or maybe her new guy has gone to the bathroom and left her alone in bed for a few minutes, and she is naked while texting with me.

Photo? I message back to her.

With all the alcohol in me, I have no ability to resist the potential of receiving an X-rated image from Amber.

A few seconds later, a photo pops up on my phone—her smooth thigh and calf poking out from under a white sheet in a neat, unadorned, dark hotel room.

My body hardens, although I wonder why she's in a hotel instead of a dorm room or an apartment. Maybe her new lover is from out of town, and they have nowhere else to go. Or maybe he's keeping her as his dirty little secret for some dark, nefarious reason.

Of course, there's an equal chance Amber simply wanted to have sex in a hotel room tonight because it turned her on.

Did you forget about your true love that quickly? my father says in my head, openly mocking me.

"Shut the fuck up," I mutter into my beer, hoping the big, muscular dude sitting next to me doesn't think I'm talking to him.

Going to sleep early tonight? I text back to Amber.

She replies with a yellow emoji head, crying with laughter.

No, baby. I'm getting fucked. Wish u were here.

My eyes widen. Amber is such a nasty thing, but she knows how to quicken my pulse.

I *heart* her last text, then drain the rest of my beer and get up to head home. Maybe Amber will visit me after she's had her way with her new beau. I don't really *want* her to do that, but I wouldn't turn her down either—not tonight.

Anything would be better than the nightmares waiting for me once I fall asleep.

Going home now, I text, as my heart pounds in my chest, waiting for her to offer a late-night visit.

But no matter how hard I stare at my phone, she doesn't respond.

I give up, leave the bar, stumbling, and make my way across the Grounds. Soon, I cross Beta Bridge and trip my way through the columns of the Colonnades. The moon shadows from the trees try to grab me as I walk past, but I dodge them as best as my semi-numb feet will allow.

I slip and slide down the stone stairs of the Colonnades and land in the Lambeth courtyard. At last, I am back in my domain, the place where I'm supposed to be the responsible one. But tonight, I keep my gaze aimed at the ground and hope that no resident wants to talk or needs my help because I am in no shape to be an RA.

I make it to my door without interruption, and once I'm inside my apartment, I lock the door behind me and head for my bedroom.

Minutes later, I'm in bed, staring at my phone, trying to force my drunken eyes to bring it into clearer focus.

There's no text from Bev, about which I'm somewhat glad because I don't want her to interact with this drunken, pathetic version of me.

But there's no message from Amber, either.

I fumble with my phone and send her another text.

Home yet?

She immediately responds, to my surprise.

LOL. Nope. Out with Susie at the corner. Come out and join us.

I nod and try to respond, but my chin drops to my chest, and my eyelids shut. Seconds later, they fly open in time to see my top sheet slither up my right arm, wrap around my wrist, and yank my hand away from my phone.

I fight my sheets as they cut off the circulation in my arm, but they wrap around my ankles and then my other hand. And soon, I'm spread out on top of my bed, naked, unable to move.

I lift my head an inch off the mattress, and a shadow passes outside my door. Someone is in the hall again.

Maybe it's Amber, I think, hopeful for the first time that night.

It wouldn't be the first time she's shown up to my apartment unannounced, stripped off her clothing, and woken me up in a way most guys could only dream of.

But that's not likely.

This time, I fear the shadow's being cast by the Devil himself, who's come to do something far worse to me than anything Amber could ever think of, even in her sickest sexual fantasy.

I shake my head back and forth, still pinned to my bed, unable to get up, awaiting the fate about to befall me.

My bedroom door creaks inward, but instead of Amber or even Satan, Bev steps into my room.

She is naked and pauses at the foot of my bed before she crawls onto the mattress and lowers herself onto me.

She rides me as she's done before, but this time, it is without emotion.

There is no kissing.

No sweet words of love.

Just pure, raw sex.

I know this is the woman I love, but with the lights out, I can only make out a hint of life in her eyes. She bucks and undulates until she finally falls forward and spasms.

With her face so close to mine, I can see her clearly at last. But even though the creature on top of me looks exactly like Bev in every detail, it is *not* her. It is only a shadow wrapped in Bev's skin. And I am in grave danger.

Her hands reach up and tighten around my neck as she grinds on top of me again, building her way toward another orgasm.

My breath sticks in my throat, and I go rigid as my body betrays me.

Black sparkles dance at the periphery of my vision as she crushes my throat with her two hands, and I struggle to breathe. I am as close to death as I have ever been, but when I force my eyes open, Bev's doppelgänger is gone, I am alone in my bed.

My sheets are on the floor, and my chest and stomach are covered in sweat.

I breathe deeply, turn onto my side, close my eyes, and wonder how I will survive until Tuesday.

CHAPTER THIRTY-ONE

MONDAY MORNING BEGINS with a throbbing headache and aching limbs. If I hadn't drunk so much the day before, I'd think I was coming down with the flu. As it is, I'm badly hung over and dehydrated.

And this is fine with me because I have no plans to attend any of my classes today.

I plant myself on my couch and stare at whatever show is on the television. Someone knocks at my door late in the morning—maybe a resident needing something. I'll never know because I don't get up to see who it is. A piece of me creates a fantasy where Bev is the one knocking, and I teach her a lesson by ignoring her. But I know that isn't reality.

My reality is far worse. My forehead is clammy. My limbs shake. And I shiver, like death is reaching for me. And Bev doesn't care.

I wonder if I will live past noon.

But, of course, I do.

When I muster enough energy to brush my teeth, my image in the mirror is as bad as my resident, Bob, sitting on his stairs, detoxing—an addict coming off his drug of choice. For a moment, I contemplate messaging Dan and asking him to deliver a pill that will bring me relief. But no drug would help me get used to living without Bev in my life.

Amber texts me twice, asking me where I was last night and why I didn't join her. I moan, remembering how desperate I was last night and glad she didn't come over.

Even though I don't want to, when I close my eyes, I see her new man throwing her against the wall, ravaging her as she smiles maniacally.

Around mid-afternoon, I amble to the kitchen and dine on a pack of instant white rice smothered in butter. It's not much, but the calories perk me up, and my brain fog clears enough so I can think straight for the first time that day.

I send a text to Amber *and* Eugene.

We good with our report? Meet tomorrow before class to discuss?

Almost right away, Amber replies to the group.

Tmrw morning not good. How bout right after class??

Before I can respond to the group text, she replies to her personal conversation with me.

Where the FWU? I was worried.

Not worried enough to stop by, I think to myself.

Meanwhile, Eugene responds to our group chat.

After class sounds good. References almost done. Amber? Summary coming along?

Done, Amber replies to the group as she waits for me to respond to her private text.

With a heavy sigh, I text her, trying to explain.

Sorry. Fell asleep. Too much boooooooze. How was ur nite?

She replies with a fire emoji and a winky face.

Great. I'm glad someone had a good time.

See u tmrw after class, she texts.

I *like* her comment, but our communications are over, and Amber has moved on to her next thing.

I reread some of my messages with Bev from a week ago. The excitement of our words. Our pet names. The gushes of emotion.

And then I boil water, make magnolia bark tea, and sip it alone in my living room.

Once again, the ritual is empty and does nothing for me, but the smell reminds me of Bev, and that gets me through the evening.

Later that night, I lie in bed, imagining distorted faces etched into the ceiling's aged, irregular surface. I've read that finding faces in randomness is a fundamental human trait, which gives me some relief. Because that suggests I am still at least partially human, despite how I feel.

At one in the morning, exhausted, I make a pot of coffee.

The tea had some caffeine in it, but I need something far more serious because I don't want to fall asleep. I can't take another night of dark dreaming.

The coffee does the trick, and it keeps me awake all night. When the sun finally rises, I am wired and bone-tired at the same time, but I force myself to go through the motions of the morning. I eat cereal, watch the news, shower, and drink more coffee.

By the time I finish my second cup, I'm as ready as I will ever be to start this day. First, I have Mooken's lecture, then I meet with Amber and Eugene. But after that comes the real business of the day because, finally, it's Tuesday.

And Bev's pain will soon end.

CHAPTER THIRTY-TWO

MY SENSE OF mission and the caffeine carry me quickly across the Grounds, and I arrive early for Professor Mooken's lecture. The urge to assure Bev that everything will soon be fine is almost overwhelming, but I don't want her to know anything in case things go wrong.

She can have no culpability in what I am about to do.

Minutes later, Bev and the two other TAs enter together through the side entrance. She doesn't even glance up to see if I am here.

My heart turns into a poisonous lead ball that plummets to the bottom of my stomach as the buzz of students grows around me.

A minute before start time, Amber walks in wearing a twisted smile—one I've seen often. Usually, after we've had sex and she's calm and satisfied.

She sits in the seat Eugene has saved for her, and at last, Professor Mooken enters the room and steps up to the podium.

"Welcome, class," he bellows.

His voice echoes above our heads with abnormal vigor.

"Today, we are talking about *drugs*. And religion, because, you know…same-same."

Requisite laughter erupts from the class, except from those who are overly religious.

"Since the beginning of known history, and likely before, humans have used potent substances to induce religious experiences," he says. "They have used drugs to see the world around them as it truly is or to glimpse and communicate with the divine existence—with God."

I'll give Mooken this much—his lectures are rarely dull.

As for myself, I've never needed mind-altering drugs. I have enough issues dealing with the reality I'm faced with every day.

The professor tells the class about *Altered States*, an old movie where the main character spends much of the time high on hallucinogens and floating in an isolation chamber. This combination ends up tapping into an ancient part of his DNA and reverting him back to the form of a proto-human—something wild and sinister. Eventually, the main character's body regresses further back in our evolutionary chain until he becomes part of the original matter of creation itself. The climax of the movie shows him almost losing himself, literally, in the cosmos.

Until love saves him and everything is fine.

Mooken's lip curls when he tells us how the movie ends.

Such a happy, sappy conclusion doesn't set well with his logic-driven brain. Still, he makes his point, which is that our states of consciousness are entirely subjective and can be altered substantially by drugs.

While Mooken continues his lecture, I study the back of Bev's head, willing her to turn and look at me.

Eventually, she looks to the left, enough for me to see her cheeks and eyes are puffy and red. She's been crying right here in class, where only the professor and the other TAs can see her. And although my heart hurts to see her in pain, a part of me fantasizes her tears are from mourning the end of our relationship.

Don't flatter yourself, my father whispers in my head. *Someone she knows probably died.*

I curse my father in silence, so no one will hear.

As soon as Mooken completes the lecture, Bev is up and out the side door before the other TAs have gathered their books.

I want to run after her, console her, and love her. But I don't. Instead, Amber and Eugene shuffle over to me, and the three of us leave the lecture hall together.

Five minutes later, we step into the room where we conducted our experiment.

We review what each other has done for the lab report, and Eugene volunteers to take the first crack at combining everything into a single, coherent draft.

That's fine with me, and from Amber's face, I can tell she's relieved as well.

"How are things with the TA?" Eugene asks. "She didn't come up and get all mushy with you today after class."

I want to slap him for stating the obvious, but he's only being his normal pain in the ass and nothing more. Amber, as usual, is blunt with her questioning.

"Is something wrong in paradise?" she asks. "I had a bad feeling about her, you know. She seems…stuck up. And she *never* says *hi* to me."

I shake my head.

"She's having a hard time…"

"Let me guess. And you need to give her some space," Amber says, interrupting.

Amber's words slice across my heart.

"Something like that," I say. "Her ex has been leaving her gifts and creepy notes. And I think he's stalking her. It's stressing her out, and she wants to take care of that before we go any further."

"See? Not all exes are as cool as me," Amber says with a syrupy, sarcastic grin.

I roll my eyes before I can stop myself, but I also laugh, which lifts my spirits briefly.

It feels good to tell someone about my problems with Bev, but I don't have time to sit and share more of my situation with Amber and Eugene.

The time I've been waiting for is finally here. I have an appointment to keep with a Russian studies TA.

As I walk across the Grounds, I am focused, on a mission. But half-way there, my phone rings. I try to ignore it, but I haven't spoken to him much lately because of Bev, and by the third ring, I cave.

"Hi, Dad."

"What are you doing?" he says, his voice already filled with disappointment and slightly slurred.

"I can only speak a minute or two. Are you okay?"

"These doctors want to kill me," he says. "Can't trust a single one of them. I can hear you breathing hard, son. You should be at the library studying."

"I have something to do first. Someone to talk to."

"Don't do it, boy. Whatever you're planning, she ain't worth it."

"I have to go. I'll text you later, Dad."

I hang up before he can argue, which he would do for the next half hour if given the chance.

Ten minutes later, I stand in the empty hallway of the Russian and Slavic Studies Department on the fourth floor of Cabel Hall. I wait outside the door where I saw Evil Jim last week. As soon as the door opens and the first student steps into the hallway, I pivot and walk calmly out the door and down four flights of steps. Once outside, I move around to the side of the building, where I wait and watch.

It's only a few minutes before Evil Jim steps onto the sidewalk and waves to someone behind him before taking off across the grass.

The instant I see him, my mind fills with loud, buzzing static. Through the white noise in my head, I follow Evil Jim, careful not to get too close, blending in with other groups of students when possible.

I am Evil Jim's shadow—one he cannot see. I follow him, turn after turn, until we arrive at University Avenue.

He moves down a narrow, graveled side street, and although it's daylight, the path he takes is secluded by large bushes and the walls of houses on either side of him.

This will be my best opportunity, and I do not hesitate.

As soon as my foot touches the gravel, I sprint, setting off on a direct intercept course with him, gaining speed with each footfall. He will hear me in a second, but it will be too late by then to stop my momentum.

When I'm ten feet away, he spins around, mouth open.

Before he can yell for help or even curse, I tackle him, folding his mid-section in half and throwing us both to the rocky ground.

"What the fuck?" he gasps, unable to understand why the same stranger is threatening him again.

"Your name," I say through gritted teeth, yelling above the din of noise in my head. "Tell me your fucking name."

"I told you last time," he says.

"Middle and last name."

"What is wrong with you? I'm calling the police."

I lean closer until our faces are an inch apart.

"Tell me."

He shakes his head and laughs, but he is not amused.

"Andrew Francis Pike, asshole. Satisfied?"

"Your wallet," I say. "Give it to me."

He starts to protest, but he surrenders, and his body drains of resistance underneath me. He reaches behind him and produces his wallet.

I snatch the leather case from him and pull out his driver's license.

It is like he said.

Andrew Francis Pike.

Shit. Shit. And Shit.

I want him to be the guy I'm looking for, but he is not *Jim.*

I release him roughly and run away, hoping he will forget me—praying he will not call the cops.

But I'm sure he will. I would if some maniac attacked me out of the blue. For the second time. In fact, he's probably already called them.

You should have smashed his phone, my father's voice says to me. *Idiot.*

As I run, I shield my face, hoping to hide, even though this won't help.

I flee across the Grounds as I review what I know and what I *think* I know, frantic to figure out where I went wrong here.

The name of Bev's ex is *Jim*. Same as mine.

She met him in Russian class.

He was a TA. Maybe hers or maybe not…or at least that's what Dan heard Bev say.

But what if he heard her wrong? Or what if her ex wasn't a TA at all? He could have been a student. But there'd be no reason for Bev to lie about him being a TA instead of a faceless student if she wanted to keep his identity a secret. There are tens of thousands of students but only a small number of TAs. It would have made more sense for her to downplay his status. But the only position at college more influential than a TA is…a professor.

The possibility hits me in the face—a stone-sized chunk of logic—as I remember the look on the Russian professor's face when Andrew pointed me out. He was surprised, but he also recognized me.

If her ex is Professor Sulke, she'd say whatever it took to keep that a secret. And Sulke would *really* want to keep it a secret.

It all fits—why she won't tell me who he is and why she's afraid of him so much.

Because in Bev's world of pursuing two master's degrees, Professor Sulke controls half of her life.

I slow down once I'm far enough away from Andrew. I'm breathing heavily, but the students around me pay no attention.

I look behind me, and neither Andrew nor the police is following. And even though I should stay away from the Russian Department, I will have to go back there to find Professor Sulke.

But first, I pull out my phone and start searching. Assaulting a teacher is even worse than threatening a TA. I have to make sure Professor Sulke has a Jim or a James somewhere in his name before I rush in and make a fool of myself again.

Too late for that, my father says. *Look what this woman has gotten you into. Nothing but trouble.*

I ignore my dad and find the professor mentioned multiple places throughout UVA's intranet and its online sites. I can't find his middle name or initial displayed anywhere, though.

Finally, I click on an article in the local Charlottesville newspaper where the reporter refers to the professor as *Johnathan J. Sulke.*

Bingo. I finally have you, asshole.

CHAPTER THIRTY-THREE

THE HEADY SCENTS of wildflowers and stale beer fill my head as I stalk the back streets of the Corner at night. I am hunting, and Professor Sulky, fifty yards in front of me, leaving a bar by himself, is my prey.

He would never do such a thing in a big city, but being at a college makes people feel they are invincible.

I track him, my hands in my jean pockets and my head bowed, studying the sidewalk while I follow his every move, trying to concentrate while my head buzzes and hums.

He's heading for his car because professors don't walk to bars. They drive.

His Honda Civic is parked on a dark side street, nestled between two other cars, under a row of leafy trees beginning to turn color with the fall.

Go home, my father yells in my ear so he can be heard over the static in my brain. *She's not worth it!*

I remain focused on the professor. I check both ways and see no one, then I take off for him at a dead run. By the time he hears the slapping of my feet, it's too late.

I wrap my hands around his throat and drag him away from his car and into the bushes.

He is taller than me but older, and I have the strength of youth and vengeance on my side. He doesn't stand a chance against my fury.

He doesn't beg for forgiveness or an opportunity to make things right with Bev. But he fights, and his desperation gives him superhuman strength for a moment—long enough for him to reach up and tear at my face.

I crush his neck so he can't yell for help. Then I rear back my head, moving out of his reach, and wait for his burst of energy to drain away. He looks deep into my eyes like he knows something I don't. But he'll never get a chance to tell me what he's hiding because I press down on his windpipe with all my weight. I push hard, locking my arms and gritting my teeth, as he sputters, chokes, then shakes with his final breath.

When he stops moving, and only then, I release his neck, and a blissful silence fills me. No more buzzing. No more darkness. For now.

I stay on top of him in case he's faking it, but after a full minute of his utter stillness, I accept that the deed is done—that Evil Jim is dead.

"Was it worth it?" I growl at the corpse. "Was it?"

Professor Sulke doesn't respond, but I know the answer he would give me. *Of course* Bev was worth it.

A wave of anxiety engulfs me like a needle pumping ice water into the back of my skull. Not because I've taken a man's life. No. He deserved what I gave him. I feel sick because I've ruined my *own* life tonight. I'm ecstatic and relieved that Bev will no longer be bothered by this pariah. Still, the fear of being caught and imprisoned for the rest of my days, denied all freedom and my ability to be with Bev, turns my blood to ice.

My mind turns analytical and studies my situation. My hands are streaked red from the blood running out of the professor's nose, and there are bruises and deep red marks on the professor's neck—tattoos of pain I gave him while taking his life.

I use the bottom of my t-shirt to wipe my fingerprints from his neck, but at best, all I do is smear the blood across his skin. This will have to be enough.

I check around me to ensure nothing has dropped from my pockets and that I haven't left a distinct footprint in the dirt. I use the light from my phone to look, but I see nothing incriminating, at least not to my eye.

I roll the professor deeper into the bushes and make sure no part of him is sticking out where someone might easily spot him. Then, I take off at a run, trying to silence my feet as they hit the sidewalk. It's the middle of the night, early Wednesday morning, a slow time, even at UVA. And thankfully, I don't see another person until I'm several blocks away.

I force myself to slow down and walk at a reasonable pace to help me blend in with the other stragglers returning from their nights of excess. But my breath exits hard from my throat and shakes my lungs. The adrenaline circulating through me is unlike anything I've experienced before. I've read that cold-blooded killers are sometimes simply desperate to feel something. To feel anything. And that they can get off on the sudden rush of chemicals released by the act of murder. But *my* internal cocktail of adrenaline and noradrenaline makes me want to vomit, cry, and run away, never to be seen by another living human again.

I make my way home via the usual route, dodging trees that reach out to grab me and stepping over shadows that stretch in front of me, trying to block my passage.

Before I make it home, with his usual bad timing, my dad calls. But I can't handle talking to him. Not now. Maybe never again. I let it go to voicemail and continue staggering home.

I try to walk as if nothing is wrong with me, but my legs are made of lead, and each step becomes more impossible than the last. Finally, I make it to the little road behind the Colonnades, and soon, I'm walking through Lambeth, and then, I am back in my apartment.

I wash up and splash cold water on my face. It stings where the professor scraped my cheeks in his dying struggles. The marks will be with me for at least a couple of days, but luckily, he didn't cut too deeply into my skin. I scrub the blood from my hands, pick the dry black-red crust from my fingernails, and let the particles swirl down the drain.

Then I stumble to bed and wrap myself under my blankets, shivering.

I think of Bev and her happiness as the darkness of sleep consumes me, but I'm only asleep for a minute before an insistent buzzing wakes me up with a start.

It's my phone, and I stare at it, terrified, as I remember what I've done tonight. I check it, worried the police have already found me and are calling to demand I turn myself in before they break down my door and riddle me with bullets.

But it's only a voicemail notification from my father.

I lift my hands and study my fingers in the pale light cast off by the phone's screen. They are clean, with no indication I choked a man to death earlier tonight. I exhale in relief as I realize the murder was another of my nightmares. It was my worst dream so far, but still only a dream.

Maybe I do need to see Mooken again. Or call the doctor he recommended as soon as the sun comes up.

My phone buzzes again, and I grab it, ready to be angry at my father for not leaving me the hell alone, but it's a text message from Bev.

Evil Jim has left her another gift, and she's pleading with me to come over.

A smile widens across my tired face and mixes with tears as I slide out of bed and escape the weight of my dark dreaming.

I text Bev back and tell her I'm on my way. And deep in my heart, I know everything will be okay.

CHAPTER THIRTY-FOUR

THE BACK DOOR to Bev's house is unlocked. I am relieved and glad I didn't really kill her ex tonight. But at the same time, I'm also disappointed and embarrassed that I have done nothing to help with her Evil Jim problem. I am still resolved to stop him, but my nightmare has served as a cautionary tale for me. I will make him leave Bev alone, but I will not take his life.

Bev greets me with tears in her eyes and pulls me to her before locking the door behind us.

"Thank you," she whispers into my shirt as she buries her face against my chest. "I'm so sorry. I don't have the right to ask you for help, but I need someone..."

"Come on," I say, and lead her back to her bedroom. "It's okay. I understand."

Once we are sitting in her dimly lit bedroom, our bodies and our lips fall into their routine, and within seconds we are entwined. I drink her in like a man lost in the desert who hasn't had a sip of water in days. She moves her hands up to face and lingers there like this is our first time together.

All my pent-up stress and all of hers merge into a single, all-encompassing tsunami, and we are soon naked under her sheets. She wants to make love with a frantic urgency I've not experienced from her before. Maybe because it will make her feel safer. I don't know. But before I do what she asks, I look into her hazel eyes to let her *feel* how much I love her.

I have to be sure she understands this before we have sex.

"I know," she says in a soft voice, answering me as if by magic, like she can read my mind.

And then we make love, flowing and pulsing together as a single organism.

In our afterglow, no part of me isn't exhausted. The night began so badly and has ended better than I could have ever hoped.

I want to ask Bev if we are *back together* now, but I realize tonight may only be a one-time deal for her, at least until her ex is finally stopped.

She makes tea for us, like old times. And I muse to myself how in college and in love, *old times* can be only a matter of days. We sit up in bed together, sipping the hot liquid, and I am not surprised by the waves of pleasure that wash through me as the tea enters my system.

"This never tastes as good when you're not with me," I say, and she nods and smiles.

"It's the same with me," she says.

I'm desperate to discuss how we feel about each other and how much I've missed her, but I don't want to ruin the evening and risk having her ask me to leave.

I'm pathetic, I know, but sometimes *pathetic* is exactly what love is.

"How were your dreams tonight?" she says. "Are they bothering you again?"

"They were horrible—the worst so far this evening. I dreamed that I killed someone."

She nods almost imperceptibly as she sips more of her tea.

After we finish our tea, she takes our cups to the kitchen while I wait in her bed and casually scan her room. On her dresser, a small wooden box catches my eye.

When she returns, she slides into bed and kisses me.

"What's that?" I ask, nodding toward her dresser.

She swivels her head to see what I'm talking about then lets out a long sigh.

"That's what he left me tonight. Inside is a handmade silver charm bracelet from Russia. One of a kind."

My brain goes numb as I remember the silver bracelet I found in her closet last week.

I want to say something, anything, to her. But I have no idea what to tell her or ask her as my mind processes conflicting thoughts and theories.

"He left that for you tonight?" I finally say, confused.

She doesn't say anything, but she nods.

I told you, my father grumbles in my head so loudly that I flinch.

Bev doesn't seem to notice my reaction. Instead, she reaches over, turns out the light on her nightstand, and darkness engulfs the room.

"Will you please spend the night," she asks. "I feel safer with you here, especially with *him* still out there. And Jim, I know I told you I didn't want you to do anything about him—that I would take care of things—but the truth is, I don't know how much longer I can stand this."

"It's okay. I'm here," is all I can manage to say as I turn on my side with my back facing her.

I pray I will wake up hours from now to discover Bev lying to me about the bracelet was only a dream—as much of a nightmare as the violent murder I committed earlier tonight.

My mind struggles to explain how the silver bracelet left by Evil Jim tonight could be the same one I found in her closet the week before.

But I know she has no answer to this.

My heart pounds faster instead of settling down as it should before sleep.

But how can I be calm? Why would Bev lie to me?

Think.

There must be a reason.

A ray of light burns through my mental clouds. Maybe she wanted an excuse to ask me over tonight—one that wouldn't require admitting she was wrong about our breakup.

That must be it.

But what if it isn't?

What if there is no evil ex-boyfriend at all, and Bev is a sociopath who enjoys toying with her lovers before she kills them?

That makes no sense, either.

This isn't a movie, and people don't go to these lengths for the sole purpose of being cruel. Real people have reasons for the things they do, even if those reasons seem crazy to everyone but them.

I try to review and parse through every detail I *think* I know about Bev, but my mind is sluggish and slows down as it gives into fatigue. I need sleep desperately, and I only have a few more moments of lucidity before I will be unconscious again.

The first night I stayed with Bev, Cynthia and Sally came to her bedroom door, and they both knew about Bev's ex and that his name was Jim. So that part must be true.

As I start to drift away, I can't keep my eyes from closing. But one last parting thought blinks on and off in my brain—a broken neon sign struggling for my full attention.

I stare at its message, and even though I don't know what to believe and what not to believe at this point, there are a few things the sign assures me are real.

Even if Bev lied about Evil Jim leaving the bracelet tonight, she *does* have an ex-boyfriend. His name *is* Jim. And for whatever reason, I think she wants me to hurt him.

Or worse.

PART TWO

BEVERLY

CHAPTER THIRTY-FIVE

Beverly Meets Mooken

PROFESSOR MOOKEN IS an amazing teacher. Intelligent, provocative with his theories, passionate about psychology, and dedicated to teaching. He is a large part of the reason I'm working on a double major in undergrad Russian and psychology.

Unfortunately for me, although he's a bit older than me, he also has broad shoulders and a comfortable way about him that's been drawing me to imagine him as more than just my teacher. But hey, I'm sure plenty of students have had a crush on Professor Mooken over the years.

To be honest, I don't think anything will come of it.

He's been my professor in two classes so far, but I've rarely spoken to him directly. Mostly, any communications have been through his TAs. But this semester, I've decided to get over my nervousness and talk to him one-on-one, at long last.

As soon as he finishes his first lecture in my Advanced Experimental Psych class, I stroll up to the podium where he's gathering his notes before I can chicken out.

"I loved the lecture," I say. "Especially the part about using real life as inspiration for psychology experiments. I mean, opportunities to learn and collect data are always around us."

Professor Mooken smiles and nods. Is he agreeing with me, the wide-eyed student, or only humoring me?

I study him and guess what's going on in his brain. He's not ignoring me. He's thinking. Processing.

"Yes, yes," he finally says, excited and focusing his dark eyes on me. "Tell me, what kind of experiment could *this* situation—a psychology class—inspire, do you think? Maybe we could have the students agree ahead of time to never laugh at their professor's jokes and see if he continues to make them. Or maybe we could ask everyone to laugh, but only when the professor says something dire and serious. But never when he's trying to be humorous. Do you think this would condition the professor to stop making jokes?"

He releases a great laugh from his chest. It's hardy, warm, and inviting. And I laugh along easily with him.

"Or we could try something more devious," I say.

"Please share your thoughts," he says. "I am intrigued."

"What if, every time the professor says something interesting and charming, the female students—and any gay men—pay rapt attention to him and fantasize about what it would be like to date their teacher. Meanwhile, the straight male students act irritated and angry because the professor's getting all the attention instead of them."

I don't think Professor Mooken was prepared for my suggestion. Brazen. Daring. And more than a little suggestive.

I savor the moment and wait until he is about to respond before I continue.

"Would that qualify as a valid experiment on operant conditioning?"

Mooken clears his throat and laughs. This time he speaks in a quiet voice.

"I suppose it would," he says as he puts his hand forward to shake. "You have an interesting mind, Miss…"

"Beverly McDane," I say. "But you can call me Bev."

He nods and shakes my hand with a firm, warm grip.

"Professor Benjamin James Mooken," he says. "At your service."

Then he leans forward and whispers to me.

"But I've never been a fan of the name *Benjamin*. It's too stodgy and reminds me of bald men flying kites. So, please. I'd much rather you call me *Jim*."

CHAPTER THIRTY-SIX

LUNCH

I MENTION MY encounter with Professor Mooken to my housemate, Cynthia, at dinner that night, and she shakes her head.

"Don't mess with a prof, girl. Nothing good can come of that shit."

"Well, maybe nothing long-term, but there are definitely some good short-term things that can come from getting to know him better."

She shakes her head again and bites into her burrito.

"Just don't get caught. The university's honor code frowns on student-teacher relationships."

She's right to warn me. But I'm fascinated with Jim on all levels. And college, as wonderful as it is, is *not* real life. A year after I graduate, my degree and my memories will be the only things from UVA worth anything to me. And the memories will last much longer than the value of my degree once I get started in whatever career I choose.

As Cynthia chews and ponders how stupid I'm being, I think about the next time I will get a chance to speak to Jim.

That following Tuesday, while he lectures on the topic of desensitization, he glances at me more than once. Nothing that lingers too long, but it's enough for me to get the message. He's interested. In what, I don't know yet. But in something.

After class, he slowly arranges his notes, giving me plenty of time to approach him at the podium.

"Hello, Bev," he says with a warm smile.

"Jim," I say, flashing my own smile. "I have a few questions about the lecture. And I'm also starving. Any chance you have lunch open today to talk, or do professors not eat?"

I see him weigh his decision. He fiddles with his hands as he debates whether he wants to take the plunge into whatever this crazy student of his is trying to reel him into. It doesn't take long, however, before he agrees.

Five minutes later, we're walking across the Grounds, heading for the Cavern—my favorite lunch-time hangout.

While we nibble on our sandwiches, I struggle to say anything coherent, and so does he. Because we are both too busy looking into each other's eyes.

Then I remember the topic of his lecture. *Desensitization.*

"I understand how desensitizing someone to a certain stimulus can help them overcome their fear of, say…spiders or heights," I say. "But what about the other way around? Doesn't desensitization have a role in addiction? Or in people who continue to make the same kinds of bad decisions over and over again?"

He scrunches his eyebrows as he chews on his club sandwich.

After he swallows, he sips from his water and tilts his head.

"Be more specific about people making bad decisions, please."

"Let's say someone shoplifts a cheap piece of costume jewelry. It's small, fits into their pocket easily. The person doesn't care too much about what she's taking, but she loves the adrenaline rush afterward. And the item costs less than five bucks, so even if she's caught, it won't be a felony. She'll receive a slap on the hand and maybe be banned from the store. Great. Now let's say she steals something cheap again the next time, expecting the same adrenaline surge. But her theft doesn't give her the same thrill as before. So, the next time, she steels a more expensive item from a nicer store. And assuming she gets away with it, she receives the adrenaline bump she was seeking. She keeps on escalating her crimes as she continues to chase the old high. The next thing she knows, she's a full-blown diamond burglar."

Jim explodes in subdued but genuine laughter, almost expelling the food from his mouth. He covers his mouth with his napkin, and his eyes are wet in a good way.

I join in and have one of the best laughs I've had all year.

We banter back and forth about what I would do with all the money from my career as a professional thief and then slip into a mutual silence.

We pick at our food before he looks up at me again.

"I'm having a very nice time chatting with you. I hope it's okay I tell you that."

"I am too," I say with a smile and flushed cheeks. "And it's very okay that you tell me so."

I'm sure he can feel the connection between us. And if he's experiencing anything close to what I am, he's got electricity shooting all through his central nervous system.

And as I'm sitting there, thinking of all the possibilities of what *this* might become, he says the words I was not expecting.

"I should warn you that I'm married," he says. "On paper, at least—even though our lives don't intersect much anymore."

And there it is.

At least he's being honest about it, which is more than most guys would do in his position.

I give him a tight-lipped smile, unsure of how to reply.

His eyes are sad, like he wishes he hadn't told me what he just has.

I should thank him for the interesting lunch, walk out, and not look back. But instead, I want to see where this ride will take me.

"Would your wife mind if you had lunch with a student considering pursuing her master's degree in psychology?"

He smiles, and some of the sadness leaves his eyes.

"No, I suppose she wouldn't."

And that is how Tuesdays become *our* day.

We don't want his TAs or the other students catching on, so we stagger our exits from the classroom and meet at the Cavern, arriving separately. That was my idea, actually. Although when I look back, it was probably part of his plan all along, and he only let me think it was mine.

Jim Mooken doesn't play checkers, but it turns out he loves the game of chess. And our lunches are where we both make our opening gambits.

Surprisingly, we play our game an entire month before giving into our basest desires and engaging in that which we're both really after.

CHAPTER THIRTY-SEVEN

SOMETHING MORE

SADNESS RETURNS TO Jim's eyes at lunch today.

"What's wrong?" I ask, speaking quietly so he knows whatever he tells me will be a secret between us.

"It's become difficult for me to...restrain myself around you," he says. "It's not right for me to feel this way, but I...when I'm with you, I am a different man. A better man. Certainly a happier man."

He looks at me, sheepish, almost coy, afraid of what my reaction will be.

But how can he wonder?

He's married, and that presents a problem for our future. But I'm *not* married.

I'm not even seeing anyone.

If we move forward with what I'm sure we're both thinking, he will be committing adultery. But the worst I'll be doing is exercising poor judgment.

This will be his sin, his decision. So I wait, letting him sort through his issues.

When we finish our lunch, instead of going our separate ways like usual, I follow him back to his office. The entire way, my heart pounds painfully, and my mouth goes dry.

This doesn't make me feel very attractive. But my mind and body are pumping so many naturally made hormones and drugs into my system, I almost stumble down the steps leading to Gilmer Hall.

Once we're inside his office, he locks the door, and we are immediately on top of each other—living a scene from a movie. When his lips meet mine, they are tender despite his urgency. After our initial kiss, I press into him, and we begin exploring each other without hesitation.

With a single move, he places me on the edge of his desk and gives me a serious look—pausing for a brief moment of caution and sanity as he asks me a silent question.

Do I really want to go through with this?

My decision has been made since the beginning, and I pull him to me.

Part of the thrill of our first time together is trying to maintain our balance on his desk without making too much noise. Shadows pass outside his office like dark apparitions peeking under his door before they continue on their way.

They remind me his career and his marriage are on the line.

But my college enrollment is also at risk because I am certainly *not* being taken advantage. I am here because I want to be, and I am all in. But the risks we are both taking only amp up the experience.

With most guys I've been with, I've been the only one concerned with my pleasure. But not with Jim. My satisfaction is his top priority. Maybe it's because he's a considerate lover. Or maybe because he's older than the *boys* I've dated by almost twenty years.

Either way, it's wonderful.

He expertly brings me to a place where wave after wave washes through my body and soul, and I have to open my eyes at one point to remember where I am.

He drugs me with my own endorphins and oxytocin. And I love it.

As the waves crest higher and their fury increases, I laugh inside when I recall Jim's lecture about desensitization. Because there's no way I could ever get used to this kind of stimulus.

Soon, my sea of joy turns explosive and combustive, and the ocean crashes over me, sending me flying toward an earth-shattering release.

I wrap my arms around him and clench tightly. I'm still on the cusp when he kisses me deeply, and my body reacts.

And holy shit.

We buck and shiver like two wild creatures fused together in a world of warmth.

Afterward, all is still and quiet, other than our huffing and puffing as we try to normalize our breathing.

We should say something to mark this occasion—should express some profound emotion to each other. But it's too soon for that. Instead, he kisses my neck, and we remain pressed against one another.

I love that he's in no rush to end our union. Compared to my last boyfriend, who enjoyed his post-coital nap more than the sex itself, Jim's intensity and attention are welcomed.

More than that, they're sexy as hell.

CHAPTER THIRTY-EIGHT

Love

AT FIRST, JIM and I are content eating lunch on Tuesdays and having sex for dessert in his office. But each time gets better and better, and after the first few occasions, he coyly suggests someplace more…comfortable.

I never thought I'd be a man's *chicken on the side.* But it soon becomes normal to stand outside the Days Inn, waiting for Jim to get a room for us.

He pays with cash so his wife won't find out and encourages me to stay and enjoy the room long after he's left to return to his family.

I don't like this part at all, but I get it. I knew what I was getting into when I started with him, but after the first month, it becomes hard to deal with. I tell my heart to remain neutral about him, that this is all my choice. I could leave him at any time.

But the reality is I don't consider it at all. Not even once.

One day, we're making love in the clean, crisp sheets of the hotel's Queen-sized bed.

I know he's not keeping score—or at least I don't think he is—but after three orgasms in a row, I can barely breathe.

My skin is covered in a thin gloss of sweat, and as we lie there in bed with my head on his chest and his arm draped across my shoulder, I've never been happier or more relaxed.

That's when I glance up at him.

"I love you," I tell him without thinking about it.

It's one of the strange things about us humans. When a feeling is strong enough, we're not very good at holding it in, even when we should.

Telling him that I love him is one thing, but waiting for him to say it back seems to last an hour. When he finally opens his mouth, I almost pass out from holding my breath.

But, at last, he answers.

"I love you too," he says, and we lie there, holding each other close for another hour.

Eventually, he turns to me, brushes my face delicately with his hand, and frowns.

"I have to leave," he says. "I know this sucks, Bev. But it won't be like this forever."

It's late in the afternoon on a Tuesday, and he has to return to his wife and kids, but when he gets up to go home for dinner, my heart cracks. I can't expect anything from him, but my insides don't understand this, and from that day forward, all my heart wants to know is when he plans on leaving his wife.

"Can't you stay a little longer?" I say. "It's still early, and I don't want to be alone, babe."

"I can't, Bev. I don't know what else to say. Cathy's expecting me."

He rarely talks about his wife. All I know is that her name is Cathy. She's shy and quiet and not interested in Jim's work or in psychology at all. They were childhood sweethearts who married too early, and in their thirty years together, I'm the first *other woman* he's been with. Or so he says.

"I've been tempted before," he's told me. "But the potential for loss was never worth the potential for gain. Until now. Until you."

I remember his words as he starts to leave. And that helps a little. But when he looks at my face, he can see how stressed and unhappy I am.

He grimaces and sets a small plastic prescription bottle on the nightstand.

"This will take the edge off if things get too difficult," he says. "There are two in there, but I suggest taking only one."

"What is it?" I say, my eyes shifting from him to the bottle.

I trust Jim with all my heart, but I've never been a fan of taking meds of any kind if I can avoid it.

His laugh is warm and genuine.

"It's only Xanax," he says. "Think of it like Valium but faster acting. Don't take it before you drive, though, until you know how it affects you. Maybe have one and settle in for a nap here, then go home later, okay? You know I love you and miss you already, don't you? I'm only giving you these to help when I can't be here with you."

He leans over and kisses me, and for the moment, his lips and his words settle my heart, ease my pain, and dull my ache. But when he leaves, my hurt returns, and no amount of free Netflix can stop me from crying.

The Xanax he's left behind is an entirely different matter.

I stare at it like it's a monster ready to pounce if I open the vial. But the pain inside gnaws at me, relentless. Eventually, I crawl across the bed, and for the first time in my life, I take a drug that hasn't been prescribed to me by a doctor.

I wash it down with some water and lie back in the hotel bed, thinking about how I got to this place with Jim. One small decision after another led to my current situation. There's no place I want to be more than in his arms, and there's also no situation I wish would end more than the one we're in.

I close my eyes and let the gray sands of weariness wash over me. After fifteen minutes of lying still and wondering what's wrong with me, my limbs turn fuzzy and weightless. And soon, I fall into a deep sleep.

CHAPTER THIRTY-NINE

REALITY

THE FIRST YEAR with Jim is filled with more fun than pain, especially since he always has a new bottle of pills for me when I get too stressed about things.

I graduate with a double major and am no longer his student. But even though this should make things easier between us, he still hasn't left his wife.

Do I leave him like any sane person would?

No.

Instead, I become his graduate TA. It's something both of us want. Even though he's the reason I first got into psychology, I love the discipline as much as he does now. And it's because of my own desires that I find myself still at UVA studying for a double master's in cognitive psychology and Russian studies.

That's a lot of work, but I live with a bunch of great girls, and since I'm not out partying and looking for men, I have more than enough time to study. Also, Room 436 of the Days Inn is a perfect place to work on my thesis material and to ponder my life, which is now even more closely tied with Jim than ever before.

I accompany him to staff functions like I'm his wife, even though I'm not.

I know all the professors, and they know me, and it feels like our relationship is out in the open.

But it isn't. Not really.

He presents me as his protégé, and I'm accepted by his peers as such. I like being known as a gifted student of psychology, but I suffer from an extreme case of imposter syndrome. And at my core, I am a lovesick young woman caught up with an older man—one who's wonderful and loving but not completely mine.

As the semester goes by, I bring up the topic of him leaving his wife more and more often. And when I do, he wants to talk about it less and less.

Soon, we fall into a rut.

The sex is still good when it happens. But often, after spending a day or evening together, he leaves to go home without us having any intimate contact at all. I'm left alone in a hotel room with nothing other than my schoolwork and some Xanax to keep me company.

I wonder what kind of marriage he and Cathy have that she doesn't worry about her husband, who is gone so often from home. For all I know, she's having an affair of her own and is happy that Jim's giving her plenty of time to indulge in her own tryst.

But when I mention this to Jim as a possibility one night, he shakes his head, aggravated.

"I wish that were the case. It would make things so much easier," he says. "But she isn't. I know her, and that's not how she is."

I laugh openly when he says this. Men always think they can tell.

It would never happen to me, they think. *I know when someone's lying to me.*

This, of course, is total bullshit.

Someone as smart as Jim should know better.

"She's happy staying home, reading and watching television," he says. "She thinks I'm working extra hours, trying to make tenure."

The more he protests, the more I think I'm right. He's not the only one unhappy in their marriage. And how could *she* be happy? Jim is with me more than her.

When he leaves, I lie in the Days Inn and contemplate swallowing a few extra tablets of Xanax, so my brain can float away on a comfortable cloud. I reach for the pills, but before I take them, I review the numerous conversations I've recently had with Jim about our future, marriage, and having children together one day.

He says he wants all of that with me. He wants what I want. He wishes things were different.

Although he doesn't seem capable of initiating a divorce with Cathy, he needs me as much as I need him. Maybe even more.

CHAPTER FORTY

A Decision

WHEN SPRING BREAK rolls around that next semester, I find myself in the same hotel bed, still thinking the same thoughts, while everyone else is at a beach. And as I lie there, I decide it's finally time to act.

Like my mom once told me—to get what you want in this world, sometimes you have to stick your neck out and go for it.

I check out of the room early, and the kid at the front desk gives me a confused look.

"Something's come up," I tell him as I return my key and hurry out the door and into the night before my courage abandons me.

Fifteen minutes later, I pull into a faculty space outside of Gilmer Hall and walk up to the side entrance of the building.

Jim would be furious if he knew I was about to snoop around his office. But I'm desperately in love, and I will risk his anger.

There's no one here to see me enter Gilmer Hall in the middle of the night. Even if there were, it's not like I'm breaking in. I have the keys to the place since I'm his TA. Actually, I've had a copy of them since Jim and I started our affair.

I lock the door behind me and proceed down the hall to Jim's office—a familiar setting I know better than his classroom.

The key to his office slides in easily, and I turn the doorknob, half expecting him to jump out at me when I enter. But his office is empty. When I flick on the lights, I realize this is the first time I've been in here by myself.

I check his coat closet, in case there is anything of use in one of his jacket pockets, but I find nothing.

As I step up to his chair, I'm careful about what I touch and what I move so I don't disturb the film of dust covering everything other than his desk and his monitor.

And that's fine because I'm not looking for any secrets about his life. I'm only trying to find his address, something that's usually easy to discover on the Internet.

But in Jim's case, I've not successfully been able to uncover that one simple thing. I know his home is in nearby Crozet, an area just outside Charlottesville proper. But other than that, I'm clueless.

My first hope is to find a piece of mail addressed to him or some other paperwork he's left in the open. But, for such a messy office, his desk is surprisingly clear. I hesitate, then slide open his top desk drawer, which is not locked. Why would it be when he locks his office? I find the standard mish-mash of items, loose change, and paper clips. My heart warms when I find a photo of my face. One of the things I love about Jim is his old-fashioned nature. He is by no means out of touch with the times, but he values a physical photo more than an image on his phone.

I settle into his leather office chair and inhale. His lingering scent comforts me, and I start to hum before I catch myself and get back to business. When I check his side drawer, it's locked.

I try all the keys on the key chain he gave me, but none of them fit the lock on the drawer.

I open the drawer on the other side of his desk and hit pay dirt—a stack of bills. Power, phone, and Internet.

Exactly what I was looking for.

I consider sifting through his bills to learn anything else I can about this man I love, but I don't. Because good, solid relationships are built on trust above all else, and I've intruded enough on his privacy tonight.

I snap a photo of his address as it's listed on his phone bill, then close the drawer and leave.

Five minutes later, I am in my car, driving to Crozet.

As the headlight of an oncoming car lights my face, I wonder if my actions tonight will ruin my entire world or make it better. There is no way to know until I go through with this.

Soon I am in his neighborhood, the house numbers increasing on my right by twos, until I finally arrive at his house. His old BMW is parked in the driveway, but it's the only car here, which makes me wonder if Cathy is even home.

I approach the front door. My throat is scratchy and dry, and I can barely swallow. I take a deep breath and exhale slowly as I ring the doorbell.

At first, there's no response. But when I ring it a second time, the doorknob turns, and the door swings inward.

Jim stands there, his eyes wide and animal-like. This is the most surprised I've ever seen him, this man who is always in control of everything. He looks almost unreal, a different person than I'm used to seeing.

"Bev?" he says, confused.

"We need to talk," I say.

He looks like he wants to protest, but I push my way in, and he steps aside, defeated.

"Where's Cathy and your kids?" I say, since he told me he would be spending the evening with his family.

He shakes his head.

"They're not here."

Great.

I'm glad the kids are gone, but I'd hoped for an all-out discussion that would include his wife. Still, I'm here, and I'm not going to leave until I deliver the ultimatum I came up with on my drive over.

It's either her or me. He has to decide.

My nostrils flare, and I get ready to spill my heart and make my demands, but before I do, I look around and really *see* his home.

It's cluttered and dense, packed with artifacts, books, and dust. Just like his office. And a sudden realization blazes into my mind like a match being struck in the pitch darkness of night.

This is the home of a bachelor.

Jim lives here by himself.

I step over to his messy but expensive leather sofa covered in books and papers, and I glare at him.

"When did Cathy leave you?"

He glances at his feet and shakes his head. I wait for him to answer, but for once, he is speechless.

I can tell he is desperately searching for the right thing to say that will placate me, the crazy woman who's intruded on his castle. He opens his mouth, but whatever's about to come out is going to be a lie.

A sudden possibility digs into my stomach—a rusty dagger of pain that guts me.

"Is Cathy a real person, Jim? Are you even married?"

To my surprise, he answers truthfully, maybe for the first time since I've known him.

"No, Beverly. I have, unfortunately, never been married."

"Kids?"

He shakes his head.

Tears fill my eyes at his blatant admission. I came here ready to lay it all on the line, for better or worse, but I never imagined the night would be this horrible.

I turn and leave before tears can roll down my cheeks, but then I stop myself.

This isn't over yet.

"I thought you loved me," I say. "But this whole time, you were lying to me? You are such an asshole."

His face takes on a stern look like he's about to lecture me.

"I did love you," he says. "I *do* love you. But it's difficult being in a romantic relationship with someone who has your…afflictions. God knows I've tried."

"What afflictions?"

"We both know," he says. "It's not my place to diagnose you. I'm too close for you to be my patient, but…"

"There is nothing wrong with me," I say, struggling not to yell. "I'm certainly not crazy. I'm just pissed off!"

"You're right. You are absolutely *not* crazy. Although you know how much I hate that word. But I will say, if I had to guess, you may be suffering from BPD or are at least close to developing into that."

"Borderline personality disorder? Don't try to blame this situation on me. Maybe I have some emotional issues. Sure. Who doesn't? But you…you're a flaming narcissist. A textbook example. And you know it."

As soon as I accuse him, he disconnects from our conversation. I see it in his eyes—a light snuffing itself out. For him, our discussion is over, but I'm not ready to let go. Not this easily.

"Why did you lie about Cathy and about having children?"

He shrugs casually, like he doesn't give a shit about me anymore.

I hate him.

"Cathy and the kids were my security blanket," he says. "I was going to tell you the truth once I was *sure* about us, but then you started harassing me about leaving my wife. You have been relentless."

"But you aren't married!" I yell.

"But *you* didn't know that, did you? And that's what counts. If you'd only been more…well, stable about things, I would have told you everything. And who knows where we'd be right now. But the truth is, I need someone who is steady and reliable. As it is…"

"As *what* is?" I say.

He gives me a closed-lip, fake smile and steps over to an antique roll-top desk. When he turns back to me, he's holding an orange-tinted medicine bottle filled with pills but with no label.

"This should hold you over until you can get yourself under someone's proper care. I did my best to treat you without actually treating you. And that was my mistake. But I can't do it anymore. It goes against my ethics. I suggest you try someone at University Health. They should be able to set you up with someone qualified and available to help. I'm so very sorry."

"What are you saying?"

"I thought that was obvious," he says. "Other than when we must communicate because of our professional relationship, I'm afraid this has to be *goodbye*."

I have so many questions and accusations I want to throw at him, but I'm crushed and can't believe he's the one breaking it off with *me* after he was the one caught lying.

"Fine," I say, enraged and stunned. "But don't expect me to keep quiet about us because you're too chicken-shit to work things out."

His face takes on a dangerous tint, and his mouth hardens.

"Do not forget you were complicit in everything we've done. Yes, I might have to move to a different university if you cause too much of a problem. But I'm established in my field, and it will be no effort for me to find a new academic home. But you…you don't even have an advanced degree yet. What do you think the university will do to you if our past affairs become public? At a minimum, they will kick you out of school, and you'd better hope no one ever asks me for a reference letter. Am I making myself totally clear?"

I glare at him, but he and I both know he has me beat once again. I have a lot more I want to tell him, but I force my mouth to remain closed. The fight is over for tonight.

But things between us are far from settled.

CHAPTER FORTY-ONE

A New Bev

I SIT ON my bed—my *real* bed in my real room. My housemates are gathered down the hall in the living room. They know something's up because it's Sunday, and I'm here with them and not with *him*.

Eventually, my stomach grumbles enough that I go to the kitchen to make a grilled cheese sandwich. Cynthia and Trisha join me almost immediately. They've been waiting, hovering like good friends, until I emerge from my solitary confinement.

"Hi, babe," Cynthia says as she gives me a side hug.

Her sudden touch is enough to topple me from my carefully constructed perch. Heat wells uncontrollably in my chest. I am sad, angry, and embarrassed all at the same time.

What was it that Cynthia told me when I started this with Jim two years ago?

Nothing good can come of it.

"You were right," I say, embracing her.

What takes place after that is what only good friends can pull off. The three of us make grilled cheese sandwiches together as a team while I tell them the basics of what's going on.

"He's such a jerk," Cynthia says.

"Oh my God, he was using you," Trisha says.

Trisha is right. He was using me, but it still hurts when she says it.

"What about his wife?" Cynthia asks in a quiet voice. "Did you meet her?"

Her question is more than I can take, even from good friends with pure intentions.

I choke out my reply.

"He was never married," I say. "He used that as an excuse to keep me at a distance. He never intended me to be anything other than his…you know."

Their eyes go wide, and their mouths open in shock.

I turn away, set down my half-eaten sandwich, and return to my room.

I fall into bed, wishing I could sleep. I'm tired enough, for sure, but my brain won't stop obsessing over everything I've believed to be true for the last two years.

Each incident I replay and unravel in my head changes with the new information I now possess. When Jim said he had plans for Christmas with his family, he was lying. He opted to spend that holiday alone or maybe with another woman, but *not* with me.

The best-case scenario is that he spent his free time with his professor buddies if he even has any of those.

Then I wonder if he knows Professor Sulke.

Shit. Of course he does.

I worry not only about what Jim may do to make my life miserable as his TA but also about what he might tell my Russian studies professor. I spend a dark hour daydreaming and imagining Jim destroying all aspects of my academic life, forcing me to quit school so he can be rid of me and move on to his next conquest.

My door squeaks open, and my bed compresses as someone sits beside me.

"I know you want to be alone," Cynthia says, "but if there's anything we can do. Anything *I* can do. I'm here for you. We all are."

I nod but don't turn around to face her. I don't want her to see my puffy face. After a few minutes, the bed returns to normal, my door shuts, and my internal musings continue.

Mainly, I focus on how the hell I'm going to get through class on Tuesday.

Hi, Professor Mooken. How are you today? Did you have a good weekend?

These are the questions I always ask him in front of the other

TAs on Tuesday mornings, even though I'm sure they suspect I already know his answers.

But on this coming Tuesday, I *won't* know.

And I won't give a damn.

As the hours pass, my spirit rallies here and there as I try to convince myself I have nothing to worry about.

Jim should be the one who's worried. He should be worried about *me*.

If nothing else, one phone call to the head of the Psych Department or the Dean would put more than a kink in his plans for tenure here.

No matter what he claims.

After all, in today's world, he'd be held accountable. He's the one with the power. Not me.

But I'd still suffer. There's no way I'd escape without some form of hefty repercussions.

Worse, I'd have to tell my parents, which would be horrible.

I lie in my bed, alternating between extravagant scenarios where I wring the life out of Jim with my bare hands and dreams where I watch him stand trial in front of the university's Honor Committee as he's forced to admit the truth in front of his peers.

And mine.

No, I won't give him the satisfaction of destroying my life. I will be stronger than that, and he can go to hell and watch as I move on without him.

Eventually, I roll over and see Cynthia left my half-eaten sandwich on my end table. The bread is hard, but much like vengeance, the sandwich tastes good cold.

The food lands uncomfortably in my stomach, but the nutrition helps. I get up, wobble to the bathroom, and open the bottle of Xanax Jim gave me. I hate him for doing that, but I'm also relieved to have enough pills to help me get through this.

I take two and return to bed. Within half an hour, at last, I fall asleep.

When I wake up hours later, my head is fuzzy, and for a brief moment, I wonder if what happened this weekend was only a bad dream.

But as my brain comes online, I know for certain everything was real.

Yesterday, I was a woman ready to march into her man's personal life and stake my claim. By the night's end, I'd learned it was all a lie.

I force myself to leave my room and join the others in the living room, watching the Food Network. I get hugs all around, even from Cynthia's boyfriend, Dan, who whispers to me what an asshole Jim is and how stupid he is to let go of someone as awesome as me.

His words help, surprisingly. And for the first time since Saturday night I feel positive about my future and about the possibility of falling in love again someday.

Not anytime soon, for sure, but one day maybe.

When I go to bed late that night, I pop another couple of Xanaxes and sleep soundly.

Monday morning starts the week like any other—stressful and busy. But I make it to my Russian class and manage to work on my thesis in Alderman Library that afternoon with all the other students—our heads bowed and our Air Buds tightly wedged into our ears.

By the time I leave the library for home, I am confident I can do this.

I am strong.

But when Monday night arrives, I lie in bed and explore horrible scenarios about what the following day will bring.

Once again, I drink my tea and take my pills. But on this night, nothing helps me sleep.

CHAPTER FORTY-TWO

A New Jim

"LET'S TALK ABOUT love," Jim says to the class.

I correct my thinking immediately. This man is no longer *Jim* to me. From now on, he is Mooken, Professor Mooken, or *asshole.*

For years, I thought he wanted me to call him *Jim* because it was a personal name, one reserved only for me. Now I'm pretty sure he wanted me to call him that so people wouldn't immediately know I was fucking my psych advisor when I mentioned my *boyfriend's* name.

My brain is all over the place as Mooken goes on about his caveman-like views of love. I've heard this lecture plenty of times, both in and out of the classroom.

I could recite it by heart.

It's a regular part of his curriculum, but I can't help thinking he's giving this particular lecture today as a message to me. Telling me to get over it—that what we had was a result of operant conditioning and nothing more.

Well, fuck you, Jim.

I correct my thoughts once again.

Fuck you, *Professor Mooken.*

"Do rats fall in love?" he muses behind his podium.

Evidently not, I think as I focus on the two rodents in the cage at the front of the class. When Mooken raises the partition and electrifies the cage floor, the rats start to have sex.

He glances at me. Making a point.

Yes, I get it.

That's all we are—rats in a cage rutting with whoever happens to be there at the right place and time. Or whenever the proper level of electrical shock is applied.

I close my eyes, flare my nostrils, and seethe.

Through my hatred, I sense someone else watching me, and I almost laugh.

There's an entire classroom sitting behind me, and half of them are male. I'm not the most beautiful woman in the world, but enough guys have come on to me over the years that I'm pretty sure at least a few of Mooken's students have fantasized about having sex with me.

It's what guys do.

Mooken finishes his demoralizing drivel about love and starts pinging the class on their upcoming lab reports. With the proper level of anxiety and stress instilled in his students, he finishes class with a reminder about the Classics in Psychological Thrillers film series tomorrow—the one I stupidly agreed to honcho when he and I were a happy couple. Back when I would have said *yes* to anything he asked.

He motions to me and goads the class into applauding my efforts with the movies.

How embarrassing.

I knew it would be awkward with him today, but I wasn't prepared for this.

As I turn around part-way in my chair, someone claps louder than the rest of the class. I raise my hand, expending the least amount of effort that Mooken will acknowledge as a wave to the students.

Or so I think.

But Mooken looks down at me, challenging me, daring me to behave like nothing has happened between us. Like everything is fine.

Reluctant, I stand and face the class full-on, even though several of the students are already packing up their laptops, preparing to leave.

I take a deep breath and tell them about the movie.

"*A Clockwork Orange*," I say. "Tomorrow's film is a tender

romance about a gang terrorizing the English countryside in their search for love."

My plot summary isn't completely accurate, but it's not incorrect, either. I'm sure Mooken wants more from me, but he can take what I give him and stuff it down his throat.

Before I finish, I throw out a half-ass request for volunteers to help me run the show tomorrow. I could do it on my own, but I don't feel like expending that level of energy right now.

When I finish my pitch, I sit down and start packing my backpack, eager to get the hell out of there.

My muscle memory kicks in as I remember how I used to look forward to lunch with Professor Mooken on Tuesdays. But those days are gone forever.

Amidst my thoughts of gloom, a guy walks up and stands—no, hovers—in front of me. His shadow is so large it blocks the glare from the classroom lights.

You're standing a little too close, Junior, I think to myself, but when he offers to help with the movie, I force a smile and thank him. After all, it's not his fault I'm in a shitty mood.

While the guy stammers, trying to say something else, I can't help but notice his face. The edges are rounder than I usually like. Still, something about him makes me want to trust him, which is weird and unexpected since I don't feel like I could trust *anyone* at this point in my life.

Especially not a man.

"Do you have a minute to talk on your way out," he finally asks me. "It's…semi-private."

I am neither intrigued nor frightened, but I agree to walk with him—anything to help me escape the classroom without interacting with Mooken.

When I stand up, ready to leave, I take a small amount of solace when Mooken gives me the eye, wondering, perhaps, why and where I'm going with this young man.

The guy opens the door for me, which is fine. But, once again, he moves in too close to me.

Outside in the fresh fall air, I've escaped one man but now must deal with another.

I stop walking, turn to face the guy, and wait for him to state his case. Inside, I wonder how long it will take before he asks me out. The sooner, the better, so I can turn him down and be on my way.

He starts his pitch, telling me he suffers from intense, dark nightmares—that he doesn't sleep well.

Welcome to the club, bro.

"I was thinking I should see a therapist, but I can't afford one," he says. "I was wondering if you had any time to talk. Maybe I could buy you a meal, and you could point me to some books that might help me? Or give me some advice. What do you say?"

I've been asked out in less creative ways, and I'm not in the mood for anything he can offer. Although, from what I can see, he *is* suffering from a severe lack of sleep. The dark, puffy circles under his eyes. The manic glint reflected in his pale blue irises. Something in him is sad *and* honest. And both are sort of refreshing.

I clear my throat and address him in my most professional tone.

"I *cannot* give you free therapy if that's what you're asking. I couldn't give you therapy even if you paid me. I don't have my degree, and I'm far from being licensed to practice. Plus, you're one of Mooken's students. As such, I'm sure you remember what Freud said about dreams since we studied it a few weeks ago. He said dreams were direct products of our unconscious minds and that interpreting them holds the keys to all personal understanding and knowledge."

The guy takes a moment and pauses, considering what I've told him. But mostly he's taken aback because I haven't responded to his invitation to share a meal with him yet.

I nod and turn away. My work here is done. But before I bolt, my damn humanity kicks in, and I feel bad for him.

And while I stew in my indecision, I make the mistake of asking him for his name.

"Jim," he says.

I laugh. Of course his name is *Jim*. If I were religious, I'd think God was showing me her shitty sense of humor. Or that meeting this student was an omen.

Instead, I'm barely amused by the coincidence.

"I have a meeting with Professor Mooken right now," I say, even though I don't.

To the new Jim's credit, he accurately reads my lack of interest, and his face drops like someone who's just lost his dog to cancer. Once again, I'm weak, and I waver from my escape plan.

I soften my rebuke.

"Look, maybe one day we can grab lunch after class and talk about your dreams, but my schedule is crazy right now, so it might be a while. Definitely not today."

As soon as I say that, a spark of hope blossoms in his eyes, and once again, he thinks he has a chance with me.

"In the meantime, you should try student health," I say, trying to refocus him away from me.

It is not this guy's fault I want to get away from him and head back home. But as I give him a half wave goodbye, a brilliant, devilish idea erupts in my head. My thought is irresponsible, for sure. But I'm long past worrying about the subtle points of ethics.

"You could ask Professor Mooken for help," I say. "He doesn't practice right now, but you never know. He might talk with you off-the-record. Maybe he could recommend a therapist who specializes in your issues."

Mooken hates when students ask him for therapy—unless they happen to be young, sexy co-eds, of course. But right now, annoying Mooken sounds wonderful—the best idea I've had all day. And any amount of pain I can send his way won't be nearly enough.

CHAPTER FORTY-THREE

A Taste of Death

I STAND OUTSIDE Gilmer Hall that night, staring at the building like it's a dead relative—one I hate but also miss.

When the side entrance door clicks and unlatches, I step back into the shadows as Mooken and a female student emerge from the building. She waits while he locks the door, and I get a good look at her face in the moonlight.

I recognize her from Mooken's Tuesday-Thursday lectures. I can't remember her name, but she's tall, dark, athletic in the most feminine of ways, and unarguably *hot.* I don't even like women that way, and I'd still have sex with her just to see what it would be like.

The woman grins and struts next to Mooken, who wears a face of smug satisfaction.

But strangely enough, I don't detect the look of love on the woman's face. Only happy, fulfilled lust.

Once they go their separate ways, I force myself to approach the building, moving closer to it with tentative steps. I linger near the door, pretending to play with an app on my phone. After five minutes of silence, I unlock the door and step into Gilmer's all-too-familiar halls.

I navigate to Mooken's door on autopilot and stand so close that I'm almost touching it. I hold the key to his office in my palm and wonder if it still works or if he's already changed the lock.

When I turn the key and step inside, the musk and the remnants of heat from Mooken and that woman slap me in the face. There's no doubt in my mind that they were fucking in here. Plain and simple.

Tears threaten to fill my eyes, and a familiar burning anger boils in my stomach. He didn't wait even a week after our breakup before he started having sex with someone else. Or maybe he was already fucking her before our breakup. That wouldn't surprise me at all.

The last time I was in Mooken's office alone, I felt guilty looking through his desk. Now, I feel entitled. I sit in his chair like I own his office, and I curl my lip at the stench from the two of them that has yet to dissipate.

I try his side drawer. It's still locked. I pull on it a few times, but it doesn't give, and I decide to save it for later. I'm not sure what I'm looking for, but I'll know it when I find it.

I re-check his other side drawer and find more bills. Nothing I care about.

I stand up and study his messy office.

A jade statuette of the Buddha is covered in dust, sitting on one of his shelves next to an old Samurai katana sword.

At my feet rests an old cedar chest. Its sides are dusty, but its top is not.

The chest opens right up, and I find something inside I wasn't expecting—a stack of old-school composition notebooks. At first, I wonder if this is where Mooken keeps the originals for his tests instead of storing them online like every other professor in the world.

But when I look closer, my heart speeds up, beating too fast.

On the cover of the first notebook, a name is scrawled in his signature wiggly script.

Amber.

It's not the most unique name, but it is one you tend to remember. And I'm positive there's an Amber in Mooken's lecture. It could be a coincidence, but I'd bet money in Vegas that Amber is the woman he just left with.

I want to open it, but I hesitate.

Mooken needs to suffer, not his students. And what if there are personal details about Amber in there? I start to place the notebook back where I found it, but then I see the next one in the pile is labeled with my name—*Beverly*—and my heart stops.

I open that notebook without hesitation and leaf through page after page of his scribbles and hand-drawn tables and graphs. The first entry is dated two years ago. I can't be sure, but this was around the time I first flirted with him after class—maybe even before that.

I expect to read a narrative about the two of us from the early days, back when he was still into me. But that is not what I find. His captured thoughts about me aren't even complete sentences. Instead, they're more like sterile laboratory notes.

Third-year student. History of personal therapy.
Above-average class performance.
Questionnaire indicator test—high potential for BPD.
Interested in psychology.
Attractive. Responds to humor.
Impulsive. Likely experimental in bed.
Perfect skin. Great smile.
Low-risk.
Single?

I arch my eyebrow at being referred to as low-risk. What does that even mean? I flip the page and find a blow-by-blow accounting of the first day we spoke. But once again, it's written not like the memories of a love-struck suitor but as lines from an academic dissertation.

I recognize the words. They are his and mine. They might not be exact quotations, but they're close enough and correct.

I speed-read through the pages until I arrive at our first lunch. All the topics we discussed are recorded here in detail.

Maybe this is only a product of his nature. After all, he *is* a professor of experimental psychology. Taking detailed notes and recording observations is how he interacts with the world.

The next page contains a graph he has added to on multiple

occasions. I discern this because the plotted points are penned in different colored inks.

The label for the Y axis makes me laugh, not because I'm amused, but because I'm in disbelief.

It is labeled *Orgasms*.

He kept track of my orgasms?

I tilt my head, not comprehending what I'm looking at.

Sometimes I felt he was trying to give me as many orgasms as possible. But I figured the man was a high achiever.

Plus, why in the world would I have complained about receiving too much sexual pleasure?

I flick through two more pages, skimming the text. His notes detail our sex life, including the positions we tried. At the end of the notes, he's penned a set of hypotheses in bold, blue ink. The first states:

Introduction of narrative-based fantasies=expected moderate increase in number/intensity of climaxes.

My mouth drops open as I remember the day he started talking *dirty* in bed. I thought he was loosening up, but it turns out it was all a part of an experiment I knew nothing about. My heart beats rapidly, and my breath grows labored as I read his next hypothesis.

Verbal reassurance of emotional bond=expected substantial increase in number/intensity of orgasms and subject's overall sexual satisfaction.

Bile floods my throat.

I'm not sure what hurts more—that he refers to me as his *subject* or the realization that when he told me he loved me, he was doing nothing more than changing a variable in his experiment.

Tears run down my cheeks. But they are not from sadness. These are tears of anger.

Was I really nothing more than research to him?

A way to test some sick sexual theory?

And for what purpose?

So he can better seduce the next student he wants to fuck?

I slam the notebook closed and open the one with Amber's name on its cover.

It's empty, and for some reason, that makes me feel better. But only a little.

I pick up the next notebook in the pile.

This one is labeled with the name *Susan*, from a year before he and I started dating. It's filled with the same types of entries that are in the notebook about me—records about what does and doesn't work for her in bed, along with graphs and annotations about their sexual escapades.

I don't want to read any more details about his past girlfriend, but I want to know how it ended with her. I turn to the last page of the notebook and read the final entry.

> *She wants me to leave my "wife," although I tell her I cannot do that. She threatens to turn me in to the university. It is time to end this. Remove everything she finds attractive about me. Stop being attentive. No more humor. Cancel lunches after class. Increase complaints about home life and job. Sharply reduce/stop climaxes.*

I pick the notebook about me again and page to the most recent entry. Much like with Susan, his notes describe how I've begun asking him more and more often about leaving his wife. After that, in black ink, the following words are underlined:

> *Begin weening?*

He may have written it as a question, but that piece of shit *wanted to break up* with me.

When I barged in on him at his house and discovered his wife and family were fake, all I did was give him a convenient excuse to do what he was already planning.

Breathing hard, I wonder again how I could have been so blind. I consider taking the notebook with me when I leave his office, but when I touch it, a wall rises inside me—a barrier of disgust that doesn't want anything to do with him.

I force myself to return all the notebooks to their places in the chest before slamming it shut.

I do the same to his office door and to the door as I leave Gilmer Hall. I am furious and hurt, and I'm not worried about someone seeing me leave Mooken's office after hours in a rage.

Let them look.

I have the moral high ground here, and searching through his office doesn't come close to whatever games he's been playing with me for the last two years of my life.

Half-way home, I am so mad I pop two Xanaxes to calm down. This won't be enough to erase my pain or my shame, but it's better than nothing.

When I finally make it to my house, I dash through the back door and avoid my housemates, who are in the living room watching television.

Once I am safely in my bedroom, I fall onto my bed and sob uncontrollably, my chest heaving. I thought I was out of tears, but I was wrong.

It takes me half an hour before I roll over and grab the bottle of Xanax from Mooken.

It would be so easy to choke down a few handfuls of these and let them wash away all my troubles for good. But with my luck, I'd wake up in a couple of hours, puke everything up, and feel like shit all day tomorrow.

Then again…

A *few* more of them won't hurt anything. And they *will* make everything hurt so very much less, even if it's only for a little while.

I give in and twist off the child-proof cap, tumble three of the little salmon-colored ovoids into my palm, and swallow them.

Or at least I *think* that's what I do.

Honestly, it's getting hard to tell exactly what's going on right now.

As I lay there, waiting for sleep—that little slice of death, as Edgar Allan Poe once called it—I fantasize about taking revenge on Mooken.

I struggle to flesh out the details of my vengeance, but there's no use. My brain turns fuzzy, about to go offline.

The last thing I see before I pass out is my hand clutching the orange plastic bottle again. My hands work the bottle cap, and all I can do is watch them—a movie-goer viewing her favorite actress perform her final scene.

And then, at last, blissfully, I sleep.

CHAPTER FORTY-FOUR

The Weekend

I DON'T WAKE up the next day until two in the afternoon. When I do, my heart is beating rapidly, and by the time I pry open my eyes, I'm lucky to be alive and to have somehow slept off my heavy drug use from the night before.

I get out of bed, drink a gallon of water, and throw up.

For once, I don't take any more Xanax. Instead, I force a piece of dry toast down my throat and crawl back into bed. I don't go to any classes that day, and I email Carl, telling him he'll have to fill in for me at the movie tonight. I'm sure I'll get shit from Mooken later, but I don't care. I spend the entire day and night at home, alone, in silence, contemplating my life and the paths I've chosen that have led me to this place.

The following day, I sleep in again and blow off Mooken's Thursday morning lecture. I need to adjust to a new norm and figure out a way to start going to his class again, but I'm too pissed off right now, and I need a breather.

I can already tell my days and especially my nights are going to be rough for the foreseeable future. And with the bottle of Xanax Mooken gave me almost empty, I start thinking about my next fix.

Luckily, Dan is more than happy to gain a new customer, and when I see him that evening, I order a big bottle of the stuff. I know I'm taking too much of it, but I'll worry about tapering off the drug some other time. Right now, the only plan I have is to stay as numb as possible until my heart stops feeling like it's riddled with rusty needles.

Friday's a little better, and I make it to my Russian studies class, but when the day is over, I buy a pack of cigarettes and amble like a zombie back to our house.

Once again, I pop two pills before I make it to the door.

As soon as I'm tucked away in my room, I start smoking. We're not supposed to smoke cigarettes, or anything else for that matter, in the house. But fuck it. I dare someone to complain.

The nicotine washes through me as the Xanax kicks in. Pretty soon, I'm chain smoking, lighting one cigarette from the cinders of the one before it.

I laugh because my actions are the definition of unhealthy coping and the exact opposite of what the textbooks says I should do.

I should go for a run. Involve myself in social activities. Break my routine. Hang out with close friends. See a movie. Avoid old stimuli.

Basically, I should try anything other than what I'm currently doing.

When I wake up Saturday morning, my mouth is dry and stale from smoking, but because of the Xanax, I ended up sleeping pretty well.

I stretch and consider taking a shower to wash the muck off me from the day before. But I don't. I still don't give enough of a shit to do that. Not yet.

Someone knocks softly at my door, and I tell them to go away without thinking twice.

"It's me," Cynthia says. "Are you okay in there? I know you're hurting right now, but I'm here if you want to hang out. All of us are. We're worried about you, sweety."

I sigh because she is sincerely concerned about me. All of my housemates are. But I'm not ready for them.

"I need to be alone," I say. "But thanks, Cyn. I love you."

"Love you, too," she says before her shadow under the door disappears, and she is gone.

Just like Mooken.

As my thoughts turn black, self-doubt and worry wring my stomach, and I think I'm going to throw up again.

Before I can, I run a glass of water from the bathroom sink and take two more Xans.

Thank God for Dan.

I crawl back under the sheets and shut my eyes. It only takes fifteen minutes before the drugs kick in.

When I wake up next, it's mid-afternoon.

I start crying and can't stop myself as my gut spasms, and my face goes full-on ugly.

At least this is good for me, I think. *Letting all this shit out and expressing sadness is healthy.*

That's the calm, rational side of me talking. But my other side has something to say as well.

Fuck him. I can't let him do this to me. I'm worth a lot more than this.

I wipe my face and blow my nose. I *am* worth more than Mooken ever thought I was, and I decide to start acting like it.

Re-energized in the moment, I roll out of bed, shower, change into fresh clothes, and escape out the back door without saying goodbye to anyone.

I'm not ungrateful for my friends, but I need to clear my head and my soul. And I need to be *alone* for that.

At first, the fresh air is too much for my system, and my stomach clenches again. It's so…*powerful* outside in the open. The scent of pine overloads my senses. But as I walk farther from my house, my breathing deepens, and I begin to feel a little better.

My feet take me where they will. I have no destination in mind, and I'm happy to let the blood rush through my veins and to move a little after spending too much time shut up in my room.

Step-by-step, I shed the lingering effects of my mood and the Xanax.

This is good, I think to myself. *I've had worse Saturdays.*

In fact, my weekends for the last couple of years—although sometimes wonderful—have also been stressful.

Some weekends I managed to do something with the girls or work on my papers. But mostly, I wasted time in that stupid hotel waiting for Mooken to show up or thinking about him after he left.

I smile at the memory of Mooken pulling random cards from a deck of Kama Sutra sex positions once and us trying whichever position was featured on each card. One time, the contortions were too much for us, and we fell off the bed and landed on the floor. Laughing and aching, it was one of the best memories I have of us.

The sun races overhead as I remember more of the good times with him and many of the bad ones, too. I stroll along Thomas Jefferson's original brick walkways and head down to the Lawn. Students play Frisbee and Hacky Sack there, and I stare at them, wondering if I was ever that carefree.

But I know the answer to that.

Yes, I was.

Until my third year when I started fucking my professor.

Stop it. Stop it.

I start walking faster, trying to push my body so my mind will shut the hell up again, and for a moment or two, it works. I'm more concerned about drawing enough oxygen into my lungs than I am about how foolish I've been for the last two years.

Stop it!

I pass through the Lawn and go down McCormick, heading for Gilmer Hall again—the building where so much of my life has played out over these last years.

It's bad enough being a grad student who has to spend so much time in a single building. But add to that the hours I've spent in Mooken's office for non-academic reasons, and Gilmer Hall is both a second home *and* a toxic dump for my soul.

I stand fifty feet from the old building, staring at its side entrance. I don't want to go inside, but observing it from out here is giving me some needed perspective. In the end, Gilmer is only a building and nothing more. But it's a place I still need because I have my studies and my thesis to worry about. And if that asshole does anything to mess with my degree or my status as a student here…

No, he won't do that, I think. *He's not that stupid.*

My eyes defocus, and I indulge in a fantasy where I burst into the offices of the University Journal and tell one of their student reporters *everything*. I even supply incriminating photos, although most of them don't show Mooken's face. He was always careful about that.

As I stand there, staring, my fantasies grow even more dramatic.

In my head, I grab the mic from Mooken while he's lecturing his class. I tell the students all about their asshole teacher—their role model who not only fucks his students but also takes detailed notes about their sex lives and gets off on re-reading his dirty little narratives.

I allow myself to wallow in the memories of all the times Mooken wronged me. And as I'm gorging on the vile juices of self-pity, Amber walks past, twenty feet away from me, absorbed in her phone, texting.

None of this is her fault. And what she's doing right now is none of my business or concern. But even so, as her smug, happy face struts out of sight, I turn away from Gilmer Hall and follow her.

CHAPTER FORTY-FIVE

Too Much

I FOLLOW AMBER to the Corner and watch from a distance as she enters the St. Maarten Cafe. Maybe she needs to rehydrate herself after having too much sex earlier with Mooken.

After fifteen minutes, I convince myself this is a foolish pursuit and a waste of my time. But as I'm about to leave, Amber exits the bar, pulling some guy behind her.

I watch the two of them step into the wooded area on the other side of the rear parking lot. Maybe he's about to be sick, and she's making sure he's okay.

A few seconds later, I realize this is not the case at all.

The guy looks around to see if anyone's watching. Why do people always do that, when they never actually spot the people who *are* watching them?

Like me.

When the guy turns to the side, I recognize him, and my eyes widen. It's the same student who asked me out to lunch last week. It's the *other Jim.*

I'm stunned as he bends her forward, and she braces herself against a thick oak tree.

The two of them go at it, and if I weren't so angry, I'd find it all amusing and maybe even a turn-on. UVA's such a big school, and yet, here I am, in a fuck rectangle where no one knows who all the players are.

Except me.

While I gawk, I become too intrigued to be mad, and my anger settles down as they finish and then part ways.

What a life that woman has.

I wonder how many other guys she's having sex with, and for a moment, I worry about those ramifications. If he was having sex with Amber while he and I were together, Mooken could be a disease vector without even knowing it.

And if he's given me something, I will straight up *kill* him.

I shake my head and leave, disgusted by everything and everybody in the world.

A few yards away, I dry swallow two more hits of Xanax, on my way to becoming numb again as soon as possible.

By the time I'm home, I am…conflicted. The long walk has helped my body feel better, but my mind is cloudy, and the Xanax is not helping.

I now have this extra knowledge about Mooken, Amber, and the other Jim, and it gives me a type of power, but I don't know what to do with it yet.

I take another pill, which is not wise, especially given the week I've had and because I almost overdosed once already.

But I need a way to be still and at peace. And I don't have another solution.

I lie in bed, staring at the ceiling, sorting through precisely who knows what in our cluster of lust.

I start with me and figure I know it all or most of it, at least. I know Mooken has slept with me and Amber. And Amber has slept with Mooken and Jim.

What about Amber? What does *she* know? She knows she's slept with Mooken and Jim, but I'm betting Mooken hasn't told her that he and I used to be a *thing*.

And the other Jim? I bet he knows *the least* of what's going on. And I can't be sure, but it looked like he and Amber knew each other and this wasn't their first time hooking up. I assume they have a history, but I also assume Jim doesn't know Amber is fucking Mooken, nor does he know Mooken and I used to date.

And then there's Mooken himself. He knows who he's fucked. But I'm willing to bet he doesn't know his new girlfriend just had sex with one of his students.

CHAPTER FORTY-SIX

A GIFT

I SPEND THE rest of Sunday immobile, toying with dark ideas of revenge, sleeping on and off. I am a mess, and I have to force myself to shower as the sun starts to go down simply because I don't smell very good, even to myself. The water pouring over my thinning body doesn't do much to lift my mood, but at least I've made it through the weekend. Tomorrow begins a new week, and I'm thankful I have an appointment with my Russian studies advisor, Professor Sulke, in the morning.

Psychology isn't the only degree I'm working on, I remind myself.

Plus, it will be good to spend an hour with a teacher I respect and who's never tried to bang me.

I only take one pill before bedtime to help me sleep. I'm not ready to taper off the drug yet, but soon I will be, and I need to be careful. Going cold turkey after being on such high and erratic doses of Xanax can cause all sorts of problems…including bouts of psychosis, which I really don't need to deal with right now.

In the morning, my eyes open after I snooze my alarm for the second time. Somehow, I get up, walk around, and find enough time to choke down a Pop-Tart before I head out for my meeting with Sulke.

The day is cooler than it's been lately, and the Grounds are fresh and crisp as I walk to Cabel Hall.

Compared to Gilmer Hall, which sets my arm hair on end at the moment, the Russian Department offers a welcome warmth. As I step through the heavy, double doors and take the stairs to the fourth floor, I regret trying to get two master's degrees simultaneously. So much of my life would be better if I hadn't.

When I arrive at Professor Sulke's office and knock, he calls out in Russian for me to enter.

As I open his door, we greet each other using official protocols, like two diplomats meeting in the Kremlin. But soon we resort to the familiar pronouns and vocabulary of friends.

Even so, I throw in a few formal words and phrases here and there to remind him that I respect him as my teacher and as a mentor.

"How is your thesis coming along?" he wants to know.

I'm honest with him when I respond.

"If I were starting all over today, I'd tackle one degree at a time," I say, with an uneasy laugh.

He wants to dig deeper into my statement, but I don't offer more details. Instead, I get down to specifics about progress on my thesis—how ancient artifacts found in today's Russia and Ukraine may have influenced early political-religious leaders in pre-Czarist Russia.

Exciting, right?

I review with him my study of ancient statues and talismans I'm citing as evidence for my thesis. Diving into my love of ancient religions and history takes my mind off Mooken for a while. And for that, I'm grateful.

"It sounds like you're managing your two degrees fairly well, from my point of view, at least. Is there a specific problem or challenge where I could help you, Beverly? Or should I let you be and allow you to finish your work? That's how students at your level often prefer to do things, and I'm not offended by that at all."

He emits a genuine laugh when he says this, and his silver eyebrows bob up and down. He is friendly with his offers of assistance, and I really wish he could help me.

For a moment, I consider confiding in him. After all, he is a professor, and he must know more than I do about how the university deals with teacher-student relationships.

I contemplate this course of action but decide to remain quiet for now. No matter how great Professor Sulke is, he's also at least casual friends with Mooken. And I don't want to put him in a tough spot by sharing my problems. But the main reason I don't say anything is that I can't think of a single version of events where I don't end up suffering consequences of my own if my history with Mooken comes to light.

"I'll be fine," I say. "I only wish there were a way to study some of these artifacts closer up and in person. It would make my thesis more…practical…and less like a research paper."

He laughs again, then squints at me, thinking.

"Tell me," he says. "How are you with handling precious objects and returning them safely to their owner?"

I'm confused, but I bite.

"I am absolutely the best. I take care of other people's things like they were my own. Why?"

He stands up and shuffles over to a glass-enclosed display shelf.

"Perhaps you would like to study this up close and personal."

When he turns back to face me, he's holding a small wooden box. He opens it to reveal a silver bracelet dripping with finely crafted silver charms from a time period I immediately recognize from my studies.

"Is that real?" I say, and he shrugs.

"I thought it might inspire some ideas for your paper."

Professor Sulke points with his chin to the box and the bracelet.

"Go ahead. Take this with you. I trust you will return it in the same condition at the end of the semester."

"I can't accept this," I say. "It should be in a museum."

He smiles and peers at me over the rim of his glasses.

"You are not the only one who enjoys holding antiquity in your hands."

After another half-hearted protest, I agree to borrow the bracelet.

When I leave Professor Sulke's office, I'm surprised to be filled with hope and floating on air. This is what I wish all of my academic interchanges were like.

When I get home, I carefully set the small wooden box containing the bracelet on my bookshelf.

I am so uplifted by my day that I even eat a little dinner with Trisha and Sally.

But by the time I'm back in bed, ready for sleep, my anxiety returns. My throat turns dry, and I cough repeatedly, stressed because I have to see Mooken tomorrow.

Before I switch off my lamp, I wash down a Xanax and wait impatiently for sleep to come.

CHAPTER FORTY-SEVEN

A New Lunch Date

WHILE GETTING READY for class, I consider making myself look as bad as I feel. But at the last moment, I slip into my favorite white silk blouse and an old pair of jeans that fits me perfectly. I want the asshole to see me at my finest and know he can't have me anymore.

I arrive early for Mooken's lecture, and as I wait in the front row with Carl and the other TAs for our *teacher* to show up, I turn around in my seat and scan the students. Wouldn't you know it? The first person I see is the other Jim sitting a few rows behind me. And sure enough, two seats down from him sits Amber.

I stifle a snarl when the new Jim looks up at me. Then I quickly turn my back to him.

Eventually, Mooken slides in—late—which I can only assume is because he wants to avoid speaking with me before class starts.

Or maybe he's late because he was fucking one of his students.

As Mooken begins his lecture, I wait, half expecting some other young, hot woman to walk into class, breathless and flushed—her blouse untucked and hair disheveled.

But nothing like that happens.

I stare at my laptop the entire hour while Mooken drones on.

By the time I look up, the lecture is over, and Mooken has made an atypical, speedy exit.

One lecture done. A hundred more to go.

I sigh and start to collect my things and load my backpack. When I look up, the new Jim is watching me from his seat like a sick little puppy who hasn't been played with in a while, even though I know he had a good time on Saturday, at least.

I have to admit, although I'm not interested in anything with anyone right now, it feels good to know someone still finds me attractive.

Before I know what my evil hand is doing, I wave him over, partly because *why not* and partly because he makes me curious. When he sees me beckoning him, he's out of his row and down the stairs almost faster than I can follow.

"I missed you Thursday," he says.

I grimace as I remember taking too much Xanax last Tuesday night.

"I was sick," I say. "I stayed home, got an early start to the weekend, and drank magnolia bark tea for four days straight."

This is not entirely untrue, since I do love my nightly tea, and I did drink quite a lot of it last weekend.

As soon as he hears I wasn't feeling well, his face changes to one of compassion, and for a moment, I'm touched. Then I remember this is what normal people look like when they hear a fellow human is in pain. I've been dating Mooken for so long—he who is always in total control of his damn emotions—I'd almost forgotten what a healthy expression of empathy looks like.

While Jim continues talking to me, Amber looms in her chair, giving both of us the eye.

I shake my head slowly without even realizing it.

What is wrong with all these people?

Turns out Amber isn't the only one watching us. Carl is packing his books more slowly than usual as he studies me talking with Jim.

I don't want to look at Carl or Amber, so I move closer to the new Jim and focus on what he's saying to me. The more he talks, the more I realize that, although not classically handsome, he has a sweet face. And something in his eyes suggests kindness.

Given my life right now, I could stand a little of that.

"How about lunch today?" I say, interrupting whatever he was saying. "We can talk about your dreams."

"I'm meeting with Professor Mooken later this afternoon," he says. "But I'm free right now if you're hungry."

I contain my shock, but I can't believe the little shit really asked Mooken to help him with his issues. More than that, I can't believe Mooken agreed. For a moment, I wonder if the professor consented to talk with Jim to fuck with me. I wouldn't eliminate that as a possibility.

"He must like you or be intrigued by what you told him," I say as we walk up the steps and out of the lecture hall together.

Once outside, Jim walks entirely too close to me again. But it doesn't seem as creepy this time around. I look at his innocent eyes and decide he's one of those people who simply doesn't have much of a personal space cushion. Plus, it's obvious he likes me, and being closer to someone you like is a natural thing to want.

For most people.

Twenty minutes later, with blissfully little small talk along the way, we end up sitting in the Cavern, the same place Mooken and I've eaten so often over the last couple of years.

"What did you say to Mooken?" I ask before biting into my sandwich.

"I told him about my bad dreams and my problems sleeping. He said he'd help me figure out who to see. He was actually nice. Not at all what I was expecting."

I laugh a real laugh when he says that.

"Now that you have Mooken to talk to, I guess you don't need to chat with me," I say.

"I guess. But he's not nearly as attractive as you are," he says.

I noticeably cringe for him and wonder how this guy has ever gotten laid. Then again, a part of me likes him telling me straight out that I'm pretty, and I smile despite my discomfort.

"Where do you live?" I say, trying to turn the topic away from me.

When he tells me he's a second-year RA who lives in university housing, I laugh again. Our living situations couldn't be any different.

I decide to ask him about his dreams.

"Are they frightening? Erotic?"

"Sort of both," he says with an unconvincing shrug.

And then, as I'm starting to enjoy our little lunch, he asks how I like being a TA for Mooken and about my plans after graduation.

I give him my standard answer about possibly pursuing a doctorate—which the university *strongly* encourages—or trying for a teaching job somewhere, perhaps overseas in Russia. He raises his eyebrows, maybe impressed. Then he mumbles something about *only* being an English Major and being prepared to make a meager salary when he graduates.

While I process Jim's vague career ambition, a man at the table across from us looks right at me. He seems familiar, and I think he must recognize me from all the times I've eaten here with Mooken. To avoid his curious gaze, I laser beam in on Jim's eyes.

And when I do, again, I'm a little taken aback. They're blue and tranquil.

"What time are you meeting with Mooken?" I ask.

He tells me he still has thirty minutes, so we finish our sandwiches without much more conversation and then leave.

When we make it to the exit of Cabel Hall, we stop, framed in the doorway, and face each other.

He asks me where I live, and I answer him in general, non-specific terms, which I'm sure is not what he is hoping for. To be kind and polite, I even offer a vague invite to stop by if he's ever in the vicinity.

He perks up at that, and I wonder, not for the first time this day, what the hell I'm doing. Why am I leading him on like this? I'm not really sure, although I'm enjoying being the one in control for a change.

While Jim mumbles something like "sure" or "that would be cool" to disguise his excitement, I notice the man from the Cavern is now standing in the parking lot, watching us and not being discreet about it.

Something about the subdued autumn light hitting the man's

face triggers a memory. He is one of Mooken's fellow professors. In Economics, if I remember correctly, although his name eludes me.

Maybe he knows about me and his buddy splitting up. Maybe he doesn't.

But I guarantee that whatever he sees me doing with Jim right now, he'll report it to Mooken as soon as possible.

When I turn back to Jim, I see him in a new light. And on a whim, I tap his phone with mine and give him my address and phone number. This could be an unwise move, but frankly, he doesn't seem like he would hurt a fly, and I *want* Mooken's informant to see me giving Jim my info.

Besides, I can't deny that I do feel *something* when I'm around this guy.

Maybe I feel safe?

I don't know. It's different from the excitement I'm used to experiencing with Mooken. But it's also nice.

Jim slips his phone gently into his back pocket, and although his mouth continues to move, he is unable to form words.

Oh my God, this poor guy.

While he's still trying to speak, I glance again at the stalker in the parking lot. He is now on his phone, texting someone.

Well, if Mooken's friends are going to spy on me, I should give them something juicy to report. But first, I have to ask the new Jim about Amber. I can't think of a subtle way to do this, so I say it directly.

"Tell me, Romeo, what's up with you and the girl who sits with you in class—Amber, right?"

His eyes go wide, surprised I know something like this about him. Little does he suspect I also know he likes to have sex with women up against trees.

I let him squirm and wait for his reply.

"We...used to date," he says. "She was my last girlfriend, but we broke up a while ago."

I remember the two of them having sex behind St. Maarten's and wonder if he does this with all his ex-girlfriends.

He sees the doubt on my face and tries to rephrase his response to make it sound better.

"I mean, we're still friends and hang out sometimes. And we're in the same lab group. But there's nothing between us."

"She's beautiful," I say.

He shrugs and nods because to disagree with me would be ridiculous and not believable. I'm not sure how I feel about being hit on by a guy who's recently had sex with the woman currently fucking my ex, but…hey, life gets complicated sometimes.

After another fifteen seconds, I've watched Jim suffer enough, and, on impulse, I step up and give him a solid, tongue-free kiss on the lips. His body stiffens, and I sincerely hope he doesn't have a heart attack right there in front of me.

Surprisingly, he tastes good, and my body responds as he draws me closer. Against my better judgment, I end the kiss with a little more intimacy than I was planning. And my body sparks with electricity when I push myself away.

Fuck. Who knew? I wasn't expecting that.

"Give me a call if the dreams get too bad, or if you need to talk," I say, and to my surprise, I actually mean it.

Jim is stunned and euphoric, which is not a bad reaction to a first kiss. But even more importantly, he's about to visit my ex while flustered and on a love-sick high that he won't have a chance of concealing.

That, plus the fact that the Econ professor is texting furiously in the parking lot, makes me smile as I turn and leave my new Jim happy, numb, and late for his appointment with Professor Mooken.

CHAPTER FORTY-EIGHT

FOXFIELD

NEW JIM CALLS me that night to tell me he's having more nightmares—bad ones. I'm surprised, but I'm fine with him calling because I can't fall asleep.

And I could use a distraction. So I invite him over.

When he shows up, he's wound tight, and for a moment, I wonder if I've done the right thing.

But then I kiss him, and everything falls into place.

I pull him into the house, through the kitchen, and into my room. He doesn't look great, so I tell him to sit while I make tea for both of us.

Having him in my room is making my heart race. So, even though I've started to taper off the Xanax, I slip one into my mouth to help me relax. And, judging from his red, tired eyes, he could use something to take the edge off, too.

I know it's wrong, but I drop half a pill into his tea and let it dissolve, knowing it won't do anything more than mellow him out.

We sit in my bed, drinking tea, making small talk. He's reluctant to discuss the details of his dreams, and that's okay with me because I'm more interested in the serious physical attraction that's growing and drawing us closer together.

To Jim's credit, he catches me off guard when he asks how it is that he's ended up in my bedroom tonight.

"Because I like you," I say, telling the truth. "And because my last boyfriend was a shit, and he hurt me. You have been forewarned."

Jim's happy because I'm opening up to him, but his broad shoulders tense when I mention my ex.

Good thing I didn't mention my ex is his psychology professor.

We continue sipping our tea, and slowly, his shoulders drop, and his breathing calms. There's not much of the drug in his drink, but his speech slows and takes on a hint of a slur, and I can tell the Xanax is affecting him.

Soon, his eyes go soft, and I wonder if he's about to pass out on me. But then he does something strange and unexpected again.

He makes me agree to a *pinky swear.*

I haven't done one of those since I was a freshman in high school, but when we interlock our little fingers and promise to never be dishonest with each other, I'm sincerely touched.

I also feel a little bad since I'm lying to him even as I agree to his oath.

When we finally set our empty mugs aside, I lean in and initiate that which he is too shy to start on his own.

Everything is perfect and feels right, but something tugs at the back of my mind. I stop in mid-kiss and push him a few inches away from me.

"You said you and Amber aren't a thing anymore, right?" I ask, and he nods.

"I promise," he says.

He doesn't know what I know—that he and Amber had sex last weekend. But something in his eyes tells me to trust him—that the two of them are a thing of the past.

We start kissing again with renewed passion, and once we get going, he takes control. In minutes, our clothes are on the floor, and as our bodies entwine, I'm overwhelmed in a good way. By each of his kisses and by each stroke of his hands. We don't even know each other, but staring into each other's eyes, we silently decide to go *all the way.*

Immediately, the sex is good, and it doesn't take long before I realize why. Because he's *not* fucking me.

He is making love.

I close my eyes and enjoy the waves of warmth as they overtake me. I try to focus on the man in my bed giving me the tenderness I haven't had in a long while. But when I do, memories of old Jim barge their way into my head.

Guilt fills me, but only momentarily, as my thoughts about both men mix together. Soon, I don't know where one stops and the other starts, and the swirling pleasure of it all is wonderful, if not slightly confusing.

After we both climax and his adrenaline wanes, the Xanax hits him full force. His eyes drift away, and within minutes he's almost asleep, and I'm not far behind him.

Until my housemates pound at my door—the neighborhood watch conducting a courtesy visit to ensure I'm safe.

When I stumble across the floor to answer it, Jim sits up, on full alert. The poor guy probably thinks it's my ex because he's clearly relieved when he sees it's only Trisha and Sally.

They heard me screaming and were worried I was being attacked.

What can I say? They didn't know Jim was here, and I'm not quiet in bed.

When I introduce them, my housemates give me a look.

Yes, he has the same name as my ex. Yes, I already told him. And yes, he is cool with it.

But I can already tell how confusing this could become, so I draw a line in the sand to get us all on the same page.

"From now on," I say, "when we talk about this guy behind me, we shall call him *Good Jim*, so there's no misunderstanding. And if we absolutely have to talk about the other Jim, he will be known as Jim the Evil, Bad Jim, or *asshole*. Agreed?"

We all nod, and I'm happy Jim and my housemates are appeased.

The following day, it's nice waking up next to someone in my bed and not in a hotel. And indeed, what harm is there in any of this? I'm an adult woman and can do whatever I like. And right now, this is what I want. It feels good. It feels healthy.

True, it's a bit sketchy with me being his TA and all, but Jim's a solid student with a 3.7 average in the class. There's no need for me to show any favor toward him, and he's not the kind of guy who would expect any special treatment from me, anyway.

After some early morning pillow talk, we have sex again before reluctantly getting ready for our classes. When we leave, we kiss goodbye, like a healthy couple would do. And I feel blissfully normal for once.

That evening, Jim shows up at my movie series, which I'm afraid will be too much too soon. But when he offers to walk me home afterward…well, to say he's sweet would be an understatement, and I'm happy to be with him as we walk along holding hands in the dark.

Plus, I'm certain Mooken sees when the two of us leave together after the movie. And even though I don't want him to know for certain that I'm having sex with one of his students, it feels good to make him a little jealous.

Fuck you, Evil Jim.

Fuck you very, very much.

Good Jim and I have sex again that night, and afterward, I make us tea like we've been performing this sacred ritual forever.

He mentions how great he feels around me and how it was such a relief the night before—sleeping without any nightmares. I love that he says this and attributes his peace of mind to being with me. But the Xanax probably helped out, at least a little.

And so, before I hand him his tea, I drop another half-pill into his dark liquid.

Jim comes over again Thursday and then Friday night, too. When I wake up Saturday morning, his gentle eyes are already on me. As we kiss, I realize, rightfully so, he thinks the two of us are in a *relationship.*

At my urging, Jim joins us at Foxfield that afternoon. Not only does he go with me, my housemates, and Dan, but he insists on being our sober driver. The entire time we're there, he gives me plenty of room to mingle and be on my own, but I keep orbiting back to him and can barely keep my hands to myself. Maybe it's the hit of MDMA I get from Dan, but there's something special about this new Jim I'm finding impossible to ignore. At the very least, he's a breath of fucking fresh air, and I am inhaling as deeply as I can.

By the end of the races that day, I'm more interested in him than I should be.

Still, I'm honest with myself. I'm not done recovering from Mooken yet. I know this. But Jim is helping me with the transition a lot more than I realized at first. Without him, I'd be lonely, taking too many drugs, and doing God knows what to myself.

When we step into my bedroom that night, even though I'm exhausted, I can't quit smiling.

However, a shadow rises inside me as we settle in for the night.

What if he ends up like every other guy I've grown to care about?

What if he loses interest in me or turns out to be another asshole?

As I start the water for our tea, I decide to do everything I can to solidify the bond Jim already feels for me. I want him to have a *really great* night's sleep tonight with no chance of any intruding nightmares. In fact, I don't *ever* want him to have another nightmare again. As long as he's with me, that is.

This is what I tell myself as I secretly slip a full pill into his tea.

We fall asleep that night without having sex, but that is okay because my heart knows there's more to us than our physical connection. I sleep with a grin on my face, happy to be next to him and because we had a good day. But when I wake the next morning, images of Evil Jim—of Mooken—flood my thoughts.

And I start to cry.

Jim stirs to life next to me and rubs my back, trying to soothe me. He's confused but also genuinely concerned. But his caring makes it worse for some reason. All I can figure is that being with him is making me comfortable and safe enough that my raw emotions are rising to the surface—artifacts of my delayed grief over how Mooken and I ended.

It's not fair to Good Jim, but the only way to deal with emotions is to let them play out and experience them, and that's what I'm doing whether I want to or not.

But I still need to tell Jim something to explain why I'm uncontrollably sobbing next to him in bed. The problem is, I'm not ready to disclose the full truth yet—that I've been in a relationship with his professor for two years, waiting for him to leave a wife that didn't even exist. I can't tell him that, but my guts tug at me, urging me to share *something* real with this man—some truth about myself that will bring us closer together.

"I don't want you to think any less of me," I say after inhaling and releasing a deep breath. "A couple of weeks ago, things got to be too much, you know? And I…I almost killed myself."

As I have come to expect from this man, he greets my complexities with compassion and understanding.

I don't go into details about how I did it or the timing, and Jim doesn't push me. Instead, he tells me how glad he is that I'm still alive. He holds me close, the way I always wished Mooken would have. And that makes me cry even more.

It makes us both cry.

Through my tears, a fist of regret hits me for sharing too much too soon. Jim likes to rescue people. I can tell that already. Women, specifically. And me being this vulnerable around him has activated his knight-in-shining-armor complex, setting it on high alert.

His eyes tell me he's already thinking of ways to help, even if there aren't any. And although this concerns me, I'm also relieved someone cares enough to want to protect me.

My cheeks dry, and we spend Sunday together before the new week starts. Already, Jim and I are falling into a rhythm of sleeping and waking up together, attending classes, and meeting for lunch if possible. In the evenings, dinner with him at my place becomes the norm, as does talking through the night, drinking tea, and making love.

That's what I'm calling our sex now. In my head, at least.

Because, even though *I'm* not there yet, and maybe won't be for a while, I can't deny that making love is precisely what we're doing.

I wonder if I've somehow lucked into the perfect man for me, and for hours at a time, I forget about Mooken completely.

But after class on Tuesday, I see a different side to Good Jim—one that puts him in a new and possibly dangerous light.

CHAPTER FORTY-NINE

FESTERING

JIM AND I are standing outside Gilmer Hall after Mooken's class, getting ready to walk to lunch, when Jim's lab mate—Eugene—joins us. In contrast to Jim, Eugene is cocky and insecure at the same time, but out of respect for Jim, I tolerate him. As the three of us chat, Eugene points out someone in the crowd, and when Jim looks past me, his body goes rigid. His kind eyes turn dark, jittery, and distant, and they remind me of the dissociation I've observed in mentally ill subjects.

For a moment, a formless fear replaces the pleasure I'm used to experiencing when standing this close to Jim, and I wait to see what happens next.

"It's Tony," he says in a whisper. "The guy who followed me to Beta Bridge."

I nod, but Jim has *never* told me about anyone named Tony before.

Still, I believe *he* believes what he's saying. Why wouldn't I?

"I can't make lunch," he says in a cold voice I haven't heard from him before.

Ignoring me, Jim cinches his backpack and secures it through both arms. All the while, he stares across the courtyard like an animal. But when I look to where he's focused, all I see is a group of students walking and talking calmly, passing the time between classes.

I turn to ask Jim what's going on, but he takes off like a lion hunting a gazelle. The sudden change in him jars me out of my stupor, and I yell for him to come back.

But he doesn't hear me or doesn't care as he turns onto the main road and runs up the hill, chasing after someone I can't see, heading toward central Grounds.

I don't know what this is all about, but I'm worried about him. And about me.

"Did you see whoever he was talking about?" I ask Eugene.

"I thought I saw this guy from one of our experiments, but maybe not," he says with a shrug.

I instantly dislike Eugene, especially if he was fucking with Jim. But I force myself to prod him for more information.

"What did this guy do?"

"Jim thinks Tony was following him," Eugene says. "Hard to tell with him sometimes, though. You know what I mean?"

I *don't* really know what he means. Not yet.

I stand there with Eugene as he tries to make conversation with me. But I hear nothing he says. All I can do is wonder what kind of guy I've become involved with.

Something is not right about Jim, but a primal part of me is excited by his ferocity. Slowly, as I stand there, I begin to redefine him. Not only as a man who's into me but also as a potential protector who's nuts enough to do whatever it takes to defend me if the need were to arise.

After all, a little crazy isn't so bad as long as it's on your side.

I turn away from Eugene in time to spot Mooken and Amber leaving the building together. They're both laughing, smiling, and walking far too close to each other.

I hate that I'm not over him and am still raw about being used for the last two years of my life.

But there it is.

As Mooken and Amber walk off together, probably for a bite to eat, I wonder if they'll return to Mooken's office later for an afternoon one-on-one session or maybe check into our favorite hotel. Or perhaps she'll fuck him in the trees behind the St. Maarten Cafe, the way she did with my Jim.

Eugene is still talking to me this entire time, and all I want to do is smack him to make him shut up. To my left, a small group of students near the street buzzes, gesturing, pointing at the road, and talking about the strange guy who stormed past them to chase an invisible foe.

And, amid all this oddity, an unwanted but darkly pleasurable thought begins to blossom in my brain.

If this is Jim's reaction to someone he thinks is simply following him around, what would he do if he found out Mooken was my ex—that he abused his position, mistreated me, and hurt me so much I tried to end my own life?

Although the scenarios dancing in my head are brutal, profane, and darkly enjoyable, I shake my head and clear them away. This is all pure fantasy because I will never tell Jim about Mooken and me.

Yes, I am angry Mooken has so quickly shacked up with a new student.

Yes, I hate him for keeping track of our sex life in his stupid notebooks and treating our relationship like an experiment.

And more than anything, *yes*, I'm hurt he was never even married. All those holidays, weekends, and nights when he had to go home to be with his family. Those were all lies, cover stories for spending time either alone in his cluttered home or with another woman.

As my anger festers, one layer on top of the next, my mind races with more dark possibilities, and this time, I embrace them.

CHAPTER FIFTY

A Plan

JIM STAYS AT his place that night to appease his head RA while I eat dinner by myself and work on my Russian studies thesis. I miss Jim, but I'm also happy to be getting some work done.

As bedtime approaches, Jim calls me on a video chat. Despite the recent bit of crazy from him earlier in the day, I light up when I see his sweet face on my phone. But his eyes are swollen and his skin ashen, and he doesn't look good.

"Did you catch that person you ran after?" I ask.

He shakes his head.

"It was the wrong guy," he says, clearing his throat and coughing, upset. "He was just some stranger. But I could have really hurt him, Bev."

As he struggles with making sense of this part of his life, which I am only now starting to uncover, a wave of guilt passes through me. Without his nightly dose of Xanax, he's not going to have a good night's sleep tonight—something he desperately needs right now.

After all, he doesn't know I've been giving him Xanax with his tea for the last week, but his body sure does.

I've increased his dose to two pills because his system is already developing a tolerance to the sedative. This might seem extreme, but it's nowhere near enough to hurt someone his age. Besides, it takes a few weeks to become addicted, and I plan on tapering him soon, once I figure out exactly what I'm doing.

Jim goes silent and doesn't want to talk about chasing that guy anymore. But when he mentions meeting with Mooken later in the day, I need to know if he told him anything about us.

A part of me wants Mooken to know everything because I fantasize this will hurt him. But I'm afraid of what he might do to me as his TA if he knew for certain I was having sex with a student. Although Mooken has no moral platform on which to stand.

"I didn't tell him about us," Jim says. "I told him I wasn't dating or having sex with anyone."

My neck relaxes when I hear this, and I ask Jim to tell me more about his session.

He shares his history of dark, over-the-top sex, which both scares and intrigues me. He also says Mooken thinks this kind of intense behavior has been serving as a pressure release valve for whatever's really happening inside him—something that likely started at a much younger age. As per Mooken's theory, when Jim isn't sexually active, his tension builds up and releases at night in the form of nightmares. That's not such an unbelievable connection, and while he goes on about his conversation with Mooken, I try to deduce what's going on inside that odd brain of his.

He has problems, obviously. He needs help, but I don't think it's anything too serious. I'd bet both of my future master's degrees he has an anxiety disorder and that Xanax is what a psychiatrist would prescribe for him, anyway.

This makes me feel better about dosing his tea, for sure.

The next day my prediction is confirmed. Jim had a horrible dream, and I feel terrible about that. But when he's back in bed with me that night, I make sure his heart is fulfilled, his desire sated, and his medication administered through our nightly ritual.

All is good in his world again. And in mine. As an extra bonus, even though Jim didn't tell Mooken directly, I'm certain Mooken knows about us by now but has decided to not do anything about it. If he were going to retaliate against me, he would have already done so. So the next time we're in class, I make sure to interact with Jim publicly and let Mooken soak it all in.

The coming Saturday is Jim's birthday, and after meeting Cynthia and Dan for his first legal beer, he takes me to Chris Greene Lake, one of his most special places.

We show up well after dark and sit on his favorite rock, reveling in the cool, fresh air. As we talk and cuddle, I can sense where the evening is going. And sure enough, after some wonderfully romantic, passionate kissing and groping, he breaks down and tells me.

Under the full moon that reflects on the still water, he lets out what he's been holding in for a while now.

He tells me he loves me.

I was expecting this and have wondered exactly how I'd respond. Because at this point, although I love being with Jim, I am not in love with him. Not yet.

Jim's *I love you* lingers in the air, begging for a response.

To buy some time, I lean forward and kiss him tenderly to show him how much I care about him, which is the truth. When we come up for air, he's still waiting for me to affirm my love for him…but I can't say those words.

Suddenly, a solution pops into my brain, and I compromise by teaching him how to say *I love you* in Russian.

"Ya vas lyublyu," I say.

He repeats the phrase back to me in a decent Russian accent. And I can tell by the way his shoulders relax, he thinks I've just told him I love him. But technically, I have not.

My words put him on an immediate high, and I have to force myself not to wince. Because I know how the rest of this evening is about to unfold.

I know what we're going to find when we return to my place.

Half an hour later, we pull into the gravel parking space behind my house, and when we approach the rear entrance, there it is, as I left it earlier.

A beautiful bouquet of flowers with a hand-written note.

The flowers are pink roses, the kind Mooken used to bring me at the beginning of our relationship. Seeing them on my porch, even though I'm the one who left them here, brings back real memories of our time together, and not all of them are bad.

The pain and pleasure from looking at the flowers steel me for what I must do next. I pretend to be shocked when I read the card that came with the flowers and ask Jim if he's the one who left them for me.

When I hand the card to Jim, he sees the message is from my ex, and the high he's been riding all night is replaced by eyes of red-tinted rage.

Jim may be stranger than any man I've been with, but he's still a man. And once in the house, he's predictably upset and wants to know more about my last boyfriend—wants to step in and solve my problems for me, as I knew he would.

I try to answer his questions carefully with only the information I want to share. But I tell him more than I first intended. Or maybe what I end up divulging to Jim is exactly what my subconscious wanted him to know all along.

He's already furious with my ex-boyfriend, and my new admissions add more fuel to that fire. I explain how my suicide attempt occurred the same day he first asked me to lunch and that I took all those pills because I was so upset about my breakup with my ex. I also tell him I got the drugs from Dan.

As expected, this saddens and angers Jim, and by the time I'm done, he is in full-on protector mode.

I'm not sure what I'm going to do with him yet or how far I want to take all of this, but right now, Jim is exactly where I want him—dedicated to and protective of me.

CHAPTER FIFTY-ONE

TWO WORLDS

ON TUESDAY, JIM cancels his weekly meetings with Mooken, which is great. Not that I don't trust Jim, but Mooken is clever, and the less those two talk, the better.

That night, Jim comes to the movie presentation of *Memento*. But before the show starts, Mooken corners me in the hall.

"Beverly, I need to tell you something," he says, and for a moment, I catch a glimpse of the charming man I used to love.

"What is it, *professor*?" I say.

He raises an eyebrow at my formal address but then nods as if validating something in his mind.

"I've reassigned Jim Straub to Carl," he says, peering deep into my eyes, daring me to complain or assume any kind of attitude with him. "It is not that big of a deal, you dating a student, although I did have to make a note of it. But I wish you would have told me instead of me finding this out from Jim. It made our last meeting…awkward. And as I'm sure you've already realized—that kid needs help."

White noise rips through my mind.

I thought I was the one holding all the cards and knowing all the secrets, but as usual, Professor Asshole is one step ahead of me. He maintains a steady face, outwardly displaying concern. But inside he is totally full of shit.

At least I don't have to wonder about it anymore. He knows for certain Jim and I are seeing each other. And the fact that a student has come to him and admitted this to him is not good at all.

I am seething mad at both of them.

"Don't lecture me about being awkward," I say through tight lips. "Trust me, I know all about *awkward*."

I turn and leave, heading for the projection room to make sure everything is set up with my laptop, but really I just want to get away from Mooken.

Throughout the movie, I barely pay attention. My mind wanders from one scenario to another. In some, I'm raging at Mooken for everything. In others, I'm chastising Jim for disclosing our secret.

When I meet up with Jim after the show, I feel betrayed. But damn his innocent motives once again. Jim swears Mooken already knew about us. He says Mooken claims I was the one who told him. In other words, Mooken lied his ass off.

"But why would he lie about that?" Jim asks.

Oh, how I want to tell Jim the real reason—that Mooken was my lover and that he's a vengeful, narcissistic jerk—but I don't need the kind of trouble that would bring.

Not yet, at least.

"Because he's an asshole," I say through gritted teeth. "And he's smart. He's a smart asshole. And those are the worst kinds."

As we walk home in silence, we don't discuss the movie at all. We barely even talk.

I don't know what Jim's thinking about, but I'm suddenly glad I left another fake gift from my ex on my back porch—one we are about to encounter accidentally. I thought it would bond him even closer to me, and it will. But it will also make him angry. And after the night I've had, my fantasies about letting an angry Jim loose on an unsuspecting Mooken are increasing.

It would serve Mooken right.

When we make it home, I force myself to switch from being irritated with the men in my life to pretending to be startled as we approach the rear entrance to my house.

There, propped up on one of the wooden steps, is a simple cross made of long black nails and crafted by Russian Orthodox monks.

"I told him how much I liked this once," I say, forcing my

voice to go soft. "He brought it back from one of his trips overseas."

Of course, none of what I say is true.

I bought the Russian cross for myself when I was in Moscow last year. Strangely, something changes in Jim's posture when I mention the object is from Russia.

Maybe he's trying to make a connection between the gift and why I taught him how to say I love you in Russian. I don't know. But he's preoccupied and thinking hard about something as we step into the house.

When we enter my room, Jim closes and locks my bedroom door, which normally would make me feel safe. But the detachment in his eyes reminds me of mental pathology again. And instead of feeling protected from the outside world, I realize I'm locked in my room with a man who holds plenty of dark secrets I have yet to uncover.

We have our tea, as usual, and I double his dosage without a second thought. These levels are still nothing that will hurt him, but he'll be out like a light soon and get some much-needed rest. Hopefully, this will give him time to reset and renormalize his brain.

As we sit on my bed and chat, I study him and speculate about what's wrong mentally with him.

I still believe he suffers from anxiety, but it's more than that. There's something inside him I don't know about that's driving whatever's going on inside that head of his.

I turn over, my back facing him. He moves in close and speaks to me, his breath licking my neck.

"Tell me more about your ex," he says. "Let me talk to him and convince him to stop harassing you."

I'm glad my back is to Jim because my mouth opens involuntarily. He is still trying to be the savior here, my heroic knight. Or maybe he's lying about wanting to talk things over with my ex and only wants to beat him senseless.

To be honest, at this point, I'm becoming more and more comfortable with that idea now that Mooken has turned our personal issue into a documented problem and reassigned Jim to another TA.

Mooken didn't threaten me with anything yet. But documenting an incident like that serves as a good insurance policy for his future.

For the fourth time that week, I almost tell Jim that Mooken is my ex-boyfriend, if for no other reason, so I can see exactly what he will or won't do when he finds out.

Even though this is tempting, I restrain myself again.

Mostly.

I ask Jim to promise me he won't try to find out who my ex-boyfriend is, which will almost certainly guarantee he will.

And would that be so bad?

After all, I can't help it if Jim figures out on his own that Mooken is my ex. And best of all, if he does, I can't be held responsible for what he would do next.

CHAPTER FIFTY-TWO

A KILLER

TWO NIGHTS PASS, and I make an excuse for not asking Jim to come over on both evenings. The first night I have plans with the girls. No boyfriends allowed. The second night, I don't feel well and need to rest. And luckily, he's also promised his lab group he will deliver some substantial progress on their lab report.

Jim must be going through hell—not only because he misses me, but because he's essentially going cold turkey on the Xanax. He tries to push the issue, suggesting he could come over to take care of me, but I remain resolute.

And after two nights by myself, with plenty of time to really think about what I want, I decide it's time to break up with Jim.

A part of me will miss being with him, but for my plan to work, I need to rip him away from everything that makes him happy. For him to be in the proper state of mind, he must be desperate and at the end of his proverbial rope.

I walk through my situation again.

Mooken is jealous. Check.

He knows about me fucking one of his students. Check.

I still have my position in the Psych Department. Check.

It is almost time to teach Mooken a lesson.

When Saturday comes, we decide to stay at Jim's place that night, which is perfect for my plans. Meeting him on his home turf triggers memories of spending all those nights at the Days Inn with Mooken, displaced from my home, my life, and my friends. And these memories strengthen my spirit for what will come next.

Surprisingly, a part of me wants to keep seeing Jim. He's fun, and who knows? One day I could develop real feelings for him. In the meantime, the sex is great, and there are worse ways to spend my spare time in grad school.

After a quiet dinner at the Chinese place near Lambeth, we walk back to his apartment under the full moon. He tries to lead us straight into his room, which would normally be exactly where I'd want to go, too. But not tonight.

This won't get any easier the longer I wait, so I sit him down and tell him straight out.

"I don't want to do this," I say. "But I have to."

His eyes tell me he knows what I'm about to say and that he wants to, *needs* to understand why. So I double down on my story.

"It's my ex," I say. "There's a lot I have to sort out with him, and it's not fair putting you through this. Maybe once it's over, we might work out, but not now. I'm so sorry, Jim."

As expected, Jim offers to talk to my ex again, but I tell him I don't want him to do that. Then, to shut Jim up, I kiss him, which leads to more…

I should leave, but my body wants to have one last fling with this guy, and it's totally worth it. But after we're done, I gather my strength and leave.

I fully expect Jim to contact me as soon as I get home, but to his credit, he doesn't.

I wait in bed, dreading his call or text but also hoping for it.

Still, there's nothing.

I wonder *what* he's doing and *how* he's doing as Sunday dawns and passes. And then Monday comes and goes, and still, Jim doesn't reach out.

Have I calculated wrong? Has he moved on from me as quickly as Mooken did?

When I finally see Jim in class on Tuesday, he doesn't approach me, and I only look at him occasionally, stealing a glance here and there. He's angry with me and well within his rights to be so.

With Mooken standing in front of me, lecturing about love, and Jim sitting a few rows behind me, I shake my head and wonder how the hell I got myself into this situation.

When class ends, I leave immediately and don't speak to either one of them.

By the end of the day, I want nothing more than to have my tea, take my Xanax—which I've given up trying to stop right now—and get some sleep.

I should remain cool and wait for Jim to come to me for this to work the way I intended. That would be best. But I am impatient and can't get to sleep that night, even with enough Xanax in me to drop a bear.

I send him a text at one in the morning.

I'm scared. Can't sleep. Can u come over? Please. He left another gift.

He responds almost immediately, which relieves me but doesn't surprise me. My heart speeds up when he tells me he's on his way.

When he arrives half an hour later, I greet him at the back door, and we move to my room, where we kiss and talk. His cheeks are red, irritated, like he cut himself shaving.

"How are your dreams?" I ask, even though I know the answer.

"Bad," he says, choking up as he talks. "Tonight's were the worst. I dreamed I murdered someone."

His nightmares have returned in full force without the nightly doses of Xanax to help, especially since I cut him off with no tapering. I shudder, thinking of how he must feel. Stopping that medication abruptly can cause all kinds of side effects, including episodes of psychosis—and that's when people know they've been taking it. In Jim's case, he must be questioning his own sanity, and I need to tread carefully around him. I can bring him to the edge, but I don't want him to jump off the cliff. Not yet.

We have sex, which helps calm him down and feels amazing, as always. I don't hate this part of the plan at all. Then we have a nice cup of tea, and for a moment I debate on whether to keep the tea clean or to dose it. But I want to hammer home his association with me to the peacefulness in his soul. I hope the pills help him tonight because these are the last I plan on ever giving him.

Jim asks about the little wooden box on my dresser that contains the silver bracelet Professor Sulke let me borrow.

"Is that what he left you?" he asks.

I nod and tell him what's inside. And he goes quiet. I'm sure by now he's had enough of my ex-boyfriend's behavior, so I let it sit there with him and fester.

Within minutes, we both fall asleep. Soon, he is lightly snoring, completely out of it.

I run through the plan in my head again and again, but eventually, I fall asleep as well.

Until the call at four in the morning wakes me up.

Jim sleeps through it since he is heavily doped on Xanax, but I wake up as soon as the phone rings.

"Bev, this is Andrew," the shaky voice says on the other end of the call.

I'm groggy as I try to understand why my Russian studies TA is calling me at such an odd time and why his voice is filled with panic and sorrow.

"A drunk fraternity guy found Professor Sulke dead, hidden in a bunch of bushes near his car. The police don't know who did it, but…"

I am immediately awake and in shock.

"What? How?" I say.

"We don't know, but a guy threatened me earlier this evening, and I think it might be the same person that killed Sulke. And Bev, I've run into this guy before, and he mentioned your name."

"What did he look like?" I ask.

"About six feet tall, light brown hair, I think. I don't know. But his eyes were crazy. Sound like anyone you've seen around Cabel Hall before?"

"That could be any number of guys," I say, but when I glance at the back of Jim's resting head and remember his *nightmare* from earlier tonight, my limbs turn cold.

Andrew exhales on the other end of the call, disappointed his lead about me is a dead end.

"That's what I thought," he says. "I mean, there are plenty of students named Beverly, I guess. But I wanted to check with you before I talk to the cops. And listen, Anderson asked me to teach the class tomorrow and to let his students know what happened, even though we don't know much at this point. I'll see you in class, right?"

"I'll be there," I say. "Thank you for calling."

When I end the call, I lie back in bed, staring at my ceiling and then at Jim's shoulders.

I'm horrified to think he may have actually murdered Professor Sulke, but I'm equally terrified I might be somehow implicated in his death. Or even worse, that his death could be my fault.

Professor Sulke was such a good teacher and a decent person; I shake with guilt when I think about him being dead. But when I close my eyes, I tremble for a different reason.

Because, as my mind races everywhere all at once, there is only one thing I know for sure.

A killer is sleeping next to me in my bed.

PART THREE

Jim and Bev

CHAPTER FIFTY-THREE

JIM

DESPITE BEING CONFUSED and angry that Bev has been lying to me, I manage to get a few hours of decent sleep. Something about being with her in her bedroom still calms me, and I am groggy but peaceful when I finally wake up the next morning.

I glance over my shoulder and see her bare back. She is still in bed with me.

"Hey there," I whisper, in case she is still asleep.

Her voice comes back strong and alert, and I get the sense she has been awake for a while.

"Good morning," she says, but her tone is flat and cold.

I roll over and kiss her shoulder. She sighs but doesn't turn to face me.

"Is there another movie tonight?" I say into her ear, desperate to force the situation to be less tense and weird than it obviously is.

"*American Psycho*," she says, her words barely audible.

I know Bev has been leaving those gifts on her own doorstep and pretending they were from her ex. And without confronting her, all I can figure is that she's been trying to make me hate her ex more than I already do.

Detailed images from my nightmare the night before flash in my mind. Mental pictures of the dead Russian professor in the dirt, stuffed in the bushes, make me cringe.

"Everything okay?" she asks, but it doesn't sound like she truly cares.

I nod before answering.

"Everything is now," I say. "I never have bad dreams when I'm here with you."

"I'm sorry I texted you last night," she says. "I was so scared. I know this is horrible to say, but…"

"You still want to break up," I say, finishing her sentence.

She nods.

"We have to. And I need to go to my Russian lecture early today. We have a lot to cover. But maybe I'll see you tonight at the show."

Another flashback from my dark dream invades my mind. The class she will be attending today is the same one taught by her Russian professor—the one I dreamed of killing.

I breathe easy, soothed by the fact that her class will go on like usual because her professor is safe.

"I'll be there," I say. "It's a good movie."

Bev rolls out of bed and pads away to the bathroom without a word.

I pick up the little wooden box from her dresser and examine the silver bracelet inside.

I set it down, then open the Graduate Directory from the top shelf of her bookshelf. When I page through to the Russian department, I see a photo of Andrew. The image of him is in black and white, but I can tell his hair is red.

I turn to the professors, and a photo of Sulke stares up at me. Even though I didn't actually kill him, I'm still filled with leftover dread and details from my nightmare. Even when I close my eyes, I relive memories of murdering this man.

I squint and look closer at the caption under his photo, and my heart skips a beat when I see his name.

Professor Johnathan Jeffrey Sulke.

His middle name is not *Jim.*

He's not Bev's ex, and I am more relieved than ever that last night was only a nightmare.

When the shower stops running, I put everything back and slide into bed again. Bev steps out of the bathroom, one towel wrapped around her body and another around her hair. She doesn't speak to me. And when she slips into her jeans, she faces away.

Once dressed, she stands close to the door with her hands on her hips.

"I have to go. Are you ready?"

I shake my head, and she huffs.

"It's too early," I say. "I need more sleep, but I promise I won't stay long."

She hesitates but finally shrugs and walks out, leaving her bedroom door open.

Once the back door closes and I'm sure she's gone, I lock her bedroom door so I can have some privacy.

CHAPTER FIFTY-FOUR

Bev

I DID NOT sleep last night.

Thank God my back was to Jim because my eyes were open the entire time. All night I worked through the possibilities for how and why he killed Professor Sulke. And even though I can't pretend to know exactly how his disturbed brain brought him to perform his terrible deeds, I know I am at least partly to blame for his actions.

When I leave my house, a part of me is relieved that Jim stayed in my room because at least I know where he is.

As I walk up the street, I realize I desperately need to talk to someone. To get some kind of trusted advice.

But from whom?

Half-way to my Russian lecture, I turn and take off in the opposite direction, heading toward the psych building.

Soon, I am standing outside Gilmer Hall, looking at the double doors like they are a pair of old friends who have betrayed me.

When I finally gather my nerve, I enter, and my feet take me to Mooken's office. I stop outside his door, listening for noises. The last thing I want to do is walk in on him while he is banging Amber. But right now, I need to talk to him about Jim. I need his advice and his help, and I can only hope he will remain professional enough to rise above our personal problems.

I knock lightly.

"Enter," comes his familiar voice.

When I step inside, he pulls his head back from his computer and blinks.

He is as surprised to see me here as I am surprised to be here.

"Jim," I say. "I need your help."

He laughs. Not a lot, but a little. Then he realizes I'm being completely serious and motions for me to sit across from him on the other side of his desk.

"Have you heard about Professor Sulke?" I ask in a quiet voice.

"Terrible," he says. "I received a phone call this morning about it. I know you two were close. How are you doing?"

I shrug. Then I shake my head.

"Not well. I need to ask you about one of your students. About Jim Straub."

His eyebrows go up.

"The same young man you've been seeing?"

I clear my throat.

"I spoke to him this morning, and he told me about a horrible dream he had last night. One in which he killed Professor Sulke."

Professor Mooken is skilled at hiding his emotions. But he is not prepared for what I just told him.

"And you worry his nightmare was more than a dream? Is that it?"

I wait for Mooken to berate me, to ridicule me for being such a stupid person. But he doesn't.

"I didn't talk with Mr. Straub enough to make a full and accurate assessment. That would require serious therapy from someone other than me. But from what he told me, along with some intense anxiety, I'd say he's been exhibiting some clear symptoms of pre-paranoid schizophrenia. Doesn't mean he'll develop into that. But onset of schizophrenia later in life is common among the twenty percent of the population that suffers from it. When I last spoke with him a couple of weeks ago, I encouraged him to see someone at the university's hospital. Assuming he is not yet under professional care, any kind of acute stressor or other intense situation could have been enough to speed up his pathology."

"What signs would he show?"

"Disturbed sleep patterns. Disorganized thinking. He might

confuse reality with the waking world or even hear voices telling him to do things he shouldn't. If these things are happening, I'd say your fears are not without basis. Is there anything else about Mr. Straub that could be causing his odd behavior?"

"I think he's been taking street Xanax," I say, hoping Mooken won't see through my lie.

He sits up straighter, concerned.

"How much and for how long? He never mentioned this to me."

Of course, he didn't. Because he doesn't know.

"I don't know," I say. "But I think he was using daily and ran out. Was forced to stop cold turkey."

Mooken's eyes expand.

"That adds a whole new level of complexity and danger to that young man. You know this, correct? Sudden cessation of that drug can cause a psychotic split all on its own, much less in patients who already suffer from other forms of mental illness. Beverly, this is serious. Do you know where he is now?"

I digest Mooken's words. Nothing I didn't know already, but hearing him say it makes all the difference. After all, I am a graduate student working toward my master's in cognitive psychology, while he is my professor—a skilled and experienced therapist with a medical degree and his doctorate. Our opinions on matters of mental health do not carry equal weight.

"I left him at my place," I say. "But I don't know if he's still there."

"I'll call the police," he says, but I shake my head immediately.

"What if it wasn't him? What if he just had a nightmare like he said?"

Mooken studies me, then moves his hand away from his phone.

"What are you *not* telling me, Beverly?"

I contemplate his question because it's a good one.

I am *not* telling him I've been stringing Jim along for the last few weeks, using him to get over my two-year affair with my professor—the same man sitting in front of me right now.

I am *not* telling him that I lied to Jim and told him my ex-lover used to be my Russian studies TA to throw him off Mooken's trail. Nor am I telling him that this was a key piece of false information that undoubtedly led Jim to assault Andrew and murder Professor Sulke.

I haven't told him these things, and I don't plan on doing so, but I have to tell him something. And since Mooken is a narcissist, I tell him what I need to so he will help me *without* going to the police.

I lower my gaze, assuming a demure, vulnerable stance before I speak.

"I do not know why," I say. "But I believe he may have killed Professor Sulke because he thought he and I…because he thought Sulke was my ex-boyfriend…instead of you."

"And you think that if you go to the police, you may somehow be implicated in Sulke's death?"

It is so like him to never include himself in any potential blame.

"Yes," I say. "Or that you might be implicated, as well."

Mooken's words come out slow and deliberate. He is starting to get annoyed and angry. I can tell.

"Why would I be associated with any of this?"

I swallow hard.

"Well, not so much that you would be implicated in Sulke's death. But if the police were to get involved, there's a good chance things would come to light about you and me."

"What about you…and me?" he says. "I am your professor, and you are my student and my TA, and a good one at that. But that is all."

My mouth opens, and I pause for a moment as I try to grasp what he is saying.

I want to yell, to strangle him, but instead, I shake my head slowly as my eyes well up with tears of anger.

"I'm not sure exactly what you are suggesting, Ms. McDane, but

I don't appreciate you trying to drag me into a situation you have caused for yourself."

There it is. The asshole is trying to gaslight me. To make me believe he and I haven't fucked hundreds of times over the last two years. If I weren't more worried about what to do about Jim, I'd jump across this desk and kill Mooken right now.

"That's bullshit," I say. "Don't fuck with me, Jim. If the police get involved in this, I will absolutely tell them about how you and I have been shacking up in that shitty little hotel for the last two years and how you lied about having a wife and kids and…and how you're already fucking another one of your students. I'll also tell them about your little notebooks where you keep all your data about your sexual exploits with your students. I'll tell them about all of that unless you help me."

Mooken sits down, his eyes wide and unblinking. He tries to inhale, like I've just hit him in the chest and punctured his lungs.

"I see," he says. "I think that perhaps we should end our discussion here and that you should handle your situation with Jim however you see fit. And remember, this conversation between you and me never happened."

He looks up at me, and his dark eyes pierce my soul.

"Even if I am questioned under oath, you and I were never more than teacher and student. Am I clear?"

"Crystal," I say as I turn to storm out the door.

"And Ms. McDane," he says. "There is one more thing. Do what you must about poor Jim Straub, and do it quickly. But make no mistake about his situation. He could be very dangerous right now. Please be careful how you handle him. For his sake and for yours."

"Oh, fuck you," I say as I fling open his door and rush into the hallway—a ball of confusion, anger, and hopelessness. My stomach is cold and tight, and I can't see any way out of this.

No way out at all.

CHAPTER FIFTY-FIVE

JIM

I SHOULDN'T BE following Bev, but as I suspect, she does *not* go to her Russian class. Instead, she makes her way straight to Gilmer Hall. That building contains many things, including the main lecture hall where all the intro psych classes are held and the lab where Amber, Eugene, and I conducted our psych experiment. But the main thing Gilmer Hall contains is Professor Mooken's office. The day is in full swing, and I'm sure Mooken has a class today, so he's likely in his office if he isn't teaching.

I count to twenty slowly after Bev walks through the door before I follow her.

When I merge into the steady flow of students, no one thinks twice about why I'm there, and no one cares when I turn down the hallway and make my way to Mooken's closed office door. The light is on in his office, and I stand closer, pretending to wait for him to finish with his current appointment.

When I do, I hear voices.

One is Mooken's, and the other one…it belongs to Bev.

I can't hear specific words, but the modulation of their volumes tells me their conversation is jumping from secretive to surprise and then all the way to rage.

Before they stop, I turn and leave, hurrying back down the hall and into the courtyard outside the building. The last thing I need is for one or both of them to catch me spying.

As I stand behind one of the monolithic sculpted shrubs, the students walking past me buzz with nervous anxiety about something. While I remain focused on the entrance to Gilmer Hall, I catch bits and pieces of what a pair of young women are saying.

"I can't believe this shit is really happening here," a short brunette says.

"Do they think the killer is still loose and walking around?" her friend says. "I heard they're going to lock down the Grounds and make everyone stay in their rooms until they find the freak who did it."

I close my eyes, and my heart pounds in my chest. Unless these students and their conversations are part of another nightmare I'm having right now, someone *was* killed at UVA, and the police are still looking for the murderer.

This cannot be me, I think.

But when I pull out my phone and browse to the Charlottesville crime report, there it is.

A homicide on one of the side streets near the Corner. The victim's name is not being revealed yet, but it's a male professor at the university. Those details, plus the location and the time the body was found, all fit my nightmare perfectly.

Air catches in my lungs, and I start to hyperventilate.

This explains why Bev was so nervous around me this morning. She must have heard about the death somehow before I woke up. And I can't blame her for thinking I'm the killer, the murderer of Professor Sulke.

But if that were the case, why would she visit Mooken, and why would they be arguing?

As my mind reels, trying to figure out what is and isn't real, Bev leaves Gilmer Hall and storms away. I see her face for only a second before she turns to make her way up the sidewalk along McCormick Road. Her eyes are red and swollen, and her cheeks are wet with tears. I keep my gaze down, focusing on my feet as I speed up and follow her for the second time that day.

With all the students and faculty moving frenetically about, I blend in and weave my way around slower walkers to keep Bev in my sights.

Bev, on the other hand, receives more than a few second

glances because of her blustery face and obvious state of distress.

Why is that student so upset?

Did she know the murdered professor?

Part-way up the hill, she pulls out her phone and makes a call. To whom, I have no idea. But it's a short discussion, and soon she's moving faster, as if she now has a clear destination in mind.

She passes the amphitheater and the Admissions Hall and makes her way to the foot of the Lawn, where she stops and looks around. Students throw discs up and down the manicured grass, running and laughing. Around here, the buzz of death I felt earlier is not as strong. Maybe they don't know yet, or maybe it isn't that big of news for them.

Bev pivots back and forth until she spots whoever she's seeking and crosses the grass. I'm a hundred feet away and separated from her by multiple clusters of students. Still, I recognize Dan's head of curly hair as she steps up and hugs him.

He greets her quickly and seems to ask her a lot of questions as he keeps looking around, trying to spot anyone who might be watching.

Eventually satisfied enough with whatever Bev has told him, he reaches into his backpack, pulls out an orange plastic bottle, and passes it to her.

As soon as the transaction is made, he walks away, and Bev makes a beeline up the middle of the Lawn.

CHAPTER FIFTY-SIX

BEV

CALLING DAN WASN'T the smartest thing I've ever done, but it was a damn sight more intelligent than fucking Professor Mooken or getting involved with *Jim the Murderer*, that's for sure.

Luckily, Dan always keeps a supply of his standards with him and wasn't far away when I called. A few convenient lies about Jim breaking up with me to explain away my tears, and I am on my way home with a brand new bottle of Xanax and a promise to Dan that I won't take too many at once.

As I rush back home, I try to figure a way out of all of this, and the concept of suicide doesn't seem like my worst alternative.

I've never been a religious person, and I don't believe in a heaven or hell. Yes, it would suck to die this young, but as soon as I'm gone, it won't make any difference to me at all. I'll be dead.

The pain of death is for the living, for the survivors, not for the dead themselves.

Jim has killed a professor. He's certifiable, in my unprofessional opinion. Either I turn him in, and he implicates me as well, or the police eventually find him some other way, and he implicates me then. Maybe Jim doesn't realize what I've been doing *with* and *to* him, but trained investigators will.

When I left Jim an hour ago, he didn't believe the murder from his nightmare was real. But if he hasn't heard yet that a professor has been killed, it won't be long.

And when he does, what will he do?

I don't know for sure. But I don't want to be around when he figures out that he really is a killer.

I walk up my gravel driveway, and none of the cars are there, which likely means I'll have the house to myself.

Even so, I walk around to the rear entrance like usual, but my hand freezes on the doorknob before I open it.

What if Jim's still here, waiting for me in my bedroom? I hesitate, standing on the creaky wooden steps outside my home.

I take out my phone and text Jim.

Hey how r u doing?

Almost immediately, the three dots start dancing as he writes his response.

Walking around grounds. Clearing my head. How r u?

I respond with a thumbs up, the universal sign of acknowledgment and of not wanting to communicate anymore. And to my surprise and happiness, he doesn't reply.

I release a breath and enter my house. The dead silence and still air of the place envelop me. I am the only one here.

When I sit on the edge of my bed and take out the new bottle of Xanax, I stare at it, remembering when I discovered Mooken's notebooks.

I thought that was a bad day, and it was. But it was nothing compared to now. I'm less emotional and thinking clearer than I was then, but I'm also more clearly screwed.

While my mind replays the events of the last few weeks, my hands get busy doing what they always do. They start to boil water for tea.

When the water is ready, I pour it into my largest mug and submerge the tea ball, letting it steep. I take one of the pills from the bottle and drop it into the water, watching as it rapidly dissolves and is soon undetectable.

A second later, I drop two more pills into the hot liquid. That should be enough, I think. Enough to make everything go away, at least for a while.

A tear rolls down my cheek, and I inhale the aroma of the tea.

"What do you think, Beverly?" I say in a quiet voice. "Do I finally do it this time, or should I take just enough of these stupid things to sleep the rest of the day and wake up and deal with everything tomorrow?"

I don't answer myself, but I know one thing for sure. My problems aren't going away tomorrow or anytime soon.

On impulse, I dump the rest of the pills into the tea. The entire bottle. They fizz madly for several seconds, and I dry swallow hard, realizing what I've done and what I may be about to do.

I set the mug on my nightstand and get up. Then I wipe down the empty pill bottle and toss it in the trash. No sense in implicating Dan in any of this.

I return to my bed and sit upright with my head propped up against the cold drywall before I pick up my mug with both hands and inhale deeply.

This is it. I'm finally going to do what I should have done long ago. I am going to put myself out of my own misery and let everyone else sort things out when I'm gone. My parents will be horrified and fucked up for a long time, and that sucks. But hopefully, Professor Mooken will be fucked up as well, and that puts a small smile on my face.

I laugh. It's too bad he has no conscience because I want him to suffer.

I lift the mug to my lips, ready to take the plunge.

And then the rear door to the house opens.

So much for privacy.

Before I can decide whether I give a shit that one of my housemates is home, my doorknob turns, and in walks Jim.

I jump and almost spill my tea. I'm amazed that, even when I am ready to end my life, my body and mind still respond with my fight-or-flight instinct. My adrenaline spikes, as does my heart rate, and I stare at Jim with wide eyes. I am a frightened child caught in the middle of an unpardonable act.

"I thought you were walking around the grounds," I say.

He nods.

"I wanted to check on you. Time for tea already?"

It takes me a moment before I register his question. But then I realize he only sees me about to have a cup of tea. He has no idea what's actually in my mug or what I'm about to do.

And that is when a possible way out finally presents itself to me. Before I can talk myself out of it, I force a smile and hold my mug out to Jim.

CHAPTER FIFTY-SEVEN

BEV

"I WILL MAKE another cup and join you," I say.

He accepts the mug and stands awkwardly at the foot of my bed.

"You can have a seat if you want," I say, forcing my voice to remain calm as I pour more water into my hot pot and face him while it heats.

He sits, hesitant, keeping eye contact with me before sniffing the tea.

"I could really use this," he says and takes a sip.

I use all my willpower to keep my eyebrows from arching in surprise as he takes another, larger drink.

"This doesn't taste as good as it normally does," he says before setting the mug down on my nightstand.

I turn my back to pour the water for my tea. A minute later, I sit on the other side of my bed as my tea steeps.

Neither one of us says anything. All is silent in my room.

Eventually, I can't take it any longer, and I'm afraid he'll be able to read the true intentions on my face.

"Do you want to talk?" I say as I sip the scalding hot liquid from my mug.

"I'd like that," he says. "I have some…things I want to ask you about."

I don't like the sound of that. But if I can get him to drink more of his tea, it won't matter what he wants to talk about.

At last, he picks up his mug, pivots on the bed so he faces me, and takes a drink of the deadly brew.

"What do you want to ask?" I say, stalling for time to let the Xanax take effect.

With that many pills in his tea, it shouldn't be long before he starts to go down.

"What did you talk to Mooken about today?" he says, more as an accusation than a question.

I'm not sure I hear him correctly at first. How does he know I spoke with Mooken?

And then I realize. Of course, he followed me.

I watch him, not answering, and he drinks more of his tea—this time a large gulp.

"Well?" he says.

I clear my throat, waiting for signs of the Xanax, but still, I see nothing.

"I had to talk with him about the lecture next Tuesday," I say. "Nothing important. He wants me to do some research for him."

Jim nods and drinks more of the tea, yet he still shows no signs of being affected by the drug.

My brain races through the possibilities that could explain what the hell is happening and why he isn't reacting.

"You followed me today," I say.

He nods.

"You saw me go into the psych building."

He nods again, confirming my fear, as he practically chugs the rest of his tea. And then I realize something else.

"You saw me talking with Dan."

"I saw you buying drugs from Dan," he says.

My mouth moves, but no words come out. So what if he knows I bought the Xanax from Dan? He still drank the entire cup of tea. Why is he not falling down?

And why is he looking at me with anger sizzling in his eyes? I've seen a lot of emotions on his face, but never hatred when it was directed at me.

"When you told me about how you tried to kill yourself after your breakup, I was...concerned about you," he says. "I was worried, so I spoke with Dan and made him promise not to sell you any more of that junk. For your own good."

Oh shit.

My body stiffens, and I prepare to run, ironically focused again on survival.

"I made a deal with him," he says. "I agreed to not turn him in to the police as long as he promised to give you placebos the next time you tried to buy Xanax from him."

He licks his lips and grimaces.

"From the taste of it, I'd say he gave you sugar pills because this tea is very, very sweet."

CHAPTER FIFTY-EIGHT

JIM

THE TEA COATS my tongue like liquid candy, and each sip makes me think of two things.

First, Bev was ready to kill herself again. Judging from the sugar levels in the tea, she must have added the entire bottle. Realizing she believes her life is bad enough to end it saddens me on many levels.

But then I think about how she gave her tea to me, believing it would kill me. I didn't expect her to do that. And the fact she did fucks me up inside.

It also makes me angry.

I told you not to trust her, my father says.

And this time, I listen to him because he's right. I should never have trusted Beverly.

I swallow the last of the tea while Bev watches me, amazed I'm not dying or at least doubled over ill. The hot liquid's sickly sweetness carves a path of betrayal in my throat.

When I set down the mug, I see Bev through wary eyes, as someone I don't know at all.

And there's an emotion on her face I've never seen before.

"Are you afraid?" I ask.

I'm confused because I'd never hurt this woman, no matter how hurt or angry I am.

"Of course, I'm afraid," she says, with a stammer. "Jim, you killed Professor Sulke. That wasn't a dream. You're a murderer."

I grimace because even though I think what she says is true, I haven't fully digested it as such or faced what I've done.

"Bev, you have to believe me," I say as my eyes fill with tears. "I don't understand what's happening to me. Maybe this is all just another nightmare. Or maybe I'm really lying in a mental hospital somewhere, strapped down and strung out on clozapine."

She shakes her head slowly.

"No, Jim. This is real," she says. "I wish it weren't, but it is. I want you to know I'm here for you. You can trust me. But you need help. *Real* help, okay?"

She's trying to place the blame for all of this on me, but she's the one who's been lying to me this whole time, not the other way around. I would never have gone after her TA and then her professor if she hadn't deceived me.

"Why did you lie about the gifts from your ex?" I ask, but she has no reply to my question.

We stand there, squaring off with one another. Neither of us speaking. Both of us breathing hard.

"You have nothing to say?" I ask as I grow impatient. "No explanation? Aren't you going to tell me how everything is your ex's fault?"

She shakes her head slowly again, eyeing the door behind me, trapped.

But a second later, the skin around her eyes relaxes, like she's spotted a ray of sunshine in this otherwise dark situation.

"I can explain," she says.

"Are you going to tell me another lie to make me think you actually love me?"

"I do love you," she says. "Or I did, at least. But I've been hurt so much by my ex I'm not sure I'm capable of love anymore."

"Don't blame this on him. I mean, does he even exist?"

She pauses for a moment and collects herself, inhaling deeply.

"Oh, he's real enough," she says. "I didn't want you to know who he was, but that doesn't matter now, does it?"

And then she tells me, at last, the one thing she's been hiding since I met her—the one piece of information that would have changed everything.

Finally, she whispers her secret.

"Professor Benjamin James Mooken," she says. "He was my last boyfriend."

I hear her words, and as I process what she's just told me, the remains of my sanity start to crumble away.

CHAPTER FIFTY-NINE

BEV

THROUGHOUT MY EXCHANGE with Jim, I'm darkly amused by how much I want to live when only moments ago, I was ready to die.

I'm okay taking my own life, but I'll be damned if I'll let someone else do it.

I hit Jim with the first ace up my sleeve, making sure he knows for sure that he really is a killer. And then I tell him about Mooken.

I am not disappointed by the results, and I continue weaving the web even tighter.

"All of this is *his* fault," I say. "He used me for so long. I don't even know who I am anymore, Jim. And when you came along, everything was good again, and I was so happy. For a while. And you're right. He didn't leave those gifts. That was me, but I had to. I needed you to protect me. I needed to feel like I was safe. And I couldn't tell you Professor Mooken was my ex because I was afraid of what you'd do to him or what he'd do to us if he thought you knew."

Jim's nostrils flare, and he looks like he wants to hurt someone. But I breathe a little easier because he's no longer channeling his anger at me. Instead, he's looking *through* me, all the way across the Grounds, to Gilmer Hall, and into Professor Mooken's office.

"Jim, Professor Mooken didn't leave the gifts. That's true. But he's done so much worse. He lied about having a wife and kids. He lied to me about everything. He never loved me. And worse than that, he kept detailed records of us when we were dating. Of our sex life, for God's sake. He used me and recorded all these things about me in a notebook like I was a part of some sick experiment! He did that with lots of his students. I was nothing special. When I finally figured out what he'd been doing to me, I confronted him, and *that's* why we broke up."

Jim is having a hard time processing what I've told him. That doesn't surprise me, given his current mental state. But I need to overload him, and he's not quite at his limit yet.

"And one more thing," I say. "He's also sleeping with Amber."

Piece-by-piece, Jim assembles things in his head. And by the look on his face, the conclusion he reaches is the one I want it to be. I know this because he balls his fists, turns away from me, and storms from my bedroom.

And finally, I can breathe again.

Mooken was right about Jim having problems. Maybe they're not full-blown yet, but the seeds of some real mental pathology like schizophrenia are definitely there. The way he confuses dreams with reality, in particular.

Combine that with the fact that his body has been going through withdrawal from the Xanax. Even with the small dose I slipped him last night, his system has got to be pretty messed up right now.

Add the fact that he's already committed one murder—*and* that it was the wrong guy.

And then top all of that off with the revelation that his trusted father figure, Professor Mooken, is the one who drove the woman he loves to attempt suicide.

Mooken is the man who messed me up so badly I can't be in a healthy relationship with Jim.

Mooken is the man who has me acting so crazy I tried to kill Jim, the one person with my best interest at heart.

Mix all of that together, and you have the perfect recipe for a volatile man in danger of experiencing a psychotic episode if pushed even a little further.

A psychological time bomb.

It's horrible for him but good news for me. Because, right now, Jim's on his way to confront the true source of my troubles—Professor Mooken. And if everything works out correctly, all my problems will soon disappear.

CHAPTER SIXTY

JIM

EVERYTHING I SEE is red.

As I stumble through the crowds of students, I do all I can to not appear drunk. The last thing I want or need is to be stopped by UVA Police.

The school day is nearing its end, and because of the change from summer to fall, the day is shorter than yesterday, which means darkness will soon arrive.

Another hour and the Psychology Department will be mostly empty, except for the professors who will be recording their notes, and in Mooken's case, maybe fucking one of their students.

I force myself to slow down. Getting to my destination too soon won't do me any good. I make a wide loop around the Grounds, and as the sun slowly starts to set, shadows all around me grow longer. Just to be safe, I step over some of the most ominous ones.

A cat darts out across the street in front of me, and I flinch. Especially when the small, furry animal looks back at me and laughs like it knows something I don't.

I pass a classroom window, and my reflection pauses in its panes as I continue walking.

When the darkness outside is finally close to black, the buildings around me light up from their insides.

What are you doing? my father says. *You're after the wrong person.*

"Shut up," I say softly enough so no one else can hear me.

Hopefully.

Take care of him for me, baby, Bev's voice says inside my head.

Stop thinking about that whore, my father says.

"She's not a whore."

What else would you call her? he says, and I hate him more than ever.

I shut out my father's voice and continue on my way, taking all the back roads, the dark paths, and the broken sidewalks. Until, at last, Gilmer Hall looms ahead of me. Its lights are on inside, but only a few students trickle from its doors, leaving for the evening.

I squeeze my eyes shut and focus.

I will talk to Mooken and demand he explains what is going on and why he lied to me about Bev. I will not hurt him. I will only talk to him.

It doesn't matter either way, my father says. *You're already fucked. You killed Professor Sulke. You're going to prison for life, or maybe you'll get the death penalty. There's no way out for you.*

Your father's right, Bev says. *Do something good for everyone before you go. Kill Mooken.*

I keep my face tight and remind myself the students I'm passing can't hear my thoughts. They don't know my intentions. I am camouflaged in my flesh, acting like a human, and they have no idea what I really am.

I enter Gilmer and shuffle down its aging halls. I know the way to Professor Mooken's office. Everyone does.

Amber knows.

Bev certainly knows.

All the students know how to get to their favorite teacher's office.

It's where they go to talk to someone they trust. To be safe. To learn about the inner workings of the human mind.

Or to have sex.

And become part of his experiments.

All these things can be done in Mooken's office.

As my breathing grows shallow, I realize I'm in the middle of the hallway, unmoving, frozen, standing in front of Mooken's door.

I've been standing here long enough for the motion-sensitive hall light to go dark. All is quiet around me, but Professor Mooken's light is on.

He is here.

CHAPTER SIXTY-ONE

JIM

I DO NOT knock on the professor's door. We are way past the point of polite formality.

I open his door, step inside, and quietly, gently shut and lock the door behind me.

Startled, Mooken looks up from his laptop, where he has been typing furiously. When he meets my glare, he is a child caught doing something he knows is wrong.

"We need to talk," I say, taking a seat across from him so only his desk separates us.

His fingers have stopped typing, but with a quick flick of his thumb and middle finger, he saves whatever he's working on.

"I don't appreciate you bursting in here, Jim," he says, turning his monitor away from me. "This is after hours, so I must ask you to return sometime tomorrow or next week. Remember, you were the one who canceled our sessions. As such, I have filled your slot with another student who is in need."

"I'm sure you did," I say. "Who would that be? My ex-girlfriend Amber?"

Mooken shakes his head.

"Please leave, Jim, before I call security."

"I wouldn't do that," I say, leaning forward, my elbows on his desk. "Because I know a lot of things I'm sure the Dean would be very interested in learning."

Stop talking to him, my father says.

Use the sword on the top shelf, Bev whispers in my ear. *Protect yourself before he hurts you.*

I grimace and ignore them both. But a distant, frightened part of me sits naked in the back of my brain and listens to their warnings.

Mooken sets down his phone and sits back in his chair.

"I was afraid something like this would happen," he says. "I suppose my young and foolish TA, Beverly, spoke to you today."

When he says her name out loud, my spine stiffens.

"She told me the truth—that you two have been fucking for the last two years."

Mooken shakes his head and tries to suppress a laugh.

"Is that what she said? I assure you she's lying. She has no proof of her claim, that's for sure. I must tell you, man-to-man, this is not the first time this has happened to me. I'm afraid it's a risk of the profession."

He studies my reaction while I try to figure out where he's leading me with his lies.

"She didn't tell you," he says. "And I can't blame her. Not everyone is as open about the topic of receiving psychotherapy as you are, Jim. Beverly was always quite secretive about our sessions, which I cannot blame her for, since that is her right as a patient."

He's trying to confuse you, Bev says. *Grab the sword.*

"She's your TA, and you were fucking her," I say. "She's not your patient."

Mooken shrugs, and his shoulders relax now that we're having a conversation instead of me threatening him.

"As you should know," he says, "more than most, I choose to go above and beyond for some of my…favorite students. Being at college is a stressful time. You have no real paycheck yet and plenty of stress. Maneuvering this period of your life is not always an easy task. I do my best to help where and when I can."

"You said you didn't give students therapy."

"I am not in the habit of doing so, but in certain cases, I make exceptions. I assure you I filed the proper paperwork with my Department Head, and everything is on the up-and-up."

"Bullshit," I say. "You two were lovers."

"And how do you know this?"

"She told me earlier today."

"You have been dating Beverly for a little over a month, as far as I can surmise," he says. "And *today*, she decides to tell you that she and I were lovers. That is rather odd timing, don't you think? Tell me about the conversation you two were having that elicited this confession from Ms. McDane."

I close my eyes and try to remember, to listen to my own thoughts, but the buzzing in my head grows louder.

"She tried to kill herself today."

Mooken's eyebrows arch up, showing true concern.

"Jim, where is she? We must call 911."

"Don't touch the phone," I say, my voice turning dark and deep.

I sound more like my father than myself, but that's fine because I want to intimidate Mooken, and my dad knows how to do that better than most.

"Don't worry," I say. "She didn't get a chance to go through with it. She tried to kill me instead. And that didn't work out so well."

"You didn't hurt her, did you?" he asks.

"I would never hurt her. She dumped a bottle of Xanax into her tea. At least, she thought that's what she did. But they were only sugar pills. She was about to drink her tea when I showed up. But then, she offered me her mug."

"I see," Mooken says.

He is somber now, pensive, and thinking.

"And that is when she told you about the two of us?"

I nod, both sad and angry at the memory.

"Isn't it more likely," he says, "that when her attempt to murder you was unsuccessful, she fabricated a lie about she and I being lovers…to redirect your anger away from her? Beverly is a very apt pupil, you know. If she survives long enough, she will make an excellent counselor one day. She's quick and thinks on her feet…despite her own battles with mental illness."

"There's nothing wrong with her mind other than what you did to it with all your lies. She's the only sane one out of all of us."

"I wouldn't agree with that," Mooken says as he rotates his monitor to face me. "Don't read the details, please—after all, this assessment is patient confidential—but take a look at the top of the document I was working on when you…interrupted."

I lean forward. The text on the screen is large enough for me to read easily. The document contains medical notes about a patient. And Beverly's name sits at the top of the page. My eyes drop down farther, to the text in the first paragraph, but he turns the monitor back around, so I can no longer see his screen.

"As a rule, I do not disclose patient notes to anyone," he says. "I take their confidentiality quite seriously. But…attempted *homicide* is also very serious. As such, I must inform you that Beverly has been a patient of mine for two years and is not mentally well. Although, recently, she decided she no longer wanted my help and canceled our standing appointments. Much the same way you did, actually. To be honest, I wouldn't be surprised if you quitting our sessions was her idea. Think, Jim. Did she suggest you stop our therapy?"

I try to recall my conversations with Bev about my meetings with Mooken. She didn't exactly *tell* me to stop my sessions, but she was happy when I did.

"She was the one who suggested I speak to you in the first place," I say.

"Ah, yes. The first day you came to me. You requested a referral to another doctor, and I told you I was perfectly happy to speak with you myself."

"That's *not* what you said. You told me you didn't give students therapy."

He smiles and tilts his head.

"Then why did we start meeting every week? That doesn't make sense, does it?"

He's right. Our weekly discussions did feel like therapy. He asked questions. I responded. He helped me dig deeper into myself and figure out what was going on inside my head.

Could he be right? Have I been his patient all along?

Was Bev also his patient? Was Mooken the doctor she recently stopped seeing?

A red-tinted memory flashes through my head—me pushing Professor Sulke's face into the dirt, suffocating him. Killing him.

"I had a dream," I say out loud before I can stop myself. "A nightmare I think might have been real. I dreamed I killed a Russian studies professor named *Sulke*."

For a moment, darkness passes across Mooken's face, but the shadow is gone before I can decipher its meaning.

"Yes," he says in a quiet voice. "We are all quite shaken about the news today. Tell me, in your nightmare, how did you…kill poor Professor Sulke?"

I tell him, and I leave out no detail. I hold out my hand to show him the dirt still caked under my fingernails. I touch my cheek that still burns from where Professor Sulke dug at it.

It was real.

I am guilty.

Regardless of whether Mooken is lying about Beverly, it doesn't change the fact that I am a killer—guilty and beyond retribution.

After I tell Mooken about my nightmare, his face softens. A tear forms in one of his eyes.

"My poor boy," he says. "John Sulke died of a self-inflicted gunshot. He committed suicide, Jim. You did *not* kill him."

CHAPTER SIXTY-TWO

JIM

I AM NOT SURE what to do with Mooken's revelation. I don't trust him, but I want to believe I'm not a murderer.

But if I didn't kill Professor Sulke, what's the other option? I dreamed of killing a man who actually killed himself that same night?

The chances of that happening are slimmer than me being a murderer.

"How do you know he killed himself?" I say.

Mooken smirks, showing his arrogance for a split second.

"The same way Beverly would have known," he says. "The head of the Russian and Slavic Studies Department emailed the teaching staff at the university and the graduate students in Russian studies. This loss is a terrible tragedy for all of us, I assure you."

If Bev received the same email Mooken's talking about, why did she tell me I was Sulke's killer?

My eyes are wide as I turn my head, looking to my right and then my left as the walls of Mooken's office grate across the dusty floor and close in on me.

"I don't understand this," I roar, so I can hear myself above the buzzing in my head.

"Of course not," Mooken says as he shuts his eyes. "Your cognitive systems are fragile right now from all the stress you've been under—the stress, it would seem, placed upon you by Ms. McDane. That and the sudden cessation of your Xanax habit have left your sanity quite compromised."

"My what?" I say. "No, no. I told you already—Bev is the one taking Xanax. That's what she used to almost kill herself. And then me. But I've never taken any of that shit at all."

Mooken's eyes sparkle, and I can see him calculating, thinking before he speaks again.

"Jim," he says. "I'm afraid Ms. McDane has been slipping you some of that drug for quite some time now. Did she ever give you a pill of any kind?"

I shake my head, thinking. She offered MDMA to me on the way to Foxfield, but that was all.

"Think," Mooken says. "Did you ingest anything with Beverly on a daily basis? Something that made you feel relaxed, almost tranquilized.

Fuck.

Our nightly tea.

I am repulsed by this simple but likely true revelation.

"I don't know," I say, lying. "But that doesn't matter to me. If I really didn't kill Professor Sulke…"

Mooken shrugs, letting his Xanax theory rest.

"Then I suggest you go home," he says after taking a deep breath. "Forget about Professor Sulke. Forget about Beverly. And perhaps watch some television before going to bed early tonight. And if you would like, because I know all of this must be tough on you, you may stop by for another session next week. I will make room in my schedule to see you again. And Jim, if I can be honest, I strongly advise you to consider my offer or to immediately schedule an appointment with Doctor Greelis. You need to speak to someone. You need help."

I'm about to take Mooken's advice and leave. Everything he's saying makes sense. It's the sanest thing I've heard all day, as a matter of fact.

What's more likely? I killed a man and don't remember it, or I've been a fool and under the influence of a woman more messed up in the head than me?

I brace my hands on the arms of the chair, ready to stand up, when the professor's door opens wide.

And in steps Beverly.

She closes the door behind her as she glares at the professor and then me.

"Don't believe a word he says, Jim. Whatever he told you, he's trying to trick you into leaving. As soon as you do, he'll call the police. On both of us. Even if he doesn't, the police will pick you up on your way home because you'll be the only student walking around and not in lock-down."

"You're the one not making sense," I say to her, anger lacing my voice. "I didn't kill Professor Sulke. When you texted me and woke me up last night, I was asleep in my bed—not out committing murder. Why did you convince me I was a murderer? What is wrong with you? You're the one I should be afraid of."

Instead of speaking, Bev holds out a shaking hand and passes me a piece of paper—a printout of an email from UVA Security. I check the email addresses and the header, and although it could be a fake, it looks real. It feels real. The message is a general student advisory from an hour ago ordering all students and staff to shelter in place wherever they are.

All evening classes are canceled.

All extra-curricular, school-sponsored activities are canceled until further notice.

And what is the reason for all this? Why is the University of Virginia shutting down this evening?

Because, as per the advisory, there is a *suspected murderer at large* wanted for questioning in the death of Professor Johnathan Jeffrey Sulke.

I finish scanning the email and drop it. It cambers back and forth in the air, and by the time it settles on the floor at my feet, Professor Mooken is backing away from his desk, frightened.

Now he's the one looking from side-to-side, searching for a way out.

Unfortunately for him, there is none.

CHAPTER SIXTY-THREE

BEV

"SEE? HE'S LYING to you," I say to Jim. "The same way he did to me for two very long years. You know Mooken. Overly confident and an ego the size of Montana—classic traits of a narcissist."

Between my words and the email I show him, Jim is now glaring at Mooken like he wants to kill him.

Mooken reads Jim correctly and punches a button three times on his smartphone, trying to make an emergency call. This is the last act of a desperate, cornered man who, for once, is unable to lie his way out of his situation.

"Stop him," I say, and Jim leaps out of his chair, jumps across the desk, and knocks the phone from Mooken's hand.

"I order you to stop this immediately!" Mooken shouts as his phone slides across the floor.

He's offended that we are daring to challenge him, but mostly, he's plain afraid.

"Look inside the chest," I say. "I want you to see I'm telling you the truth. That's where he keeps his notebooks filled with all the dirty secrets about him having sex with his students."

Jim turns to the cedar chest behind Mooken's desk. It's old, like everything else in this office, but it stands out from its surroundings because it's free of dust and grime.

"Do *not* touch that," Mooken shouts. "That is a priceless antique from Papua New Guinea."

Jim ignores him and pushes Mooken into one of his bookshelves.

Between the impact and his frenzied attempts at keeping his balance, a handful of turquoise and onyx statuettes fall to the floor, as do two framed photographs—one of Freud and one of Skinner—that shatter when they hit and shower the floor with glass. The authentic katana sword on his top shelf also rolls off, drops, and lands at his feet.

Jim looks from the wooden chest to the fallen sword, but he ignores the weapon and opens the chest—the same one I opened a month ago.

When he lifts the lid, the old iron hinges creak, revealing Mooken's secret resting place.

Jim hovers over the opened wooden box and reaches inside.

When he pulls his hand back out, I expect to see the notebook with my name on it or the one with Amber's name written on its front.

Instead, his hand is empty, and Jim's face darkens with confusion and distrust, once again directed at me.

I curse out loud. This was my best chance to pull Jim back to my side, and I've wasted it.

Mooken shows the hint of a dark grin again because he knew what Jim would find inside the chest—absolutely nothing.

"Where did you put them?" I say, trying my best not to scream.

Mooken ignores me and addresses Jim. He's the one Mooken is worried about. Not me.

And that is his mistake.

"If we could all calm down," Mooken says, his arm outstretched toward Jim. "As you can see, I have nothing to hide. No dark, hidden secret that will reveal my *evil scheme.* Both of you need counseling, and it is clear to me now that you need dedicated therapists. I thought I could help you both, but I can see now that is not the case."

Mooken straightens up, thinking he has the advantage again, but I am far from conceding this battle.

While he pacifies Jim, I scan his office. He's re-homed a stack of notebooks somewhere in his office, and I need to find them before Jim turns on me.

I run through the likely candidates.

His filing cabinet. That would make the most sense. It's large and has a lock on it. But knowing Mooken, it would have been filled to the brim already with no room for anything else. And those notebooks take up space.

He could have taken them home with him, but from his scrunched-up face and the sweat on his brow, I'm certain they're somewhere close by.

A wave of anger rolls through me, but I tamp it down because I need my mind to remain clear and efficient.

I scan the items scattered on his dusty floor and note the trails each made when they fell. Then I search for any other place, besides the chest, with an obvious lack of dust.

His bookshelf. No. There's dust everywhere.

The pile of books on the old wooden table in the corner. They haven't been moved in a decade.

A stack of three cardboard boxes in the other corner. Same. None have been opened or moved in forever.

My mind races back to the night I first discovered the notebooks. I remember checking his desk drawers and finding one of them locked.

"Jim, the desk drawer on the left side," I say. "The notebooks have to be in there."

Jim shakes his head. He's tired of believing me and thinks I'm stalling for more time. But Mooken's eyes go wide with terror.

And it's then I know I've guessed correctly.

I step toward the desk, and Mooken reacts. His body tenses and coils—a dragon ready to defend his treasure.

Thankfully, Jim understands Mooken's reaction, too. He sits down at Mooken's desk and grabs the handle of the locked drawer.

Mooken glares.

"No!" he yells, giving up all hope of pretending there's nothing there for Jim to find.

Jim turns back to Mooken and growls—a wide-eyed dog with

bared teeth.

Mooken freezes, but his mind continues to churn, trying to figure his next move.

And I wait, anxious but hopeful Jim will finally realize Mooken is his enemy. Not me.

Jim tugs on the drawer handle again and again with increasing strength until something inside the desk snaps, and the drawer flies open.

When Jim reaches inside, I focus with everything I have, trying to will the image of the notebooks into existence.

But he retrieves a black three-inch binder filled with paper instead. I scream inside, worried Mooken has destroyed the notebooks with the damning evidence or hidden them somewhere I'll never find.

But when Jim opens the binder, he tilts his head to the left, confused.

"These are the questionnaires everyone had to take," he says.

There's nothing damning about those, I think.

We all know about those stupid questionnaires with their pain-in-the-ass behavioral questions. Mooken *should* have those, and they *should* be hidden and locked away because they contain students' and lab subjects' personal information.

My heart goes cold. Because even though I know something here is foul, I don't know what it is.

Mooken speaks in a cracked voice.

"I keep those locked away to protect the privacy of my students, and you should not be looking at them. They are confidential."

Ignoring Mooken, Jim thumbs through the binder to the first tab, reads something, then pages to the next tab.

"Is my questionnaire in here?" Jim says, glaring at the professor.

Jim doesn't know what he's found yet, either. But Mooken's obviously uncomfortable and still afraid, and that must mean there's something here to discover.

Mooken says nothing but takes a half step toward the sword on the floor.

But why?

The questionnaires are standard with him—five pages of fill-in-the-blank, multiple choice, and rating questions. Mooken has been very open about using the responses to perform statistical analyses on the types of students who take psychology classes and those who participate in psych experiments. He plans on using that data for an upcoming textbook he's authoring.

So what's the big deal?

Jim pages through more of the tabs in the binder, and I step closer to the door, my fight-or-flight reflex going into overdrive.

Jim rips one of the questionnaires from the binder and holds it up for us to see.

"Professor," he says. "Why is my questionnaire labeled *Pro-Schiz-26*?"

The air is sucked out of the room, and Mooken's face turns ashen.

I have no idea what the number *26* is for, but *prodromal* is the earliest phase of schizophrenia—difficult to detect but good at predicting a later emergence of schizoid behavior in certain people.

I struggle to grasp what Jim has uncovered. But as best I can tell, Professor Mooken has not been using his questionnaires—the ones I myself administered to hundreds of students—to determine the types of people who volunteer for psych experiments.

Instead, he's been using them to diagnose students with mental health issues and not telling them. But that can't be all. That alone is unethical and dubious but not enough to warrant the look of fear on Mooken's face.

There's still something I don't know.

CHAPTER SIXTY-FOUR

JIM

"TELL ME WHAT this means," I say, filled with rage.

Mooken's mouth opens, but nothing comes out.

"It means he thinks you're showing symptoms of being in the early stages of late-onset schizophrenia," Bev says. "That's not good."

I turn on Mooken, beyond angry.

"So not only are you Bev's ex-lover," I say. "But you think I'm going to develop schizophrenia at some point in the future? Were you ever going to tell me about this?"

Mooken's face is stone, and my words pass through him without effect.

"Is that what's happening to me right now? The nightmares, the shadows…"

"Yes," Mooken says in a flat, matter-of-fact tone. "Those are only previews of what is likely still in store for you. Unless you get help right now, which is what I was trying to…"

I raise my hand, silencing him. I don't want to hear any more of his double talk.

"What about the other students and the volunteers? I'm sure I'm not the only one your questionnaire diagnosed. Do you plan on letting any of them know they need help?"

I flip to the next page in the binder and see a guy named Jerry Parks. His questionnaire is labeled *BPD* at the top, but there's no number after those initials.

The next questionnaire has the number *20* written after its three-letter code. The one after that and the one after that both include numbers next to their codes as well, but the numbers are in no apparent order. Maybe if I could take the time to go through the entire binder, I could figure out Mooken's coding system, but I already know enough to be worried.

Shoving the binder away, I glance back to the open drawer and see a stack of notebooks. If they're the ones Bev was looking for, one of them should be filled with details about her sex life with Professor Mooken.

Sure enough, the notebook on the top of the pile has Bev's name written on it in black ink. Seeing that is enough to make me believe Bev and to lose any last bit of trust I had in Mooken.

He and Bev *were* lovers.

Bev was *not* his patient.

I was not his patient.

But worst of all, if everything he's told me is a lie, then I really *am* a killer.

I push the notebooks aside and search the hanging files in the back of the drawer, wondering what other lies I might uncover.

From the very last folder, I retrieve a thick document held together by a metal clip.

When I do, Mooken dives for something on the floor. By the time I read the title of the document and turn to face him, he's standing between Bev and me, arms flexed, holding the katana.

Usually, that would get my full attention. But I ignore him and his drawn sword and reread the title of the document I'm holding.

At first, I think I've stumbled across a draft of his new textbook or maybe a journaled paper he's working on.

But no scientific paper I've ever read would have a name like the one typed in large font, centered in the middle of the title page.

Love Sick: Romances Among the Mentally Ill.

CHAPTER SIXTY-FIVE

JIM

I SPEAK THE title of his document out loud, and from Bev's slack jaw, I assume she is as lost as me. Mooken is the only one who doesn't seem confused.

I move the pieces around in my mind, frantic to solve this puzzle, as desperate as the students in our lab experiment. I don't know how, but something in the back of my thoughts tells me there's a connection between this manuscript and Mooken's mysterious questionnaires.

"What do the numbers on the questionnaires mean?" I ask. "Why does mine have a *26* on it?"

"Return everything to my drawer and close it," he says to me before he turns to Bev. "I rarely make mistakes, but I should never have gotten involved with you. Especially after seeing the results from *your* questionnaire. But, then again, borderlines are very alluring. And also great in bed. Isn't that right, Jim?"

The professor stays focused on Bev, his body coiled and ready to pounce.

Before he can act, I do the only thing I can think of. I throw his own manuscript at him and dive for his legs.

Luckily, the professor is no samurai and has no real skill with a sword. He swats at the flapping pages with the blade as he turns to face me. At the same time, I collide with his knees, pushing into them hard with my shoulder and toppling him to the floor.

His head hits the oak planks with a crack, but he's only stunned and disoriented. At least he's released the sword, which I pick up and press edge-side down against his neck.

I don't know how to handle a sword any better than he does, but it wouldn't take much skill to push the blade harder against his skin and take his life. It would be as easy as cutting into a slab of meat.

Professor Mooken knows this as well. I can tell from the loss and surrender in his eyes.

"Tell me what the number on my questionnaire means," I say through gritted teeth. "I've already killed one professor, and I'll do it again if I have to."

Mooken closes his eyes and exhales, defeated.

Or so I think.

Then he smiles maniacally and shakes his head.

"You won't do this," he says. "Here is the truth, Jim. Yes, I suspect you did kill Professor Sulke. But I have no doubt it was during a psychotic episode, which you mistook as one of your nightmares—a horrible one, I'm sure. And even though you're holding a sword to my throat at the moment, and despite Beverly's best attempts to send you into a psychotic state this evening, you remain quite cognizant. And the *sane* part of you, Jim, is *no* killer. If you do this now, however, you will become one. Please, let me get you the help you need."

"You keep saying I need help," I growl. "But I'm fine. You just said so."

Mooken pauses before speaking again. When he does, he talks in a whisper.

"When was the last time you spoke to your father?" he asks.

Why is he bringing that up? I think, confused by his question.

"I don't remember," I say. "A couple of days ago, maybe. Don't bring him into this."

"Jim, as your teacher and counselor, I was allowed to review your student file."

"So what?"

"As part of the financial assistance you receive, you were given a position on the resident staff to help offset the cost of your room and board. You are a recipient of what is commonly known as a hardship scholarship."

"I don't understand."

"Your particular hardship is your family situation, given the loss of your mother and father at such a young age."

"Stop lying to me," is all I can muster as the buzzing in my brain turns frantic.

"You asked about your symptoms, Jim. Your father, with whom you have daily conversations, has been dead for a very long time. Look inside yourself, and you will see you already know this to be true."

I take my phone from my pocket and stare at my recent calls list. My father's number appears again and again, but the log shows that each call was outgoing and lasted only a few seconds.

This means nothing to me, but Bev's eyes are wide and full of fear because of what Mooken just said about my father.

I try to understand her reaction as the static in my head gets louder, making it almost impossible to concentrate.

"Put the sword away," Mooken says. "And let us discuss how to move forward from this. Each of us has something we don't want the authorities to uncover. You have the blood of Professor Sulke on your hands and are in dire need of help. And our dear Beverly has been having an affair with me, her professor, in a very consensual relationship for quite some time. And after it ended between us, she began having sex with you—one of her students—in an attempt to weaponize you against me. The university will not look favorably on any of that, I can assure you."

"Don't blame everything on us," Bev says, her voice raising in pitch. "You're in the wrong here, professor. Like you said, you and I were consensual."

"Well, it's true," Mooken says with a low laugh. "Professors have affairs with students all the time, you see. The only real crime is when we get caught."

"Listen, asshole," Bev says. "If I go down, you're going with me."

"Oh, I will be reprimanded," he says, with more than a hint of his usual arrogance. "But I won't lose my position, and I certainly won't go to jail, especially once the police and the Dean understand your part in Sulke's murder. The Dean will do her best to keep me quiet. No one wants a bunch of bad press about an already horrible situation."

"Maybe so," Bev says. "But you *will* lose your job when they find out you're testing students for mental illnesses without their knowledge or consent."

At that, Mooken's eyes widen. He doesn't seem too worried for a guy with a sword to his throat. But when I turn to look at his desk, his body tenses beneath me.

"If you won't tell me what the numbers are for, what's your book about?" I ask him, practically shouting so I can hear my own voice above the din between my ears. "The dating lives of mentally ill people doesn't sound like a textbook to me."

As soon as I hear my own words spoken out loud, the connection becomes obvious.

Images flash through my head.

I see myself sitting in Mooken's office, telling him about my past girlfriends, keeping the fact I'm dating Bev a secret.

But what if he already knew? What if he manipulated things to set the two of us up in the first place?

More images rush in.

I watch a memory of Bev when she first suggested I talk to Mooken, and I see Mooken's curious look when I tell him—right before he changes his mind and agrees to see me.

I hear his *helpful advice*, telling me to go for it with Amber, that having sex with her will be good for me.

I look at Bev and nod to the binder sitting on Mooken's desk.

"Find your questionnaire," I say, squinting, desperate for this noise in my head to stop.

She sits down at the desk and picks up the binder. She hesitates at first, then leafs through the pages, whipping each one to the left until she finally stops.

"What does it say?"

"BPD," she says slowly. "Borderline personality disorder."

"Is that it?" I say.

She turns to me as if to say, *Isn't that enough?*

"There's no number following my diagnosis if that's what you're asking."

I was sure Mooken had set the two of us up, but now, once again, I'm lost. Until Bev rustles through more pages and stops at another questionnaire.

"Amber's has the number 26 on it," she says. "Right after her diagnosis. *ASPD.* Antisocial personality disorder."

I register without much surprise that Amber is either a sociopath or on her way to becoming one, but her mental health is not my first priority tonight. I am only worried about Bev and me.

"Why do Amber and I have the same number?" I say, gripping the sword tighter. "Tell me!"

"Statistical coincidence," Mooken says, trying to shrug and show me he is retaining his cool.

Bev pages through more and more of the binder, frantic.

"No one else has a 26 on their questionnaire," she says. "Only you and Amber. What the hell are you doing, professor? Playing matchmaker with mentally ill students? And why try to match Jim with Amber when you're busy fucking her yourself?"

"That is ridiculous," Mooken says. "You have not been listening to me. I am *not* having sex with Ms. Louder. I am seeing her as a patient, the same as I did with you. The same as I did with Jim."

As Mooken continues to weave his excuses, I struggle to breathe like I'm being suffocated by a warm, wet cloth over my mouth.

"Jim, you must listen to me," Mooken says. "I understand now. Yes, I may have overstepped some bounds as your counselor. But I had only your best interests at heart. Now, Beverly, on the other hand. Why don't you ask her why she chose to date you in the first place? After all, you are—no offense—an underclassman *and* one of her students. Whatever her reasons, you should assume she's been lying to you about many things. To do so is part of her psychological constitution. It's what borderlines do."

"Don't listen to him," Bev says. "He's trying to turn you against me again."

I wish to God everyone would shut the hell up.

"He's not lying about everything, though, is he?" I say to Bev, snarling. "You told me your ex-boyfriend was your Russian TA. And he wasn't. *And* you lied about him leaving you those gifts. And because of your lies, I killed that professor. Why did you make all of that up? So I would protect you? You were already the most important thing in my life. I would have done anything to take care of you—to make sure no one harmed you. I would have even *killed* for you."

"I know," she says softly as she steps toward Mooken and me. "And I'm so very sorry."

"And what about our nightly tea?" I say. "That wasn't just tea, was it? What were you trying to do? How could you get me addicted to that Xanax shit?"

"I…wasn't trying to do that, Jim. You needed to relax and get a break from your nightmares, and I thought it would help you. And it did, didn't it?"

"Shit, you sound like Mooken!" I say. "Yes, it helped…until you stopped giving it to me. You turned me into a junkie."

I stay where I am, on top of and pressing down on Mooken, the sword's edge still against his throat, but inside, I am trembling and absolutely losing my shit.

"I'm so sorry for everything I've done to you," Bev says as tears fill her eyes. "You're a good guy and don't deserve any of this, but you have to know I loved you…that I *still* love you…with all my heart. And I need your help. We can fix things between us. Trust me. We were meant to be together, but if we let Mooken go right now, he'll turn both of us in. We'll both go to prison. My life will be ruined. Both of us will be destroyed. But together, we can take care of this right now and return to our lives before this asshole fucked everything up. We can be together again. And in love. Don't you want that?"

That is a stupid question.

Yes, I want that.

I would *love* that.

"Do this for us," she says.

I re-focus on the trembling professor and press the blade harder into his flesh—enough so a red stitch blossoms across his skin and droplets of blood roll down his neck.

I don't want to go to prison. I don't want Bev to go to jail, either. I feel wretched about what I did to Professor Sulke and for what I'm about to do to Mooken. But the fact that I feel guilty at all means I'm *not* a sociopath, right? Not even Mooken thinks I am.

Then, what am I doing, and why am I doing it?

I'm not in the middle of a psychotic episode now, am I? Maybe not, but this reality is as bad as any of my nightmares.

I am so confused and fed up, I stop caring either way. I only want the noise inside me to stop.

And I can only see one way out of this. I raise the sword high and aim its pointed tip at Mooken's neck. I don't know if I can do this, but I'm about to find out.

CHAPTER SIXTY-SIX

JIM

MOOKEN'S EYES GO wide. He is an animal trapped with nothing to lose, tensing his body, ready to rage one final time against his imminent death.

Only a millisecond passes, but my neurons engage in a complex game of justification and reasoning.

I can't take his life.

I'm in control of myself right now, and I'm not a murderer.

But I killed Sulke with my bare hands.

Of course, I can do this.

Do this for Bev.

Do this for me.

I tense, ready to swing the sword, but Bev exhales sharply behind me.

When I turn, she's reading something on Mooken's computer screen, her fingers hovering over his keyboard.

"Do it!" she says, glaring at me. "Give the bastard what he deserves. He doesn't give a shit about either one of us."

I turn back to Mooken. I want to do what Bev tells me, for her, for us. But when I envision cutting into Mooken's soft flesh, nausea rises in my stomach, and I wretch. My father would be ashamed of me for being so weak, and my mother would be saddened.

I am not sure why, but I know that to be true.

But I am neither of my parents. I am the living embodiment of not having the stomach for what I want so badly to do.

And this is the safest way out for Bev and for me.

But I...just...can't.

Instead, I flip the sword around and bring the katana's hilt crashing down, through the loud sheet of noise in my head, and onto Mooken's skull as he bucks his hips in a feeble attempt to free himself. The hilt tears into his forehead, sending his eyes rolling back into his skull and his head flopping to one side.

His chest still rises and falls. He isn't dead, but he is unconscious. And I relax my grip on the sword for the first time in what feels like hours.

Now Bev and I can talk and figure a way out of this together.

I exhale, but when I turn to her, she's standing only a foot away from me.

She holds Mooken's jade statuette of the Buddha, gripping it tightly, her knuckles white.

She locks eyes with me, and for a moment, I see the end of *my* life.

But I am not her target. Instead, she pushes me off Mooken and straddles his motionless body.

I open my mouth to ask what she is doing. I want him dead, too. But I don't want her to throw her life away. Not for him.

As I look at Mooken one last time, he is no longer my psychology professor staring up at me. He is my father. And Beverly is my mother, sitting on top of him like she did that night so long ago when I was nine years old.

"Mom?" I say quietly.

But neither my mother nor Bev answers.

Being married to my father, my mother has survived more than she can take. And this time, finally, she's the one on top. She straddles him, holding her knitting needle as a weapon, gripping it with the same intensity and sense of purpose as Bev, who holds tightly to the jade Buddha raised above her head.

Now, as then, I turn into stone, unable to move. And I watch, horrified.

Bev's hand speeds down and slams the heavy statuette into Mooken's head at the same time that my mother impales my father's neck with her knitting needle. Mooken's cranium caves in, and globules of brain matter spill onto the floor, while my father chokes on his own blood and turns, in his last moments of life, to see nine-year-old me standing there, watching everything.

Leave that memory alone, my father says in my head, his deep voice booming through the static. *You need to get away from here right now before she kills you.*

The gray, tattered memory, released after so long, now plays over and over in my head. And with each repetition, it grows clearer.

I am nine years old, living in our small apartment, and Mom and Dad have closed their door for the night—my signal to stay in my room and pretend I don't know what they're doing.

The scent of beer is strong in the air, and there are screams like there always are, but this time, it is not my mother who is making noise.

It is my father.

You've really done it this time, boy, he growls in my head.

The child in me opens my mouth, desperate to speak. I have so many questions for my father—so many answers that would help me understand what I saw when I stormed into their room that evening. But when Bev finally stops bludgeoning Mooken, before I can make reason from the chaos in my head, the blood drains from my brain, my vision crackles, and the static erupts inside me like a cannon.

In an instant, the darkness closes in on me, squeezes my cranium, and prevents me from breathing.

I see nothing except smothering, hot blackness, and then I am gone.

PART FOUR

THE PRESENT DAY

NOW

CHAPTER SIXTY-SEVEN

JIM

WHEN I OPEN my eyes, it's close to four in the morning, and all is quiet in Professor Mooken's office.

My professor is still slumped over in his chair in front of his laptop. He is still dead.

Scenes from the last month continue to play in my head. They repulse me, but at least I remember the truth now.

When I scan the office, I see it with new-found clarity. I know why the chest is open behind Mooken's desk and why the katana sword and the jade statue of the Buddha are on the floor.

I remember it all.

I *did* kill Professor Sulke, but not Mooken. Beverly is the one who took his life.

Yes, I am guilty.

But so is Bev. And she is nowhere to be seen.

And Professor Mooken. He was guilty as well.

There are no innocents here.

Remorse fills my throat, choking me, but I stuff it back down. There will be time to deal with my emotions later. I will torture my soul and pay inside for what I've done the rest of my life, but I will not do that behind iron bars.

I'm sorry for what has happened and for my part in it, but I'm not stupid. And like Mooken said, I'm not a killer as long as I'm not in a psychotic state.

And right now, fully in control of my mind, my top priority is to save Bev, despite how much she has wronged me, and to save myself.

Once I find her, together we will leave this place.

This office.

The Psych Department.

Maybe even the university.

Forcing myself to stand, I amble over to Mooken and look again at the file on his screen. Nothing has changed, but with a calmer mind, and clear memories, I read his assessment of me more thoroughly.

Mooken writes how I have been exhibiting symptoms that suggest the early stages of schizophrenia, the precursor symptoms to this awful mental sickness.

Visual hallucinations.

Shadows that move on their own.

Talking daily to my father, who has been dead for almost half my life.

Sudden bursts of uncontrollable rage fueled by things true only in my own mind.

All of this syncs with my newly revived memories and the three-letter code written on the front of my questionnaire.

But the document on Mooken's screen is not the same one he showed me earlier. That was an assessment of *Beverly's* mental state.

I continue reading about how I killed Professor Sulke. How my psychotic episode was brought on by excessive stress and going cold turkey on the Xanax.

I read the document from the top again, carefully, and word-for-word. And it becomes clear that someone has altered the text from what it originally said.

And with Mooken dead, Bev is the only potential culprit.

With my chest aching, I try to come up with another reason the document has been transformed into one that accuses me of murder.

But I can't.

My eyes fill with tears as I select all the text, including the hundred pages of *mmms,* and delete everything. Then I save, close the file, and delete it. As I shut down Mooken's laptop, I realize this may not do much good if someone performs a thorough forensics check on his files, but hopefully, they won't.

Someone whispers, and I turn, expecting to find Bev waiting for me, but the office is still empty.

Finding her is my next task, for better or worse. But first I need to think. There's no way I can begin to erase the evidence of my presence from this place completely, so I won't even try.

But that isn't a bad thing.

I've been coming to see Mooken every week for the last month. It would be odd if my DNA somehow *weren't* found here. And from the number of students, including Amber, who have been here, there's going to be plenty of DNA evidence for the police to sift through.

I pick up my balled-up questionnaire from the floor and stuff it into my pocket. Next, I look for Beverly's questionnaire in the binder on Mooken's desk, but I can't find it.

She must have taken it with her.

My stomach clenches and sours. Bev has fled and left me here, abandoning me to take the blame for Mooken's death on my own.

I stop all movement and listen closely for the wail of sirens but hear nothing. At least she didn't call the police. If she had, they would already be here.

I pick up the draft of Mooken's future book from the floor—the one he'll never complete, and I leaf through what he's written—pages and pages of printed-out rough case studies, narratives, and humorous anecdotes. He doesn't use real names, as far as I can tell. But he was writing this for a broad audience, and he includes plenty of observations and details to support his theories. I'm sure the public would have loved it.

One chapter is labeled: "The Tides of Love: Bipolar Depressive and a Generalized Anxiety Disorder."

Another is about a student with obsessive compulsive disorder dating a student with PTSD.

And at the back of the binder, I find a mostly blank chapter composed of only hand-written notes about what happens when a prodromal schizophrenic becomes involved with a sociopath.

This is the chapter about Amber and me, or at least it would have been if Mooken had lived to finish and publish his book.

I glare at my professor's cold body, waiting for him to elaborate, to explain why he thought this was okay to do.

But he doesn't say a thing.

"Was this the real reason Amber started dating me? Because you convinced her to? Eugene would be overjoyed."

I inhale and let the air leave my lungs slowly and with purpose.

I close the draft of Mooken's book and slip my questionnaire inside its pages for safe keeping.

It's almost time for me to leave.

But first, I wipe down the hilt of the katana and return it to the floor. When I check the statue of the Buddha Beverly used to cave in Mooken's head, it's still bloody, with a patch of fleshy scalp and a tuft of gray hair attached.

I think about whether to clean that as well, but I leave it as is. If Beverly wasn't smart enough to wipe it down before she left me, that's her problem.

I've done what I can, and now I must leave.

As I stand at the door to Mooken's office, I turn back and frown as I survey the scene one last time.

There is a certain strength in knowing who I am and what I've become. I don't consider myself a murderer, though. That's for sure. Everyone dreams of doing terrible things. The only difference is that some of my dark dreams turned out to be real.

I can and will seek *real* psychological help for all of this someday. So I can better learn to cope with and treat my impending schizophrenia. So I won't be forced to end my days in a facility somewhere, drooling, strung out on meds.

But as I said, that is for another day.

When I reach for the doorknob, ready to leave this evening behind me, finally, my foot slips on something wet.

On the floor, my sole has smudged a small pool of dark red blood.

This is strange, I think.

This blood is far away from Mooken's desk and the rest of the carnage. I kneel and study it closer and see that it has seeped out from under the door to Mooken's coat closet.

My limbs turn to ice, and I shiver as my hand reaches out to open the closet.

When I pull back the door, I am greeted by a surprising density of coats.

Sports coats.

Winter coats.

Raincoats.

Why would a professor keep so many of these in his office?

I follow the cut of a black London Fog raincoat that hangs almost all the way to the floor, and there, hidden behind its folds, I find Beverly curled up like she is sleeping.

Her body is peaceful, but her head is flat and concave in places where it should be smooth, and lovely, and round.

Darkness rushes into me, threatening to fill me completely and send me away again. But I fight it as hard as I can and force myself to remain in control.

There is only one question I need answered. If Bev killed Mooken, who killed her?

Who took the life of the woman I love?

As soon as I ask this question, images assault my soul—memories pounding inside me, demanding to be seen. Grainy film clips jump and jerk in my brain as I release a menacing growl that fills Mooken's office.

As my guttural noise subsides, I am still here, physically, but not really.

Jim is gone.

I am a boy standing behind my mother, confused and lost as she withdraws the knitting needle from my father's neck.

I am my father as Beverly turns to me, her mouth open, screaming words I cannot hear over the noise of the buzzing.

I am even Mooken's ghost for a moment as I grab the blood-covered Buddha in dark mockery of the sin Beverly has just committed.

And finally, at last, I am a killer bringing down the chunk of jade and smashing it into Beverly's head, watching through tears that blur my eyes. I lift it and strike again. When I raise the statuette one last time, my hands become those of my father's. The last blow is his as he delivers the cold vengeance to Beverly that he was never able to give my mother.

It is with his hands that I set the Buddha down and stand on shaking legs. And when I do, at last, the film in my head stops playing. All around me and inside me is quiet.

CHAPTER SIXTY-EIGHT

EPILOGUE

THERE ARE STILL no sirens in the distance—only cold quiet as I stare at Bev's lifeless body in the closet, trying to make sense of her and why she isn't moving.

"Father, help me," I say. "I don't understand."

I wait and wait, but the one time I want to talk with my dad—the one time I *need* to talk to him—he doesn't respond.

I check my phone, but there's no call from him. I scroll through my call history for the last few months, and it is devoid of any incoming calls from my father at all. Even our text thread contains only my parts of our conversations.

I am shocked and feel like throwing up at first, but then my thoughts clear, and a lightness washes over me.

Somewhere in my mind, I wonder if Bev's ghost will call me one day from the grave, as my father's did, although I doubt it. I know there are no such things as ghosts—only painful memories my brain has struggled to process all my life.

I close the coat closet door softly and give up any hope of ever leaving Mooken's office. With Bev gone, there is no reason to do so anymore. Instead, I will remain here with Mooken and Beverly for all time.

I sit down in Mooken's guest chair. I lean back, close my eyes, and find a small plastic cylinder in my front jeans pocket—a gift forced on me by Dan, who swore to me how much I might need it one day.

Perhaps one day, I will awake to realize all of this—maybe my entire existence since age nine—has been only a single, bad dream.

But that is not likely.

Then again, my nightmare, the one in which I killed Professor

Sulke, where I ended a man's life, turned out to be real. And since that could happen, isn't it reasonable the opposite could occur as well? That there is a chance, however slight, that Bev's death was only a nightmare.

I pray for this with all my soul. But I give up after only a few minutes because my wish is a desperate fantasy belonging to a fool.

With my last hope gone, I tumble two of the pills into my palm and dry swallow them. I crave the relief the pills will bring, and in fifteen minutes, my body starts to relax.

Numbness fills me, and I am at peace as I sit there, surrounded by the quiet of the dead.

Without thinking about it, I tip the plastic bottle up and swallow hard. I do this again and again, forcing the pills down my throat as tears burn my face.

Then I sit there as the second hand on Mooken's clock ticks, ticks, and ticks.

Another fifteen minutes pass before the howls of sirens emerge outside the building. I smile sadly as my brain turns warm and soft, and I start to drift away.

The authorities—or someone—will soon discover me. They will find the three of us here, and they will figure out what they can, whether it ends up being the truth or not.

I have no power over any of that now. And releasing the illusion of control is the best thing I have done for myself in a very long time.

Slowly, darkness seeps in and engulfs me, and warm black crude oozes through my veins. But unlike the times before, this is not the darkness of my approaching insanity. No, *this* blackness promises a restful slumber more absolute and freer from nightmares and noise than any I've ever known.

I slump in the chair, unmoving. For how long I do not know.

The buzzing in my head is gone.

The voice of my father is quiet.

My heart makes less and less noise with each beat.

I am becoming absolute nothingness. And the last sound I hear after the crack of Mooken's door being forced open is the whirring of an empty pill bottle as it rolls away from me across the dusty wooden floor.

The End

NOTE FROM THE AUTHOR

This novel began its life when I was an undergrad at the University of Virginia, many, many years ago. For a very long time, I had only an inkling about what it was supposed to become other than a book about a psychology student who found himself in the middle of a murder. Up until a month before this novel was published, it was called *Blown Out of Proportion*, mainly because the younger version of me liked the name and because it had an amusing acronym (BOOP).

But as I started writing the story and diving into Jim's and Bev's past, I realized that saying the characters blew things out of proportion wasn't fair to them. Both of them had mental health issues, and I wanted to make sure the story treated those with due seriousness. Hence, the new title, *The Control.*

The story's building blocks were taken from different pieces of my life and from my psych classes at UVA. Of note, when I was in second grade, I was recruited by my teacher to participate in a college student's psychology experiment. I was to be his control subject. After a few signatures from my parents, I was placed in an observation booth with the worst of the worst troublemakers the school had to offer—classmates who were, in retrospect, suffering from…well, something.

We repeated the experiment three times, and during each pairing, the other student and I sat on the floor facing each other. We were given a set of wooden blocks and told to build towers from them as tall as possible. My job in the experiment was to reach over and knock down the other guy's blocks as soon as they were a certain height and to do so in the most nonchalant, casual, stoic manner possible. As I did this, over and over again, Mr. College Student, safely behind his observation glass, recorded the kid's behavior.

Needless to say, these disturbed children were none too happy about me knocking down their blocks. Long after the college student left, I had to deal with these kids who held grudges against me for quite a while. But, hey, it was interesting, and I was paid in model kits, which was fine by me.

The last thing I want to include here is a note about UVA. I went there for four years as an undergraduate, and I loved my time at "The University." But, as any reader who is familiar with the Grounds knows, I took some liberties in this novel with the placement of buildings, names of bars that have long been closed, and such. In the end, I created a university that was a combination of today's UVA and the university as it was when I attended.

ACKNOWLEDGMENTS

Thank you to everyone who encouraged me to write this novel, my first Psychological Thriller.

Special thanks to Kristen Paul for all the conversations and suggestions over the last year. Your insights were numerous and priceless, and I couldn't have created a book this good without you.

Ron Mason, you read more versions of this novel than anyone should ever have to! All your observations and suggestions were invaluable.

Jerry Carr, thank you for all the chats about the intricacies of the plot and helping me sort out what worked and what didn't. Shaka, brother.

Thank you so much to Noelle, an amazing author and inspiration. And thanks for always being there to provide feedback on my latest cover!

Special thanks to Juli. Your reactions, good ideas, and support were on target and gratefully appreciated. And Dawn! The head of the best Psychological Thrillers group on Facebook, thank you for being so welcoming to me and all the other authors and readers to whom you provide an online home.

ABOUT THE AUTHOR

Mike grew up as a military brat, traveling around the world and the country before landing as an adult in the suburbs outside of Washington, D.C. He currently lives with his writing buddies, Elsa and Baloo, the wonderful pups who make sure he takes plenty of breaks.

Word-of-mouth is crucial for any author to succeed. If you enjoyed "The Control," please leave an honest review online by going to the product page where you purchased this book. Even if it's only a line or two, it would mean a lot.

For more information about Mike and his books, to sign up for Mike's e-mail list, or to purchase directly from the author, please visit:

writerlayne.com.

Printed in the USA
CPSIA information can be obtained
at www.ICGtesting.com
LVHW040203171223
766611LV00003B/290

9 798869 037886